D0448706

"YOU CAN RUN, BUT YOU CAN'T HIDE."

■ ■■■■■■■ ■

McCann was cooing at the images on his MFD. The central MFD now had the Skyray attack screen on with the selected target firmly locked.

"No interference from the cloud?" Selby asked.

"Nope. Our boy's as clear as a face without zits."

"You have a way with words, McCann."

"He is dead meat. You can take him on the HUD. He's all yours."

Selby maneuvered the ASV 130 from the cloud band. It was unnerving to think that the little Hawk's pilot, way below the grayish mass and beyond visual range, thought he was safely out of reach. Under normal circumstances, he would be.

Selby watched as the targeting box on the HUD came into the missile ranging ring. The pulsing diamond froze then glowed, signifying a solid lock-on.

"Here goes," Selby said to McCann, and pressed the missile release button on the stick.

Also by Julian Jay Savarin

Trophy

Published by
HarperPaperbacks

TARGET DOWN!

Julian Jay Savarin

HarperPaperbacks
A Division of HarperCollins*Publishers*

If you purchased this book without a cover, you should be aware that this book is stolen property. It was reported as "unsold and destroyed" to the publisher and neither the author nor the publisher has received any payment for this "stripped book."

This is a work of fiction. The characters, incidents, and dialogues are products of the author's imagination and are not to be construed as real. Any resemblance to actual events or persons, living or dead, is entirely coincidental.

HarperPaperbacks *A Division of* HarperCollins*Publishers*
10 East 53rd Street, New York, N.Y. 10022

Copyright © 1991 by Julian Jay Savarin
All rights reserved. No part of this book may be used or reproduced in any manner whatsoever without written permission of the publisher, except in the case of brief quotations embodied in critical articles and reviews. For information address HarperCollins*Publishers*,
10 East 53rd Street, New York, N.Y. 10022.

Cover art by Attila Hejja

First printing: December 1991

Printed in the United States of America

HarperPaperbacks and colophon are trademarks of HarperCollins*Publishers*

10 9 8 7 6 5 4 3 2 1

for Dieter, edgerider, VF 74-er, MFG-er. Folkhard and Klaus, edgegivers, and the gentlemen of the Maple Five, edgeriders all.

Beginnings

1965.

The English Electric Canberra PR-7 flew high above the Mediterranean. Originally designed as medium bomber, the specially modified twin-engine aircraft maintained a steady altitude of 48,000 feet. On this day, its training mission had little to do with bombing.

Fifty miles behind but a good 20,000 feet lower, a stablemate aircraft stalked it. This was also a twin-engine aircraft, but they could not have been more different. The English Electric Lightning was a hot rod of an airplane. Its mighty, after-burning Avon engines mounted shotgunlike one above the other in its tubular airframe, it was twenty years ahead of its time in sheer accelerative power. An F-2A modified to F-6 standard, it was unique; for neither version possessed its avionic pack or its weapon fit. On this day, it carried a single air-to-air missile that was itself so advanced, no competitor existed. The missile was shorter than would have been expected—just over a meter in length—and was slim. It was a prototype, with a projected range of sixty miles. This was to be its first live firing. It was meant to be the template for missiles that would eventually have ranges of well over a hundred miles. The Lightning's own fire control radar was also nonstandard and was designed specifically for use with the missile. Though the pilot had trained intensively with it, he was anxious not to get anything wrong; but this did not disturb the calm he felt. A thorough professional, he did not doubt his own capabilities.

His quarry was not the Canberra, but a target drone twenty miles from the larger aircraft. The Canberra's task was to monitor and record the shoot. To allow for a wider safety margin, the Canberra was to move a further ten miles after being alerted by the Lightning of the intention to fire the missile. The target drone would be emitting a signal that would be recognized by the missile to achieve lock-on. The drill had been rehearsed so often, each of the four men—the Lightning pilot plus the three crew of the Canberra— was totally familiar with his role during the exercise. Nothing had been left to chance.

The Lightning pilot gently tapped a button beneath the single radar screen in the center of his instrument panel, in place of the normal, circular radar usually positioned at top right. The unit went into search mode, covering a range of one hundred miles. The pilot marveled. If only all Lightning pilots had access to a piece of kit like this! But only those involved with this particular project would ever get to see it. No one would know for some time yet whether such equipment would be cleared for operational use by Royal Air Force squadrons. The whole system, weapon and avionics, was under the tightest of security embargoes. Supposedly, only two members of the government were aware of its existence: the minister directly involved and his deputy.

What the pilot did not know was that the deputy had since changed from support for the project to barely concealed hostility. It was too expensive, and dedicated fighters were on the way out. Surface-to-surface missiles would decide the outcome of future wars. The deputy was not a pilot and felt what he saw was a waste of taxpayers' money.

The Lightning pilot continued his search from his altitude of 20,000 feet. Both the Canberra and the drone, with their respective altitudes and headings, were clearly shown. You beauty, the pilot thought with satisfaction. This was nothing like the Airpass AI-23 radar mated to the Red Top missile, which was standard fare for less fortunate Lightnings.

The pilot now began the series of maneuvers that had been laid down for the flight. He slammed the throttles forward. The twin Avons went into reheat-after-burning-mode with an explosive roar. A double plume of white-blue flame torched its way from the engine nozzles as the pilot reefed the aircraft into a steep climb. The Lightning stood on its tail and seared upward. In less than a minute, it was at 60,000 feet.

As the pilot eased back on the throttles and leveled out he again studied his radar. The traces were still there, firmly captured.

The pilot rolled the aircraft onto its back and hauled smoothly but firmly on the stick. The Lightning plunged seaward, unaided this time by the afterburners. When the pilot had leveled out once more, he was just five hundred feet above the water.

He gave the radar another look. The traces were still there. He felt very pleased. The radar was performing as expected. Now for the missile.

He armed the weapon while still at five hundred feet and watched as the targeting box began hunting for the drone. Everything was still going smoothly. The box began to get excited as he closed the range. Soon he got the tone that told him the missile had locked onto the drone. The range was almost seventy miles. Fantastic, the pilot thought. Much, much better than expected. The people on the ground would be pleased with themselves. They had created a superb weapon system, far in advance of anything around, or on other drawing boards.

The agenda called for a high-level shoot at a low-flying target, so the pilot once again put the Lightning into its spectacular climb. At 50,000 feet the pilot informed the waiting Canberra he was about to fire at the drone. The Canberra acknowledged and took its arranged position.

The pilot called a second warning. Again the Canberra acknowledged and gave the okay for the shoot. The pilot called the launch and fired.

"My God!" he said as the Mach 3-capable missile streaked away from his aircraft at a phenomenal rate of acceleration, the bright white trail of its exhaust seeming to paint itself across the heavens within the blink of an eye. Within moments, he could no longer detect movement. Only the white, seemingly frozen writhings of the missile's trail kept him company; an oddly frightening signature in the sky.

He glanced at the radar. The drone was well and truly targeted. The box framed it solidly.

The Canberra had no warning as the missile, curving upward from the lower altitude it had previously attained, slammed explosively into its bright yellow-and-black-striped belly. The stricken aircraft was instantly turned into an expanding fireball. Pieces fell toward the water five thousand feet below the Canberra's last altitude.

Fifty miles off Malta, a man and a small boy in a fishing boat recoiled in shock and fear as a helmet splashed into the water next to their small craft. The head was still in it. It rolled grotesquely. The head seemed to look straight at the boy.

He screamed.

In the Lightning, the pilot saw his kill confirmed on the radar.

"Target down!" he reported smugly.

He was unaware that his target, the drone, continued to fly quite unharmed until its fuel, meant to last barely longer than its intended moment of destruction, ran out.

The subsequent inquiry absolved the pilot of any blame for the loss of the ill-fated Canberra and its crew. Nevertheless, he asked to be relieved of his post, a request that was swiftly granted.

Further development of both the missile and radar was halted.

1

Moscow. Late Autumn, 1990.

Winter seemed in a particular hurry this year, the man thought as he walked slowly through the park. The trees about him had virtually shed their foliage and looked dead, rather than preparing for the long hibernation. The man shivered in his shabby overcoat. There was a sickly pallor to his gaunt face, giving him the look of a recent prisoner, which, indeed, he was.

He was not eager to arrive at his destination, though he knew the place well. The last time he was there, he wielded power. Now he was unsure of himself and a little afraid; mostly of the man he was going to see.

Why had the general arranged his release from the Siberian hellhole, the very same general who had caused him to be sent there in the first place? What was important enough to justify returning his freedom to him?

He was under no illusions. The freedom was tenuous, and its price would be heavy. The general wanted something badly enough to secure the release of a disgraced former colonel in the KGB.

Hands deep within the pockets, he gripped his

coat tighter about him as if for protection against something much more ferocious than the coming Russian
winter. As he walked on he noted the faces of passersby.
Old habits died hard; but he was noticing something
new: open discontent, a strange grimness, a latent
anger.

So much for the new freedoms, he thought, allowing himself a fleeting twinge of malicious pleasure.

Everything had a price . . . as they were only just
beginning to find out.

"And where do you think you're going?"

The belligerent challenge came from the uni-
formed KGB guard who stood at the entrance of the
short tunnel that led to a wide courtyard. The courtyard belonged to one of the most forbidding structures
in the city.

The guard was peering at the unwelcome visitor.
As recognition dawned the guard's mouth opened and
closed soundlessly.

At last he said, "Comrade . . . Comrade Colonel
Stolybin! I . . . I had no idea. . . . I mean, you don't look
. . . What I want to say—"

"You're becoming more embarrassed by the second, Sergeant," Stolybin interrupted in a neutral voice.
"For your information, I am no longer a colonel. . . ."

"Well yes, Comrade. I know, but . . ."

Stolybin waved a dismissive hand. Even now he
could not quite forget his former standing, and the action was unconscious. The sergeant could easily have
taken offense, but he had known Stolybin well.

"There is no need to apologize, Sergeant. You
were not responsible for what happened to me. I'm here
to see the general." Stolybin gave a tight grin that held
no mirth. "He got me out."

"I see, Comrade Colonel. . . . I mean . . . Of course you may go in."

"Thank you," Stolybin said dryly.

As he walked past, the sergeant called out. "Comrade . . ."

Stolybin paused to look back.

"It's good to see you again," the sergeant said, a trifle awkwardly, as if afraid of showing emotion. "Things are coming to pieces all over the country. We need to have order restored." The sergeant stopped suddenly, as if afraid he'd said too much.

"I know exactly what you mean."

Stolybin turned and walked on.

To the guard, it had not been an open expression of solidarity; but such a comment, even from the ragged-looking former colonel, made him feel strangely better.

Now that the colonel was back, perhaps he and the general would start sorting out that bunch that seemed to have taken over the Motherland.

"Welcome, Sergei Grigorevich!" the general said expansively. He took Stolybin by the shoulders and kissed him on both cheeks.

If Stolybin thought it was a brazen act of hypocrisy, he gave no indication.

The general stood back to survey his visitor critically. "You look a little"—the general paused—"lean. Yes. That's it. Lean." He stubbed out his cigarette when he saw Stolybin's nose wrinkling distastefully.

"I was not exactly at a dacha on the Black Sea," Stolybin retorted with the air of a man who considered he had nothing further to lose. The general could always send him back to Siberia, despite the rash of peace and openness breaking out all over the place. He didn't care. "The Comrade General knows this. Or should I address you as Citizen?"

The general's eyes suddenly turned hard. It was as if he had never welcomed Stolybin. "Don't make the mistake of thinking you have suffered as much as is possible and that there is nothing more in store. You lost the nation its most advanced aircraft prototype and allowed the successful defection of its test pilot—"

"General . . ."

"Don't interrupt! I will not have insubordination from my junior officers."

Stolybin was not intimidated. "If the General will permit, I am not his junior officer. My rank was stripped from me."

The general glared. "I stripped you. What I take, I can return. Before you left on your twelve-month . . . sojourn, you were a lieutenant-colonel in the KGB. You have been reinstated"—the general took his time—"as a full colonel, with full pay and privileges, as of today. Any objections?" Given the general's position, it was an empty challenge.

Stolybin harbored a sense of betrayal, and nursed a seething anger, but he was not stupid. "No, Comrade General."

The incident that had cost him his rank and his freedom had occurred just over a year before. An operation that he had planned had not ended well. He still thought its conception brilliant, but unforeseen factors had made him the loser. The prototype had not made it to the West, but had run out of fuel over the Norwegian Sea. It was now in pieces 12,000 feet below the surface. The pilot, however, had been rescued by the West. He had never returned. In addition, there had been combat. Four top-of-the-line fighters—two MiG-29s and two Su-27s—sent to stop the pilot, had been destroyed by fighters from a special NATO squadron.

They had cost Stolybin his operation. The anger against them flamed in his pale cheeks.

The general observed the sudden rush of color with satisfaction. "You're remembering where to direct your anger. Good. You will like the reason for my decision to give you a second chance. Count yourself lucky, Colonel. I don't give second chances easily; in fact, you are the first. Fail me a second time, and you will be a very unfortunate man indeed.

"The Motherland is in chaos," the general went on, "and I am certain it will get worse, unless something is done to stop it. We have granted the republics a certain degree of freedom. But what happens? They begin to kill each other. This is peace? This is freedom?" His contempt was palpable. "We have made the West a present of what they call Eastern Europe; our armies are in retreat and now, what are we about to do?" The general answered his own question, thumping his regulation-issue desk suddenly. "We're throwing away our weapons! Weapons that we need for our own defense."

Knowing that if past practice was anything to go by the sacrificed weaponry had already been superseded by better quality, Stolybin chose discretion and remained silent. Whatever the general said to him would not make him relax his vigilance. His neck was on the line. If the general dumped him again, the general would be coming down, too. Stolybin knew this was dangerous thinking. He kept his expression attentive as the general continued to rave.

"The Wall is down," the general continued in a razor-edged tone, "and everyone is happy; or so it seems. But mark my words, Colonel. Europe, the world, has become a more unstable place. Before long, people will be wishing for the certainties of the status quo. There are those among us who are not prepared to wait for this enlightenment, whenever it may choose to return. Our land is coming apart. It's a comic opera out there. Deputies arguing with each other like a rabble on a street corner while the Motherland creaks into immobility. You, Colonel, can have your revenge on those who defeated you, and serve the Motherland while you're at it. Well?"

"I am still here, Comrade General, and I await your orders."

The general stared at Stolybin unblinkingly for a long moment.

"I have not offered you a drink, Colonel. What would you like? I hope it's vodka. Our people appear to be succumbing to Western tastes. You have returned to a land fit not for heroes, but for hamburgers and cola."

"Vodka, Comrade General."

"Good. Sit down, Colonel. You look almost dead on your feet."

Stolybin gratefully sat down on one of the two chairs available for visitors in the sparsely furnished room. They were "interview" chairs, which meant they were not particularly comfortable. The general had a more opulent room where the real visitors were entertained. The general went quickly out to that room through a connecting door to get the drinks.

He returned, not only with two generously charged glasses but with a dark, bulky file tucked beneath an arm. He handed a glass to Stolybin, then with his freed hand placed the file on the desk. A cigarette dangled from his lips. A quick puff, then he put it out.

He held up his own glass. "To the Motherland."

Stolybin got to his feet. "The Motherland."

They drank, the general downing his in one gulp. Stolybin tried to do the same and was seized by a fit of uncontrollable coughing. The severe regime in the Siberian prison had ill-prepared his body for the potency of a regal vodka.

The general waited patiently until the coughing had subsided. "In a few days," he said, "you'll be able to do that without blinking. Of course," he went on, as if only just remembering, "you only like scotch, don't you?" He pointed to the dead cigarette. "And hate these."

Stolybin, not fooled, replied: "I've always liked good vodka, Comrade General. But I have been out of practice." He ignored the rest.

The general nodded. "You have a new apartment, new uniforms, and new civilian clothes. Those, I'm afraid, are not the Western kind you usually prefer; but if your work requires Western travel, allowances can be made . . . within reason. You will also be given a car, and a driver." The general paused long enough to note Stolybin's look of surprise. "Oh yes. Colonels can still get a car . . . at least *my* colonels can. You'll like your driver," he went on, permitting himself a twitched smile that was more of a smirk. "I believe you know each other. Tokareva."

Stolybin tried not to react. Tokareva! He certainly knew her. Nearly 180 centimeters tall, twenty-three years old, and a pneumatic whirlwind. Memories of her glorious body taunted him. He wondered how she had managed to return to her old job. The association with her former boss could not have helped during the past year.

As if he had read Stolybin's mind, the general said: "I kept her out of harm's way . . . just in case a chance came for you to redeem yourself."

And what price had she been made to pay? Stolybin wondered, hoping the thought had not outwardly betrayed him. He tried not to think of the general launching himself upon that wonderful young . . . He drove the obscene vision from his mind.

But the general was accurately following Stolybin's train of thought. "She was . . . grateful."

And Stolybin hated the general. Weakened by his time in prison, he had not yet regained full control of himself. He used to be very good at thinking one thing while displaying something quite different. He vowed to retrain himself. But for the moment, his feeling of hate showed briefly.

"Good," the general was saying. "Good! I want you to hate me. I want you to channel that hate into giving me the results I expect from you." He tapped at the file on the desk. "When you have read all of this, you will understand the high stakes you are playing for. Yes, you. Because if you fail, I will not hesitate to take my revenge." Suddenly cold eyes bored into Stolybin's already shaken soul. "There is to be no failure. There will *be* no failure. Am I clear?"

"Very clear, Comrade General."

The general's voice became less hard as he continued: "Tokareva is loyal. She sees the dangers to the State. Even so, no contents of this file—not even the smallest part of it—will be made known to her. As far as she is concerned, it does not exist. Very few people know of its existence. You are the first new person in decades, making a total of five who are still living. There is not to be a sixth. Whatever the operation you devise after studying it, whatever manpower you choose to employ . . . *no one* is to know of this file. Your life depends upon it."

Stolybin looked steadily back at the general and said nothing.

"The file will never leave this office unless taken away by me," the general went on, "or I ask you to bring it to me next door. You will study it here, and each day when you're finished, I shall retrieve it."

The general was a Georgian. Stolybin was Russian and found he suddenly hated the way the general spoke the language. He hated the traces of the accent. It was a petty attitude, he knew; but he could not forgive the general for sleeping with Tokareva.

"Several years ago," the general's Georgian voice said, "when I was about your age, I was given a very important job to do. I succeeded. It's all in the file. You will study the subject thoroughly, and base your operation upon it. I have put in an outline about what I want done. A broad canvas, if you like. You will paint me the detailed picture, and act upon it. This will be your office for the duration. No one will interfere with your work. I'll make certain. Have a quick look now, then you may go out to the courtyard where Tokareva is waiting with the car.

"She will take you to your new apartment. Spend the night with her, if you wish. But in the morning, sharp and early, I want you in here in a smart uniform, ready to begin. Consider tomorrow to be the first day of the operation." The general moved toward the connecting door and paused. "Remember, I do not expect failure. You will see why." He went out, leaving his empty glass.

Stolybin stared at the closed door for what seemed years, conflicting emotions going through him. He was alternately attacked by a sudden hunger for food, and for Tokareva. Yet a part of him was revolted by this desire for her. She was the general's leftover. But it had been a long, long twelve months. . . .

He went over to the desk and sat down behind it. He pulled the file toward him. Though bulky, it was neatly arranged. He began to read, and within two pages, he was hooked.

* * *

Two hours later, Stolybin slowly closed the file. He felt a new and grudging respect for the general. He had no intention of forgiving his superior the sexual blackmail he had used on Tokareva. It was an obvious trick, fouling a disgraced subordinate's territory; but the general's earlier operation had been brilliant. It had been a stroke of genius. Stolybin knew the general was challenging him to do better, or at the very least, equal him.

But what the general wanted was frightening; and monstrous in its cold-blooded calculation. Stolybin was no hypocrite. He could be as calculating as anyone the general could put up against him.

Yet this operation made something deep within him balk at the thought. The fear he had felt in the park returned. He had read the file. He was in. The general had neatly trapped him.

Stolybin stood up. At that moment, the general entered.

He must have been watching me on a monitor, Stolybin thought sourly. A tiny camera or two would have been planted in the room as a matter of routine.

"Well?" the general said, lighting up a cigarette and daring Stolybin to object.

"That was a brilliant operation, Comrade General," Stolybin remarked truthfully, ignoring the smoke the other blew into the room.

"I know that." It was not a boast. "What I meant was have you any ideas?"

"There are several possibilities . . ." Stolybin began.

"Good." The general picked up the file. "Don't tax the mind for the moment. Attend to the needs of the flesh." He walked out, again leaving Stolybin to stare at the closed door.

After a while, Stolybin stuck his hands deep into

the shabby coat he had been given on leaving the prison and made his way out of the room, heading for the courtyard.

It seemed to him that what the general wanted was a war; a foreign war to unite the people, and to overthrow a government. From well before Caesar's time, generals and politicians had done that when there was trouble brewing at home. It always worked.

But in Caesar's time, wars did not engulf the planet, threatening it with destruction.

As he went out into the courtyard and saw the welcoming smile on the face of the tall, young woman waiting for him, Stolybin felt that perhaps the best way to temporarily forget the nightmare he had been asked to create was to bury himself deep into Tokareva's warm and energetic body.

And as for the people, he thought with some contempt, they never seemed to learn. Like people everywhere, they fell for it every time.

Suddenly he smiled, grimly. Colonels could be dangerous, too.

"What is the problem?" Tokareva inquired solicitously.

Stolybin was standing near a window in the darkened bedroom, looking out upon the Moscow night. He was naked. After half an hour of trying, he had found to his immense chagrin that he had been unable to make love to her. Tokareva was the daughter of a Finnish mother and a Russian father and she had inherited the best of both worlds. The seemingly translucent blond hair and pale skin, the fine features of her mother, had been coupled with a sturdiness inherited from her father's peasant stock. The result, in someone of her height, made the pulses race. She also possessed fathomless black eyes that seemed to draw at the very spirit.

But the naked body reclining so invitingly upon the new bed supplied courtesy of the general could not entice him. Just one year before, it was another story. They would have been at it almost the moment they had come through the door.

He knew what his problem was. Without turning to face her, he said, "The general . . ."

"Ah. Now I understand. What did he tell you?"

"That you let him sleep with you."

"I let him!" She sounded indignant. "Was that his sick version of what happened?"

Stolybin shrugged. "You let him, he made you. Does it really matter who did what?"

"Yes! It does!" She was sitting up in the bed now, staring at him through the gloom. "Why don't you ask *me* what happened?"

"All right. What happened?" He sounded indifferent.

There was a long silence that was charged with her anger.

At last, she began quietly. "I wanted to be around when you came out. I didn't know how long they had sent you for. The general offered me protection. . . . I . . . I—"

"I don't need to hear this."

"Yes, you do!" she said fiercely. "You should know the truth before you judge me. It was all a pretense. I went around, not denying he was screwing me, but not saying he was either. The general was the one who made a show of it. So people left me alone."

Stolybin turned. "What are you saying?" he asked softly.

"I'm saying nothing happened. The general is impotent. At least, with me."

Stolybin was torn between his glee at the news

and the cutting knowledge that Tokareva had indeed been to bed with the general. How else could she have known of the older man's lack of potency? Despite this, he could feel the beginnings of a response in his body.

Tokareva's eyes picked out a subtle movement in the glow from the city's lights.

"Ah," she said. "Some life is returning."

"You were in his bed," he accused. "That's the only way you could know."

"I had no choice. After trying just that one time, he never touched me again. He was too embarrassed. What more do you want? You've got me as you left me. Do you think I would have enjoyed having that old man, with all his stinking cigarette smoke, on top of me every night for a whole year? *Do you?*"

Her anger had the effect of arousing him. "You have dangerous knowledge," he said after a while. "You must not let him suspect you've told me."

"I won't. Now come here."

He returned to the bed and got in slowly. She was ready for him, but entry into her seemed to go on forever.

"Oooh!" she said. "Come home, come home!" Her arms wrapped themselves strongly about him. Her body began to heave. "Sergei, Sergei . . . oh . . . I missed you. I missed you." Her speech was thick, punctuated by short gasps of pleasure.

Stolybin felt himself driving into her. Twelve months of pent-up fury was pounding into her. He wanted to pay the general back; the prison guards who had enjoyed having a KGB man to shove around; and Tokareva for letting the general touch her.

He knew he was being unreasonable about that part. The general would have left her no choice. But he didn't care. He was working out his frustrations. A detached part of him told him he must be causing her some pain; but she didn't seem to mind, and he was well past caring.

They scrabbled at each other on the bed, gasping and grunting. Then she rolled him over, straddled him, and plunged her lower body frantically. Her voice rose to a scream, mingling with his long-drawn-out growl. Her damp body collapsed slowly upon his.

"Oh Sergei, my comrade colonel. That was so good. You have lost nothing."

Stolybin lay back, mind crystal clear. He knew exactly how to produce what the general wanted.

Still lying on top of him, Tokareva stretched, a great, satisfied feline.

Stolybin was up bright and early. The long, pleasurable night of hectic lovemaking, instead of wearing out his gulag-slimmed body, had served to energize him. Smart and sharp in his new uniform and new colonel's shoulder boards, he stared at himself in a full-length mirror. There was a little looseness here and there, but nothing that was conspicuous.

The prison regime had removed all excess fat from his big frame, and save for the pallor of his sunken cheeks and the strange fire in his eyes, he considered himself quite fit for action.

He touched his cropped head reflectively. The hair was in bad shape, but it would soon recover.

"Pleased with yourself?"

He swung round. Tokareva, in her own uniform of a lieutenant, had entered. The night before, she had worn civilian clothes.

"A commission," he said in mild surprise. "You never told me."

"You had other things on your mind."

"The general pulled a few strings, I suppose."

She nodded. "Screwing a lieutenant is better for the ego."

"Don't say that. I don't even want to think of the two of you—"

She came forward to halt his words with a long kiss. They had made love before and after breakfast.

"And now," she said as she stood back, "we must be distant. We must look as if we had a terrible night, and you must be the cold, aloof KGB colonel. You must look as if you despise me, for all to see; especially the general."

On entering the apartment for the first time last night, they had thoroughly searched it for bugs and cameras. Having wired a few rooms in his time, Stolybin had checked every cranny. He felt pretty certain the general would not have been so obvious; but that in itself could have been what the general had hoped he would think.

Before leaving, he gave the entire apartment another check. If he did find anything now, he thought ruefully, it would be too late to do him any good. But there was nothing.

He put on his brand-new cap and followed an efficient-looking Tokareva out.

2

"Yo, buddy."

In the front cockpit of the Air Superiority Variant Tornado, the F.3S, Flight Lieutenant Mark Selby sighed.

"McCann," he said to his backseater, "you're a highly educated man, an American, to be sure . . . but we won't hold that against you—"

"He loves me, really," McCann said to the empty sky 40,000 feet above the cold North Sea.

"—so why do you insist on talking like some street urchin?"

"'Street urchin.' Boy, you Brits kill me sometimes."

"What did you want to tell me, McCann?" Selby asked with heavy patience.

"Ah. Interested, are you? Just that the boys have come out to play."

"Christ. Why didn't you tell me?"

"I just did," McCann said smugly. "Aaah shiiit!" he yelled in an aggrieved tone as Selby suddenly rolled the aircraft onto its back and pulled firmly on the stick. "Warn a guy, will you?" Then his complaint turned into a grunt as he worked against the G-forces pressing at him. Suddenly, the forces relaxed.

The ASV was now in a steep dive.

The "boys" who had come out to play were a pair of Belgian air-force F-16 Falcons. This was a test combat. The F-16 pilots had been selected to compete for one place in the November Project. The idea of the November units was the brainchild of Wing Commander Christopher Jason, RAF, who had felt that changing realities on the international scene required a fully integrated defense structure, starting with air forces, and initially made up of personnel from the NATO countries. The first of these squadrons, November Zero One, was already operational and had been blooded in combat with the MiG-29s and Su-27s sent to shoot down a defecting pilot in the stolen prototype.

Selby and McCann, of Zero One, together with fellow members Axel Hohendorf and Wolfgang Flacht—both formerly of the German *Bundesmarineflieger*—in a sister aircraft, had defeated the MiGs and Su's in combat. None of them dreamed that their actions had resulted in Stolybin's Siberian holiday. They did not even know of his existence.

As the ASV plunged seaward both men's minds were occupied only with ensuring neither of the F-16s got the better of them. The F-16 pilot who best acquitted himself would be the chosen candidate to join the next squadron being formed, November Zero Two.

This was not going to be a long-range intercept. With the ASV Super Tornado's reach of over a hundred miles, even in a simulated combat, the F-16s would be dead ducks. The test was to be in a close-in knife fight, where the Falcons would be able to use their legendary agility. But the ASV was agile, too. Formidably so. But Selby had no intention of taking the F-16s for granted. Overconfidence could, like familiarity, breed contempt, which in turn bred carelessness, which in *its* turn meant *you* were the dead meat. In true combat, that was a recipe for a shortened life span.

Selby began to gently pull the diving aircraft into level flight, easing back on the stick. As the sleek nose came up toward the horizon his left hand slid the twin throttles back. Virtually at the same moment, the two-engine rpm indicators at the lower right of the main instrument panel registered 85-percent power on both turbofans. Uprated by 30 percent on the standard F.3 power plants, they gave the ASV, lightened by the substitution of tough but weight-reducing composite material in strategic areas of the airframe, a thrust-to-weight ratio that was well over unity. At this better than 1:1 ratio, the engines were virtually flying themselves when at full thrust, canceling out practically all aspects of weight. It served to give the ASV a performance that outstripped its nearest competitor. In the hands of a good pilot, it was formidable. In the hands of a superb pilot, it was magic and seemed invincible.

Nearly all the November pilots were superb men at the stick; but there were those who surpassed all others. A tiny group, of which Selby was one.

"Have they seen us yet?" he asked McCann.

"Patience, my pilot," McCann said. "Ol' Elmer Lee has everything under control."

"That's what worries me."

"Like I said, he loves me really."

Despite the banter, both men had the greatest respect for each other in the air. They were a very tough team and had proved it in combat. Those who were prepared to overlook McCann's apparently uncontrollable attraction for trouble, would admit he was a genius in the backseat. The son of a Kansas City, Missouri, banker, he had been born into reasonable wealth, and there were those unkind enough to say it had ruined him as a responsible human being. Some of the pilots looked upon Selby with pity; but he would not change McCann for anything, despite Elmer Lee's penchant for towing disaster in his wake. There were quite a few senior USAF officers who heaved a great sigh of relief when McCann was selected for the November program. The Brits were in charge of the concept, and if they were crazy enough to want a nut like McCann, those officers thought happily, they could have him for a lifetime.

Even though McCann had been promoted to captain for his performance during the fight, his national air force seemed in no hurry to have him back.

No decorations had been awarded to either crew. That would have signified a public acknowledgment of the battle that was not supposed to have taken place. However, their confidential records marked the event.

In the backseat, McCann had called up Target Search and Acquisition on one of his three multifunction displays. He studied the grid pattern on the MFD as the radar plots of the incoming F-16s moved on the screen. They were still just under a hundred miles away. Their less capable radars would not yet have made them aware of the Tornado's interest in them.

"Lambs to the slaughter," McCann said, only barely managing to keep the smugness out of his voice. "Good thing we're doing a close-in engagement, otherwise we'd have zapped them before they knew we were there. I wonder which of these hotshots is going to make it to Zero Two?" he continued thoughtfully, asking the question more of himself.

"We'll soon find out," Selby remarked, doing one of his frequent searching sweeps of the sky about him.

To those who didn't know, the area in the immediate vicinity of the aircraft would seem lonelier than the empty quarter in the deserts of Saudi Arabia. To him, it was one of the most crowded places on earth. A pair of aircraft approaching each other at a thousand miles an hour from one hundred miles would be in serious danger of a terminal meeting within three minutes, if their pilots were not on the lookout. Less time, he mused, than it would take to order a cup of coffee in some cafés he could think of.

Captains Pierre Garrier and Max Polken flew their F-16s with the subtle ease of true professionals attuned to their aircraft. They knew what was required of them and fully understood that only one of them would go through to the new international squadron. Each wanted the posting, and since they were members of different squadrons, there was an extra keenness to their rivalry.

As pilots of what many thought to be still the best dogfighter in the world, they intended to use its astounding agility to the full. Like the Tornado that was to be their opponent for the exercise, they had no direct linkage between themselves and the control surfaces of their aircraft. Control inputs fed by the pilot via the stick and throttle were interpreted by computers at speeds that gave no perceptible time lag between command and result. Control was thus instantaneous and gave the impression that one merely had to think the aircraft into its maneuvers. To its pilots, the F-16 was the electric jet.

Both Garrier and Polken felt they would need a very special aircraft to seduce them away from their Falcons; but if either man could place himself in Selby's shoes, he would think differently. To Selby, flying the Tornado ASV was a kind of nirvana; a total union with his aircraft.

* * *

While the three aircraft were setting up their positions for the coming mock combat, three hours further east Stolybin looked up from his desk as the general strode in. A cigarette dangled from the general's lips. Stolybin kept his face neutral.

The general looked at him as if expecting comment and, when none was forthcoming, seemed almost disappointed. The general glanced at the file that was lying open near Stolybin's right hand. A sheet of paper on a large pad before him was full of scribbled notes.

"You've been busy," the general remarked. The cigarette danced perilously. A fine tracer of ash floated to the floor. Without asking, he reached over to pick up the sheet of paper and read it through before replacing it, drawing on the cigarette as he did so. Some ash landed on the spotless desk. The general did not brush it off.

"Good," he said approvingly. "I like the beginnings of what I can see here."

"Something I'd like to know, Comrade General . . ."

"Forget the 'Comrade General' in here. I am Vasili Vasilievich and you are Sergei Grigorevich."

"I would like to know . . . Vasili . . . whether this man"—Stolybin tapped a name he had written down—"is still alive, and accessible."

The general actually smiled, though a tethered goat awaiting the attentions of a hungry tiger might have detected a similarity of expression.

"Going for the throat," the general said. "I like that. I've always considered you the best of my operatives, Sergei. That was why it pained me to send you out there in the cold. But you had to understand that the privilege of working for me and *with* me bears a high price for failure. You always knew that. I gave you much more autonomy than any of my staff. I used to get

regular complaints from those of greater seniority
about it. Naturally, they took a kind of shameful pleasure in your being sent away." The general gave a sudden cackle. Ashes flew all over the place. "Now, of
course, they are again put out. You are in favor again,
and they cannot understand it."

Stolybin ignored the flying ash and the soft soap.
The general in a friendly mood was even more dangerous than when he was nasty, and it was a wise man who
knew it. Stolybin awaited a reply to his question.

"He is alive," the general said after a while, nar-
rowing his eyes through a thin plume of smoke as he
looked at Stolybin. "And accessible."

Stolybin nodded, pleased. "Do you like my basic
idea so far?"

"I like it very much. There are risks . . . but then,
there are risks in every undertaking, as you well know.
But this is a far greater prize than anything you have
ever gone for."

The general turned away, straightened his back,
and stood absolutely still. He seemed far away as he
stood in silence, the still-dangling cigarette sending its
thin stream of smoke signals to the ceiling.

Stolybin watched him, in no hurry to disturb the
apparent reverie.

At last, the general drew once more on the cigarette and turned back to face Stolybin.

"This country of ours could very quickly degener-
ate into civil war. It would make Lebanon look like a
child's picnic. All that is happening now is a result of
the last one. Despite seventy-three years, the scars are
still raw. It seems to me that all we had was a kind of
truce in between. I can smell old attitudes returning. If
you're wondering how I know this, I lived it through my
grandparents. They were deeply involved in the fighting. My grandmother was a true warrior. She was not

afraid of doing her share. She would recognize the symptoms today. We must not be made vulnerable again. We will stop this slide into chaos."

The general stopped suddenly, as if returning to the present from a far time. He turned to go.

"Comrade General . . ." It was time to be formal again.

The general paused, but did not turn round.

"I may have to go abroad to arrange some aspects of this," Stolybin said.

"Of course. You have a free hand, within the limits I have set."

The general went out.

Stolybin stared at his notes. Finally, he circled one of the many names he had written. Then he paused, noting for the first time something the general had left. It was the crumpled front page of a daily newspaper. The headline was all about the Nobel Peace Prize being granted to the Soviet Union. The general had circled a word of his own, in thick red. It was the word "Peace." Stolybin carefully smoothed the page with slow hands.

"MIRAGE!" was scrawled across it in large letters.

"Do you think Axel and Wolfie will come back to us?" McCann asked.

Kapitänleutnant Axel, Baron von Wietze-Hohendorf and Oberleutnant zur See Wolfgang Flacht, pilot and backseater respectively, had gone home to Germany on leave.

Selby, preparing to commence battle with the F-16s, did not have those two on his mind. "What do you mean, 'come back'? Of course they'll come back. They're only on leave."

"I dunno. Germany being one again and all that. Maybe they'll want to stay."

"McCann," Selby began with a sigh in his voice, "this is not the time to discuss German unity. I'll talk it through with you later. Okay? We've two F-16s to thrash. Let's concentrate on that, shall we?"

But McCann wouldn't leave it. "I suppose you wouldn't mind if Axel did stay over there. He'd be out of your hair and well away from your sister."

Selby's voice had suddenly lost a great deal of warmth when he spoke again. "Whatever goes on between Hohendorf, my sister, and myself, is not for public discussion. Got it?"

"You mean you want me to shut up?"

"Yes!"

"You sound weird, shouting in an oxygen mask."

Selby made a sound that could have been one of sheer exasperation. It was a bit difficult to get at your backseater's throat when trussed up like a chicken to the front seat of your fighter.

"McCann!"

"Fight's on!" McCann called as the F-16s were suddenly in visual range.

Selby forgot all about Hohendorf and his sister and everything else not connected with the fight as he metamorphosed in an instant into the razor-edged aerial warrior he really was.

"Let's go get 'em!" McCann crowed as the Tornado was reefed into the attack. "Yee haarrr!"

As luck would have it, Pierre Garrier had the dubious pleasure of being Selby's first intended victim.

The Super Tornado, wings swept fully back, hurled itself toward the speck that was Garrier's Falcon like a hungry gray shark. The close-in fight, intended to take place within short-range missile and gun range only, would depend heavily upon the maneuvering skills of the pilots, and the agility of their respective aircraft.

Under normal circumstances, no one in his right mind would want a close-in tangle with an F-16. But these were not normal circumstances, and the Tornado ASV was no ordinary ship.

"Keep an eye on his pal," Selby now said to McCann. "They may be going for a sandwich."

"I give people indigestion if they try to eat me."

"Then let's ruin their day."

As part of the constant evolutionary process that had gone into the initial planning of the November Project, ongoing updates of the aircraft were an integral element of the program. Thus, the aircraft that Selby and McCann now flew, though it was the same one they had used in combat, was already subtly different.

Its air-superiority gray paint scheme for example, incorporated "intelligent" crystals within the paint structure. In each cockpit, there was a special alphanumeric keypad whose codes would call up a series of commands that would cause the paint to alter its tones and shades and even color. Electrical signaling would excite the crystals, making them respond to a particular command's instructions. Under most conditions, giving the instructions was the backseater's job. There was an automatic mode whereby the aircraft's sensors could work their way through a limited repertoire, but the crews were not so sure they were happy with that.

"Imagine," McCann had said on being told of it, "here you are, cruising nicely mottled over a snowfield in the mountains when the goddamn kit thinks it's over a jungle and turns you green. Fat target for the other guy. Shitsville, huh?"

Others were less graphic, but the feelings were

the same. Everyone felt happier maintaining manual control.

McCann now tapped in a code that gave him Air Superiority Shift from the menu. This meant that the aircraft would appear to be constantly shifting its color scheme through various shades of blue gray. To someone looking at it at a distance, it would seem to disappear from time to time.

At first, Selby had been doubtful of the value of the system, which had been dubbed Optical Stealth. Then he had practiced dissimilar air combat against Canadian CF-18 Hornets. The Canadians had utilized the novel idea of painting dummy cockpits in the mirror position on their aircraft's underbelly. Selby had found that in a fast-turning fight close-in, split-second visuals of the darting Hornet were confusing under certain lighting conditions, giving fleeting impressions of the aircraft turning away when it was in fact heading toward him, and vice versa. While such devices were not foolproof against aircraft sensors, it was still the Mark One Eyeball, the best sensor of all, that counted. Seconds, like speed, was life and if Optical Stealth gave those vital extra seconds, then he was all for it.

McCann also switched the attack radar to standby, giving the Falcon nothing to home on to. The ASV's radar, however, kept the F-16s last position in memory and was working through its likely future positions in relation to the Tornado. When McCann decided to switch on again, no matter how briefly, the radar would run through its options and come up with the right answer within nanoseconds. Sneaky stuff, and McCann loved it.

Garrier hauled his Falcon into a steep climb, deciding to use height from which to begin combat. His radar had shown him a brief position of the opposing Tornado, but he had lost it in the climb. He couldn't know that the ASV's stealth properties had been enhanced by the inclusion of the composite materials in its structure. Thus, its radar cross section, or RCS, was a lot less than his Falcon's, a smaller aircraft.

His first knowledge of his adversary's presence was the sudden and strident warning of his radar receiver telling him he was being tracked.

The F-16 was the kind of aircraft that had been specifically invented for dogfighting, and had been constructed in such a way as to make the pilot feel at one with his mount. Its reclined seating position gave better G-tolerance. Stressed to 9G, the Falcon could break its pilot under maneuvering stresses, rather than the other way round. Unlike most other modern fighters, it did not have a central control stick. Instead, a short sidestick that fitted neatly into the hand was mounted on the right side of the cockpit. In his large bubble canopy with hands on the throttle and the stick, the F-16 pilot in full control of his potent machine could take on all comers.

Except aerial sharks like Selby.

As soon as he'd received the radar warning, Garrier had twitched the sidestick to the left, pulled back, reversed the turn, and pulled again. The Falcon described a twinkling path through the air that went left and down, right and up, displacing itself across a considerable portion of sky.

He broke lock briefly, but the sound was soon back.

Garrier strained and grunted against the punishing G-forces as he hauled the F-16 in a painful, right-hand turn. The aircraft almost seemed to pivot about its tail.

Now I have him, he thought.

But there was nothing in his sights.

Bip.

The merest hint of a lock-on. Garrier sent the Falcon skyward, standing the nimble aircraft on its tail, rolling in the climb, and pulling at a forty-five-degree angle from his original course. He pulled into a dive, rolled in the dive, and pulled upward into a barrel roll to describe a brief climbing helix pattern, before reversing and heading back down again at right angles to his most recent path.

Bip.

I don't believe it, Garrier thought grimly.

He put all his inventiveness into his maneuvers and the strenuous fight continued—for years, it seemed to him—but always, the infernal *bip* was there to greet him. He felt dampness on his forehead beneath his helmet, as if his body moisture was being pumped out of him. There was also the feeling that he was being toyed with.

Where the hell was Polken? Why didn't he attack the impossibly elusive Tornado?

Beeeeeeeeeeeee . . .

The continuous tone told Garrier he had lost the engagement. He felt a sudden wave of frustration and chagrin take possession of him as he acknowledged the defeat by flying steadily and calling, "Knock it off, knock it off."

Confirmation came from the other aircraft, which had suddenly appeared next to him, from below.

"You were pretty good," an American voice said to him. "Sorry." The voice didn't sound sorry. "But good fight. Good fight."

Garrier looked at the sleek aircraft that kept station with him, then looked around for Polken. Polken was nowhere to be seen. It was then that he realized that he had been shepherded well away from the other F-16.

Despite his defeat, he found himself smiling grimly in his mask. It had been cleverly done. Well, Polken was on his own now, to face that gray nemesis that appeared to have a strange paint scheme. Garrier decided that the lighting conditions were playing tricks with his eyes.

He gave his victors a snappy fighter-jock salute, rolled his aircraft smartly right to peel stylishly away, heading for home.

McCann watched him go.

"That guy was pretty good," he remarked to Selby. "He knew how to handle his little hot rod. Too bad. We just happen to be better."

"Remind me never to call you modest."

"You never do."

"Just in case I forget. Now, let's sort his mate out."

Selby had to watch it with Polken, who was in danger of becoming a handful. He had to work for his eventual victory, but in the end, sheer skill and advanced equipment won the day.

As Polken too called "Knock it off" and departed the fight area McCann passed his own comment on the capabilities of the two Belgian pilots.

"Both those guys are good," he said. "The Boss is going to find it hard to choose when he checks out the fight videos and the replays from the range screens back at base."

McCann was talking about the huge screens in the control center at the Moray coast unit, which was the home of the November Project.

"Better him than me," Selby said. "I believe those

two were chosen from a hundred possible candidates."

"Many are called, but few are chosen," McCann intoned. *"Yeeharr!* C'mon pilot, baby. Get me home. I need a bar to prop up."

"Give me strength," Selby muttered.

The Grampian coast, Scotland.

Wing Commander Christopher Tarquin Jason, Royal Air Force, and holder of the Air Force Cross and a master's degree in the arts, had watched the entire fight on the main screen of the control center. He was most satisfied. Selby and McCann were one of the three top crews on the squadron and their performance from Zero One's inception had served to vindicate all he had striven so hard for.

The November Project was Jason's brainchild. He was the Boss to all the crews and they had great respect for him. They also knew he could be tough, and no one in a reasonable state of mind would get on the wrong side of him. McCann excepted; for no one could ever be sure when McCann's mind was in a reasonable state.

A pilot of great skill himself, Jason set standards the November pilots had to equal or better. No one who achieved less than that was retained. Those who did not make it were not left with a feeling of failure. Jason did not give that impression to them, for he knew that anyone who came to his unit was already above average. Some November failures had gone on to other operational units, where some of what they had learned during their brief stay had served them well. Jason also left them with the option to try again. One or two had taken that route and had made it. The fact that they had tried a second time had impressed Jason and had been a plus during their subsequent interviews. Jason's standards for the navigators, the backseat riders of which the troublesome McCann was one of the undoubted stars, were no less stringent. McCann was in because he was so brilliant at his job, even Jason was prepared to tolerate the Kansas City Kid's foibles. Within limits.

Jason was in his thirty-sixth year, but there were times when he felt ten years older. Today was not one of those. If one did not know Jason and what he did for a living, he would seem unremarkable. Medium build, clean-shaven, receding sandy hair. "Blame it on the bone dome," he would say when the retreating hairline was remarked upon. His "bone dome" was his flying helmet, the aerial warrior's casque. It was Jason's dark eyes set in the regular features that held attention. It was the intensity and power of that gaze that said this was not an ordinary man.

Jason had fought long and hard for his November Project. Well before the Berlin Wall had come down; long before the effects of *perestroika* and *glasnost* had caused the Hungarians to begin cutting holes in the wire, he had worked on the idea of a fully integrated defense system, evolving from its NATO genesis. Beginning with the November air defense project, he had felt this was the way to create an efficient, tightly professional force that could respond swiftly and coherently to any given threat. It was better, he felt, than having individual nations within the NATO and EC framework so bogged down by their own perceived requirements both defensively and financially, that the changes in Eastern Europe had left them all at sea.

The November system not only spread the cost and manpower, it also produced a far more effective organization, capable of dealing with anything that might arise in a changing world, and would give the nations breathing space while the November units held the line. Simple and easy, Jason had thought.

Not so. Detractors had fought tooth and nail to

prevent the project from becoming a reality, and even now, with its brand-new base on the Grampian coast performing smoothly and with the second squadron, November Zero Two, in the process of being worked up to strength, the wolves were not far from his heels.

With him in the control center was Air Vice Marshal Robert Thurson, a tall and slim aesthete of a man whose general demeanor belied the steel beneath. Thurson was Jason's former flying instructor, and was also his most ardent supporter. Thurson had defended the wing commander's ideas, even at some risk to his own career. He believed Jason was right. However, Thurson had his own Machiavellian tendencies, which he would use without compunction when dealing with adversaries. While Jason appreciated this, he did not always escape the fallout from such incidents.

With complaints about low-flying and the onset of the mythical "peace dividend," the November Project's existence, far from being seen as a natural evolution to the new situation, was again at risk from its opponents. An expensive luxury, was the current battle cry, terminate it.

It did not help that during the early days Zero One had lost a crew and aircraft in spectacular fashion. The Super Tornado's twenty-three-year-old pilot had suffered G-loc—G-induced loss of consciousness—during a hard-turning air combat practice. The backseater, one of November's best, had also perished. Worse, the whole tragedy had been watched in all its detail on the screens, by a group of local dignitaries and MPs who had been invited to the unit as a courtesy for the day.

Jason closed his eyes briefly as he remembered. Not the best way to gain the support of skeptics.

Thurson, on one of his periodic visits to November One, was standing close by and noted the action.

"Anything I should know?" he queried mildly.

"I was just remembering young Palmer and Ferris, sir. I was just thinking how precarious we still are. How finely balanced it all is. I'd have thought that the changes in Europe would have shed some light, given our doubters a clearer picture of what this is all about."

"My dear Christopher, don't expect rational thought and behavior from a people who have been living under an enormous cloud for the past four decades, and who perceive that cloud to have disappeared without trace, so to speak. You cannot tell them traces may remain, or that other clouds will take its place, and that being able to contain such threats is vital. You cannot tell them these things because they will not listen. They do not want you spoiling the dream. If human beings learned anything from history, man's very first conflict would have been his last. He would have said, 'Wait a minute, this stuff's insane. We must stop it.' And he would have lived happily and peacefully thereafter."

"Do you seriously believe that?"

"Of course not. Which brings us right back to where we are."

"I believe Europe to be a more dangerous place than it's been for some time. All those disparate states armed to the teeth, with old scores to settle. I mean, they're at it already. Any serious conflict between them could easily drag in more heavyweight supporters on one side or another. Then there's the Soviet Union itself, or what's left of it. A civil war there and . . ."

Jason let the words die into silence. Thurson was looking at him.

"You do realize, don't you," the AVM began, "that if you say such things to the people you'd like to convince, they'd only tell you that you're just looking for something to justify your existence." Thurson waved an arm about the control room. "And this. Expensive toys, you will be told. We can't afford it."

"We're not the only ones paying," Jason said.

"Don't think our partners are immune to their opponents of the scheme, even after what happened to Kuwait."

Thurson turned to the screen. A ceiling light in the underground room gleamed briefly upon the individual broad and thin rings denoting rank on the shoulders of his olive-green flying overalls. Without the usual accoutrements of G-suit, immersion suit, leg restraints, and lifejacket—essential for the continuing survival of the relatively fragile human body in the Tornado's arena—he seemed undressed. But even wearing this basic clothing, the air vice marshal managed to look nattily turned out. The attire fitted his slim frame neatly, with not a wrinkle showing. Upon his left breast was the familiar white-bordered, dark aircrew patch with its RAF pilot's wings beneath which was the legend "Bob Thurson."

Still looking at the screen, Thurson continued. "It will be little use speaking of the Balkans in the earlier part of the century when those states fought each other, and what happened in its wake; nor that what is now happening appears to carry a rather worrying echo. They won't listen. Everything's changed, you will be told." Thurson appeared to be almost speaking to himself. "But don't worry, Chris. I'm in your corner."

He stood, legs apart, studying the screen as Selby's combat with the two F-16 Falcons was replayed. Electronically etched wingtip trails streamed behind each of the aircraft images, graphically displaying the maneuvers carried out by each combatant. A series of rolling displacements, for example, like the ones Garrier had performed in his unsuccessful attempt to evade Selby, were shown in ribbon form so that every part of the moves could be minutely scrutinized.

As he watched Selby's countermoves Thurson said, "I like the way that man works. Incidentally, where are his European alter egos, Hohendorf and Bagni?"

"Hohendorf, with his backseater Flacht, is in Germany," Jason replied, "and Bagni's aloft on combat air patrol with one of the newer boys as his number two. His backseater's still Stockmann, our resident hard-nosed American marine. Those two get on very well. Like Selby and McCann, and Hohendorf and Flacht, they are one of my top teams."

"It was Bagni, wasn't it, who was flying against young Palmer the day he went down?"

Jason nodded. "Bagni blamed himself for the crash, which was, of course, nonsense. Stockman was aboard that day and talked him into sorting himself out to make a good landing. I've left them together ever since. In his remorse, Bagni confessed to me that he had always been terrified of landings. . . ."

Thurson was looking at his subordinate steadily. "You thought not to mention this to me?"

Jason stood his ground. "As CO, I made a judgment of his real capabilities. Bagni's a superb pilot. His landings are always perfect. If I thought for one moment he was a danger to himself or the unit, I'd ground him so fast it would take years for his breath to catch up. I flew with him immediately after the crash, in a single-stick ASV—"

"One set of controls. Was he worth such a risk? Had he cooked it, you would have had no option but to eject, as you could not have been able to take control and so attempt to retrieve the situation. I might have lost one brand-new, pricey aircraft, one pricey pilot, and had the ejection failed, one very pricey wing commander. I would have had to explain to the Italians, the minister, assorted members of Parliament—"

Jason took the liberty of interrupting. "Sir, you would have done the same in my place. I am your pupil."

"—not to mention equally assorted Eurocrats." Thurson halted in midflow. "Damn you, Christopher. You fight dirty."

"Yes, sir. I had a good teacher. And Bagni was definitely worth it. He's no more afraid of landings than I am."

Thurson's gaze remain locked upon the wing commander. "As you've just said, you are the CO. You'll carry the can. As the one behind the November program, that can you may have to lug around is of substantial size. It's not only your neck, but mine too. And never forget, the wolves are always ready to pounce."

"I never do."

Suddenly Thurson gave a fleeting smile. "The devil with it. I always enjoy a good scrap . . . within reason, of course."

Which in Jason's interpretation really meant, "Get me into trouble and I'll have your guts."

Thurson glanced at his watch. "My word. It's well past my lunchtime. Thank you, Christopher. I will be your guest in the mess."

Jason, who'd had no idea whether the air vice marshal had intended to stay for lunch, said, "A pleasure, sir."

As they went out a couple of noncommissioned fighter control assistants followed their movements with curious eyes.

"I wonder what they were talking about so anxiously," one, a member of the RAF, said thoughtfully.

His companion, a Frenchman, said, "And here I am thinking all the English are models of reticence. If they had wanted us to know, they would have said hello Airmen Roland and Williams, please join us. We need the advice of two such wise men as you. You are the backbone of the unit."

"Just my luck. A comedian on my shift."

"You asked."

"Serves me right. And besides, I'm Welsh."

"Ah," the Frenchman said, which could have meant anything.

3

Thurson said: "I missed seeing Caroline Hamilton-
Jones down there. How is she progressing?"

They were walking toward the officers' mess.
Thurson had decided he fancied a stroll, and as a result,
everyone who passed them gave him salutes, which
came in a variety of styles, depending on the national-
ity walking past. As the most senior rank in the entire
unit, he inevitably collected the lot.

"Doing well, and liking it," Jason replied.

Thurson had to answer yet another salute with a
casual one of his own. "Perhaps walking was not such
a good idea. Doing well, is she? Good." Another salute,
right hand waving briefly in the direction of the field
service cap set centrally atop his head. "Remind me not
to walk about this place unless absolutely necessary.
My arm's getting tired."

Jason had the grace not to smile.

"So she's made it to the Hawks at Brawdy," Thurson went on.

"Yes, sir."

"Who would have believed it? Women on advanced Hawks."

"I recommended her, sir. But you backed me up.

She never would have got as far as the selection board if you hadn't put your weight in. As it turned out, she has an excellent aptitude for flying."

"You're turning me into a very rash person indeed, Wing Commander. I can almost feel the noose tightening around my neck. When the Royal Air Force decided to allow women into the piloting and navigating aircrew ranks, I don't think anyone intended them to go into combat flying. It occurs to me that Flight Lieutenant Hamilton-Jones is not the type of young woman who can easily be fobbed off with flying transports, VIP aircraft, tankers, and so on, challenging as those duties might prove to be. It occurs to me that she would like to go on to fighters." Thurson paused to look at Jason. "I don't suppose a certain wing commander hinted that if circumstances changed, he'd give her a shot at becoming a November pilot."

Jason was innocence itself. "Would I ever?"

Thurson walked on. They were almost at the mess.

"Glad to hear of it," he said. "You've got enough trouble without looking for more. Besides, it would never happen. Women fighter pilots indeed. And don't say it—I know the Americans have got female naval pilots who fly A-4 Skyhawks and A-7 Crusaders, and yes, I know some of them give male pilots a hard time during air combat practice, and so on. They are, after all, Americans," Thurson added, as if that answered everything. They had arrived. "All this walking has made me hungry. Let's see how we can augment your mess bill."

As they entered, Jason thought of Caroline Hamilton-Jones. She had just begun to love Ferris, Palmer's Australian backseater, when the fatal crash had occurred. Privately, he admired her determination. He knew many people, not necessarily weak, who would not have wanted to go near an aircraft after what had happened. To actually want to *fly* one took a special kind of drive. He had indeed told her if circumstances allowed it and she could meet the standards required to join the November squadrons, he would give an application from her serious consideration. But that was for the future. No point ruining the air vice marshal's lunch.

While they were walking down a corridor toward the dining room for their informal lunch, the aircrew, mainly dressed like the AVM, went by. They came loosely to attention as the two architects of the November program passed through.

"Speaking of Americans," Thurson began, "is Lieutenant McCann still your enfant terrible?"

"Very much so, I'm afraid, sir. He's a lost cause as far as that goes. And he's a captain now."

"Captain, is he? By George! Such wonders to behold."

"The Americans were happy to let him have his promotion, as long as we promised not to send him back to them."

"They obviously know a good thing when they see it."

"To be fair, McCann is a genius in the backseat, and Selby knows how to handle him."

"After what happened with that defecting aircraft, and seeing the way they operated today, I've got to agree with you. He's still an unruly beggar."

"Our unruly beggar now, sir."

"For our sins, yes."

"My ears are burning," McCann announced as Selby joined the circuit prior to landing. "Someone's talking about me."

"Probably tearing his or her hair out as well," Selby told him unsympathetically.

"You can give a guy a complex. You know that?"

"Impossible."

Selby carried out a smooth touchdown. The aircraft barely jolted as its main wheels made contact with the runway.

"One of these days," McCann began aggrievedly, almost like a prayer. "One of these fine days you'll make a lousy landing and boy, will I crow!"

"You've got a long wait, Elmer Lee, old son." The sleek nose of the ASV Tornado held off for some moments then lowered itself gently. The nosewheel touched and the thrust-reverser buckets, preselected, shut themselves like clams behind the jet nozzles. The throttles went forward to Max Dry, slowing the aircraft powerfully, locking the seat harnesses with the force of the retardation.

Selby eased the throttles to idle. The buckets went back to the open position.

"And another fine landing," he said. "Give the man a big hand."

"I hate goddamned pilots," McCann said as they taxied off the runway. "And I hate smart-ass pilots even more."

"I know, Elmer Lee," Selby responded good-naturedly. "It's a tough life."

McCann was himself a frustrated pilot. Dreaming of carving the skies with his passage in an F-15 Eagle, he had joined the US Air Force. After some very hairy landings during training, often one of which an instructor swore he'd never fly with McCann again, the Kansas City Kid was washed out of pilot training. The USAF hoped that would have been the last of him, but McCann did not give up easily. Offered what he had then seen as a very second best, the chance to fly in the backseat of two-crew aircraft, he had accepted, to the chagrin of those who had hoped he wouldn't. Against all expectations, he had proved to be, as Jason had indicated, a genius with the electronics, coupled with the soundness of his spatial awareness during air combat.

Inevitably, being McCann, he had clashed with many pilots, his most serious incident occurring when he was a very green lieutenant being piloted by a major. He accused the major of making a wrong move, in terms that were less than mindful of the disparity in ranks. It did not help the major's disposition when later analysis of the fight had proved McCann correct. It did not help McCann, either.

Selby taxied the ASV to its hardened aircraft shelter so that the inertial navigation and attack system could satisfy itself it had returned to the point it had started from.

"We've got a couple of days off, Elmer Lee," Selby now said as they shut down the aircraft's systems. "What are your plans?"

"I'm taking the Vette down to London."

"You're going from here to London, just for two days, by *road?*"

"Sure."

"In that gas guzzler?"

"Careful. You're talking about the car I love: 1990 Chevvy Corvette, the best set of wheels in the world, from the world."

"No accounting for taste, I suppose. We're up on the Grampian coast of Scotland, McCann," Selby went on. "That's over six hundred miles each way."

"So? That's no distance in the States."

Selby released his harness and began to climb out. He paused, looking at McCann still in the backseat. "This isn't the States. You've got six hundred miles of traffic-congested, mainly narrow roads. Don't get caught speeding, or the Boss will have your balls. We're low-profile people. Just remember that. And when you get back, I don't want you asleep in your cage when you're up top with me. I'm talking like this to you for your own good."

"You could have fooled me."

McCann freed himself of the aircraft and followed Selby down.

McCann drove the Corvette fast along the A98, heading for Inverness, Perth, Glasgow, and Carlisle, for the fast motorway run to London. A shortish man, he had seen his twenty-fifth year, but looked more like a teenager. This was enhanced by the fact that he possessed a round chubby face and a crop of corn-colored hair that became unruly beyond the length of one inch. People sometimes called it Kansas corn, a description he hated. He was no farmer, he would be at pains to tell them. He was a city boy.

"Kansas *City,*" he would say furiously. "You know, you deadheads. Where the pretty little women come from . . . like the song says."

There was a cockiness of manner that sometimes rubbed people the wrong way, and his bright blue eyes and button nose gave him the appearance of a slightly malicious imp, and a deflator of pomposity.

Even in November in northern Scotland, he drove with the windows down and the roof panels stowed in the back. True to form, he wore his aviator sunglasses, despite the now overcast sky. On the car stereo, the old song "Kansas City" was playing loudly. Scotland was getting a dose of the McCann treatment.

Though he had not indicated it to Selby, he was not really looking forward to the drive to London. But it was that, or have his father come up to see him.

McCann Senior had warned in a letter he'd be "crossing the pond" to see his boy, and for the first time in his life, McCann had found he was not so keen to see his doting father. Suddenly a brand-new Corvette every birthday since his twenty-first was not such a big deal. He wanted to keep the one he had for a while longer. He hoped his father was not going to tell him the '91 model had been ordered.

McCann did not analyze the change in himself and probably would not have come up with a coherent answer had he chosen to do so. All he knew was that he was subtly different. The boy had at last left home for good. It was not going to be easy to tell the old man.

He thrust the gloomy thoughts from his mind and enjoyed the drive and the Scottish scenery.

Selby was also on the A98, but instead of continuing on the A96 to Inverness, he would turn left at Fochabers for Aberdeen, where his sister Morven was studying to become a marine biologist at the university. He intended to make only a brief stop. His real destination was Edinburgh, where Kim Mannon was already waiting.

Up ahead was McCann's stone-gray Corvette, being driven with verve. Selby's own four-wheel-drive Ford Sapphire Cosworth could easily have the legs of it, particularly because of the Ford's phenomenal grip on the road, but Selby was in no mood for a challenge with McCann. When the junction came up, he flashed a farewell to McCann, who replied with a flash of his hazard lights before speeding away.

Selby settled into the new route, letting the Cosworth have its head on the way to Aberdeen. He had two major concerns, both women. Morven seemed to be determinedly serious about Hohendorf, despite the fact that the latter's estranged wife appeared to have no intention of divorcing him. And as for Kim Mannon, what had months before appeared to have been a foregone conclusion now seemed increasingly less so.

After the combat over the Norwegian Sea, he had been so relieved to have survived that everything he had previously taken for granted had suddenly become infinitely precious. Against his own belief that fighter pilots should not marry, he had rushed her to Edinburgh's Holyrood Park and, in a wildly romantic gesture quite out of character, had taken her up a hill to propose. She had said yes.

"That was then," he said to himself. "This is now."

The cause, Sir Julius Mannon, big wheel in the City of London and father of the intended bride. Sir Julius had his own ideas about a suitable husband for his only daughter.

Selby had met her at a function he had attended under duress. Morven had been invited to an autumn ball in London, before he had joined November One. She'd needed an escort, and he had conveniently provided it. Though Morven could have had her pick of escorts from among her university friends, she had not wanted someone who might get carried away with the spirit of the occasion. A brother fitted the bill nicely for a woman who did not want to get involved with anyone. Morven liked to choose her men when it suited her.

"So she chooses Axel Hohendorf," he said aloud as the road took him through Speymouth Forest.

Despite the fact that both he and Hohendorf had been through real combat together, and that once he had even contributed significantly to the saving of Hohendorf's life when the German pilot's aircraft had suffered a severe birdstrike, he still found it difficult to come to terms with Morven's involvement with his squadron colleague.

He thought of his other problem with Kim Mannon's father and smiled briefly, without humor, at the irony of it all.

He could picture her exactly as he'd first seen her that evening. He had been standing well away from the crowd after the tables had been deserted for dancing in the ballroom of the pricey hotel that had been booked for the occasion.

The small, neat body, the short black hair, thickish eyebrows, and wide-apart dark eyes brimming with mischief and daring; the small sharp nose and the generous mouth; the black gown with gold highlights that hugged a delightful form; the gold necklace at her throat that would have cost him several months pay to purchase; the black earrings hanging from small lobes; the black-dialed wristwatch with its slim, golden strap; and the golden sandals upon her feet.

She had been appraising him boldly, perfectly in keeping with the persona she presented to the world. Horrendously expensive, he had thought, and no territory for a hardworking fighter jock.

Though struck by her smoldering beauty, he had not warmed to her on this first meeting. In fact, he had gone out of his way to be offhand, considering her dangerous to know. But she, like Morven, had made up her mind and had pursued him. Bewildered initially by her, he had soon fallen deeply in love, despite a determined rearguard action. He had certainly been right about the danger. Being in love with Kim Mannon was no easy thing.

But dear God, she was so exciting.

Thinking about her, seeing her in his mind's eye, made him eager to arrive in Edinburgh. He thrust the thoughts of Sir Julius out of his mind. Kim was no weakling. She knew how to fight even someone as powerful her father; and Selby was himself determined not to be intimidated.

Sir Julius had tolerated, almost benignly, his daughter's dalliance—as he had chosen to see it—with Selby.

Selby tightened his lips grimly as the older man continued to invade his thoughts. Sir Julius had been quite happy to go along with what he had perceived as a fling of the moment. Then he hit the roof when Kim had told him she'd said yes to Selby's proposal. Mannon intended to marry his daughter off to an old flame of Kim's, one Reginald Barham-Deane, the "financial barracuda" of the Mannon empire, as Sir Julius had himself once called his employee. Barham-Deane had only tenuously been a flame, as Kim had merely allowed him to tag along with her. Nothing had really happened between them. But it was cold comfort. Barham-Deane was a tangible shadow that had to be dispersed.

Lafayette, Indiana, USA.

Representative Amos Gant was visiting his mother. With some months to go before his thirtieth birthday, Gant looked several years younger than his real age. There was no sign of a receding line to mar the rich brown of his hair, which was cut just short enough to avoid the tag of looking like a pansy while still managing to present an air of military efficiency.

Gant was that most exotic of politicians, a formidable hawk that had become dovish. Most observers remained skeptical of his apparent conversion. Political opponents, who had said of him that the appearance of a real dove would have had him reaching for a hunting rifle to blast the unfortunate bird out of existence, were even more skeptical. Gant wanted to be president one day, and no path was too inglorious to achieve that goal. Gant's road to Damascus had been the sudden collapse of all those Eastern European regimes.

He had, in the merest blink of an eye, metamorphosed from a Cold War hawk to a Peace Dividend dove. He had made trips to Moscow, a city he had once called a den of iniquity. He had even befriended one of the newly elected deputies, a former dissident who had once received the dubious ministrations of the KGB. The deputy, Alexei Ivanovich Belov, was a firm believer in drastic arms reduction, apparent music to Gant's ears. He arranged to have Belov visit the United States, entertained him at his own home in Indianapolis, where Belov spent some time, and generally ushered the bemused Russian just about everywhere.

Gant collected a lot of media attention. Hardened journalists went along with what they saw as a panto-mime, while hanging on to their skepticism. Gant's opponents became worried. The man was scoring high points at their expense. Like the journalists, however, they refused to accept that Gant had really changed. But Gant seemed to be unerringly in tune with the spirit of the times. He had become a powerful advocate of arms cuts and even seemed prepared to ignore comments of friends that his current stance was akin to heresy.

But there was no stopping him. He and his new-found friend, it seemed, were determined to increase the momentum toward a significant cut in weaponry by both sides in the ertswhile arms race. He made a point, however, of stating that because the Soviet Union already possessed such a disparity in numbers, it was only right that the Union should make the biggest cut. Belov readily agreed.

Neither man appeared to have official sanction for their meetings and discussions, but undoubtedly they generated great interest both within the corridors of power and, more important, among their respective electorates. They were beginning to affect the way those with the votes now looked at international relations. Overt criticism of their efforts to achieve arms cuts was beginning to be counterproductive. It was an incautious politician, whether in Washington or Moscow, who would choose to castigate them in public. One big-city mayor in the States, with his own eye on Washington, had made the mistake of pillorying Gant, calling him a hypocrite, during a reelection campaign. He lost.

On a Moscow street corner where Belov had been holding a meeting, he had been heckled by a man who had called him a traitor and accused him of being in the pay of the Americans. The man had been set upon by the crowd. Undercover KGB personnel who had infiltrated the crowd saved the heckler from serious injury.

As they hustled the man away one of the KGB men was heard to say about Belov, "In the old days, I'd have shot the bastard. Save everyone a lot of trouble."

They had set the heckler free, without so much as a caution.

"Are you sure you can't stay longer?"

Gant looked across the breakfast table at his adoring mother. His baby-blue eyes twinkled at her. The dark brown hair and the eyes were a powerful combination, as he'd known from an early age. He had used them for effect for as long as he could remember, from childhood through school, into adulthood and politics. They had served him well. His tall frame, slim and athletic, had enabled him to become a champion runner, in both high school and college. Now, clothed in well-made suits that were not cheap, he made a stylish figure on Capitol Hill.

"Mom," he began with patience but genuine affection, "we've been through this. I've already stayed longer than I should have. I'm a day overdue in Washington, and I've got to got to spend a few hours in Indianapolis first."

She smiled at him, looking proud. "If only your father could see you now. So busy. He would have liked to see you in the White House one day."

"I know, Mom. I'll get there. Don't you worry."

"I know you will. It's just—"

"Now, now, Mom. Dad's been dead for fifteen years, and for every one of those years, you've said how he would have liked it every time I succeeded at something. Don't you think I know that?"

"Of course you do. But it would have been nice if he could have seen all this."

Gant nodded and said nothing. She would never let go of the memory of his father. Gant did not himself remember his father with much affection. Gant Senior had wanted his boy to be a football player and had been openly scathing of the then slight frame of his son. Sissy, he had called him once. Gant had never forgotten. After all, his father had said, a football player had once become president.

"Are you seeing that Russian friend of yours in Washington?" his mother now asked.

Gant shook his head. "He's in Moscow right now. But we'll be meeting again in a few months. Serious things to discuss." He did not elaborate.

A horn sounded once.

"And there's Jack Hagen," Gant continued, standing. Hagen was both chauffeur and bodyguard. Gant picked up his jacket from the back of his chair and put it on.

His mother stood up and came around to make minute adjustments to its fit. "You must get a wife soon. A president needs a wife."

Gant gave her a brief smile. "Plenty of time, Mom. Plenty of time."

She gazed up at him. "And plenty of young women who would like to be your wife. I've seen the way they look at you."

He kissed her on the forehead as the horn sounded again. "I'm out of here, Mom. Jack's getting impatient. See you soon. We'll talk on the phone as usual."

She watched him leave, the pride shining in her eyes.

As Gant entered the car he looked back at the modest but comfortable house. His mother was at a window, looking down at him. He raised a hand briefly as the car started down the short drive. He saw the return wave before she went out of view.

Gant was not a poor man, but he was not rich. However, many of his sponsors and backers were. His campaign funds were thus always in plentiful supply, and despite his apparent switch in attitude, there was as yet no danger of sources drying up. Those sources had agreed to fund a special meeting with Belov, to discuss ways of creating a program for arms reduction that would be presented to both the White House and the Kremlin. Though this was unofficial, Gant was sure his ideas would find favor with Washington, and if things went as expected, he would make a powerful impression on the Hill. People would not forget that in a hurry.

There were many people who did not like the manner of Gant's hungry lunge for the top.

They were not all on Capitol Hill.

While Jack Hagen was driving Gant south to Indianapolis, Stolybin was laboring beneath the lights of his KGB office. The file he had begun for his planned operation was growing. It lay open on one side of his desk. On the other was the general's original file. A months-old page of a Moscow newspaper was now before him. A single photograph took up most of the page. In among a crowd of people, there were two faces that interested him.

They belonged to Belov and Gant.

Stolybin smiled thinly. He recognized other faces. Among the supposedly eager crowd were those of KGB operatives.

The general entered, trailing smoke and ash. "It's after six o'clock, Sergei. I know I want you to work hard on this, but even you must have some rest. I believe you were here all lunchtime."

Stolybin nodded. The general did not "believe." The general knew. "I can eat later, Comrade . . . er . . . Vasili."

The general looked pleased by the use of his name. "Don't starve yourself."

"I lived on less during the last twelve months."

The eyes of the two men locked. Neither appeared to blink.

Then the general smiled through his cigarette smoke. At least he seemed to. He looked down at the spread page. "You have been busy. Ah yes. Deputy Belov." He sounded as if he wanted to spit. "And his Amerikanski. They interest you?"

"They must have interested you, too," Stolybin countered. "There is plenty of paperwork on them, and they inhabit several computer disks."

The general's eyes narrowed, but it could have been the smoke. "Everything interests the KGB." He paused. "Belov." He spat the name out. "The fool believes Gant is serious."

"Oh, Gant is serious . . . about *our* reductions." Stolybin's eyes were cynical in the extreme. "I remember him from my time in Washington. He made the other American hawks look like chickens. This man has not suddenly turned into a chicken, unless it's to eat one. He's hiding among the doves. For a purpose."

"Which is?"

For an answer, Stolybin thumbed through the notes he had made, then stopped. "I see Lieutenant Grashin nearly got his head kicked in at one of Belov's street meetings. Our own people had to save his skin. Lucky they were there."

"What are you trying to say?" the general asked softly.

Stolybin took the bold route. "That was clumsy. Getting someone to heckle Belov was not a good idea. I suspect very few people in that crowd thought he was genuine—the heckler, I mean—and they would have been even more convinced by Belov's words. Now he's a deputy. . . ."

"You're saying you would have done better?" The general had taken his cigarette between forefinger and thumb, and now he drew strongly upon it, eyes fastened upon his subordinate. He took the cigarette briefly from his lips. For a moment, it looked as if he wanted to stub it out on Stolybin. Then slowly he returned it to his mouth, as if he couldn't bear to be without it for much longer.

"I would not have done that at all," Stolybin said calmly.

There was a long pause during which all that could be heard was a faint wheezing from the general, whose eyes remained locked upon Stolybin's.

Here it comes, Stolybin thought with resignation. He's going to remind me of my past failures. So it's back to Siberia. But if he wants me to do this properly, obvious stunts like heckling have got to stop.

At last, the general spoke. "You had a bright idea with that defecting pilot friend of yours. Now he is living off American fat, after first spilling his guts to the British."

Stolybin said nothing and waited for the ax to fall.

But the moment was postponed, for the general continued. "I expected you to say that. So what will you do? How does Belov fit into your plan?"

For reply, Stolybin passed the older man a sheet of paper.

The general took his time to study it, then a slow smile creased his rough features. The cigarette performed a brief dance about his lips while remaining clamped between them.

"You do have your faults, Sergei, but I still like the way you think. This is good. You're creating a maze. You're sure there isn't Byzantine blood in you?"

It was the general's way of giving a compliment.

"I shall destroy all of these notes, of course," Stolybin said, "at the end of it all."

"Of course," the general said. "It is what I would expect."

The A96 skirted the River Don as Mark Selby approached the compact city of Aberdeen. He'd always liked the place, not for its reputation of being the oil city of Scotland, but for its university enclave. He liked Old Aberdeen.

Unlike virtually all nonlocal students, during her first year, Morven had landed on her feet in the accommodation game. Not for her the halls of residence or the student flats of Hillhead. She had been befriended by a fellow undergraduate in the same year, Tricia Balcombe, whose family owned a small house that had been used for generations by those Balcombes who had attended Aberdeen. Tricia was the latest and had invited Morven to share. Every Balcombe in the past had apparently done the same with a contemporary.

Selby was happy Morven had met Tricia Balcombe, for it was Tricia who had invited her to the autumn ball that had subsequently brought Kim Mannon into his life.

He now pulled up in the quiet street where Morven lived. He got out of the car and went to the door. His visit was not to be a long one. A quick hello, a cup of tea, then it was on to Edinburgh and two glorious days with Kim, to be spent mostly in bed.

The door opened before he knocked. A pretty blonde he did not recognize smiled at him. She seemed a cheerful sort of person.

"I saw you drive up," she greeted. "You must be the fabulous fighter pilot brother. She's got your photo, with all your gear on, in her room. Do come in." She stood aside to let him enter, eyes surveying him with frank approval. "The real thing's even better."

"Bet you say that to all the boys."

"Only to those who merit it, and there aren't many. Can I get you a drink?" She pushed the door slowly shut.

"Anything nonalcoholic, thanks. Is Morven in?"

"She's not, I afraid, so you'll have to make do with me. I'm Zoe Patterson. Your look at the door tells me you expected to see Tricia, if not Morven."

"Well . . . yes. You're . . . unexpected." McCann would go ape, Selby was thinking, if he could see you.

"Just 'unexpected'?" she asked boldly. "Don't look so shocked. I feel as if I've known you for a long time. Morven talks about you a lot."

"She does, does she? And you don't have to put on an act for me. I'm not going to bite."

She blushed suddenly. Oh yes, he thought. McCann would go bananas.

"Is it that obvious?" she asked, looking slightly unsure of herself.

"You look as if you're steeling yourself to say something. Where's Morven gone? Germany?"

Zoe nodded to herself, confirming something. "She said you'd be quick. Everybody's off somewhere. Tricia's gone to East Africa—she's been there since August—which is why I'm here. I've got her place in the house for a year."

"And Morven?" Selby could feel his voice hardening.

Zoe quickly went out of the room and returned with a sealed envelope, which she handed to Selby as if afraid he would indeed take a bite out of her.

He ripped it open and read the note.

Brother dear [it began]
  No time to let you know. I called the base, but you were up in the blue yonder. I'm off to see Axel—he called last night—and to meet his mother. We discussed this before, so please don't be cross, and don't bite Zoe's head off. By the way, isn't she absolutely gorgeous? She fancies you like mad, but I told her Kim Mannon would do unspeakable things to her. Two women! I'll have to lock you up! And please, don't worry, Mark. I'll be all right. Really. Just wish me luck. Okay? Now go and have fun with Kim . . . or Zoe, if you feel brave!
Lots of love,
Mo

Selby wanted to crumple the note, but restrained himself. He folded it carefully and replaced it in the envelope. Then he put it in a pocket.

Zoe was regarding him warily. "You'll still have that drink?"

"Oh yes. Thank you. And I won't bite you. Promise. Morven's ordered me not to." His smile was friendly.

"Thank goodness," she said. "There are times to be bitten, but this isn't one of them." She paused, as if wondering whether she should say more, then decided it was safe to do so. "I've met Axel, you know."

"Oh yes?"

"He's nice." She said it with feeling.

"He's all right."

She gave up. "Fine. I think I've got the message. Tea?"

"That will be fine, thanks."

As she went out and he took a seat Selby decided it was not the best way to start two days' leave.

When he left to continue on to Edinburgh, the tension had long eased and he'd promised Zoe he'd come to a dinner she was having for some friends. Bring a friend, she'd said, meaning a fellow flyer. He wondered if it would be safe to bring McCann.

His arrival in Edinburgh did not improve his mood. Reggie Barham-Deane was there, grinning smugly back at him. The reasons were quite legitimate, but it did not make Selby feel any better.

The large Princes Street house was also used by Sir Julius as temporary accommodation for the top executives of Mannon Robinson who traveled to Edinburgh on business, and Barham-Deane had just completed a week in residence. He was, however, due to return that day. Kim Mannon had known this and had arranged her own arrival to coincide with Selby's. She had expected Barham-Deane to be long gone.

"Hullo there, Selby," Barham-Deane began with overcheerful bonhomie. "How's the flying business? Little airplane behaving itself? I thought you'd be somewhere exotic like the Gulf, getting all keyed up to zap an Iraqi johnnie, or three."

The physical contrast between the two men could not have been greater. Though just under six feet, Selby's compact frame made him seem shorter. His closely trimmed dark hair set off a face that just avoided being too square in shape and a well-defined jawline that was barely saved from being too prominent. It gave his features a precision that was enhanced by piercing blue, distant eyes. A neat mustache underscored his nose. His strong hands were broad, seeming too peasantlike for the delicate art of flying a high-performance, complex fast jet like the Tornado ASV. Yet anyone who knew his flying capabilities would say that his touch lived on the very razor's edge of perfection.

In his navy Savile Row suit, the plump but sleek Barham-Deane was the epitome of the new breed of go-getter that inhabited the financial jungles of the City of London. He had the air of a man who saw himself as a supreme predator. The food chain ended with him. Like Selby, he was not yet thirty. He was equal in height to Selby and his gleaming blond hair, tended carefully in a longish crew cut, was frequently caressed by an apparently absentminded hand.

His eyes were deep set, their color indeterminate. The tan he sported had been obtained well out of season for lesser mortals. His beardless face was so smooth, it was difficult to tell whether he actually bothered to shave. His smile was a strange one, making him look as if he were sucking a boiled sweet. When he was feeling mean and particularly nasty, the corners of his mouth would turn down so severely, his lips would appear to be trying to form themselves into a horseshoe.

Selby stared at him silently, despising his comment. Selby had friends out there who might well not be returning.

Knowing what it was like to shoot another pilot down before *he* got you, Selby said coldly, "It's not a game, Barham-Deane. People tend to die."

The boiled-sweet smile came on. "Touchy, touchy. It was only a lighthearted comment."

"You chose the wrong subject about which to make it. I've a very good friend in that 'exotic' place, as you call it. We were in the same university air squadron and were together right through to Tornado conversion, after which we went on to different units. I'd like to think that even if he does go out hunting, he'll make it back."

"So do we all, dear boy. So do we."

Selby looked as if he did not believe Barham-Deane to be of sincere.

"You lead such a high-risk life," Barham-Deane said. "Why not quit and come to fly the company jet? We've got a brand-new HS-125. Plenty of perks," Barham-Deane continued without looking at Kim, "and lots of money. A lot more than Her Majesty's government pays you."

Flying a twin-engine executive jet for a living, even one as excellent as the BAe HS-125, was not Selby's ideal, but worse, the offer from Barham-Deane had carried with it the poisoned sting of a veiled insult. Barham-Deane had known exactly what the effect upon Selby would be.

Selby chose not to rise to the bait. He gave the other man a hard stare before turning to Kim.

"I'll help myself to a drink, if I may," he said to her. "I think I need it."

Her eyes widened slightly at the underlying tension in his voice, but she said nothing as he left for one of the reception rooms.

Barham-Deane waited until Selby had shut the door before saying, "Knows his way around, I see."

Kim's dark eyes appeared to be on the point of combustion.

"You bastard," she said to Barham-Deane. "You

shit. You know how he feels about his flying. You deliberately—"

"Dear me, dear me! I've actually made you angry!"

"You always make me angry. And as for that false offer of a job . . . not everyone worships money the way you do."

Barham-Deane pointedly looked about the sumptuously decorated hall in which they were standing. "I think all this cost a pretty penny. You may not think you worship money, darling, but I can't see you trading all this for sparse military quarters."

"So you've told me, a million times before."

"Slight exaggeration, but you get the drift."

Kim took a deep breath and let it out slowly, controlling the exasperation she felt. "Please go, Reggie. You should have been gone before I got here. If you were hoping to extend your stay, forget it. Besides, Daddy always likes personal reports from his senior executives. He'll be expecting you. Don't keep him waiting."

"I concluded the deal two days earlier than expected, so—"

"Well, don't think you're going to spend them here."

Barham-Deane made no move to go. "A house in Chelsea, a Buckinghamshire mansion, this pile here in Scotland, assorted homes in Europe . . . oh no, my dear. I can't see you giving all this up for our skybound hero in there. What can he possibly give you to compete with all that? What can he give you that I can't?"

"You have nothing that I want, Reggie."

The boiled-sweet smile came on. "I can wait." He seemed quite unperturbed by her blunt rejection.

"Then you'll grow very old waiting." The dark eyes had taken on a slatelike look, shutting off all her emotions from him. "Your car's been waiting out there to take you to the airport. Be a good boy and leave."

"As someone once said, you can run, but you can't hide. Your father's made up his mind that you'll marry me."

"I don't understand your thinking. You want to marry me, knowing I don't love you, knowing I've just spent the best part of a year sleeping with Mark, and knowing that in the next two days, I'll be spending as much time in bed with him as is physically possible. Yet still . . ."

The smile remained in place. "Of course."

"You're sick."

"Have fun," Barham-Deane said, and walked out, slamming the door behind him.

"Bastard," she said, and went angrily to join Selby.

She found him with a neat scotch for company. He was not much of a drinker, she knew, so she assumed something more than Reggie Barham-Deane was on his mind.

He raised the glass briefly. "The only one for the next two days. I just felt I needed this."

"Are you all right?"

"I didn't expect to be welcomed by Barham-Deane."

"You can handle Reggie. It's not just that, is it?"

For reply, he handed her Morven's note.

She was wearing tight, black designer jeans and black, flat-heeled shoes of very soft leather. A rich burgundy sweater with a low-cut V neck completed the outfit. Her favorite watch was on her wrist, but that was all the jewelry she wore. She stood, legs slightly apart as she read the note. A silence descended.

When she had finished, she folded it as slowly as he had and handed it back.

"Good on her," she said.

Selby stared. *"What?"*

"Good on her," Kim repeated. "She's right. You have no reason to worry. She's a grown woman, Mark. She has a right to make her own decisions . . . just as I have."

"Oh no. Now wait a minute. You can't equate us with her problem."

"Problem? What problem? You think she has a problem with Axel Hohendorf, and my father thinks you're a problem. What is it with you men?" Kim went on in exasperation. "We're not your property, you know. Father, brother, lovers, husbands, you're all the bloody same!"

"Hey, hey, hey! Why are you getting angry with me?"

"Why shouldn't I? I've just had a toe-to-toe with Reggie. Every time you two meet, you're like a couple of stags fighting over territory."

"That's exactly what we are."

"I'm not anyone's territory!" she said furiously. "I'm *me*, Kim Mannon. And Morven—"

"Is my sister, the only one I have. I've looked after her since our parents died. She's involved with a man who's still married and whose wife, a full-blown countess in her own right, won't give him a divorce. The man is himself a baron, why would he chuck over a countess?"

"Do you think so little of Morven?"

"Don't be ridiculous. I think the world of her."

"Then let her make her own decisions."

"You don't understand," Selby began with some frustration. "My father had a reasonably successful business—not in your father's league, of course—light-years from it, in fact, but he gave us a decent living. I've told you before how just over nine years ago the office cleaner found him dead at his desk when she came in to work the next morning, with his heart pills spread near an outstretched hand. He hadn't been quick enough."

"I know that, Mark," she said quietly, "and I know how long it took you before you told me. I know how hard it must have been for you, especially after what had happened to your mother."

The winter before his father's death, his mother had been knocked down and killed by a skidding lorry, not far from their home. The tragedies had made him very protective of Morven, perhaps overmuch; but as he'd said, she was his baby sister, and the only one he had. He had to look after her.

"I know you feel a great responsibility toward her," Kim was saying. "But she's not a baby. In fact, from what I do know of her, she's pretty tough-minded. She'll be all right. Look. I'm on my own, too, you know. I've lost my mother and my brother." Kim's mother and brother had been killed in a helicopter crash in Portugal's Sierra Estrella. The company pilot had died, too.

Kim waved her hand briefly. "Look at this place. Think of all the other places my father owns. All that wealth does not stop me feeling alone. That's why, like you in a way with your attitude to Morven, my father is sometimes overprotective. He wants to preserve me—"

"Yes. He told me when we first met." Selby's voice was less than enthusiastic. "His way is marrying you off to the barracuda."

"You seem to forget, I have a say, too."

Selby looked about him. "The man who owns this, and the only other house I've seen so far, Grantly Hall, is not someone who will give you any say. As you've just said, you're Kim Mannon, Sir Julius Mannon's daughter. It makes a difference."

The dark eyes were looking intensely at him. "Mark?" she began in an uncertain voice. "What are you trying to say?"

He placed his glass on a low table that looked as if it had cost half his year's salary, and rose from the deep armchair in which he had been sitting.

"God knows," he said. "When I left the base, I was full of anticipation. Then in Aberdeen I got Morven's note to tell me she'd gone off to join Hohendorf—"

"He's introducing her to his mother. Doesn't that say anything to you? I thought you liked him."

"Well . . . I do. He's a bloody good pilot." And we've been in combat together, he finished silently.

"You saved his life, too, when his plane hit that flock of birds."

"Anybody on the squadron would have done the same."

"The way Elmer Lee told it, when we finally got him to admit that anything had actually happened, is quite different. He doesn't think anyone else could have shepherded Axel back. He also said you were very worried for Axel."

"Bloody McCann should learn to keep his mouth shut."

"Don't be hard on him. He thinks the world of you, just as, in a different way, you think the world of Morven, and me too, I hope. Now come here. We haven't kissed each other hello."

They met halfway, and she pressed her body against his as her arms went about his neck. She stood on tiptoe, as if to obtain greater purchase. She moaned a little as his hands traveled slowly down her back to cup the firm curves of her behind.

"Why don't we," she murmured against his

mouth, "do this more comfortably? I think you're getting ready, and I know I am."

"You don't have to ask twice," he said.

The two days were not as blissful as Mark had hoped. The shadow of Barham-Deane continued to put a pall on the proceedings, and his continuing worry about Morven caused Kim to snap at him impatiently. At the end of it all, he left to return to base almost wishing he had not come, while her eyes had held a strangely distant and thoughtful look in them when he had bid her good-bye.

He traveled back to November One, taking the Cosworth through lonely highland routes, driving the surefooted car fast along the near-empty roads. On the compact disk player, "After Hours" by Swing Out Sister was streaming through the car's six speakers. The mood of the song, he thought, suited his perfectly.

The next song was even more in keeping. Entitled "Blue Mood," it was nevertheless an enjoyable companion. He turned up the volume as the car hurled itself forward.

It was dark when he arrived at the airfield, the reflective markings on the edges of the long access road giving the impression of runway lighting. One of the guards at the main gate, Corporal Neve, was a solidly built man who knew Selby by sight.

He went up to the car and leaned toward the driver's window. " 'Evening, sir. Had a nice time?"

"No," Selby replied, and as the barrier was raised he drove through after a brief wave to Neve.

Staring after the receding taillights, Neve said dryly, "Yes, thank you, Corporal Neve. Hope you had a nice time, too."

Soon after, McCann's Corvette turned up.

"Bet you had a nice time, sir," Neve said to him.

Captain McCann always had a nice time. The whole world knew that.

"I had a lousy time," McCann said. "Believe it."

"What a cheerful pair," Neve muttered to himself as the Corvette went through.

"What was that?" Neve's fellow guard was standing on the other side of the centrally positioned sentry box.

"Just thinking about the mystery of officers."

"Oh, that lot," the guard said dismissively. "Don't worry about it, mate." He waved an outgoing personnel van through.

4

Selby was in the mess having a cup of coffee when McCann walked in.

"Didn't expect to see you till tomorrow," Selby remarked by way of a greeting.

"I couldn't take it any longer," McCann said.

Selby looked at him in surprise. *"You* managed to have a bad time?" He poured McCann some coffee from the nearby percolator.

"I had a bitch of a time. You?"

"Not so good."

It was McCann's turn to be surprised. "I don't believe it. Things not so hot between you and Kim? The couple of the century?"

"Leave it there, Elmer Lee. It's rather more complicated."

"Well, I'll tell you about my lousy time."

Selby said nothing and waited.

McCann confessed his reluctance to meet his father in London and explained why.

"But do you know what he did?" McCann went on, then answered his own question. "He had a brand-new '91 Corvette waiting outside the hotel. He's had it shipped over. They're not even out in the States yet."

"So now you've got *two* Corvettes?"

"Yeah."

"McCann, you're the only person I know who could be unhappy with two cars. So where is it?"

"With the importer. I told him to sell it. My father went home, pissed off with me. He couldn't understand I wasn't rejecting him. Now I've told the importer not to sell it. It means I've got to pay to keep the goddamned thing garaged." McCann stared into his coffee. "You know, the last time I saw the old guy so upset was when I told him I wasn't going into the bank, but into the air force; but he got over that soon. He even came around to liking the idea. You'd think he wouldn't be so bent out of shape over a thing like a new car. Hell, I'm saving him money."

A silence fell, and after a while Selby said, "Look . . . I think we should get some sleep. We've got that missile systems test tomorrow afternoon and we've got to put all our personal problems on hold for a while." He clapped his navigator briefly on the shoulder. "C'mon, old son. I need you hot and cooking in that backseat tomorrow. We've got a couple of really tough jockeys for the DACT. I used to be on the same squadron with both of them. Believe me, they're hard nuts."

The prospect of taking on a couple of aggressive crews in the forthcoming dissimilar air combat training mission energized McCann.

"I'll be cooking," he promised.

"That's more like it. Now let's head for the land of nod."

The November day was bright and cold, but in their full kit, which included their immersion suits, Selby and McCann felt warm as they walked to their waiting Tornado in the hardened aircraft shelter.

Recessed beneath its flat belly was a single, slim

missile. It was the Skyray B, a modified version of the original Skyray highspeed advanced medium-range air-to-air missile, which had been given even longer range and was designated HALRAAM. Together with the advanced short-range Krait, this, with the Super Tornado's internal six-barrel 20mm rotary cannon, gave the aircraft a quite formidable weapon load. The relatively small proportions and weight of the missiles now made it possible for the Tornado ASV to go into battle with no less than twelve missiles and a full load of cannon shells, when all tooled up.

With four each of long-, medium-, and short-range weapons plus the gun, the ASV could engage and hit its targets from 130 miles out down to an eyeball-to-eyeball knife fight in gun range. The performance envelopes of all the armament overlapped, thus leaving no gaps in the aircraft's reach. Its attack and search radar could see for over 150 miles.

The missiles, with their multiple seekers, were not easily fooled by decoys. The seeker or seekers would busy themselves with the decoys—infrared or radar—while remaining locked onto the designated target.

Selby began his preflight walk-around of the aircraft while McCann climbed aboard and into the backseat to start warming up his avionic systems. The ASV began testing itself with its built-in test equipment. If it wasn't happy, it wouldn't fly.

Selby reached beneath the airplane to make sure the inert missile was secure. The only other external store carried was the elongated instrumentation pod with its plungerlike proboscis, beneath the left wing. These two, inert missile and pod, would perform as if the forthcoming engagement was real, with all information transmitted by the pod, while the missile would behave as if in combat, without actually releasing itself from the aircraft. No one was going to die.

The briefing had disclosed that the Skyray family of missiles owed their genesis to an experimental model some twenty-five years earlier. Skyray B was closest to that experimental weapon, for it contained advanced versions of the original components. This was to be its first use in air combat maneuvering, and its performance under all flight regimes was to be closely monitored. There were to be no G-limiting conditions to its release. It had been designed to operate at the highest G that could be sustained by aircraft and crew, and beyond.

For the fight, two Phantoms and two Hawks had been designated. The Phantoms, F-4Js (UK), were from the few still-remaining in RAF service, while the nimble, single-seat Hawks came from one of the advanced weapons conversion units. All the aircraft were being flown by instructors, so Selby knew he was going to have his work cut out for him. To add to his problems, two of the aircraft—one Phantom and one Hawk— would be carrying a small recognition unit upon which the Skyray was meant to home. The attack was to be made upon those aircraft only. These units were intended to act as ident systems to be carried by allied aircraft in a theater of combat. The missile's job was to interrogate the system and, if it liked the reply, ignore that particular target and search for one that was hostile. Lack of an answer would seal the target's fate.

Selby found himself thinking he would not like to be in the aircraft whose intentions were benign, but whose reply was rejected by a rogue missile. Imagine, he thought as he completed his checks, being chased round the bloody sky by a missile that was supposed to be your friend, while the bogey got away scot-free, with plenty of time to achieve lock-on and blow you away.

"Not good," he said as he climbed the ladder to the

front cockpit, after signing the form that now made
him responsible for the plane.

McCann, strapped in with helmet on but oxygen
mask still hanging loose, looked up questioningly.
"What?"

"Just talking to myself," Selby replied as he eased
into the roomy front office.

McCann raised his eyes briefly heavenward. "Oh
Lord, I got me a pilot who talks to himself."

"Be thankful you've got a pilot at all," Selby retorted, and began doing up his harness, helped by a
member of the ground crew who had followed him up.

McCann winked at the crewman, who smiled
briefly in return. He was accustomed to Selby and
McCann's comments to each other.

"Truss him up nicely," McCann said to the crewman. "Can't have him loose up front. You never know
with some guys."

"I'll do my best, sir," the crewman said, entering
into the spirit. His job completed, he went back down
the ladder and moved it out of the way.

Canopy shut, the Tornado ASV nosed its way like a
gray bird of prey, out of the hardened shelter. Its twin
engines spooled up briefly as Selby momentarily slid
the throttles forward to gain some extra thrust for a
mild increase of taxing speed. He pressed a gentle foot
against the left rudder pedal, feeling the resistance of
its self-centering pressure as he steered the aircraft left
onto the taxiway, aiming the ASV along the yellow taxi
line.

Selby hoped the Skyray would work without
hitches. Theoretically, once you had identified your adversary at long distance, popping off a long-range missile at him should not be a problem. But everyone knew
that actual warfare tended not to have read the same

books as the theorists. A missile that could additionally discriminate between friendly and hostile targets during flight was bound to be a big plus, if it worked at extreme distances.

The choices for the program were the top three November crews, Selby-McCann, Hohendorf-Flacht, Bagni-Stockman. Selby and McCann had drawn the first mission. None of the crews knew the full history of the Skyray's genesis. None knew of the downing of the Canberra by the Lightning over the Mediterranean all those years ago.

The Skyray could be configured to home on to or ignore particular signals, and in warfare, this would enable the change of signal capability to enhance security. Code for the day would simply be programmed into the missile arming system just before takeoff or in the air.

The aircraft came to a halt at the threshold of the wide main runway, nose aimed northward. Beyond the base, the runway direction pointed past a ruined castle to the sloping, two-hundred-foot-high cliff face of Strathmarchin Bay. Beyond that were the cold November waters of the Moray Firth. Despite the time of year, the day was calm, with no signs of the kind of ferocious storms that could sometimes lash this part of Scotland.

"Good day for it," Selby said to McCann as he swiftly went through his pretakeoff checks.

"I'm ready to cream those suckers."

"Just make sure you give me the correct targets. The Boss will have our guts if we screw up, but I'll be after yours first."

"Aw, gee. You say such nice things to me."

The corners of Selby's mouth twitched into a brief smile in his mask as he spoke to the control tower. "November, Verdant requesting takeoff with a zoom climb to flight level three-five-zero."

"You are clear for takeoff, Verdant," a young female voice replied. "Wind is one-eighty, three knots. Zoom climb to flight level three-five-zero."

"Verdant," Selby acknowledged.

A negligible tail wind, and a clear airspace for the fast climb to 35,000 feet. Couldn't be better.

"You have inbound traffic," the voice was saying, "low-level, bearing zero-four-one at thirty miles. Striker One and Striker Two."

"Verdant," Selby again acknowledged as he swiveled the rudder pedals downward to hold the Tornado on the toe brakes. The Boss was returning from an early sortie with a baby pilot in tow. It wouldn't do to get in the way, even though the trainee would have an experienced backseater to hold his hand.

He pushed the throttles firmly to Max Reheat. The engine nozzles opened wide as blue-white flames speared backward, signifying a clean light of the afterburners. Selby released the brakes and the ASV hurled itself forward, a fierce beast unleashed. In fleeting seconds, the digital airspeed symbols were showing 130 knots on the head-up display. The nose was eager to rise as the phenomenal acceleration sent the numbers whirling. At 140, he eased the stick gently back. The aircraft seemed to leap joyfully off the restricting ground, gaining speed more swiftly as the landing gear was immediately retracted.

Selby held the ASV at low level, letting the speed build. By the time it had reached the bay two kilometers later, the green symbology of the HUD glowed 400.

Selby gave the stick a firm, backward pull. The ASV stood on its tail and hurled itself skyward. He eased the stick to its central position, unloading the G-forces of the pull-up. The Tornado continued to accelerate in the climb, heading for 35,000 feet.

"Byee!" McCann said to the tower. "Must love you and leave you."

"Please maintain correct radio procedure, Verdant," the controller admonished.

"Don't you just love it when she talks dirty?" McCann, unrepentant, said to Selby, deliberately making the conversation public. "So sexy."

"I just hope the Boss didn't hear that," Selby said, wisely staying off the tower frequency.

In the control tower, the young flying officer blushed from neck to hairline.

While Selby and McCann were catching the early-morning sun at 35,000 feet, Morven was looking out at the long paved drive of the Schloss Hohendorf, with its twin ranks of tall trees made skeletal by the approach of winter. Her bedroom window gave her a perfect vantage point from which to view the grounds of the castle.

She had been given a large, comfortable room, one of whose two windows was a wide, turreted bay. From where she now stood, she had the slightly unnerving impression of being suspended in midair above the gently flowing stream that had been diverted centuries ago to split itself about the castle in a natural moat. It became one again beneath the narrow bridge that allowed access to the graveled courtyard from the drive.

The room, though big, was warm and cozy. It was at the front of the fifteenth-century building that, though much-updated through the years, had nonetheless retained a substantial part of its origins. By going to the left-hand pane of the tall window, she could see the white clock set in its own steepled tower at the center of the shallow U of the castle.

Morven Selby had the strong frame and clear complexion of someone used to working in the open air. Her thick and lustrous hair was long, and fell in a dark curtain well past her shoulders. The luminous green of her eyes, the heart-shaped face with its firm chin, the high and curving forehead, the strong nose contrasting with the soft, vulnerable mouth, would make an observer realize he was in the presence of considerable beauty. Her smile, which she could use to devastating effect, often generated a twinkle in the eyes.

She rubbed a hand absently down one thigh. The movement was sensual in the extreme, perhaps more so because it was unconscious. Her thin, but opaque nightgown moved loosely about her body with the action of her hand. She had not slept in it, but had put it on to go to the window.

She had slept alone, for Axel had suggested, and she had agreed, that they should resist their desire to sleep together while at the *schloss*. At least for this, her first visit. But they had seized every private moment to embrace, kiss, and caress each other.

A movement in the courtyard attracted her attention. Still continuing to rub her thigh slowly, she peered down. A fully dressed Axel was walking with slow steps, in deep conversation with Hans, the family retainer.

She had thought Hans looked almost as old as the building itself, at their first meeting. He had greeted her formally, back ramroad straight. Even now, as he walked with Axel, his posture was absolutely correct. He kept deferentially to one side and a little behind the younger man. Morven had suddenly realized the kind of family she was getting into when Hans had addressed Axel with a very respectful "Herr Baron," despite Axel's later explanation that years of trying to get Hans to drop use of the title had been to no avail.

As if knowing of her presence at the window, she watched Axel pause, then turn back to look up directly at her. Hans remained firmly looking forward.

* * *

Hohendorf smiled with pleasure and waved. He saw her brief answering wave before he turned again to Hans.

"I am a very lucky man, Hans," he said to the older man.

Correct as ever, Hans said, "I am glad the Herr Baron feels happy with his life."

"Must you be always so formal, old friend? You know you never liked Anne-Marie."

"It is not in my place to like or dislike the Herr Baron's wife. But I will say that the young lady is a person of beauty. There is life in her beauty." Hans then closed his mouth firmly, as if he felt he had pushed the bounds of propriety too far.

"Thank you, Hans," Hohendorf said dryly. "Coming from you, I know that is a rare compliment."

Hans gave a slight nod. "Herr Baron."

Hohendorf gave him an affectionate touch on the shoulder. "All right, Hans. Thank you."

Again, the old man nodded. "Herr Baron." He went back to the *schloss* and entered by a side door.

Hohendorf looked up again at the window, but Morven had moved out of sight.

Schloss Hohendorf was within its own secluded grounds just outside Tecklenburg, on the edge of the largest piece of forested land in Westphalia, the Teutoburg. After breakfast, Hohendorf suggested a bicycle excursion of the area.

Morven readily agreed.

The day was crisp, but there was no wind to speak of, and no frost. A cloudless sky made the sun brighten the day. Morven had decided to wear a lightweight tracksuit top, but felt the cycling would make her warm enough to risk wearing shorts. Hohendorf did the same.

The sun's rays filtered through the skeletal trees to speckle the ground. Hohendorf kept glancing at Morven as they rode down the long drive between the tall ranks of beech.

"Stop staring at my legs," she told him, though pleased by the attention, "or I'll go back and change into the other half of my tracksuit."

"Would you do that to me?" He stole another glance. "They are so beautiful."

"They're fat, you mean."

"Nothing could be further from the truth."

Morven's legs were a source of wonder to him. They were long, richly full, and swelled into thighs that made him want to touch and caress at every opportunity. As she pedaled, the muscles in her calves and thighs moved provocatively. There was an air of wildness about her that intoxicated him.

"You're going to fall off that bike," she warned, "if you don't look where you're going." But the flushes that appeared on her cheeks were not due to the exertion of riding. "So where are you taking me?"

"To see my beautiful forest."

The green eyes glanced at him. "And then?"

"And then . . ." His own glance was sufficiently eloquent.

"Whatever will Hans say?" she said. Her eyes teased.

"Are you still worried about him?"

Morven shook her head. "I was never worried, but he has been a little formal."

"That is his way," Hohendorf said. "I have explained about how he treats even me, whom he has known since I was a baby. He likes you."

"Even though I am not Anne-Marie?"

"The reason I love you, Morven," Hohendorf began seriously, "is precisely because you are *not* Anne-Marie."

She waved briefly at the passing trees. "All this is very different to what I'm accustomed to. I'm no countess—"

"Stop it. I will not have you talking about yourself in this way. To me, you are a princess."

She gave a little sideways nod, tentatively accepting the compliment, a pleased expression upon her face.

"You do like it here?" he asked anxiously.

"It takes getting used to, but yes . . . I do like it. And your mother's been wonderful. I wasn't sure when I came, you know. I felt a bit like someone usurping—"

"You're usurping no one, and my mother thinks you are perfect."

"I wouldn't go that far, but she can't ignore Anne-Marie. I dread meeting her. I hope she doesn't turn up while I'm here."

"There is no chance. She will not find out before we return to Scotland. And even if she does, there is nothing she can do."

"Even so, I'd rather not meet her just yet." A sudden frown appeared upon Morven's forehead. "Mark would just love it if that happened. God knows what he made of that note I left."

High above the waters of the Greenland-Iceland-UK gap, Selby was not thinking about his sister and Hohendorf. More pressing matters were upon his mind.

"Anything, Elmer Lee?"

"I got diddly-squat here."

Selby heard his own sigh. "In plain English, I suppose that means nothing."

"You've got it, buddy."

"Well, check those screens of yours again. Those Phantom boys out there are wily. They're not going to make it easy for us . . . and they'd just love to catch us with our knickers down."

"Not while I'm back here."

Which was true enough. In the backseat, McCann reigned supreme. Even so . . .

"Well, well," McCann was saying softly. "Someone's heard your prayer. We have company."

The tension of alertness was in Selby's voice as he said, "How many?"

"Just a singleton so far."

"One? They're playing silly buggers. The others are lurking somewhere. And watch out for those little Hawks. Those little sods are cheeky, just because they regularly tap F-15s and F-16s."

"Yeah. Well, we're no goddamn Eagles and Falcons. There's going to be a shark on their tail today. Go high. I want to light up some area."

Selby put the Super Tornado into a gentle climb to 40,000 feet, from their original altitude of 35,000. McCann briefly turned on the radar in track-while-scan mode. The TWS mode had a beyond visual range well in excess of 150 miles, and even switched off, the computers would continue to plot the targets it had picked up, giving their likely positions in real time, based upon the data received from the brief sweep. McCann could call up a display from the menu of one of his multifunction display units, which would show where the computers thought the targets should be, giving a choice of positions. Another brief radar illumination of the target area would effectively confirm one of the computers' suggestions.

"I've got them all," McCann now crowed. "One Phantom and one Hawk," he went on as target identification was shown as both a readout and a generated image, "at high and medium levels, and one Phantom and one Hawk, both at low level. They haven't seen us. How can they? The poor guys are blind. It will be a lot of miles before their radars can pick up anything—if they know where to look. Hell, those Phantoms are blind at forty miles."

"Don't underestimate them," Selby cautioned. "That guy I told you about is a cunning sod. He'll try to get close."

"Oh no, you don't," McCann said sharply, clearly not speaking to Selby.

"What?" Selby inquired. "Come on, McCann. Don't keep it all to yourself."

"I just gave another flash and got an update. One of the Phantoms disappeared."

"I told you. Which one?"

"The guy on the deck. It's all right, I've got him again. I did a little work on his last known position and dug him out."

"Just make sure you don't lose him. What altitudes have we got for them?"

"I'm patching the display over."

On one of Selby's own three MFDs, a computer-generated display of the positions of the four targets appeared with all relevant information. The Phantom and Hawk were at 30,000 and 16,000 feet respectively. The low pair were both at 500 feet. Each was traveling in a different direction, but suddenly they changed course and began to move toward each other, only to break and change course once more. Heights had changed, too. The low pair were climbing, the high pair diving. They passed each other, then split to go into four separate directions.

They did not stop there. The choreography was constantly shifting, but each pair was covering the other.

"They know we must be seeing them," Selby remarked. "Changing speed, course, and altitude is intended to confuse the radar."

"Not *my* radar. I've got these guys hooked but good. They're going nowhere, except to get zapped."

"As long as that's what happens eventually," Selby commented, still cautious. Overconfidence did not bring success in combat; but neither did hesitation. "Interrogate them, Elmer Lee. Let's see who's carrying the codes."

McCann selected the inert Skyray by tapping a button on the weapons control panel in the bank of panels on the left console. The square button had two warning lights, one of which now glowed amber to denote that selection was complete. Next to the button, the legend LRAM glowed in bright amber. McCann next slaved the missile seeker to the tracking radar. Immediately, a targeting box, with a flashing diamond within it, appeared upon the display. It began hunting out the targets passing directly over one, which it ignored. At the top left of the display, an alphanumeric code was reeling off symbols as the box hunted.

Suddenly the box stopped. The flashing diamond froze and a continuous tone sounded in both their helmets. The code had stopped on a series of numbers and letters.

"There's one," McCann said triumphantly. "Hawk, heading three-zero-one, bearing ninety, height 650 feet and climbing. Speed four hundred knots."

On his own MFD, Selby verified McCann's reading of the tactical situation. The Hawk was heading to the northwest in a shallow climb and crossing from the right. It was a hundred miles out.

He reefed the Tornado into a tight left-hand turn as McCann went on searching for the other coded target. The ASV wheeled on a wingtip to come around on the Hawk's tail. McCann grunted with the brief onset of the sudden increase of G-force.

"I've got the other," he informed Selby. "Goddamn. It's the second Hawk! We've been suckered."

"The Boss keeping us on our toes," Selby commented.

"You don't sound surprised," McCann said aggrievedly.

"I didn't think it was going to be easy. This is a new missile and mistakes at long range could have all sorts of nasty little consequences, and some not so little. He wanted to make certain we got the right target, under any conditions. After all, no one's going to say come and get me, in combat."

"Goddammit."

"And don't forget, Elmer Lee, after we've made successful interceptions, the codes will be switched. We've then got to take out the targets *without* codes. They may not be the two Phantoms."

"Goddammit," McCann said once more. "No one suckers ol' Elmer Lee. We're going to have ourselves a ball. The score's going to be four zaps. That's a promise."

Selby did not doubt McCann's determination and knew that in the air at least, he could count on his backseater to deliver; but it still did not mean all would go well. He was, however, equally determined to ensure all the simulated firings produced the best possible results. If the new Skyray was really all it had been talked up to be, then his crew would be the one to prove it.

At November One, Wing Commander Jason was in the underground main operations room of fighter control. He was taking a great interest in the display screen, watching the images and traces of the five aircraft as they maneuvered both aggressively and defensively.

He watched keenly as the Tornado performed its preattack dance. Selby and McCann were about to launch their first attack from 50,000 feet on their first selected target, which was skimming the cold sea at a mere 200 feet. This was going to be through a bank of clouds whose base was 1,000 feet above the sea and topped out at 14,000 feet. A readout at the bottom of the display had identified the cloud as a massive cumulonimbus, a storm cloud. If the missile could seek effectively through that to maintain its lock, despite the ferocious discharges of electricity in there, then it was the sort of weapon the November squadrons could use.

Jason watched the screen intently and awaited the outcome of the first encounter.

"You can run," McCann was cooing at the images on his MFD, "but you can't hide."

He had switched one of the other MFDs to Tactical Evaluation Display, holding the Track While Scan display on the third. The central MFD now had the Skyray attack screen on with the selected target firmly locked.

"No interference from the cloud?" Selby now asked.

"Nope. Our boy's as clear as a face without zits."

"You have a way with words, McCann."

"He is dead meat. You can take him on the HUD. He's all yours."

Selby maneuvered the ASV 130 miles from the cloud bank. It was unnerving to think that the little Hawk's pilot, way below the grayish forbidding mass all that distance beyond visual range, thought he was safely out of reach. Under normal circumstances, he would be.

Selby watched as the targeting box on the HUD came into the missile ranging ring. The pulsing diamond froze then glowed, signifying a solid lock-on. The modulated tone of the missile sounded eager and slavering, as if itching to be launched. He suddenly found himself with the vision of a monstrous hound, unable to bark, straining at the leash.

"Here goes," Selby said to McCann, and pressed the missile release button on the stick.

Now it was the turn of the simulation computers. Having satisfied themselves that the parameters for missile release had been achieved, they brought up displays that were the exact replica of a live firing. Missile speed, continuously computed range to target, target course and bearing, missile tones, and so on. It was all there. Selby and McCann were fascinated. According to the electronics, the Skyray had now achieved Mach 6.1, or over six times the speed of sound. That was faster than any other air-to-air missile he knew of. The nearest was the American weapon carried by the F-14 Tomcat, which had a speed in excess of Mach 5.

"Jeez . . ." McCann said in awe. "If this thing performs like the kit says . . . for real . . . boy, have we got something."

The missile countdown continued. Distance to target blurred in a tumble of numbers. In the distant Hawk, the pilot would not get the warning tone from the incoming "missile" until it was already much too late, despite the fact that his simulated warning receiver would be on. One hundred and thirty miles at Mach 6 plus was no distance.

McCann's MFD showed time to impact from launch as 1.7333 minutes and was counting down. Terminal speed of the missile would be 4,500 miles an hour.

"If this were for real," he now said to Selby, "it

would blow the target away even without a warhead. You ever hear of anyone surviving a collision at four and a half thousand miles an hour?"

"Ah yes, but a near miss is as good as a mile, especially at that speed."

"And there she goes!" McCann exclaimed suddenly. On his MFD, the image of the Hawk had disappeared. A hit. "Well, we know it works."

Selby had tuned to the Hawk's frequency just in time to hear a chagrined voice say, "Shit!"

"I think he just found out," Selby said. "That was just the first shot, Elmer Lee. We've got a whole program to get through. Don't count your chickens."

But the rest of the program went smoothly. Selby carried out releases in a variety of flight regimes; at high speed, slow maneuvering, with the helmet sight, or the HUD, inverted, at low level shooting high and vice versa, at high G-loadings and at negative G, even during a rapid rolling sequence. The Skyray B, or rather its simulations, performed without a single hitch.

Feeling rather pleased with themselves for having scored on both Phantoms and Hawks each time, they headed back to November One, cruising at 20,000 feet in formation with the Phantoms. The shorter-legged Hawks had already departed, guarding their fuel reserves jealously.

"And they never saw what hit them," McCann remarked somewhat smugly. "Shouldn't play with the big boys. Hey, Mark, ol' buddy, what say I put some music on the spare channel? I've got a new tape here. Played it on the way up from London. It's pretty good stuff."

On Selby's headphones came the opening bars of "After Hours."

"Turn it off," he said.

"What?"

"Turn the bloody thing off, McCann. Besides, I've already got a copy."

"Don't you like it?"

"I like it, but I don't want to hear it right now. Okay?"

"Okay."

The music was switched off and Selby was left to the sounds of his own breathing and the subdued noises of the aircraft. The bright November sun beat down from a cloudless sky upon the tinted bubble of the canopy. Far below, the sea was a still plateau of slate, and hundreds of miles to the north was the storm cloud beneath which they had hit the first Hawk.

In the backseat, McCann's head was moving in slow rhythm. He had switched the music off to Selby, but had kept it on his own helmet phones.

With oxygen mask on and visor down, he looked like a strange nodding figure from a bizarre dream.

Suddenly a new voice broke into the music. "Tiger One to Verdant. Our gun sights need calibrating. Will you help?"

McCann instantly stopped the tape and said to Selby, "Sounds like a couple of tigers needing blood after what we just did to them."

"Sounds very much like it. I've heard some excuses for a fight, but this one's the corniest of the lot. Gunsight calibration indeed!"

"Well? Do we teach them a lesson?"

Before Selby could reply, Tiger One was at them again. "What's the matter? Only play at long range, can we?"

"That the guy you know?" McCann asked.

"That's the one. He's mean in a knife fight, even in that tub out there."

Despite calling it a tub, Selby knew that the aging,

cranked-wing Phantom had reigned supreme for many
years, and was still formidable in the hands of someone
who knew how to use it well. The pilot of Tiger One was
such a person, and his wingman was no doubt highly
skilled, too. In a two-against-one fight, those two would
be dangerous.

"Well?" McCann was urging. "Do we do it?" He
tapped a button on one of the multifunction displays.
An aircraft status menu came up, showing current fuel
state and flow among the other items of operating status. The touch of another button highlighted the fuel
readings. "We've got plenty of gas. Enough for a ten-
minute turn-and-burn, with a good margin left before
bingo."

Bingo state was the amount required to make it
safely back to base with sufficient fuel left over for a full
diversion to another airfield if circumstances at November One warranted it.

Selby glanced at the two Phantoms with their
black tails riding shotgun on either side of the Tornado.
The crews were turning to look at him every so often.

"Get November on the data link. Ask for permission."

"Now you're talking," McCann said, and quickly
contacted home base. Data-link transmission would ensure that the Phantoms knew nothing of what was sent
and received.

McCann's message owed nothing to operating procedure. PERMISSION TO TEACH TWO BLACK-TAILED TIGERS
A LESSON, was what he sent.

GRANTED, came the reply.

"We're in business," McCann said enthusiastically. "Let's go get 'em!"

Selby had checked his own instruments to satisfy
himself that his fuel state did give him the required
margin to engage in close-range air combat practice.

Happy with the conditions, he called, "Fight's on! Fight's on!" on the open channel, simultaneously pulling the stick firmly back and slamming the throttles into combat afterburner. The ASV stood on its tail and hurtled skyward, wings sweeping back at it climbed.

The sudden move had taken everyone by surprise, not least of all the Phantoms. They snapped into quick rolls to the left and right, displaying the great plan views of their bellies as they went. One climbed in a sweeping turn while the other curved downward.

"Oooh shit!" came a rueful exclamation from one of them.

As for McCann, he had felt himself pressed into his seat by the sudden onset of the powerful G-forces.

"Gawd," he muttered as the pressures eased. "I really hate it when he does that to me."

"This is going to be a quick, embarrassing lesson," Selby was saying.

"For whom?" McCann asked, pushing his luck. "Them or us? Uhh—"

His words were cut off as Selby rolled the aircraft 180 degrees in the climb and pulled on the stick once more. The control computers, responding almost faster than Selby's inputs, sent the ASV into an inverted dive. Before it became vertical, Selby rolled the aircraft upright and eased the stick back. The Tornado rocketed in a gentle climb. It was at 40,000 feet, well away from the Phantoms, who had gone the wrong way.

In his mask, McCann grinned. He had primed Selby. The Phantoms were dead meat.

"They'll try for a sandwich, with us in the middle," he now said to Selby.

"They've got a hope. Camera's on, to record their folly."

The ASV's color video gun camera was slaved to

the HUD; it was fully automatic and would have every fleeting moment on film.

McCann's head was moving this way and that, searching the airspace about the hard-maneuvering Tornado, grunting against the sudden pressure of the G-forces as Selby jockeyed for advantage.

"I've got one low down," he warned Selby, "two o'clock and turning in."

"He's not the one to worry about. It's the other sod. The guy up front's the attention getter, while his mate intends to sneak up on us. I'll keep my eye on this one. You watch out for the sneaky one. He's the one who spoke to us. It's an old trick of his."

"Going to use the helmet sight?"

Before replying, Selby deliberately switched to the open channel, knowing the Phantoms would be listening. "No. Let's give them a chance. They're going to need it."

"You're the one who's going to need it," a hard voice said.

"Sounds like you struck a nerve," McCann said gleefully.

Back on the cockpit channel, Selby said, "Just keep looking for him."

They had decided not to use the radars, so it was eyeball stuff.

"Aha!" McCann said. "I've got him. Coming up on our six."

Behind the Tornado, a horseshoe of superheated air hung like a white sculpture in the deep blue of the sky. A thin trail linked it umbilically to a tiny, swiftly moving shape. The second Phantom, curving down from above, barrel-rolling to bleed speed and stay behind.

"He's giving us a fancy barrel roll," McCann continued, looking over his left and right shoulders alternately, to keep the other aircraft in sight.

Selby suddenly rolled the ASV onto its back and pulled into a steep dive. Then he was climbing again, arrowing upward, burners blazing.

The two Phantoms shot past in opposite directions, neither of them able to gain a single advantage. The barrel-rolling Phantom was now in a steep left turn, standing on a wingtip as it hauled itself round. It was still some distance away.

Selby pulled the throttles right back. The ASV gradually began to slow down in its vertical climb. Soon, the wings began to spread.

"Here beginneth the sharp lesson," Selby murmured as the aircraft continued to slow down. He opened the throttles gradually, but only enough to maintain the smoothness of the deceleration.

"Hey!" McCann began. "What are you doing? It will be very embarrassing if that rhino nails us. I'll never be able to hold my head up in the mess!"

"It's touch and go as it is . . . with your head, I mean."

McCann sat back in his harness, watching as the ASV was virtually held upright by the power of its engines. The wings were barely providing lift; soon it would start to slide down, tail-first.

"Hey, man," McCann said. "This is not an airshow. MiG-29s and SU-27s do that shit."

"What Fulcrums and Flankers can do, we can," Selby retorted.

"Yeah, but not in goddamn combat, even if it is a practice."

"Shut up, McCann. I'm concentrating."

Then Selby did what seemed impossible. He moved the stick slightly to one side. The aircraft rolled through 180 degrees, still keeping its nose upright as he checked the roll. The tail began to slide more quickly.

"Jeez," McCann said. "We're sitting ducks. No energy—"

"Shut it. This aircraft needs a mod. A remote, pilot-only-operated mouth zip for backseaters."

The nose began to drop through an arc, and there, smack in the HUD, was the Phantom. Selby got the gun tone instantly, the row of green dots that showed the fall line of the shots—had he fired—straddling the other aircraft perfectly, from nose to tail.

The Phantom had gone into a frantic break to the right, but had been too late. All it had succeeded in doing was presenting its vulnerable underbelly for the shot.

"Bang, bang, you're dead," Selby said as the Tornado's nose fell through into a dive. He opened the throttles fully. The engines came smoothly on power and he eased out of the dive.

Very little altitude had been lost.

"Fuck," someone said disgustedly, then: "Knock it off. Knock it off."

The fight was over.

The Phantoms joined up in formation briefly before banking hard to head for home. They had a rendezvous with a tanker before heading for their home base in the southeast of England.

"There go a bunch of pissed-off guys," McCann said with satisfaction as he watched the two aircraft depart. "That was a pretty hot move Mark, baby. But do me a favor—don't ever pull that stunt with a Flanker, or a Fulcrum, if we find ourselves mixing it with one again. Not while I'm back here. Okay?"

Selby said nothing.

"Promise me," McCann insisted. "An old rhino is one thing; but a red-hot, let-it-all-hang out Flanker is another ballgame. Do I hear an affirmative coming from the front seat? Do I?"

"Don't worry, Elmer Lee."

"Now I'm really worried. Hey, you Flanker and Fulcrum pilots out there," McCann suddenly shouted. "I've got a real nut up front. Don't come near us. Please?"

"I don't think they heard you," was all Selby said.

5

"Are you cold?"

Morven shook her head as she leaned across to where their solid-framed mountain bikes lay to get her thermos from its mounting. She unscrewed the outer lid that would serve as a cup, then removed the stopper. Steam rose as she poured the hot tea. She offered the cup to Hohendorf.

"You first," he said. He watched in some amusement as she sealed the thermos, then took a cautious mouthful of tea. "You did not expect us to have tea."

"Not good tea," she said as he raised an eyebrow at her. "I've drunk the stuff they serve in cafés."

"Ah, but you see my mother has always liked tea. My father, of course, never. For him, it is always coffee."

"I suppose we won't be seeing him before we leave for the UK."

Hohendorf looked away, to study the landscape ahead.

"No," he said. "We won't." He did not sound particularly disappointed.

They were sitting on a small travel rug brought for the purpose, high up on a slope in the Teutoburger

Wald. Before them stretched the wooded hills and valleys of the forest. Down the slope was an open patch of ground, at the edge of which a track curved before disappearing into the woods. Over to the right and north of where they sat, the A30 autobahn, unseen and unheard, took a steady stream of traffic toward Holland.

Morven finished her tea, filled the cup again, and handed it to Hohendorf. Then she placed the sealed thermos on the ground and lay back, hands behind her head, knees slightly raised. There was such an air of quietness within the forest, it seemed the nearest living thing was hundreds of miles away.

Hohendorf was sitting upright, holding the cup in both hands. He took a brief drink before saying, almost to himself, "I would not like anything to happen to this place."

She turned her head slightly to look at him. "Why should anything happen to it?"

He did not make an immediate reply, but instead took another mouthful of tea.

After a while, he continued. "Europe has become a more dangerous place than it has been for the last forty years. It sounds crazy, I know. Everyone is happy—or was happy—about the eastern countries getting their freedom. They forgot, or chose to forget, about all the old hatreds. I think we are going to have to be very careful."

"Aren't you happy that Germany is again united?"

For a second time, Hohendorf paused before replying. "Of course. But, I am a little worried. We must not allow ourselves to fall into the trap of history. If that happens . . ." He gave a strangely philosophical shrug. "If that happens, there will be no more Germany. Ever."

"You're worrying me," Morven said. She sat up, clasping her knees as she looked at him. "You can't possibly think something's already going wrong."

"If we are clever, and very watchful, we shall be all right. We must make quite sure that the Western European nations become a solidly integrated group. That will help. That is why I believe very strongly in what we are doing in Scotland. Way to go, as our friend Elmer Lee would say." Hohendorf looked at her and grinned suddenly, looking much younger than his twenty-nine years.

When he had first gone into the Marineflieger and had been measured by the examining medical staff, he had ventured the information that he had been precisely constructed and was thus exactly 1.8288 meters, or six feet. The staff had not been particularly amused to prove him right, despite several measurements to find a discrepancy.

He had a crop of fine blond hair that was cut in the fashion of Hollywood's idea of a Roman, and the palest of blue eyes. His body was slim, but tough looking. The unlined face looked like a teenager's, until you looked at the eyes. There was an awareness and knowledge of a life experience that had turned the teenager into a man. At times the eyes looked far older than their years.

As she looked at him Morven remembered the portraits of the generations of von Hohendorfs she had seen hanging in the *schloss*. Of all the males, it was his maternal grandfather he resembled most. That particular portrait, of a Second World War naval commander in best blues, cap at a rakish angle, was the one next to which Hohendorf's, in full flying kit with helmet beneath his arm, was hung. Two generations of warriors. According to Axel, she now remembered, his father had never been happy with that portrait arrangement, preferring his son to be next to the paternal group.

"If anyone," he was now saying to her, "tries to take Germany back to the old days, I shall oppose him and his kind." He placed the now empty cup on the ground and leaned over her. "As I shall oppose anyone who tries to take you away from me." He kissed her gently on the lips.

"Including Mark?"

"Including Mark, and Anne-Marie, and my father . . . anyone."

"Is that why we're not waiting for him to return?"

"No. That is not the reason. My father has gone to the east to survey business opportunities."

"You don't sound as if you approve."

"I neither approve nor disapprove. Anne-Marie's family own a very successful domestic airline, Ettling Luft. All sorts of opportunities are possible with the opening up of the east. My father desperately wants me to leave flying for the military and join the board of the airline."

"I certainly can't compete with that."

Hohendorf laid a restraining finger upon her lips. "You have already forgotten. I won't have you saying such things about yourself. They cannot buy me from you."

He kissed her again, this time with some passion. She squirmed with pleasure beneath him.

"What if someone comes?" she murmured against his lips.

"This is a favorite place of mine. No one comes here. You are the first person to have come here with me since I discovered it. I have never seen anyone in all the years I have come. I do not say they don't. Just that I have never seen them."

She giggled suddenly. "Today will be the day."

"Stop thinking about it. Your legs have been driving me crazy."

"I can feel they have," she said, opening her mouth wider to kiss him fully.

She felt his hand reach for her shorts and she raised herself a little to ease his progress. Her own hands were working at his shorts. They both succeeded in undressing each other's lower halves at about the same time, and by then, Hohendorf was as eager to enter her as she was to receive him.

Morven moaned softly. "I . . . I can't tell . . . you how much I have wanted this. I . . . I—"

Her voice ended in a high but faint squeal as he went deeper into her with firm, yet gentle strokes. The legs that so enamored him had opened wide then locked upon his back.

"And I . . ." he murmured between low grunts, "I've been wanting, too."

"I can tell. I can *tell!*" Her voice shook with a tight urgency.

She made high whimpering sounds as her body began to tauten, her legs gripping him with a strength he would not have thought possible. It drove him to greater heights of ecstasy. Their bodies heaved at each other in the cool of the November forest air, and the moisture of their exertions covered their skins with a fine sheen. Sounds of soft suction came from between them.

Hohendorf locked his arms beneath her upper body, squeezing her to him as a great convulsion took hold of him. It seemed to go on forever as she pulsed beneath him, the heat of her pelvis overwhelming him, locking him into her. They clasped each other, straining as if to fuse themselves into one.

Morven gave a high keening wail before her body slowly, reluctantly, began to relax.

"Oooh," she said in a long-drawn-out whisper. "I didn't want that to stop."

He was still within her, equally reluctant to accept the end of the wave of passion that had so recently possessed him.

Then, as he started to withdraw, she held on to him. "No," she said softly. "Don't go yet."

"All right," he said, and kissed her long and gently.

About them, the forest was quiet.

At Schloss Hohendorf, a big, gunmetal-gray BMW 850 coupe, brand new, crunched over the gravel of the courtyard to a self-assured stop. It carried Munich license plates. The wide left-hand door opened and a tall, patrician blonde climbed out from behind the wheel.

Anne-Marie, Countess von Ettlingen und Hohendorf, had arrived. She glanced at the red Porsche 944 Turbo near which she had parked, recognizing it as her estranged husband's, and began walking purposefully around her car.

At the front of the schloss was a wide patio about two meters above ground level. This was flanked by two broad flights of steps that made a curving descent to the wide gravelly circle of the courtyard.

Hans was slowly making his way down one of the flights, barely disguised reluctance in every step. Anne-Marie paused at the bottom.

"Ah, Hans," she began imperiously. "My luggage is in the back. Please have it brought to my room. The car is open."

Hans nodded stiffly. *"Jawohl,* Frau Gräfin."

Anne-Marie began to make her way up the steps before pausing to turn sideways and look down. "Is my husband in, Hans?"

Poker-faced, Hans said, "He has gone to the forest, Frau Gräfin."

"And taken one of those dreadful bicycles of his, I suppose." She gave a dismissive toss of her fine mane of blond hair. "All very healthy, but never one of my pursuits. Thank you, Hans."

She continued up the steps as Hans, eyes giving nothing away, went to take her luggage out of the BMW.

November One, Scotland.

After the debrief, Wing Commander Jason pointed at McCann. "A word in your shell-like, Captain McCann." He glanced at Selby. "Just McCann." To McCann, he continued, "My office, if you please."

Puzzled, McCann surreptitiously glanced at Selby as Jason turned away. Selby's own glance was equally puzzled. Selby briefly spread his hands in a gesture that told McCann he was just as much in the dark.

Jason had paused to look back. "You won't need Mark Selby to hold your hand, so tear yourself away."

Looking like someone who felt certain he was just about to be dropped upon from a great height, McCann feverishly ran through his mind any misdemeanor he might committed within the last twenty-four hours.

He couldn't think of any.

In the office, Jason took his seat behind his large service-issue desk, while McCann stood before him, legs slightly apart, hands clasped behind.

"I'll come straight to the point, Captain," Jason began. "I've received a complaint from SATCO."

As soon as McCann heard mention of the senior air-traffic-control officer he knew what was coming and wished he could kick himself.

Jason was staring at him unblinkingly. "I see realization has dawned. My difficulty with you, McCann, is that you're bloody good in the backseat. Almost too good. You have it in you to be an instructor one day, though God knows I can't see how you could impart some of your wizardry to eager sprogs without killing them in the process.

"But to more immediate matters. You have seriously embarrassed one of the ATC officers with your nonprocedural transmission. For your information, I was inbound at the time and heard you. Denial would be pointless."

"I was not about to deny it, *sir.*"

"Thank God for small mercies. Explanation?"

"I hadn't heard that voice before, sir, I was sort of welcoming her to November One."

"Welcoming her? It may have escaped your notice, Captain, but *I* do the welcoming around here. The Group Captain gets the first crack, and I the next, in his absence."

"I thought she'd find it funny, *sir.*"

Jason shut his eyes briefly. "Funny. Well, I'll tell you something, McCann. The young lady is new to us. It was her first time in the tower, and she had the bad luck to run into you. And no, she did not find it funny at all. Tell you what I shall do."

"Yes, *sir.*"

"I suggest that you apologize to the young lady forthwith. You will go to the tower where you will present yourself to Flying Officer Karen Lomax and humbly apologize for causing her such embarrassment among her colleagues, some of whom were noncommissioned personnel. Further, you will be ADO for the week."

"Air duty officer for a whole week, sir?" McCann could not help himself. "There's nothing to do but sit in a corner and watch people take off and land."

"ADOs are a vital complement in the tower, Captain." Jason's tone was stern. "If someone gets into trouble, your expertise will be needed."

"But sir, I thought pilots—"

"And furthermore, I believe Flying Officer Lomax will be on duty for the rest of the week."

"That's a tough deal, sir."

"Consider yourself lucky. SATCO wanted parts of you on a silver platter. She absolutely hates aircrew taking liberties with her young ladies." Jason held up a hand. "Forget it, McCann. This is not negotiable. That is all."

Jason busied himself with the papers upon his desk. McCann had no option but to leave. As the door clicked shut Jason looked up. There was the barest hint of a smile about his lips.

McCann met Selby in the aircrew kitting room. Selby had already removed all his flying gear and was in overalls.

"Well?" he began. "What did the Boss have to say?"

"I'm deep in the brown stuff." McCann began to remove his own gear. "The Boss was inbound when we took off—"

"And he heard your little sweet nothing."

"You got it. But that's not all. SATCO made a complaint and it seems my balls on a plate was the bargaining chip."

Selby was grinning. "So?"

"So I've pulled ADO for a week."

"And what about your flying?"

"Boss said nothing about being off flying for the week, so I guess I fly *and* do ADO duty. There's more."

"I can hardly wait."

"Seems the lady in question is new. New to November One, that is. Karen Lomax. Heard of her?"

"I'm afraid not. Haven't seen her in the mess. Perhaps she's married. You certainly know how to put your foot in it, Elmer Lee."

"Well," McCann said unhappily, "I've got to go to the tower and apologize. There's a whole bunch of enlisted people there, too. Goddammit. Why do I do these things?"

Selby slapped him on the shoulder. "Talent, old son. Talent. Cheer up. She might only bite your head off."

"She's probably a weight lifter and looks—"

"Elmer Lee. Naughty, naughty. You were about to make a sexist remark."

"God*dammit,*" McCann fumed helplessly.

Flying Officer Lomax was anything but a weight lifter. Slim and graceful, she was elfinlike, with auburn hair that she wore in a single braid she had then coiled and pinned neatly in place. Wisps of hair had escaped the braid and curled softly about the base of her neck.

When McCann had made himself climb the narrow, winding steps to the glass cage of the tower, the first person he saw was the lady in question. Her back was to him, and she was busy talking to an aircraft in the circuit. Her slim neck was visible as she leaned forward to press a switch, prior to speaking to another aircraft.

A sergeant looked round to see McCann standing there awkwardly. McCann did not know he was looking at Karen Lomax, since another, slightly older female officer was sitting at at the opposite end of the traffic control desk, busy with her own aircraft.

"Can I help you, sir?" the sergeant asked.

"Um . . . ah . . . yes. I'm here to see Flying Officer Lomax."

"She's talking to an aircraft at the moment, sir,

but as soon as she's finished I'll let her know you're here." The sergeant did not say which of the two officers was Karen Lomax.

"Thank you," McCann said, and found his eyes straying to the wisps of unruly hair on the graceful neck.

The sergeant seemed not to be interested in him further. Then the slim officer stopped talking and the sergeant leaned over to say something.

The back straightened suddenly, and then McCann found himself looking into the shyest eyes he'd ever seen. Words instantly failed him.

"Yes, Captain?" she asked in the voice that had driven him to make his incautious transmission.

McCann cleared his throat. "I'm . . . I'm . . ." He paused. "I'm Elmer Lee McCann," he went on quickly. "I . . ."

Suddenly realization dawned. "It's you! I know that voice." Color came to her cheeks as the memory of the incident returned. The shy eyes widened at him.

By now the whole tower seemed to be listening. McCann found himself wanting to get out of there with as much dignity as he could.

"I've come to apologize," he said, the words almost running into each other. "It was a stupid thing to do."

"No harm done." She turned quickly away, the back of her neck pink.

McCann glanced around the tower. No one was looking at him, but he sensed they were all hiding smiles.

"Um," he said.

She turned again to look at him, waiting.

"I'm ADO for the week," he told her sheepishly. "Penance."

"It's not that bad up here, surely?" The warm voice was killing him.

"Ah . . . no. No."

"Good," she said, and turned away once more.

"Thank you," McCann said. "I'll be in tomorrow."

The sergeant looked round. "Very well, sir."

McCann hastily went back down the steps. He didn't see Karen Lomax's eyes follow his progress until he was out of sight.

Later in the mess, McCann was talking enthusiastically to Selby. "Oh God, Mark, she's a doll. A real doll. A beauty."

"I think I'm getting the message."

"She's cute."

"You'll be running out of vocabulary soon."

But McCann was not to be put off. "And I'm up there for a week."

"I'm very happy for both of you."

"But how come we've never seen her in here?"

"As I've said, perhaps she's married."

"Hell. I sure hope not."

Selby gave one of his long-suffering sighs. "Elmer Lee, first your father and your two Corvettes, now you think you're falling in love. Listen, old son, don't clutter your mind. I want you firing on all cylinders while we're doing the Skyray program and especially when we go to the Med for the live firing."

"I'm sometimes a little crazy on the ground," McCann said quite seriously. "At least, that's what some people think."

"*Some?*"

"Okay. So maybe more than some. But in the air, I'm number one. You know that."

"I know that, Elmer Lee. But if it turns out she's married to a seven-foot weight lifter, just keep that mind of yours sharp as a razor. We can't afford distractions."

"The best goddamn cutthroat in the business. That's me."

"I'll drink to that. You're buying."

"Coffee is what you get."

"There speaks a rich man's son."

Hohendorf and Morven were cycling back to the *schloss* in a buoyant mood, feeling languorous after having made love for most of the afternoon in the forest.

Their mood vanished when Hohendorf spotted the BMW, waiting like a nemesis for their return.

"Scheiss!" he said tightly, before he could stop himself. There was still some daylight left, so the car could be clearly seen at a distance.

"What's up?" Morven asked, her own voice tense in reaction to his.

"That car. The BMW."

"Your father's back from the east?" It was an understandable mistake. She was not familiar with Anne-Marie's taste in cars.

"Anne-Marie." He could barely speak her name, so great was his feeling of outrage. "What is she *doing* here?"

"Oh God," Morven said. She looked stricken.

"Do not worry. I want you to go up to your room, have a bath, relax, then change and come down when you feel like it. By then I will have attended to Anne-Marie. Please, my darling. Do not worry," Hohendorf repeated.

As they drew closer they saw that matters were not going to go as smoothly as he had hoped. From wherever she had been in the building, Anne-Marie had spotted them. By the time they had crossed into the courtyard, she was already determinedly coming down the steps.

Anne-Marie was a classic Bavarian beauty. Her

blond hair was a burnished gold. The fine bones of her face proudly displayed the noble breeding, with eyes so pale, they were almost white. She was elegance itself, tall and, though slim, possessed a highly curvaceous body. Her voice had a dark and sensuous timbre to it. She was, by any standards, a formidable presence.

They got off their cycles and took their time walking their mounts into the courtyard, where Anne-Marie was waiting at the bottom of the steps.

She had drawn herself to her full height, arms stiffly at her sides. Her eyes fastened upon Morven, but it was Hohendorf to whom she made her first comment.

"Hans said you were out riding in the forest," she began in perfect English, her slight accent making the rich voice even more alluring. "I never realized how true those words were." The near-white eyes raked Morven's body with slow contempt. They lingered on the bare legs. There was just enough light to see the marks upon them. "You look as if you've been rolling about on the ground. Didn't you find it a little chilly?"

Morven's green eyes had begun to smolder.

Hohendorf stepped in quickly, touching her arm briefly. "Don't give her the satisfaction. Do as I suggested. Leave this to me." He gave the arm a gentle squeeze.

Morven was reluctant to give in. Her eyes were blazing now, but she yielded to Hohendorf's advice and walked slowly past Anne-Marie, coldly ignoring her.

Anne-Marie flashed a haughty expression at her, turning a head that tracked her movements like a radar antenna. If eyes were laser beams, Morven would have been fried on the spot.

Hohendorf waited until Morven had gone through one of the tall wooden doors to one side of the courtyard before turning his livid countenance upon his wife.

"Your behavior is unforgivable!" he said to her in German.

Her eyes widened at what she saw as sheer nerve on his part. *"My* behavior?" she snarled at him. "You have just spent the whole afternoon with that . . . that—"

"Be very careful of your choice of words," Hohendorf interrupted with dangerous calm. "Be very, very careful."

Something in his eyes checked her. She cocked her head slightly to one side to study him.

There was a hint of surprise in her voice when she spoke. "You still believe you are in love with that woman? Oh, Pauli . . ." She never called him Axel, and was switching her attack in her time-honored way. "Generations of von Hohendorf's have had their fun with plump peasant women. . . ."

"Anne-Marie, you have just crossed the boundary. I want you out of here. Find yourself a hotel." Hohendorf began to walk away.

She lost control. "How dare you! How dare you walk away from me while you've got your whore in *my* home!"

Hohendorf turned swiftly to grab her shoulders so suddenly she recoiled, eyes now widening in genuine fear.

"You have done enough to me," he said tightly. "When I was with the Marineflieger, you walked out on me, because you did not want to be a service wife. Your own words. I lived for months in that house on my own while you were conducting your affair with Gerhard Linden, one of the senior pilots in your father's airline. What's the matter? Has he found a nice little stewardess? Is the taste of a countess too rich for him now? I'm not finished!" he added as she struggled to move away from him.

"You're hurting me!"

"Don't worry. I'm not going to beat you up. You won't drag me so low. But you will listen. I have lost count of the number of times you have embarrassed not me, but yourself. You don't love me. You never have. Our marriage was a joke and still is a joke. I don't know what possessed you to come up here today. I can't believe it was to see how I'm doing. You never wrote to me before I met Morven. Now, because you think I may have found a little happiness, you want to spoil it. Forget it, Anne-Marie. No one is going to spoil this for me. No one!"

He pushed her away from him so abruptly that she took a couple of stumbling backward steps.

"You are a fool!" she said at his retreating back. "Warriors are not needed anymore. There is peace now. You are throwing away the second highest position in the airline for what? Germany is whole again. Your place is with *me.*"

He looked back at her. "My place is where I choose to be, and with whom."

"You are German. Have you forgotten that?"

"I am German, and I am proud of it. I also know where my responsibility lies."

He went through the same door Morven had, leaving Anne-Marie alone in the darkening courtyard.

From her window, Morven had seen the last part of the argument. She had not heard what had been said, but the antagonistic stance of the figures below had clearly signaled what had been taking place.

"This is not how I want it," she said to herself softly.

She was still in her shorts. She rubbed her inner thigh reflectively, still feeling his touch upon her skin, still feeling him within her. Her body gave an involuntary twitch, remembering.

She moved away from the window to go into the bathroom, where the water for her bath was running. As she undressed she came to a decision. It was not one that made her happy.

A couple of hours later, there was a knock on her door.

"Come in," she called. "It's open." She knew it would be Hohendorf. His knock was distinctive.

He entered. She was fully dressed and he stared at what she was doing.

"Why are you packing?" he asked, hurt in his voice.

She paused. "Oh Axel . . . I can't stay here. Not now."

"But Anne-Marie is gone. Didn't you hear the car?"

"I was in the bath, and anyway, these are solid walls. You don't hear much unless you open a window."

"Morven, Morven." He came close and put his arms about her. "It was so wonderful out there in the forest."

"Yes, and she spoiled it. She made it cheap."

He held her away from him, looking directly into her eyes. The light in the room appeared to make his own eyes darker.

"Anne-Marie can spoil nothing if we do not let her. And you are not cheap. Stop saying these things about yourself. I must also be cheap then, because you know I love you."

She moved closer to him once more, to hold on tightly.

After a while, he said, "We'll both go. I've got an important training program back at the base. Perhaps I should cut this holiday short and go back."

"But that's not fair to your mother. She's enjoyed having you here."

"She will understand. I would not feel so good after you left. We'll leave tomorrow."

Red Square, Moscow. The same day.

Stolybin, in civilian clothes, had mingled with the crowd watching the parade. Suddenly he'd heard the sound of firing. Over to his right he'd seen a scuffle with men in zipped padded jackets struggling with someone they soon bundled away.

Stolybin had remained where he was. It was dark when he eventually returned to the office. The general was waiting.

"Did you see what happened?" the general asked.

"I heard, then saw him taken away."

"Shots for the president," the general said, adding darkly, "there will be more before the country gets out of this mess. How is the project going?"

"Progress is good. I intend to go to England soon."

The general squinted through his haze of smoke, as if doubting Stolybin would return.

"All right," he said at last. "Take Tokareva with you." He gave a fleeting smile that had more than a touch of a leer in it. "You can travel as man and wife."

"Why can't I go as a diplomat?"

"You can go as a diplomat . . . with a wife. Tokareva's English has improved greatly. She speaks it very well now."

"She has been busy."

The general's shrug was deprecating. "I helped a little." He turned and went out.

Watching as the connecting door swung shut, Stolybin found himself wondering whether the general had anything to do with the shots in the square.

* * *

Twelve days later, the general stormed into the office. Stolybin rose from his chair as the general slammed a sheaf of papers on the desk.

"The first signatures are down on the treaty!" he snarled. "Look at these figures. See what we're giving away. Nineteen thousand tanks! Forty-nine percent of our armor. Thirty-eight percent of our artillery, and 20 percent of our combat aircraft. This is monstrous! We are being bled dry. I want action from you, Colonel. The Motherland is going to be in serious trouble this winter. We have got to be ready to act. We'll have to move the program forward."

"I would advise against it, Comrade General." As the general appeared to have decided on formality, Stolybin thought it best to do the same. "If we hurry the pace, things might go wrong."

The general glared at him. "I do not expect things to go wrong. You are a colonel in the KGB. You can adapt to changing circumstances. We all have to."

The general went out, leaving the papers with the breakdown of figures for the arms reduction treaty with the West.

Stolybin sat down slowly and stared at the papers. Then he flung the pen he'd been using across the desk in frustration.

The pen rolled off the desk. He got up, went around to pick it up carefully. He laid it across the papers the general had brought.

"All right, General," he said. "You want things to happen more quickly? Fine . . . but not at risk to my neck."

Whitehall, London.

Charles Buntline, in a well-tailored City suit, knocked on the door to the minister's office. Despite recent upheavals in government, the minister was still in his old job.

"Come in."

Buntline entered an office that looked like the inner sanctum of an exclusive club.

"Ah, Charles," the minister greeted. "I gather you have some intriguing news."

"Yes, Minister. Stolybin has been seen in Moscow."

"Do you mean that chappie you bested over the defecting pilot business?"

Buntline nodded.

"But I thought," the minister said, "he was out of circulation. If I remember correctly, you indicated at the time that he'd been sent on an extended holiday to one of those dreadful places they keep for such occasions, even in these supposedly enlightened times."

"That was not a mistake on my part," Buntline told the minister calmly. "Stolybin was sent into internal exile. Now he's back. He was seen two days ago in Red Square."

"So they've let him out." The minister was puzzled. "But why? These people don't forgive failure easily, despite *perestroika* and *glasnost,* which are themselves beginning to look decidedly tattered."

"I've been giving that some thought, Minister. Whoever's let him out has done so for a specific purpose . . . not because he's in favor again."

"And that purpose?"

Buntline placed his hands in his pockets and paced the opulent carpet of the minister's office.

Then he paused, turning again to the minister. "Before this new openness hit the Soviet Union, Stolybin and I frequently sparred over the years. I know some of his methods. If there's one thing he's good at, it's destabilization. The heads of governments in many countries have reason to thank him for their sudden departure into the political wilderness and, sometimes, a wilderness more terminal."

"And whose government do you think he is now preparing to give his undivided attention?"

Buntline's reply came without hesitation. "His own, or what's left of it."

The minister stared. "Oh, come now, Charles. What is he? A lieutenant colonel in the KGB? You don't seriously—"

"He's a full colonel now. That much I do know. Only someone with plenty of clout could have got him out and bumped him up a rank. Someone who has set him to work."

"And who, in your estimation, is that person?"

Buntline began pacing once more and, when he had stopped for a second time, said, "I have my suspicions, though not hard facts. However, this particular individual is one of the hardest of hard-liners. He was the one who put Stolybin away in the first place. I have no evidence that he is involved, but equally, I find it very difficult to believe he isn't."

Buntline began to warm to his theme. "The Soviet Union is coming apart at the seams. The Russian people are facing a winter of starvation. There are growing signs that we in the West may well face an influx of economic refugees not only from former countries of the Warsaw Pact, but from Russia itself. We are talking millions, Minister. Add to that a sizable chunk of very dissatisfied hard-liners who see what is happening as nothing less than the dismemberment of their society, you have a recipe for a quite ferocious civil war, which could very easily engulf other nations. Despite the arms reduction treaty, nothing serious will move in that direction for some time. We therefore have, on our doorstep, a very powerful nation lurching into instability, a nation with its massive arms stockpile intact. Am I making my point clear, Minister?"

"What you're doing, Mr. Buntline, is scaring the daylights out of me."

"Good. I intended to. If Stolybin and his sponsors are planning to give this whole nightmare a push, I feel we ought to try and find out or, at least, be on our guard. You can be certain whatever he's planning won't be obvious. Let us not forget how he fed us that story about the defecting pilot while scheming to have the thing shot down by his own side and drag us into the mess at the same time. Using that experimental squadron up in Scotland saved the day."

"Yes," the minister agreed reluctantly. "We had to lean on the air vice marshal to get use of the aircraft." Turning from the large window through which he could see the traffic-packed thoroughfare of Whitehall, he glanced at Buntline, who was stony-faced. "You don't much like him, do you?"

"He mollycoddles that unit. If, as is being touted, it's meant to be the new edge of the changing defense requirement, he should not be so reluctant to use it."

"I do have some sympathy for him," the minister said, hedging his bets. "That first squadron had only just been declared operational. Had matters gone wrong . . ." The minister paused. "Questions in the House and all that."

"But it didn't. And though the defecting aircraft ran out of fuel and was lost, we did gain some quite valuable information."

The minister said nothing for some moments, seemingly content to look out of his window. "Something really must be done about the awful traffic in London." He turned to Buntline. "Very well, Charles. Thank you for keeping me informed. Stay on it. Let me know of developments. Nothing much we can do at the moment. See if you can find out what is actually happening."

"I'll keep on it," Buntline said.

Buntline was a true Whitehall mandarin: anonymous, of indeterminate age, with an indeterminate job that had taken him to all corners of the globe.

He let himself quietly out of the minister's office.

6

In the two weeks that followed, work continued apace at November One, on the testing of the Skyray B missile. The crews of Selby, Hohendorf, and Bagni, detailed for the testing program, continued to achieve excellent results. There were no hitches. All systems performed better than expected, and the crews were in top form.

McCann spent his week in the tower and, most unusual for him, behaved himself. He was no nearer discovering more about Karen Lomax, though he had glanced at her frequently when he thought she wasn't looking. His relationship with her was strictly professional, even more so than with the other personnel in air traffic control.

Unknown to him, she had stolen her own surreptitious glances, to the hidden amusement of her colleagues.

It was after a particularly successful flight that Selby, while they were getting rid of their flying gear, gave him some news.

"I've found something out about the love of your life," he said.

"What love of my life?" McCann countered.

"Dear, oh dear. Listen to the studied indifference. The doll. Remember? The one who had you using up the dictionary to describe her. A certain flying officer."

"Yeah?"

"Yeah," Selby mimicked. "The reason you don't see her in the mess is because she lives in married quarters."

"Goddammit. So she *is* married. Just my luck."

"I didn't say that."

"You just said she lived in married quarters. Single officers do not live in married quarters."

"They do, if they have permission to live with their parents."

McCann looked confused. "What parents?"

"Use that much-vaunted wizard brain of yours," Selby urged with some amusement. "Forget electronics for a moment and think names." He tapped briefly on McCann's forehead with his knuckles. "Anything popping up in there?"

"Names," McCann repeated. "Lomax? I don't know any other—" McCann's voice died suddenly.

"Aha. Daylight."

"Not Wing Commander Lomax," McCann said at last, like someone who had just had a present taken from him. "Boss of the Engineering Wing?"

"The same."

"Oh hell. He hates pilots."

"So I've heard. Thinks we abuse his airplanes. I've got more news."

"I don't think I want to hear."

"She's got a boyfriend. Fiancé, in fact."

McCann gave his pilot a hard stare. "You're a sadist. You know that?"

"Just trying to keep you out of trouble, Elmer Lee. You ought to know who the boyfriend is."

McCann gave in. "All right. Hit me with it."

"Flight Lieutenant 'Geordie' Pearce."

"Dammit. Another engineer officer."

"More to the point, he's the command rugby star. Big and mean."

McCann pondered this piece of news while he hung up his flight gear.

"We're not due to fly for forty-eight hours," he said when he'd finished. "I think I need a drink. I'm off to the mess. If the bar's open, I'm buying. Coming?"

"Spoken like a man," Selby said. "Lead on."

"She's got no right going out with a gorilla like that," McCann said, staring morosely into the one drink he'd nursed for the last thirty minutes. "It just isn't fair."

Selby frowned at him. "You're beginning to worry me, Elmer Lee. I've never seen a woman do this to you. I'm off to Aberdeen in the morning to see Morven. Why not come with me? Take your mind off Karen Lomax. Meet Zoe." He waggled his eyebrows at McCann.

"I dunno." McCann would not be cheered.

"Oh, come on. Have a ride in my Cosworth. It's a great car."

"Nothing beats a Corvette in my book."

"This will change your mind. Sink into soft leather and enjoy."

"Anyway, isn't Axel going to be there?"

"He's flying," Selby answered neutrally. "He's got our slot for the next two days."

"I see. So that's why you're going. You guys are going to have to talk to each other sometime."

"We work well together."

"That's not what I mean, and you know it."

"Put a sock in it, Elmer Lee. I'm not looking for a lecture. Are you coming with me, or not?"

"All right," McCann said after a while. "I'll come

. . . if only to stop you from giving your sister a hard time."

A cold rain was falling when they left the base the next morning. The Cosworth 4x4 was surefooted in the rain, the glistening road surface holding no terrors.

McCann, however, looked uncertain as Selby took bend after bend at speeds that would have had most other cars making unwanted acquaintance with the landscape.

For his part, Selby had given his visit to his sister much thought during the night. He had not spoken to her since her return, and his conversations with Hohendorf had been mainly restricted to operational requirements. He was now wondering how best to handle the coming meeting with Morven.

Taking McCann along had not been wholly altruistic. McCann needed to forget his gloom; but his presence would also ease some of the inevitable tension.

"Jeez, Mark!" McCann was saying. "We're not going to take that corner."

The winding road, wet and empty, streamed beneath the wheels of the Cosworth.

"Of course we are," Selby assured him calmly.

The car clung to the road like a leech.

"Jeez," McCann repeated softly.

"You should talk. I've seen the way you drive, McCann."

"Hey. I'm pretty good. I know my Corvette like the back of my hand."

"And I know this car like the back of *my* hand. Now, are we going to argue all the way to Aberdeen?"

"Nope," McCann said, watching as another bend seemed almost upon them.

But he didn't say a word.

* * *

When they arrived, McCann had a look of surprise on his face, unable to believe they had made it in one piece.

Zoe was there to greet them, brightening when she saw Selby.

"Well, hello again," she began. "Do come in. You're in luck. I'm studying at home today." She turned to McCann.

"Elmer Lee McCann," Selby said by way of introduction. "My backseater."

"Hello, Elmer Lee. So you're the magician in the back."

McCann smiled at her and held out his hand. "The best in the business."

"He always says that," Selby said.

"That's because it's true," McCann retorted.

She gave a little laugh. "Come on in, you two. Morven did warn me you were a double act."

"I'm sorry we've sprung this on you," Selby said as they entered. "We didn't know we'd got the time off until late afternoon yesterday. I did ring, but there was no one at home."

"Oh, don't worry. It's nice that you could come. What's more, Morven's going to be here soon. I was speaking to her just before you arrived. She's returning from a short field trip and is putting some of her material away in the lab. Tea, or coffee?"

"Coffee, please," McCann said.

"Tea, please," from Selby.

They had answered simultaneously.

"Well . . ." they both began hesitantly.

"It's all right. No problem. Morven has tea and I have coffee, so I'm quite accustomed to making both."

As she left them to go into to kitchen Selby glanced at McCann to gauge the effect of Zoe's presence upon his backseater. There was a look of appreciation upon McCann's face, but not one strong enough to obliterate the memory of Karen Lomax, if only temporarily.

Oh dear, Selby thought. This is bad news. Elmer Lee in love is all I need.

They were on their second cups when Morven arrived, in anorak, thick sweater, jeans, and field boots. She had a backpack that she carried by its straps. She put the pack down by her feet.

"Hello, Mark." Her voice was cool, eyes watchful.

He stood up and went up to her. "Mo."

"I know I look a mess," she said as he gave her a quick but warm hug.

"You look great."

"You've got to say that. I'm your sister." She looked past him, at McCann. "Hi, Elmer Lee. Behaving yourself?"

"I'm trying." He grinned at her. "And don't say 'very.'"

"Since you've put it so nicely, I won't." Using Selby as support, she began to untie her laces. When the boots were loose, she kicked them off to reveal thick grayish socks. She picked up the boots and the pack. "Excuse us for moment, you two," she said to Zoe and McCann. "I want to have a few words with this brother of mine. Right," she said to Selby. "Upstairs."

She went out into the compact hall without waiting for a reaction.

Selby glanced back, his expression blank, before following her out.

Morven had placed her boots on a corner mat and was already making her way up the stairs. There was a purposeful manner in the way she moved.

She began as soon as they had entered her bedroom and had shut the door.

"All right, Mark. Explain."

"Explain what?"

"You know what." The green eyes were on fire.

"I've been back for two weeks or more, and not a word.
Don't tell me you didn't know: unless Axel's suddenly
become invisible. You must have known when he returned, that I was back in Aberdeen. You may not
totally approve of my seeing him, but I don't expect you
to cut me off like that. You and I are the only two left
in the immediate family, Mark."

"Do I get a word in edgeways, or what? We've been
very busy. We've got an important program on."

The eyes were not mollified. "Not good enough.
Axel's been flying as much as you have. We've seen
each other three times since we got back."

Selby was looking hard into her eyes, as if searching for something.

"This isn't quite like you, Mo," he said. "You've
had rows with me before, but you've never sounded
bitter. Something's wrong. What is it? I can tell with
you, just as you can tell with me. I know something's
worrying you. What is it?"

She turned away from him and began to empty
her backpack carefully.

"Mo? Has he . . ."

She rounded upon him. "Why have you always got
to blame him? The poor man's doing his best!" The
green eyes were filming over with moisture. "You
know, I've thought maybe I should call it a day, but it
only feels worse."

Selby put his arms about her. "Oh God, I'm sorry.
I don't want to hurt you. You know that. I'm just worried about you. Come on. Tell me. What really happened out there?"

"Anne-Marie. That's what happened."

"His wife? *She* was there? Is he crazy? How could
he . . ."

She pushed herself away. "There you go again.
Why don't you *listen!* He had nothing to do with it. We

were having a wonderful time. The castle's old and warm, his mother's lovely, and generally, although it felt a little strange, I was made very welcome. Then out of the blue, *she* turned up and made a scene. It spoiled everything then and I decided to come back. Axel cut short his time with his mother because he didn't want to stay without me."

"This is the very thing I hoped would not happen to you," Selby said. "It doesn't matter how good, how noble Axel von Hohendorf is. The bottom line is that he *is* married, and to a woman who obviously has no intention of giving him up, whatever her own behavior might be. She's going to make life hell for the both of you. That's what I've been trying to tell you all along."

"You don't like Axel, do you?"

"How can you say that? Hard as it may be for you to believe, I actually do like him. I think he's a great pilot, and if I have to go into combat, he's one of just two guys I'd feel safe with as my wingman, or in the lead. But I can't let that cloud my judgment of this thing with the two of you. What's more, if he's got heavy emotional problems, it could affect his flying."

"What are you trying to tell me?"

"I'm saying that the job we do is not forgiving of mistakes. Mistakes can cost lives. I once said to him fighter pilots should not marry."

"Is that why things are less than okay with Kim Mannon?"

"That does not come into this conversation. It's not relevant."

"I think it is."

Selby ignored the comment. "What I'm trying to say is this: if Axel makes a mistake that costs him, I'll lose twice over. I'll lose a top-class squadron colleague, and I'll lose you, too."

The green eyes looked at him for long moments. She said nothing for a while.

"That's the best you can do?" she asked quietly.

"It's not how I want to see it."

Another silence passed while she continued to hold him with her eyes.

"I never thought I'd ever be saying this to you Mark, because I know how much it means to you. But right now, I hate your bloody airplanes more than any thing I can think of—even more than Anne-Marie."

Moscow.

Deputy Belov was alone in his small, basic flat when a knock on the door sounded. There was a sizable gap between the door and the floor that let the cold in, and a rolled carpet, small and threadbare, had been placed against it.

Belov stood up and went to the door.

The carpet had been pushed some way in by a large brown envelope.

He stared at it, wondering if it were a letter bomb of some kind. He had enemies. People who did not like his politics. Even before *perestroika,* he had been active in one of the underground movements. Being elected deputy did not take away all the risk. There were those with long memories.

Since being made a deputy in the new parliament, he had, from time to time, clandestinely received information that had enabled him to unmask some of those determined to obstruct the path of reform, or worse, abuse it. On one such occasion, information he had received had helped to nail a notorious black marketeer.

Was this, he wondered, more information? Or a present from the marketeer's friends?

No police protection was available to him, and he

did not expect any. He continued to stare at the package.

Carefully, he opened the door. The dim corridor was empty. The large envelope inexorably drew his eyes to it. At last, he picked it up, then shut the door slowly after another quick look up and down the corridor. No one.

He went back to the small desk he'd been sitting at and, after a few moments of cautiously feeling the package for irregularities, gingerly began to open it.

What came out was as explosive as any bomb. The papers that he spread on his desk gave full details of the hard-liners' plan to circumvent the requirements of the arms reduction treaty. How they would put obsolete and obsolescent matériel into the pile while replacing them with fewer but much more advanced weaponry. New, advanced aircraft would fill the new inventory. Many of those would be going into naval service, where the numbers of aircraft had not been calculated into the requirements. It was all there. Even design modifications of the aircraft in question.

Belov placed the papers back, hardly daring to touch them. He had to let Gant know. But not by telephone, or by letter. He would have to go to America secretly, and not by a direct route. Perhaps he should go via Switzerland or Germany to make contact first with the Americans there, who would then contact Gant.

He decided on Germany.

Two days later, he was on a flight to Frankfurt. No one stopped him. He did not see the hard-eyed man who took a reserved seat some rows behind him after the aircraft took off.

* * *

In his office, Stolybin received a phone call. He spoke softly to whoever was at the other end, then replaced the receiver, tapping thoughtfully at it for a brief moment.

Then he withdrew his hand and continued working. There was no need to tell the general as yet.

Washington. Three hours later.

Representative Gant received a signal via classified channels saying that Belov was coming over. No other information was forthcoming.

In his office, Gant stared at the signal.

"What the hell?" he said softly, then quickly began making preparations.

The next day, Belov arrived. He was met by Gant's people and taken to a safe house well away from prying eyes. On the way they lost the hard-eyed man who had followed Belov from Moscow. The men guarding Belov had taken it for granted there would be a tail and had acted, even though they had not discovered one.

The hard-eyed man drove around for a while before returning to his hotel. He was not particularly bothered.

His embassy did not know of his presence in Washington.

"My God!" The exclamation had come from Gant.

He and Belov were alone in comfortable study in the house that had been selected for Belov's temporary stay. Gant studied the papers carefully. He selected a detailed drawing of an aircraft.

"Su-27 with foreplanes, folding wings, navalized," he said quietly. He put that down, selected another. "MiG-29, also with foreplanes and folding wings, also navalized. How *many,* did you say?"

"According to my source," Belov replied, "at least twice as many each than has been indicated, some of which will operate from land. Again, according to my source, some are already fully operational. The source promises more information. My friend, we must bring our meeting forward. And it must not be in your country. I was not stopped this time, but we should not take chances. Things are very bad in my own country and we must act soon."

Gant was sympathetic. "I've seen the food lines. Where do we meet?"

"Europe, I think, or perhaps North Africa. Yes. I think North Africa. Only our own people should know of this. People who think like us. When we have got all the evidence, we shall each present it to our respective governments . . . on the same day."

Gant nodded. "Agreed. I'll make the arrangements. We'll get word to you."

Belov gave a hesitant smile. "This will be good for you, if we succeed."

"Good for you, too. Good for your country."

"I am not so sure," Belov said, a little sadly. "Now I would like some sleep. I must not be away from Moscow too long. I would like to leave tomorrow."

"No problem."

Belov looked steadily at Gant. "No problem. Ah. What it is to be American. To be so sure of everything."

"Perhaps it's because we are not always sure of ourselves."

"Very profound, but I think, my friend, you are very sure of yourself. Now, I will say good night to you, Amos."

"Good night, Alexei."

Belov's return trip to Moscow was without incident, but he was still oblivious of the hard-eyed shadow that trailed him all the way back.

* * *

On the morning after People's Deputy Belov's departure for Moscow, Gant was having a late breakfast in his Washington apartment with a close friend, Frank Benno. Benno was an ex-USAF major who currently flew Boeing 747s for a living. The breakfast was strictly private.

Benno had a wide and varied experience of jet flying, having flown both fighters and heavy multiengines during his service career. He was now studying the documents that Gant had placed before him.

"How hard is this info?" he asked.

"As hard as it's possible to be, given the circumstances. My source is impeccable," Gant said.

"But you won't say."

"Sorry, Frankie. You know I can't do that."

Benno gave a wry smile. "Okay, okay. I've been there. Well, if this stuff's really genuine, you've got a hot one on your hands."

He picked up first a detailed drawing, then a photograph of the Su-27 Flanker, and laid them side by side. The familiar graceful shape of the Su-27 was instantly recognizable. But just beneath the cockpit on either side were the fully movable foreplanes, which, if the information was correct, should give the already highly agile Soviet fighter formidably enhanced agility.

"I would not like to be the pilot who comes up against this baby," Benno said. "This is bad news for any fighter jock coming head-to-head with a guy in one of these. Of course," he went on, "any plane is only as good as the guy with his hands on the stick."

"Meaning?"

"You can put the best plane in the world in the sky, but if the guy flying it is no good, he's still going to get creamed by a hotshot in a less maneuverable ship. I've used a Phantom to outfight F-14 Tomcats, and

I know of at least one lady pilot who flies A-4 Skyhawks and regularly zaps Tomcats and F-16s."

"But would you expect them to allow mediocre pilots to fly this plane?"

"Nope," Benno replied. "Not unless they've gone to all that trouble just to let some dipshit get nailed in combat."

"Which means we've got trouble if things come apart over there."

"That's about what I think. Have you passed any of this on to the intelligence boys?"

Gant shook his head.

"What?" Benno was amazed, and worried. "You're sitting on this?"

"I need more facts, Frank. I'll be getting them. I want a watertight case to put before the man on the Hill."

Benno looked at Gant with sudden understanding. "I had a feeling this dovish conversion of yours was all bullshit. You want to prove that the Peace Dividend is all wishful thinking."

"Don't you think so yourself?"

"I'm not in Congress. I'm just a flying bus driver."

"You left the air force because defense cuts would mean you wouldn't get to fly as often as you'd like."

Benno said nothing.

"I'm going to need you to fly Mamie for me," Gant went on, "in a month or so."

Benno nodded. "Fine by me. I can fix the time off. Where are we going?"

Benno, whose multiengine jet experience in the air force had included flying the Boeing 707–based RC-135 electronic intelligence aircraft in their many versions, had flown Gant's specially modified 707 on campaign and fund-raising trails. The aircraft's name was that of Gant's mother, while the 707 had itself been donated by Gant's wealthy backers.

The aircraft's interior had been totally stripped and refurbished to a high-executive, head-of-state standard. There were staff seating areas and lounges that could be sealed for both privacy and security. There was a dining/conference room, four luxurious cabins, lavatories, and a totally private master study with its adjoining large bedroom and private bathroom at the forward end of the plane. Leather upholstery was everywhere.

"We're starting in Europe," Gant was saying in reply to Benno's question, "but we won't be stopping there."

"Sounds like a major trip," Benno said thoughtfully. "Perhaps I ought to arrange for a vacation."

"Ten days should do it."

"What kind of a flight plan do we file?"

Gant understood the question. At times, Mamie had flown to places that had not adhered strictly to the documented flight plan.

"We'll file one that takes us to Cannes in the south of France. I'll let you know the rest later. I can tell you we'll be leaving Cannes at night. We won't have a noise problem because of Mamie's hush kits."

The hush kits were modifications to the engines that enabled them to operate with a substantial reduction in noise. The 707 was also equipped with an up-to-date avionics package that gave a precise, long-range navigation capability. Its storm avoidance instruments enabled it to be flown in the least turbulent of areas, ensuring a smooth flight for its passengers. It could carry forty people in relaxed splendor. But for his proposed trip, Gant intended to have no more than fifteen people aboard, including crew and staff.

Benno was now studying the MiG-29, which, like

the Flanker, possessed foreplanes on either side of the cockpit.

He tapped at a photograph. "What gets me is that the guys who designed these birds have been able, just by making some mods to the basic besign, to give their planes an angle-of-attack capability that's way ahead of anything we've got right now. Hell, we've only just had a decision on the ATF, though it can be flown in the poststall regime, if the specs are all they're said to be. But so far, there's just one flying prototype for each contender. It will take years before they see operational service, if at all."

The ATF, the advanced tactical fighter, was meant to be the next generation fast jet.

"My feelings exactly," Gant said. "Which is why we've got work to do. Defensewise, people are going around in circles."

Benno carefully stacked all the papers together and placed them back in the shallow file Gant had brought.

"Yeah," he said. "I can see you're going to need something pretty dramatic to convince people we can't let our guard down too quickly. But this ought to do it. You've convinced me."

"Except you're not the guy holding purse strings. He's the one we've got to convince. To be more precise, his boss."

"If this is not for real," Benno said cautiously, "you're going to be in deep shit, Amos. You can forget about the Senate then, and a possible presidency."

"This is for real, Frankie. Believe me. Now, do I still have a pilot? I don't want to use the regular guy on this."

"Sure you do. I wouldn't miss this for anything."

"Thanks, Frankie. It's good to know I can count on you."

"Hell, I miss flying the Elint 135s. Doing the schedules can get pretty boring, even though it pays well. So your little spook flight's just what I need to get the adrenaline going."

Gant put the file away. It had been a good morning's work.

7

Southeast England. The second week in December.

The large house near Sevenoaks in Kent with its twenty acres of well-kept grounds had two unexpected, early-afternoon visitors on a quiet Tuesday. Though the day was cool, there was a bright sun, for winter had not yet decided to make its presence felt in this southeastern county. The house, with its eight bedrooms and three reception rooms, was substantial by any standards. The visitors admired it as they approached its unbarred gate.

They walked along its wide, neat drive, which bordered a vast lawn that was punctuated by strategically placed clusters of shrubs and flowering plants. In preparation for the coming winter, many had been pruned and cut back, while the perennials looked carefully trimmed. A woman in her sixties dressed in trousers, Wellingtons, and a Barbour was working in one of the clusters. The visitors walked across the lawn toward her.

She did not turn around until one of them, the man, spoke to her.

"What a magnificent *Helleborus corsicus,*" he said appreciatively.

"Oh!" She straightened with a start and turned to face them. "Oh dear," she went on with a sheepish smile. "I *am* sorry. I didn't hear you." She glanced at the plant she had been tending. "You know the garden." She touched the pale green, cup-shaped flowers gently. "I am rather proud of my Corsican Christmas roses. They're a bit early this year. But all the better, don't you think? They do make the garden look cheerful when most other things have gone to sleep for the winter. We were very lucky, of course. Last week's heavy snow did not touch us. The rest of the country was not so fortunate."

"Christmas roses do indeed cheer things up."

"Do you garden, Mister . . . ?"

"Hemming," Stolybin lied smoothly. "I'm afraid I don't, but I do love a garden that has had care lavished upon it." His English was perfect. "I'm too lazy to give a garden the attention it really needs."

"I'm sure you're not. You're young, and busy. Gardening is really for the old."

He smiled at her. "You are not old. You look very fit to me."

"Thank you, young man, even though I do know better. Now, how can I help you?"

"I'm Michael, and this is my wife, Diane. We're friends of Alan's and we promised him we'd drop by to say hello if we were ever in the area."

"Oh. I see. Alan's always having his friends drop 'round. Are you from his squadron?"

"I'm army," Stolybin said apologetically. "We met on a joint exercise."

"Don't apologize for being in the army. We are on the same side, after all, even though the services do have their rivalry."

"My feelings exactly."

"Do go up to the house. My husband's there. If you don't mind, I'll just finish here, then I'll be in to have some tea prepared."

"That will be fine. Thank you."

"All right. I'll see you later."

They smiled at her and went on to the house.

Stolybin looked about him as they walked. "Not a guard in sight. I don't suppose they think he needs guarding."

"Why are we here, Sergei?" Tokareva asked.

"I'm Michael," he said sternly, "and you're Diane. Remember that always, and speak only English. I cannot tell you why we're here. Your job is to keep the wife occupied while I talk to the old man."

The home of Sir James West was staffed by two people, a husband-and-wife team that had been with the family for years. A contracted gardener looked after the heavy work in the garden.

It was Sir James himself who opened the door to Stolybin's ring. He looked at the younger man and the exotic beauty of Tokareva with a puzzled expression. Despite nearing seventy years of age, he held himself erect and looked much younger.

"Yes?"

"Sir James," Stolybin began, holding out his hand, "I'm Michael Hemming, and this is my wife, Diane. We're friends of Alan. He suggested we look you up if ever we were in the area."

There was a slight pause, then West shook both their hands.

"Well," he said. "Are you air force?"

"No. Army. Met Alan on joint exercises."

"I see. Er . . ." He seemed to be searching beyond them. "My wife's out there in the garden."

"Yes. We've met her. She told us to come up. She's doing some work on the *Helleborus corsicus* and will join us soon."

"Ah yes. She quite likes her Christmas roses. Do come in. Do come in." He led them into a large, comfortable reception room that overlooked the garden. He glanced out of one of the huge windows. "Ah, there she is. Loves those things," he went on to them. "Please take a seat. Drink?"

"Scotch, if I may," Stolybin said as he sat down in a deep armchair.

Tokareva took a settee. "Vodka and tonic, please."

"Ah," he said to her. "The good Russian stuff. No doubt we'll soon be able to buy the genuine article more freely now that things are easing over there. I always drink it neat, but I suppose a young lady like you prefers it slightly milder."

Tokareva was at her most demure. "I don't think I could handle it neat, Sir James."

Stolybin forced himself not to glance at her. Tokareva, he knew, always took her vodka neat.

"Quite right, too," West said, and went to a cabinet to prepare the drinks.

They made small talk while they waited for Lady West, the subject being mainly the son, Alan. Stolybin had been well briefed, and could lie most convincingly until, by the time tea was brought, the atmosphere was quite genial.

At the end of tea, Tokareva said to Lady West, who had insisted they call her Madge, "If it's not too much of a bother, Madge, would you mind showing me 'round the garden? It's very beautiful and I know Michael would like to talk about the army and airplanes."

Margery West was delighted at the chance to show off her garden. "No trouble at all," she said. She glanced at Tokareva's feet. "What size do you take?"

Stolybin glanced surreptitiously at her, hoping she would not make the mistake of giving a metric measurement.

But Tokareva was on the ball. "Eight," she answered sheepishly. "I do have rather big feet."

"Nonsense. Your feet suit you. You're a tall young woman. Nothing worse than tall women with little feet. Come with me. I'm sure we can get a pair of Wellingtons to fit you. The ground's a bit damp in some places and you wouldn't want to soil your shoes."

Tokareva allowed herself to be ushered out.

Stolybin waited until he could see them making their way across the garden before dropping his bombshell.

"I come from friends," he said quietly, "from Moscow."

"What?" West's eyes jumped in their sockets like startled colts. "What are you talking about? Moscow? You're in the army."

"I am in a sort of army . . . yes. Let us not beat about the bush, Sir James. Perhaps if I say 1965, that will crystallize your memory."

West suddenly went pale and looked his age.

"My God," he muttered after a while. "After all these years." He stood up, went to the liquor cabinet, and poured himself, almost without thinking, a neat vodka. He took a long drink and slowly swallowed. "After all these years," he repeated, not turning around. "Why now? What could your people want of me? I'm an old man. There's nothing I can do for you."

"You underestimate yourself. There is plenty you can do."

As if making confession to a priest, West abruptly explained, speaking to the cabinet, "I had seen warfare at first hand as a very young officer. I did not want my country sucked into another. I believed the manufacture of a highly advanced missile would cause provocation. I wanted it stopped for that reason only. I did not betray my country. I was fighting for its continuing survival."

"I do not doubt it. I've read your file. I fully understand your motives."

West turned to look at Stolybin. His eyes had become sunken. It was clear the years had not dimmed his feelings of guilt, despite what he had just said.

"You have a file on *me?"*

"Not I, specifically," Stolybin said. "Someone who knows you well. I've been given access to it."

West looked as if a bad smell had suddenly entered the room. "KGB," he said with distaste. "That's what you must be. Don't you people ever give up? Haven't you heard? The Cold War's over. We have peace in our time. There is freedom of movement. The Wall is down!"

"I know the litany. I'm afraid like so many people, you're swallowing the myth whole. The game has merely changed. It's evolved into something much more complex and dangerous."

West shook his head defiantly. "I'm an old man. There is not much you can do to me. Whatever it is your masters have sent you here for, tell them to forget it. You have come to the wrong place. Now I must ask you to leave, and . . ." He glanced out of the window. Neither his wife nor Tokareva could be seen. "And take that woman—who is no doubt KGB as well—take her with you."

Stolybin made no move to go. His eyes had become mercilessly cold. He looked about him pointedly. "Fine living for a socialist."

"I don't know what you mean by 'socialist.' Whatever it is, it's something I am not. Now please leave my house, before I call the police. Nothing you can say will change my mind."

Stolybin's smile was feral. "No? At the end of the war, you were a liaison officer with a Soviet unit in Berlin."

"So? Many British officers were. French and American, too."

"We are not here to discuss other Allied officers. We are discussing you. I believe you expressed certain sympathies with our Soviet ideals for the future."

"I was young and gullible. I had just experienced a terrible war. All wars are terrible, but mine seemed especially so. As long as your people felt war should be avoided at all costs, I found sympathy with such views."

"So when the new air-to-air missile was being tested years later, you helped to ensure it failed."

"I've already told you. At the time, I believed it to be a destabilizing factor. I was not so much helping your people as trying to keep my country out of a possible war it could ill afford. Wars can be started for the most innocuous of reasons."

"Three men died," Stolybin reminded him, plunging the knife into a long-festering wound, "and another suffered a ruined career."

West shut his eyes, clearly remembering vividly. "I have lived with the ghosts of those young men all these years. You cannot possibly torture me more than I have already done to myself. Expose me, if you must, but I will not do your bidding."

"Brave words," Stolybin said with contempt, "but empty." He indicated the window with a brief movement of his head. "Does your wife know of your treachery? And what of your son? He is a Tornado pilot, I believe. He flies the low-level bombers. We will not expose you, not in the way you believe. If you do not agree to help us, both your son and your wife will receive detailed information of your part in what happened twenty-five years ago. Let me see . . . Alan must have been about five years old at the time." Stolybin gave another of his unpleasant smiles. "I was not much older myself."

"Get out!" West's voice was a low whisper, almost pleading. "*Get out,* damn you!"

"I am sure that is not what you really want. If I leave here without getting what I've come for, you will be responsible for destroying your son's career, and as for your wife . . ." Stolybin deliberately left his words hanging.

"I will gladly pay for my grave mistake, but leave my son and my wife out of it."

"Unfortunately, that is not possible. You have but one choice: do as we ask. And please don't believe you can escape by blowing your brains out when we leave. The documents are already prepared. They would go to your wife and your son, should you decide to take your own life. I do not believe you would be so cowardly."

West's eyes gazed upon Stolybin with undiluted hatred. "Even in suicide, you would pursue me. What do you need of me?" he asked stiffly.

Stolybin ignored the palpable hostility he could feel emanating from the older man.

"Another new missile is being tested."

"If your channels of information are so efficient, why do you need me? I know of no such missile."

"We believe you do. This missile owes much to the one you helped terminate. But it is much more lethal and has a far greater range. To use your own words, we believe it to be a highly destabilizing factor. The missile is being developed for use by a special unit being created to coincide with the restructuring of defense postures. We feel both the unit and the missile should come to an untimely end."

"You have indeed come to the wrong man." West actually looked pleased. "I have no influence whatsoever."

"You have many old contacts."

"Useless for your purposes. You already know much more than I do."

"You must find a way, Sir James West." Stolybin used the title like an insult. "During the tests of the missile, a special recognition code is used by both the launch aircraft and the target. This is, of course, changed frequently. What we need is the basic code. We can do the rest. We can break it down to whatever permutation is used on a given day . . . provided, of course, we have the primary numbers of the code and the order in which they fall."

"You're asking the impossible."

"I think not. Your son, as I've said, is a Tornado pilot. A good one, too, I believe. The new unit requires good pilots. Arrange it so that he becomes a possible candidate for selection. That would give you an excuse to visit the unit and to observe a test. You must then find a way to observe how the code is implemented."

"You're mad."

"Your son does not even have to succeed in becoming a member of this unit. Once you have found the basic code, pass it to us. You will be contacted at the appropriate time."

West continued to try to avoid the inevitable. "This cannot work. I won't be able to have access—"

"You had access in 1965."

"That was 1965. Things were very different then."

Stolybin was implacable. "Matters are, if anything, easier for you now. You are respected. You were once a junior minister, closely involved in defense. Many remember you as having had an excellent war record. You do not do yourself justice, Sir James. I am

certain you will find a way. You will not see me again,"
Stolybin continued, clearly brooking no resistance,
"but someone will be in touch. Of course, we shall be
keeping an eye on you." He stood up, ready to leave.
"I'd better go and find Diane."

He smiled briefly at the glare of hatred in West's
eyes.

"Cheer up, Sir James. Haven't you heard? After
all, the Cold War is over. No one is going to suspect that
you, a pillar of society now approaching your seven-
tieth birthday, intend to pass secrets to us. Information
is supposed to be freely exchanged these days. Such
clandestine work is now redundant. Why, I suspect
they may even be quite keen to show you how their new
toy works." Stolybin's eyes were like lumps of stone. "I
have every faith in you. Don't bother to see me to the
door. I can let myself out, and thank you for the
scotch."

He walked out, leaving West seething impotently.

He found Tokareva and Madge West at a far end
of the garden. Tokareva was carrying her shoes. She
looked at Stolybin with disguised relief.

"Going so soon?" Madge West said.

"I'm afraid we must," he told her regretfully.
"Back in harness tomorrow, and I've got some things to
prepare. Thank you very much for tea, and for showing
Diane your beautiful garden."

Madge held out her hand. "A pleasure. Do come
again."

"We shall," he lied, shaking hands.

Behind her, Tokareva raised her eyes briefly skyward, then bent forward to kick off the Wellingtons and
put on her shoes.

She shook hands with Madge. "Thank you for everything. I enjoyed the garden."

"Thank you, dear. As I've just said to Michael, do come again."

"We will."

Later, in their car back to London, she said, "I don't think I could have lasted much longer. She was boring me stupid with her garden."

"Silly," he corrected. "The term is boring you silly."

She stared at him. "Is this important? We are in the car. There is no one to hear."

"It's important. Remember it."

They were silent for a while, then she said, "All this is making me very tense. I want to make love. When we get back to our hotel, let's make love."

Madge West found her husband in the same room, staring out at the garden with a faraway look in his eyes.

"James," she began. "Who were those people, really?" She had to ask him twice.

He looked at her as if seeing her for the first time, then recovered himself quickly.

"Alan's friends."

She shook her head slowly. "I think not. He may have been English, but she wasn't."

"That's not so odd. Servicemen have always married a wide range of nationalities. Comes with the job, you might almost say."

She knew he was keeping something from her. "If you feel it's something I ought not know about, I do understand." On occasion, during his political career, there were matters he had chosen not to discuss with her. She had accepted it as par for the course. She did so now. "Whatever it is, tell me only if you think it necessary."

He said nothing for a while, then he looked at her with a great warmth in his eyes.

"Madge, I cannot begin to tell you how much I have loved you over these past years."

It was then that she realized that whatever was on his mind was a source of worry for her, too.

Stolybin and Tokareva were back in Moscow the next day.

"You've got bags under your eyes," the general greeted him. "Tokareva must be keeping you awake at night."

Stolybin did not tell the general that Tokareva's sexual activities were not restricted to nightfall.

"So, you've succeeded?" the general was saying.

"I've got him." Stolybin sounded as if the issue had never been in doubt. "I pointed out his options, and he saw the wisdom of cooperation."

The general's wreaths of smoke drew slow-motion patterns before Stolybin's eyes.

"You pointed out his options," the general repeated, savoring the turn of phrase. "I would have liked to have been there. I can be a hard bastard, but I think when you're in your stride, there is no one to touch you, Sergei."

"Am I to take that as a compliment?"

"It means I am pleased with you. *That's* a compliment."

London. Thursday, the same week.

The minister received a call from a senior colleague.

"James West? Yes. Sir James, isn't he? What? Yes, yes. I think he was in Defense. Before my time, of course. Ha-ha. I'm not *that* old. His son? Well, I'm not sure about that. I'd have to have a word with our not-so-tame air vice marshal. Very particular about selection for that unit of his. I suspect he probably hates being pointed in any direction, if you see what I mean. I could try, but I promise nothing. The old boy would like a visit? I suppose that could be arranged, but it will be harder recommending the son for selection. Almost a law unto themselves as far as that goes, that lot. What? Ha-ha. I may be the minister, but you wouldn't think it sometimes. But it should be simple enough for the old boy. Drink in the club? Say no more. You're on. Goodbye."

The minister replaced the phone and continued working on some routine papers.

Thurson was up at November One on another of his many visits the next day. It was a prearranged visit, but he brought news he felt sure Wing Commander Jason would not welcome.

"I've had a call from the minister," the air vice marshal said in Jason's squadron office. He looked at his subordinate speculatively, as if gauging the other's reaction before continuing. "He wants us to do a bit of public relations."

Jason held back a sigh. "Not another visit from some VIP, sir. We've got work to do up here, not show people around."

"People pay taxes, allocate funds, some of which comes our way. We've got to do these things, Christopher. We've got to keep the minister sweet. The continuing survival of the November Project is still a precarious thing. Besides, this is not one of these shoals of MPs and local dignitaries affairs. Just an old former junior minister. Used to be in Defense, of all things. Perhaps we should be a little accommodating." It was more than a suggestion.

Jason knew he had to give in. "Who is he, sir?"

"Sir James West."

"West," Jason said thoughtfully. "West. The name's familiar."

"Of course it is. I've just said, he was formerly in Defense. You're bound to have seen and heard mention of him in service correspondence and discussions."

"I have. Skyray B."

"What?" Thurson was surprised. "I was not aware—"

"Oh, I don't mean Skyray itself. But the missile from which Skyray was developed. James West, as he was then, was very much against the original missile. Too expensive and too unreliable, he said at the time. Events, of course, subsequently proved him correct."

Thurson said quietly, "Nineteen sixty-five. I remember. I was on Lightnings then. Flying officer. Green as anything, but very keen. We all hoped the new missile would work. Knew the pilot who did the shooting. My old flight commander. Odd, how life can sometimes turn out."

"Sir James West is the last person we need up here," Jason said. "His antipathy toward the old missile might still be strong. If he thought that one was expensive, God knows what he'll think of Skyray B, despite its being cheaper than most of its contemporaries. He might convey his feelings to the minister. We've got enough problems without inviting a potential enemy into our camp."

The air vice marshal looked thoughtful, then stared pointedly at the empty mug he held. "I think I could do with a refill."

Jason knew the ploy. The AVM was about to go into persuasion mode. He pressed a button on the intercom unit on his desk.

"Sergeant Mason, could you organize another mug of tea for the air vice marshal, please? I'll have another as well."

"Yes, sir," a female voice said.

As they waited the AVM said "Young Sergeant Graham was at the end of that line last year. How is she doing?"

"Not Sergeant Graham anymore. Pilot officer now. She's fine. Went to pieces a bit after Palmer's death, but pulled herself together. On my recommendation, she accepted a commission. She's another one I hope to see back here."

"Caroline Hamilton-Jones the other?"

Jason merely gave the briefest of shrugs.

"I know you believe in pushing frontiers back, Christopher, but you're doing enough here. I don't think our world's ready yet to see women in the cockpits of ASVs. One thing at a time, eh?"

Jason was saved from making comment by the appearance of Sergeant Mason, a slim blonde, with the fresh tea.

"Thank you," Thurson said to her pleasantly.

"Sir." She handed a mug to Jason, who thanked her with a smile.

"Do you specially select your assistants, too?" Thurson asked after she had left.

Jason grinned. "Luck of the draw, sir."

"Hmm." Thurson took a drink of his tea.

"To continue," the air vice marshal went on. "Sir James may, in fact, turn out to be just what we do need. We should give him a demonstration of Skyray. Prove to him how efficient it is. I'll check his clearance with the minister. Shouldn't be difficult, given his background. If he does happen to be the minister's chum, it will do us no harm at all if he's impressed. We need as many people a we can get on our side—even ex–junior ministers approaching seventy."

Jason did not look convinced, but he was philosophically resigned to the inevitable. In the past, the

AVM's instincts on whom to have on visits had proved accurate. Thurson knew how to play the PR game, even when things had gone wrong, like the accident to Palmer and Ferris.

"I leave it up to you, sir. There is something else, however, that I do remember about the name West. As you've said, life sometimes takes some strange turns. I remember another West, Flying Officer Alan West. Instructed him at Cottesmore, on Tornadoes; the IDS, of course. I actually thought of him for future consideration for the November program, but decided against it. He's a stable officer, but a trifle heavy-handed on the stick. I seem to remember his consistently hard landings. In virtually all other aspects, he was fine. Yet he lacks that extra element needed to fly the ASV at the levels we require."

"He's a Flight Lieutenant now," the air vice marshal said, "and is doing quite well. He's a deputy flight commander on his squadron, and I believe he's in line for promotion to squadron leader in the not-too-distant future."

The AVM's knowledge about Alan West confirmed a nagging thought. "I do hope, sir," Jason ventured, "that Sir James's visit has nothing to do with a possible request to consider his son for a November squadron posting."

The air vice marshal cleared his throat. "It was suggested—"

Jason took the liberty of interrupting his superior. "No."

The AVM let it pass. "My sentiments exactly. I told the minister that I would not interfere with your selection process. But of course, we shall have a small price to pay."

Jason nodded. "We let Sir James come."

"Exactly. We need to keep our masters happy,

Chris. Many are not convinced that what we're doing is evolutionary, and despite what may or may not happen in the Middle East, swingeing defense cuts is the fashionable buzz. It's no use telling people that being peaceful and having a minuscule defense capability will not necessarily save you from future aggression."

"Very well, sir. We let Sir James experience our hospitality."

Outside, two Tornado ASVs stood on brightly flaming tails and hurled themselves skyward.

Both Thurson and Jason wanted to get the visit over with as quickly as was possible. Thurson subsequently informed the minister that the November unit would be happy to invite Sir James as soon as he was able to come. Security clearance was granted.

In deference to his age and former position, he was flown to November One in an HS 125 CC, the military version of the BA twin-engine executive jet. Thurson accompanied him.

He was taken down to fighter control, where Jason was waiting.

"I know your son," Jason said after they were introduced. West impressed him as remarkably spry for a man approaching seventy.

"So the air vice marshal tells me," West said cheerfully. He looked about him. "Things have changed since my day. My word. Coming over, I was most impressed by what I could see of your establishment. Quite astonishing aircraft, too. Four of them took off after we landed. They went like bullets." He shook his head in wonder.

Jason permitted himself a look of satisfaction. "Yes. They are rather impressive, as are their crews. We've laid on a bit of a demonstration for you today."

"You did not alter your daily program just for me, I hope."

"We . . . er . . . modified it, Sir James. It is part of a scheduled training mission. If you'll come this way, please."

Jason led him to the large operations room with its huge tactical situation screen. The air vice marshal brought up the rear, content to let Jason control the proceedings.

Jason indicated a large bank of consoles at which several operators were sitting, with keyboards and small monitors before them. One was in civilian clothes. Jason noted the older man's questioning look.

"That's our Mr. Eldridge, the resident missile genius. He's responsible for the special code that guides Skyray B to its selected target. It becomes totally autonomous on leaving the launch aircraft."

"Isn't that rather frightening? It could hit anything, some inoffensive light plane, for example."

"We won't be doing a live firing today, of course. We are some way from conducting a live shot. At the moment, we're putting it through its simulated paces. However, to answer your question about the identification of the correct target, that is precisely Mr. Eldridge's province. The code he has devised ensures such mistakes are not made. We would not like a repeat of what occurred twenty-five years ago."

"Ah," West said calmly. "So you know about that."

"I had to study Skyray's genesis and all matters relating to it."

"Naturally. So you know of my own position on the matter at the time."

"Indeed, Sir James."

"Yet you are happy to invite me up here."

"As you yourself have said, things have changed,

out of all recognition." Jason picked up a remote from
a nearby console and pointed it at the screen. He
squeezed an apparently random selection of buttons on
it. Various graphic windows appeared onscreen. Using
the remote's pointer, he guided West through the dif
ferent views.

"The four aircraft you saw taking off," he went on
"are here, and here. Two of these are departing for
patrol, while these two will be demonstrating the simu
lated missile shots. Over here, two hundred miles away
are their intended targets, a pair of IDS Tornadoes, on
a low-level transit. On each Tornado is—let's call it—
black box receiver. The missile will recognize the code
and, according to the in-flight instructions given by the
backseater, will attack or ignore a potential target.

"In a combat melee, for example, where the aver
age missile would not be able to distinguish friend from
foe if launched without a solid lock-on, Skyray would
attack only those targets without the recognition code
It can be programmed to attack in response to the code
or in absence of it. The code can be altered, as long as
there is communication between base and the aircraft
via secure data link. The backseaters then reprogram
the weapon. If there is a change of code, but for what
ever reason, this cannot be communicated to any par
ticular aircraft—say because of battle damage—the
missile's standard systems will revert to normal operat
ing requirements. In effect, a damaged aircraft will stil
be able to fight, and Skyray's advanced specifications
will still make it more lethal than its nearest competi
tor.

"For the purposes of our live tests, only the re
sponse code will be used. The target drones will carry
the code for the day"—Jason gave a brief smile—"thus
making quite certain your light aircraft going about its
business does not attract Skyray's attention. In any

case, such tests will be carried out well away from areas of other aviation activity, and well beyond the missile's range. Does that answer the question?"

"Fully, and most comprehensively," West replied. Then almost offhandedly he went on: "But how does it work?"

"The code?" Jason glanced swiftly at his superior. When the air vice marshal nodded barely perceptibly, he continued, "Mr. Eldridge can give you a demonstration."

They went over to Eldridge's console.

"Paul," Jason said, "Can we give Sir James a demo?"

"Certainly," he readily agreed. "It won't be the real thing, of course."

"Understood," West said, desperately wondering how he was going to discover the genuine article.

"But I can easily demonstrate the principle," Eldridge was saying. "The basis is an alphanumeric genetic code we call the primary. This is made up of twelve characters, say like this." He tapped in a random series of letters and numbers. "Now I'll put in the secondary code." Another set of characters appeared beneath the primary. They were the same numbers and letters, but in a very different order. "Now the primary," he went on, "will interrogate. The secondary then has to identify itself by correctly knowing its position on the original code. For example, the '2' will identify itself as being in the fourth position, and a '4' will appear, and so on, until the entire secondary code is displayed as a series of numbers. Those are the ones now appearing above the primary, in the box."

The new digits came rapidly onscreen until all twelve characters of the code had been identified. The box glowed, then froze.

"Code accepted," Eldridge said. "Because we've

got twelve characters in the code, we in fact gain access with sixteen digits, as '10,' '11,' and '12' are themselves double digits. The system allows only one error before it shuts you out. If, for example, you wanted to break into the code and by some method you were able to gain access to the secondary, a single identification error would put the system on immediate alert and you'd be shut out. So if say the '2' were in the sixth position but in trying to find out you gave it any other, that would be your lot. Total shut-out." Eldridge looked somewhat smugly at West. "And all this happens within nanoseconds. No time at all."

West commendably gave no indication of the turmoil within him. The man who had called himself Michael Hemming had demanded the impossible. There was no way he could gain access to the primary code, or any of the codes, for that matter. This was not like all those years ago when he'd had access to all that had been happening within the program. In any case, that particular code had been simplicity itself, a recognition pulse that had been easy for the lurking submarine to intercept, and then redirect. The result had lived in his nightmares ever since.

"Now, Sir James," Jason was saying, "if you'll come over to observe the screen better, you'll see the simulated attack." He highlighted the test aircraft as West followed him. "These two will be hunting for the possible targets, who are now three hundred miles away. The red images in the lower corner over there." Four target aircraft were onscreen. The hunters were blue.

West looked on with great interest. Perhaps there would be something he could eventually use.

"Who's up?" the air vice marshal said.

"Hohendorf and Flacht in Blue One, Bagni and

Stockmann in Blue Two." Jason glanced at West. "Two of our best teams."

West nodded, but was silent.

After the demonstration, West felt his trip had yielded him no information he could pass on to his KGB tormentors. The interceptions were carried out with a skill he found he had no option but to admire. The simulated missile firings worked without a hitch, and though the identification codes were displayed in a special window on the tactical screen, only the secondary code was actually shown. The primary remained within the recesses of the main operations computer.

Though he gave no outward indication, he felt a great weight descend upon him. Inevitably, he would be unmasked and would have to face the odium not only of the nation, but of his son, whose career would undoubtedly be finished. Within his despair, West also felt a strange sense of relief. He had lived with his guilt for long enough. Let the KGB do its worst.

8

As West was resignedly pondering upon his imme- diate future, the pair of returning Tornado ASVs were on a low-level transit, on their way back to base. As detailed in their flight plan, the homeward leg contained such a stage for the final run-in to November One.

Their route had taken them across North Uist in the Outer Hebrides off the west coast of Scotland, then southwest of Skye in a direct line for Loch Awe in Argyll, on the Scottish mainland itself. They had maintained an altitude of 4,800 feet on the way in, but now, as the loch approached, they descended to 200 feet, which they reached as they swept over the ax-shaped body of water. Loch Awe pointed roughly northeast, the way home.

Hohendorf, who was in the lead, seemed to be going even lower as they banked hard left to follow the line of the loch.

In the backseat, Oberleutnant zur See Wolfgang Flacht was keeping an alert survey of the airspace about them. Bagni, in the second aircraft, was neatly tucked in just behind Blue One's starboard wing. Flacht could see both crewmen clearly. They seemed close enough to touch. Stockmann, the U.S. Marine flyer and Bagni's backseater, turned briefly to look at Flacht. With visor down, he looked like a giant mutated fly.

Flacht said calmly to Hohendorf, "We won't forget the cables, will we? We're approaching the pylons."

Near the head of the loch were two pylons, one on either side, which rose to 210 feet. The cables spanned the loch, which was familiar to the crews of both aircraft. Everyone knew of those cables. Everyone also knew that a Tornado IDS, from a unit that had no connection whatsoever with November One, had made the national news by hitting a power line and tearing it off, at sixty feet. The incident had occurred just eighty-five miles south of their current position, and no one wanted the November units hauled publicly over the coals. Not the best way to keep a low profile. More importantly, no one in his right mind wanted to incur the Boss's wrath.

"Don't worry, Wolfie," came Hohendorf's equally calm voice from the front. "I won't be adding pylons to today's score."

Flacht was keeping a sharp eye on his displays.

"Well," he said. "You may have to add some new scores. We've got company."

"What kind?"

"People out for revenge. They're trying a sneaky bounce."

The warning radar had picked up four aircraft, all heading their way. Phantoms they had beaten were out for blood.

"How far?"

"A hundred miles and descending. They haven't picked us up yet, but they know the flight plan, so they can guess where to look."

"They tried something on Selby and McCann and

got zapped. They cannot be thinking we're easier meat. Can they?" Hohendorf sounded hopeful, eager for the challenge.

Flacht was more than willing to take on the incoming Phantoms. "Why don't we find out?"

The Tornadoes rose slightly to clear the cables, sweeping down again as they neared the head of the loch. Here it branched to the left, and they banked hard over the remains of a castle that stood in solitude on a small island that was almost at the center of the junction. On either side of the water, high ground rose, clothed in the white of fresh snow. Visibility, however, was perfect.

Another hard bank, this time to the right, and they were curving toward Cruachan Reservoir, threading between two ramparts of granite that soared to three thousand feet. Ahead of them was the rising speckled flanks of Ben Cruachan itself, its summit of snowcapped peaks at just under four thousand feet.

"Do the others know?" Hohendorf was saying.

Flacht glanced at the other aircraft, and just before Bagni moved smoothly to line astern, holding station just slightly above and behind Blue One, Stockmann looked toward them and pointed upward. Flacht's proficiency in the backseat was second only to McCann's. And as for Stockman, he was snapping at Flacht's heels.

"They know," Flacht replied.

The rising wall was almost upon them, and Hohendorf raised the nose of the aircraft to skim the steep slope. Though the ASV's terrain-following systems could have been used, he always liked flying the contours manually. He now rolled the Tornado onto its back and continued up the incline.

Flacht craned his neck to look through the top of the canopy.

"Kapitän leutnant Hohendorf," Flacht began with studied formality, "why is there a rock face above my canopy?"

Hohendorf cleared the summit still upside down, skimmed a brief patch of level ground before he eased the stick very gently back. The Tornado went down the equally steep opposite slope, still inverted.

"You're seeing things, Wolfie," he said to Flacht. "Besides, I'm maintaining positive G."

"Is that what you're calling it these days?" Flacht kept looking at the ground rushing past his head. He was certain he could touch the rocks, or even grab a handful of snow. Behind the ASV, a billow of white trailed as its passage disturbed the loose surface.

"Best way to clear a ridge," Hohendorf was saying. "Positive G all the way, and less exposure."

"I believe you," Flacht said, fervently hoping Hohendorf would roll the aircraft upright soon.

In the following Tornado, Stockmann had watched aghast as Hohendorf's aircraft had rushed up the side of the mountain on its back.

"Holy shit!" he said to Bagni. "Did you see that crazy German?"

"What crazy German?" Bagni said by way of reply, and promptly followed suit.

"Aaah goddammit, Bagni!" Stockmann exclaimed as lumps of Scottish real estate whizzed past the top of his head. "You crazy Europeans!" he finished helplessly.

In the lead aircraft, Hohendorf rolled upright, to Flacht's immense relief, and took another mountainside conventionally. Flacht looked back to search for Bagni's Tornado and was just in time to see it descending, upside down.

"You're giving Nico bad habits," he said as he turned to study his displays once more. "He just came down inverted." Another glance back. "Now he's rolled upright."

"El Greco is a good pilot, and a fine wingman. There's nothing I can teach him."

Though a native of Tuscany in northern Italy, Bagni's ancestors originally came from Siracusa in Sicily, and his former colleagues in the *Aeronautica Militare Italiana*—the AMI—had nicknamed him "the Greek," which soon took on the more artistic connotations of "El Greco" when his remarkable flair in flying became apparent.

Flacht now made a sound that suggested he doubted Hohendorf's protestations.

"Where are those black-tailed Phantoms now?" Hohendorf asked.

"They're still on top, but they can't find us down here."

"Let's put the cat among the pigeons, as Mark Selby would say." Hohendorf switched to the frequency that would give him communication with Bagni's aircraft. "El Greco."

"Sì," came Bagni's voice.

"You take the high arena, and I'll take the low."

"On my way."

Flacht again glanced rearward as an arrowlike shape of indeterminate coloring seemed to erupt out of the mountains. Bagni and Stockmann's ASV, wings swept, was heading for the heavens.

"Now we'll see what that does to our waiting friends," Hohendorf said with satisfaction.

There was not long to wait. Studying the threat warning display, Flacht watched as the four radar traces suddenly split in various directions, like minhows becoming aware of a predator in their midst.

"Fight's on!" came Bagni's voice.

"Nico's going for them," Flacht said.

"We'll wait our turn," Hohendorf said. He stood the ASV on a wingtip and threaded his way between two high walls of granite. He was now on a reciprocal course, heading for the Phantoms. He stayed low.

"Two have stayed up with Nico," Flacht informed him, watching the display, "two coming down. They still don't know where we are. Ten miles." Another display had positively identified the adversary aircraft as the same Phantoms they had earlier fought with the inert Skyray B.

Hohendorf knew that no other combat aircraft in existence could handle the lower levels of denser air with the same stability as the Tornado. It had been optimized for such altitudes, and was far less susceptible to low-level turbulence. The flight control computers would be making constant minute adjustments to the flying surfaces, keeping the aircraft steady. Other airplanes, like the Phantoms now heading down for a hopeful kill, would be bouncing all over the place, giving their pilots an extra work load, and affecting their ability to achieve a gun solution. Instead of concentrating solely on the fight, they would have to worry about keeping control of their own aircraft as well.

That was Hohendorf's intention. He was dragging them down into his own arena, where he could take them in his own good time, which would not be long.

For Flacht, it would soon be head-out-of-the-cockpit time. Once the fight was close-in, his job would be to watch out for the opposing aircraft. He selected a channel that would allow them to eavesdrop on the Phantoms. He did this just in time to hear someone say disgustedly, "Oh fuck!"

"I think Nico's just scored," he told Hohendorf. "It will be our turn soon. I have one bogey dead ahead, at four thousand feet, five miles. He must be skimming that ridge."

"I've got him," Hohendorf said. He saw the fast-moving shape skirting the top of the ridge. "He's high. Too high."

He set off after the Phantom, maintaining his low altitude. Though the Phantom was perhaps mere feet from ground level, its real altitude was still four thousand feet or so, if you took away the mountain. As far as Hohendorf was concerned, that made the searching Phantom a beacon to be homed on to.

"I can't believe the backseater hasn't picked us up," Flacht was saying. "We're almost sitting on their tail."

Flacht had briefly "lit" the Phantom with the radar then had put it on standby, where it constantly updated the Phantom's position with a series of possible future solutions, based upon the information it had gleaned. Thus the Phantom would have no idea it was being tracked, even though its backseater might have been warned by that brief sweep of the Tornado's own radar.

"We're being masked by all this high ground," Hohendorf said. "Even this close, his radar won't get anything. Now that we're behind him, he's sweeping in the wrong direction, in any case. He's blind until his warning receiver picks us up. By then, it will be too late for him."

The Phantom was still keeping high, as if reluctant to chance it among the deep valleys below.

"Watch out for his friend," Hohendorf warned. "This one may be the bait for a trap."

"The same thought is in my mind." Flacht was now dividing his attention between his displays and the world outside. Everything was on-line, waiting. If the second Phantom was lurking out there in an ambush position, he would be ready.

Flying between the high walls, Hohendorf closed

in on the still apparently unaware Phantom. Mere seconds had passed since the sighting. He did not select the gun until he was virtually on the other aircraft. Instantly, he got the tone.

"Bang," he said.

The Phantom leaped skyward as if jabbed with a high-voltage cattle prod. Had it been for real, a gunshot would have shredded him.

"Check six," Flacht admonished, turning round to look behind, checking their own six to make sure the second Phantom had not sneaked up while they'd been occupied with his companion.

There was no Phantom.

Nothing's that easy, Flacht was thinking. Hohendorf was very good, but either the Phantom crew had . . .

Instinctive as ever, Hohendorf interrupted Flacht's thoughts.

"You're wondering if it was too easy."

"Yes. I was."

"They were springing a trap," Hohendorf said, "but we got there before they could close the door. His friend is down here with us, but in the wrong place."

"How do you know?"

"It's the only answer. If you haven't got him on the radar, it means he's down, but he misjudged it. Now to find him."

The Tornado was now hurtling along Glen Kinglass, heading for Glen Orchy.

Then Flacht was saying urgently, "I've got him! He's coming through from the right, between those two mountains. Low down."

Hohendorf had reacted fast to Flacht's visual sighting, banking hard toward the Phantom. The other aircraft was indeed low down, hiding in the narrow space between two steep-sided chunks of high ground that towered a good 2,200 feet above the valley floor.

The Phantom, aware it had been spotted, rose swiftly to gain height. Hohendorf let it go, then pulled tightly behind, climbing on full afterburners.

The Phantom wasn't having any of it. Its great cranked wings biting at the cold air, it pulled onto its back from the climb, rolled upright, and hurtled the way it had come, hoping to come down behind the Tornado. Hohendorf canceled the burners.

Flacht swiveled his head around. "He's turning, coming back at us."

Hohendorf was unperturbed. Still in the climb, he rolled the ASV ninety degrees, wings spreading. He pulled the stick toward him. The aircraft came onto its back, leading edge root extensions giving its airframe extra lift as it moved at right angles to its original path.

Hohendorf kept a firm pressure on the stick. The nose began to curve downward. He eased pressure and the nose held in a shallow dive; then he rolled left ninety degrees and hauled the stick firmly back. Up on the head-up display, the G-counter whirled to 7, indicating that Hohendorf and Flacht were being loaded with seven times their own weight as the Tornado ASV racked itself into a tight turn to come round on the Phantom.

It cut beautifully into the opposing aircraft's turning circle, its nose staying just ahead of the Phantom's, whose pilot was having a hard time trying to make his own turn tighter.

Hohendorf had suckered the other pilot into a climbing turn, forcing the heavier aircraft into an energy penalty. The climbing turn was costing the Phantom in speed and power. Soon it would be wallowing. The ASV, however, with a height advantage, had converted that to speed and energy. With its already vast reserves of power, there was no need for Hohendorf to reengage the afterburners.

The glowing line of snaking dots that represented the fall line of the shots moved inexorably toward the straining Phantom. Both aircraft were now a little above five thousand feet, well clear of the razored edges of the mountain peaks, some of which showed through their incomplete blankets of snow.

Then the Phantom was flying helplessly through the line of dots. The continuous tone of the "shoot" cue seemed full of glee.

"Bang," Hohendorf said, relaxing the turn at last.

"Sod it!" came from the other aircraft. "Knock it off. Knock it off."

Hohendorf acknowledged the end of the engagement by breaking hard right and climbing.

Over the airwaves, a chagrined voice said, "One day we'll thrash these bastards good and proper."

Another voice had a question. "Where the hell's Raven Three?"

Raven Three was pursuing Bagni in a steep descent and feeling lucky. The pilot was certain he was going to nail at least one of these fancy people who thought they were so good.

In the Tornado, Stockmann watched the mountains draw closer with alarming speed and hoped Bagni knew what he was up to and did not overcook it. Stockmann vividly remembered how Richard Palmer had died. In the practice air-to-air combat that fateful day, it had been Bagni and himself versus Palmer and Ferris. Bagni, using all the wiles at his command, had dragged Palmer low. But Palmer had not had the experience to counter in time and had himself gone dangerously low, turning far too hard, without straining sufficiently against the onset of G. He had thus lost consciousness, leaving Ferris with little time in which to initiate command ejection. Bagni had naturally blamed himself.

Stockmann now wondered whether Bagni was remembering, and had become fixated by the onrushing landscape. For one terrifying moment, the thought passed through his mind that Bagni was at last about to purge the guilt he felt by plowing into the ground. Stockmann found he had to consciously stop himself from reaching for the command ejection selection lever on the far edge of the right-hand console. He knew of a case where a backseater, in another air force, had used command eject, mistakenly believing his pilot had been incapacitated. One very irate and very surprised pilot had wondered what had happened when the canopy had suddenly disintegrated above his head.

Stockmann forced himself to remain quiet as the mountains came ever closer. Their peaks looked hungry.

He glanced around. The Phantom was still coming down, eager to get into the slot behind their tail for the shoot. The Phantom's pilot was clearly determined to succeed. It was equally clear that Bagni was aware of this and was about to deliver his his surprise. Stockmann just wished the ground was not coming so close.

Then Bagni popped the brakes. The spade-shaped panels rose from each side of the rear fuselage near the tail, and the ASV seemed to decelerate as if someone had thrown out a giant anchor. Stockmann again glanced back at the Phantom. The other aircraft was suddenly very near, caught out by the abrupt cut in speed of its apparent prey. Stockmann could see the Phantom waver slightly as its pilot tried to maintain separation. Stockmann was also quite certain the other pilot had become very aware of the increasing proximity of the ground.

"He's beginning to worry," he said to Bagni.

"Good," Bagni said. "That is what I want."

Stockmann felt a sense of shameful relief that Bagni was in full command of his faculties. Even so, the ground was not going away.

Down they went between two mountain peaks, heading, it seemed, for a very steep slope. The Phantom, weaving a little, followed. It still did not have a gun solution.

Bagni set the Tornado up for a skim up the slope, then flipped it onto its back.

"Oh Christ," Stockmann muttered.

In the Phantom, the pilot saw the Tornado flip over and made a strangled sound in his mask.

"What's up?" came from the backseat.

"That mad bastard's going up the slope, upside down."

"You're joking."

"I kid you not. I'm not into this game. That mountain's too bloody close." He pulled on the stick. "Up we go," he said with relief, leaving the claustrophobic proximity of the ground and reaching thankfully for the upper air.

Bagni cleared the slope, rolled the Tornado upright, and continued the climb. There, bang on the nose was the Phantom, following a slightly curving path as it angled onto its back.

He slammed the throttles into combat burner. The ASV swept its wings and leaped upward, gaining rapidly on the other aircraft. Soon it was within gun range. He gave a slight back pressure on the stick to bring the nose of the ASV just ahead of the Phantom's cutting into the slight curve in lead pursuit. Were the gun to be fired, shells and Phantom would arrive at the same spot, at the same time. A certain kill.

Bagni slid the throttles out of burner. The Tornado maintained the speed of its climb.

"Buon giorno," he said. The tone confirmed the kill.

The Phantom jerked as its pilot rolled out of the way, much too late.

"That wasn't exactly fair," came an aggrieved voice. "We nearly hit the deck."

"All's fair in love and war."

"You guys are mad. D'you know that?"

Bagni laughed. *"Arrivederci.* Nice to do business with you. Please have a Merry Christmas."

"There's still a week to go," the disgruntled voice retorted.

Bagni laughed once more, then hauled the Tornado around to catch up with Hohendorf and Flacht, whose own aircraft was flying slowly over Loch Ericht, waiting for them to rejoin. In tight formation, they headed for November One.

They came in low and tight over the main runway to go into the classic fighter break prior to landing. In the tower, Karen Lomax watched with approval.

"Very stylish," she remarked. "Who's up?" She had just come on duty and had not yet taken her place at the control desk.

"Hohendorf and Flacht in Blue One," a sergeant replied, "and Bagni and Stockmann in Two."

"I see. Not McCann, then."

"No, ma'am," the sergeant said, with due respect for her rank. He glanced at his colleagues. "He's not due to fly today."

Karen Lomax shrugged self-consciously. "Oh

. . . I was just wondering . . . that's all. Never know what to expect with him."

"No, ma'am." More surreptitious glances.

The only other officer currently present was a French captain, formerly of the *Armée de l'Air*. He observed the covert signals bemusedly, having no idea what they were about; but McCann's name stuck in his mind. The captain was ADO for the shift.

"I'll take over now, Chas," Karen Lomax said to the sergeant who had spoken.

"Right you are." The sergeant quickly made room for her. "We've got that HS 125 CC on hold, waiting for takeoff clearance."

"Fine," she said, took her seat, and put on her headset to begin talking to the aircraft.

They landed smoothly, Bagni's touch feather light. His terror of landings, of spreading himself and his back-seater across the runway in an explosion of flame and burning fuel, now seemed a thing of the past. No more shaking hands and sweating palms in the privacy of his darkened room, where he used to fight his quiet battle. He had come a long way.

He followed Hohendorf's aircraft as they taxied off the runway toward their respective hardened aircraft shelters on Zero One squadron, feeling good. Hohendorf's trick of going up a slope upside down held no terrors for him.

After they had shut down the aircraft and were walking back to the squadron buildings, he caught up with Hohendorf.

"Thanks for showing me that move, Axel," he began. "It frightened that Phantom."

Hohendorf was modest about it. "I could not have shown you how if you did not already have the skill, Nico."

Bagni had to quicken his step slightly to keep up with Hohendorf. About five inches under six feet, he was not a big man, but his body was compact. For a man of Sicilian ancestry, he had a true Roman face with strong planes, a high forehead, and a proud nose. His dark brown eyes were lustrous in the reflected light that came off the banked snow that had been cleared off the taxiways. Short, dark curls adorned his head. Despite the quickness of his step, he did not appear to be hurrying. He was a man at ease with himself.

He wondered what Hohendorf would say if he knew how terrified Bagni had once been of landings.

"It is kind of you to say this, Axel," he now said.

"Not at all. There are two men in this squadron, apart from the Boss, with whom I will fly anywhere. You, Nico, and Mark Selby."

Bagni glanced speculatively at his colleague. Ahead of them, Stockmann and Flacht were in deep conversation.

"Ah yes," he said. "Mark."

Hohendorf did not look around. "We have our differences, of course. But up there"—he raised the helmet he carried in his right hand to briefly point at the now overcast sky—"up there, we work tightly. That is what matters in the end."

They did not look up as the BA 125 CC carrying Sir James West flew over their heads on its way back south.

McCann was in another HAS in the backseat of his aircraft, doing a check on his equipment. He always spent time in the ASV, even when not flying, checking to ensure that incipient failures could be caught on the ground instead of in the air, where he needed everything to be at 100 percent. He believed in prevention. So far, nothing had shown itself to be amiss.

Movement was caught on the periphery of his vision. He moved his head slightly sideways to look out of the rear cockpit and along the nose of the aircraft. A large man was standing at the entrance of the HAS. From where he was sitting, McCann thought the newcomer looked enormous.

The man entered and walked over to a crew chief. They stood talking while McCann studied the large man, who wore an olive-green, padded anorak over his RAF No. 2 uniform. He bore the rank of a flight lieutenant. A large, square face that seemed as hard as granite turned briefly to look in McCann's direction before once more concentrating on the crew chief.

A member of the ground crew came up the ladder. "Everything okay, sir?"

"Perfect," McCann replied. "You guys do a good job, as always."

The ground crewman looked pleased. "Just keep saying that to the new boss, will you please, sir?"

"New boss? When did that happen?"

"Yesterday, sir. Our old boss got his promotion through. He's got command of Zero One's engineering squadron now. Our new engineer flight commander is over there, talking to Chiefy."

"Him?" McCann said weakly, with a sense of foreboding.

"Yes, sir. Flight Lieutenant Pearce. He's the one. We're pleased to have him. Did you know he's the command rugby star?"

"Someone did mention it," McCann said faintly.

"Great, isn't it, sir?"

"Oh sure," McCann said. "Great."

Later in the mess, McCann said to Selby, "I've just seen the future, and I don't like it."

"Seen the future. You lucky man. What's so bad about it?"

"What's so bad, the man says—"

"Before you go on, I've got some news that should cheer you up nicely."

"Impossible."

"Why not wait to hear?"

"Surprise me," McCann said, unconvinced.

"It seems that someone very close to your little heart was talking about you today."

"If you mean Flying Officer Karen Lomax, was she spitting at the time?"

"Oh dear," Selby said. "We *are* depressed. I thought that would have cheered you up, you miserable colonial."

"You don't know what I've seen."

"The future."

"Yeah . . . and it's a mountain that walks."

"Come on, Elmer Lee. Don't keep it all to yourself. Give."

"The engineering boys have got a new flight commander," McCann said unenthusiastically.

Selby was surprised. "A new one? What's happened to Jurgen Reinecke?"

"Got promoted. He's boss of Zero One's engineer squadron."

"Nobody ever tells us anything. Aircrew are always the last to know. So who's mountain—" Then Selby saw the expression on McCann's face. "You've got to be joking. Not our resident rugby star."

"Give the man the wooden nickel prize. Yep. It's Pearce."

"Bad luck, Elmer Lee, old son. Bad luck indeed. Look at it this way. Forget Karen and think of Zoe in Aberdeen. She'd love to see you. Morven says she's always asking when I'm going to bring you next."

But McCann would not be deflected. "How can someone who looks so delicate go out with something like that? The guy's built like a truck."

"And they say he likes to hurt people, too. Ask anyone who's played against him."

"That's it. Cheer me up."

"Elmer Lee, Elmer Lee. Forget the lady, especially when you're up there with me. Think of Zoe instead, but not up there, of course."

"Forget Zoe," McCann said.

Selby shook his head in defeat. "You have got a problem, and that, Elmer Lee, worries me."

"You can count on me when we're up top," McCann said firmly. "One hundred percent. As for down here . . . I can handle it. No sweat."

Selby was not so sure, but he let it go.

In the squadron crew room, Hohendorf finished his mug of coffee, placed it near a collection to be washed, and prepared to leave. Flacht had already gone home to married quarters to his wife and small son, while Stockmann and Bagni had departed for the mess.

Jason appeared in the doorway and beckoned with an imperious finger. "My office, if you please, Kapitänleutnant."

Hohendorf followed. Jason stood aside to allow him to enter.

"I've just received a signal," Jason began, shutting the door behind them. "Quite amazing how quickly bad news travels." He did not go to his desk. Instead, he leaned against the door, as if barring Hohendorf's means of escape. "The others have gone, I take it?"

Hohendorf nodded. "Yes, sir. Shall I have them called back?"

Jason raised a hand briefly. "No need. You're here." It sounded ominous. "I've just received a signal," he repeated, "by way of the air vice marshal, who received it virtually as soon as his executive aircraft had landed. This signal had in turn come from a minister of the Crown, who had himself received a complaint from a member of Parliament on behalf of one of his constituents, who had phoned *him*, in a state of high dudgeon. Are you with me so far?"

"Yes, sir," Hohendorf replied uncertainly.

"Said constituent reported—and I quote—that six aircraft were seen cavorting dangerously close to the ground in an abandoned manner, disturbing the peace of his guests, who had come to the mountains for some solitude and quiet.

"It would appear that the gentleman in question, a person of some considerable wealth who mainly lives in the south of England, has built himself a substantial mountain abode where he entertains guests during the winter months. He had a large group up there today, and it would seem that you have caused them some discomfort. The minister wants to know what I'm going to do about it. Or to put it more correctly, the minister wants to know what the AVM is going to do about it. The AVM wants me to sort it out so that the minister can get the MP out of his hair."

"And I suppose the member of Parliament wants his constituent out of *his* hair."

Jason looked at Hohendorf unsmilingly. "Was that perhaps a joke?"

"A weak one, sir."

"Quite."

Hohendorf tried to explain. "We were on our way back at low level, when the Phantoms bounced us. At least, they tried. We laid a trap for them instead."

"You won the engagement, I trust? I had left the ops room to see another of our VIP guests off the station."

"Yes, sir. We did."

"I should hope so. So what am I to tell the air vice marshal?"

"We did nothing you would not expect us to, sir. Air combat is not a game, and even in practice, it must be done seriously. We used our aircraft to the full extent of our abilities."

Jason thought about Hohendorf's words for some moments. "The problem that someone in my position has is convincing people that what we do is necessary. The man who was so quick to phone his MP little realizes that the reason he is able to enjoy his wealth and build his mountain fastness is precisely because there are people like us around. And if he does not believe that, he should have a quiet word with the next ex-wealthy Kuwaiti he passes in the street. Trouble is, I can't put it quite like that to the minister. Wing commanders are not supposed to say harsh things about their wealthy constituents to ministers."

"Why not, sir? It's the truth."

Jason gave a brief smile that was without humor. "Oh that it were so simple. All right, Axel. Thank you. I'll think of a suitable reply for the AVM so that he can mollify the minister. And I meant what I said at debriefing. That was very good work with the Skyray program. Both our guest and the AVM were impressed. I think we're ready for the live tests. I'll lead the detachment of four aircraft to the Med, but your crew and Selby's will have the first slot. My crew and Bagni's will serve as backup."

"Thank you, sir."

"No need to thank me. You've earned it. All of you. And now, I've got to do some work on my diplomatic language."

Hohendorf took the cue and left the wing commander to his difficult chore.

2

The very next day, West received a telephone call from someone whose voice he did not recognize. Even so, he had no illusions about what the voice represented. He was ordered up to London. Within an hour, saying little to his wife, he was on a train, and by 10:30 that morning was reluctantly getting out of a taxi near the northern end of Hammersmith Bridge. He paid the driver and strode erectly along the walkway toward the borough of Barnes, on the other bank of the Thames. Few people were using the walkway.

A man was standing halfway along the bridge, staring down at the river. A cold breeze came up the water, sharp enough to claim attention, but not sufficiently strong to cause discomfort. Along the bridge, traffic rumbled continuously.

The man straightened just as West reached him.

"Sir James West," he said. There was no doubt in his voice, which had been pitched at the precise level to be heard above the noise of the traffic but not overheard by anyone who might have been approaching.

West stopped.

"Please lean against this railing. Here. Next to me. Let us look at the river." The man resumed his position, not waiting to see if West complied. He again stared down at the water. "They'll never get it clean."

West, with more things upon his mind than the ecological state of the much-abused Thames, did as he'd been told.

"Now tell me," the man ordered.

"I discovered nothing that can be of use to your people."

"That is not good news . . . for you."

"I tried," West began with foreboding, "but it was impossible to discover anything of value."

"So apart from going on a nice little visit, you have wasted our time?" The words were spoken ominously.

"Did you not hear me? It was impossible."

The man turned eyes of stone upon West. "You do not have the luxury of deciding what is impossible and what is not. Tell me everything that happened while you were there."

West recounted in as much detail as he could all that he had observed, including the code demonstration he had been given by Paul Eldridge.

The man listened impassively, and when West had finished, he said, "We'll be in touch." Then he walked away, going toward Barnes.

West stared at the departing figure. "Is that all you've got to say?"

The man either did not hear, or chose not to. He did not turn around. He continued his casual pace, as if out for a morning stroll.

West remained irresolutely where he was for long moments, staring after the man, until at last he slowly began walking back the way he had come. As he walked it occurred to him that nothing about the man had marked him out as not being British.

West came to the end of the bridge and cautiously

checked the traffic before crossing to the other side of the road to wait for a taxi. He stared at the bridge, as if seeing it for the last time. He suddenly looked very old.

"Going somewhere, guv?"

The taxi driver had to repeat himself before West realized he was being spoken to.

Moscow. 1600 hours, the same day.

Stolybin carefully studied the report that had been brought over by special courier. There was no expression upon his face. Anyone watching would have found it impossible to gauge whether the news was good or bad.

The general, watching him on a monitor in his own office whose opulence constrasted sharply with the spartan furnishings of Stolybin's, could wait no longer. He rose from his desk and barged into his subordinate's adjoining room, trailing cigarette smoke.

"Are you going to stare at that all day?" he began. "What does it say?"

Stolybin stood up slowly, and wordlessly handed the report to the general, who puffed furiously as he read it. The more he read, the less happy he looked.

At last, he slammed it down. Ash billowed from the tip of his cigarette. "This looks like a failure to me." Mean eyes squinted through the smoke at Stolybin. "This looks like *failure*! Your trip was useless!"

Stolybin was remarkably unperturbed. "On the face of it, Comrade General, it does look like failure—"

"What do you mean 'on the face of it'?" the general interrupted harshly. "You have either failed or you haven't." He waved an aggressive arm in the vague direction of the city streets, where a heavy snow was falling, then pounded the desk with a clenched fist. "Out there, people have no food. We're on our knees, *begging* the capitalists for scraps from their table. In the republics, they are not only killing each other, but they also want to dismember the Union. Chaos is around us. Do you hear me? *Chaos."*

Stolybin said nothing, biding his time.

The general's cigarette, after valiantly hanging on during the tirade, gave up and fell onto the report, where it proceeded to burn a small hole. The general watched it, as if daring it to continue. He did not remove it. That was left to Stolybin, who picked it up, stone-faced, and stubbed it out in an ashtray he had prudently acquired for such an eventuality. The burn was not serious.

The general stared at the dead cigarette as if expecting it to relight. Then he looked up at Stolybin.

"I was not finished with that."

"With respect, Comrade General, you were. Most of the cigarette was ash."

The general again looked down at the ashtray. Only the smallest butt was left. Without another word, he went out and was soon back with a fresh one sticking out of his mouth. When he began to speak, his voice was calmer.

"The Western allies may think they have won the Cold War, but they may soon find it a bitter victory. One of my people was in Berlin not so long ago, having coffee in a small café. His German is, of course, perfect. He listened in on a conversation that was not very discreet, all things considered. A group of men were complaining, not so quietly, about the sudden crowding of their city. One said, in a joke, that perhaps the Wall should never have gone." The general took a long drag of the new cigarette. "Mark my words, Sergei. There was seriousness in that joke." He gave a brief smile that was sudden, and grimly feral. "Perhaps in a way, we have also won. Now, tell me why you think you have not failed."

Stolybin chose his words carefully. "James West," he began—he did not believe in the use of imperialist titles—"may have done better than is at first apparent."

"I don't see how you can say that. He was able to discover nothing."

"If the comrade general will permit, I do not agree."

The general's eyes showed a dangerous stillness as he waited for Stolybin to continue.

"West has told how the code is implemented," Stolybin said.

"What use is that without the code itself?"

"I have an idea."

The general was skeptical. "Another of those."

Stolybin decided to press on. "Before I was, er, sent on extended"—his eyes held the general's—"leave, there was a captain I knew—one of our own people—a genius with computers."

Stolybin paused, momentarily unsure of how to continue. The man in question, Ivan Vannis, was a Latvian, and given the state of things in the Baltic republics, he may well have gone nationalist, or perhaps may have been removed from his post, or even imprisoned.

"Captain Ivan Vannis," he said, taking the plunge.

The general scowled. "A Latvian."

"If he's still with us, he must be sound. He could certainly help with this."

"How?"

"That's what I want to find out."

The general gave Stolybin another of his long stares. "All right. Find him. It's your neck."

"So you keep telling me," Stolybin muttered to himself after the general had departed, leaving the usual cloud of smoke hanging in the room.

Stolybin emptied the ashtray expressionlessly.

He discovered that Vannis was still operational and currently based in Leningrad. Within a day, Vannis was standing before him, looking bemused, and not a little apprehensive. A small, dark-haired man of about thirty who wore glasses, Vannis, it was clear, thought he had been brought to Moscow to be questioned about his loyalties.

"Do you remember me, Ivan?" Stolybin commenced by way of a greeting.

Vannis swallowed. "Yes. Yes, Comrade Colonel."

"Relax, man. You are not here to be grilled about your loyalty to the Union. I need your help. I want to put that brain of yours to use."

Vannis brightened. "I am at your service, Comrade."

"I never doubted it." Stolybin pushed a modified version of the report he had received toward Vannis. "Read that carefully, then tell me how we're going to get into it. Take a seat. Make yourself comfortable."

Vannis took the papers and gingerly sat down on one of the hard chairs in the office. Stolybin watched him speculatively, permitting himself a wry smile as Vannis seemed to forget his uncertainties as the problem began to hook him. He read the papers through twice.

At last, he looked up. "We can do something."

"Good. Good. How?"

"I'll have to work it through, of course . . . but there is a way to get in. Although we do not have any of the codes, that is almost not important. In any case, everyone changes codes at random. The trick is to get the code of the day while the missile is in flight."

"That does not give us much time. That thing's very, very fast."

"Ah yes. But you see, Comrade Colonel, to computers, what we may think of as fast is incredibly slow. A second, for example, could be a whole epoch, or more. Nanoseconds can be stretched into days, years, centuries. It depends on the speed of your computer. So while we don't need the code, we do need the *method* of its implementation. According to this report, we have it."

Stolybin looked pleased. "You're telling me we can burn through to the missile's secondary code while it is in flight."

"Yes, Comrade. We can burn through, find the code, get at the primary, and fool it . . . in theory."

"In theory. I don't like the sound of that."

"We would need the right equipment and a very powerful computer. We would need a terminal with access to the most powerful machine in the Union."

"I'm certain that could be arranged," Stolybin said, knowing the general was listening. "Leave that to me. All you have to do is prove to me you can make your system work. You'll be given the facilities when you've done that."

Vannis looked anxious once more. He clearly realized that once he'd committed himself, there was no turning back. It would have to be success or failure. Failure would most likely be a terminal one.

Stolybin's years of interrogating people told him fairly accurately what was going on in Vannis's mind. Good, he thought. Let him worry. Nothing like anxiety for one's safety to concentrate the mind.

"Please continue," Stolybin said.

"According . . . according to the report, the system gives you just one try at the code before shutting you out. I do not believe this to be correct. I think your informant was misled."

"Do you see proof of this?"

Vannis shook his head. "There is nothing in here. I . . . I find it difficult to believe that the crews would not be given at least one chance for error. In the heat of battle, a change of code in the air may not always be correctly punched in first time around. I am almost certain the program has allowed for one error. That's our window. We can get in while the code is trying to sort itself out. As we know how the code works, I can run my own program to see how long it takes for an error to be tolerated before shutdown. The time between hitting the key and the computer's recognition of the character can be lengthened to give us the window within which to insert the correct identification."

"Are you saying that if I tapped a computer key, the length of time it takes for the character to appear onscreen is sufficient for you to enter?"

Vannis nodded. "Yes, Comrade Colonel. To the right computer, it could be several centuries of time. More than enough for a search. We must have at least one that is fast enough."

Stolybin pondered Vannis's words, then said, "Very well, Ivan. You shall have your equipment. We will find a place for you to work and a place to live. In fact, I believe living quarters have already been allocated. Someone will be waiting outside this office. Thank you."

Vannis stood up, placed the papers carefully back upon Stolybin's desk, then saluted. "Thank you, Comrade Colonel."

After Vannis had gone, the general came in. "Can he really do it?"

"He seems to know what he's talking about."

"If he can, he is a little genius. Why is he still a mere captain?"

Almost before the general had finished speaking, they both understood why.

The general said dryly, "We spent years boasting to the West that we had no ethnic problems while laughing at their own. They must be laughing now."

"I think, Vasili," Stolybin began, risking informality as the general seemed to be in a good mood, "that we may well be in one of our rare accords with the West. They are as worried about an explosion as we are."

"They're worried about their skins, you mean."

"Aren't we worried about ours?"

Within three days, a workroom had been set up for Vannis, with all the necessary equipment. The general, pulling strings and calling in secret favors, was able to meet all requirements. On the fourth, Vannis had a graphic model to show Stolybin.

Stolybin went to the room alone. The general had decided this was for the best. Stolybin knew it was because the general did not want to be seen having anything to do with the captain.

The room was fairly spacious, and was in an area of the building that was strictly out of bounds to all but authorized personnel. Entry was gained by sliding a data card into a waiting slot. There were five computers of varying power in the room, plus a terminal linked via secure modem to one of the main defense computers.

The five autonomous machines had power ranging from a one-megabyte unit of the home-computer type, to a forty-megabyte PC clone. Vannis, in a white lab coat, was keen to show off his work.

"We shall start with the least powerful, Comrade

Colonel," he began as soon as Stolybin had entered, "so as to better illustrate the principle behind the interception of the keyboard commands. This one." He was like a boy with wonderful new toys.

Each of the autonomous machines was attached to its own monitor, while the terminal for the defense computer possessed a large screen of about 1.5 meters square.

"Here, Comrade," Vannis went on, stopping by the one-megabyte computer. "Tap a key. Any key."

Stolybin dutifully did so. A character appeared onscreen.

"How long would you say it took between key press and the screen's response?"

"Instantaneous?"

"Oh no, Comrade. It was very slow indeed. Now watch."

Vannis tapped a few keys. The screen changed to show a figure with a soccer ball at its feet, with two vertical lines acting as goalposts, some distance from it.

"These are basic graphics," Vannis continued, "but they'll do for our purposes."

"You're going to show me a game of soccer?"

"Ah, but it's a very special game. Please tap this key." He showed Stolybin.

Stolybin did so. The figure kicked the ball swiftly, speeding it between the posts.

"That seemed quite instantaneous to me," Stolybin remarked.

"Not at all. Compared to the other machines, that was a snail's pace. Now watch." Vannis's fingers flew over the keys. "Now hit the same key."

This time, the ball took longer to reach the posts. Vannis slowed the action down until the ball seemed to hang, floating toward its destination.

"The passage of time is the same as at your first

key press," Vannis explained. "We have, if you like, the same thing in slow motion. That's putting it a little crudely, but easier to understand."

"You wouldn't be patronizing me, would you, Ivan?" Stolybin asked mildly.

Vannis, anxious to dispel such a belief, said urgently, "No! I would not dream of it, Comrade! I was merely—"

"All right, Ivan. Don't get worked up. Please continue."

"Yes. Yes, of course. Er . . . as I was . . . er . . . saying, the same period of time is being stretched to allow possible manipulation of the . . . er . . . window of opportunity. Now, if we move to the next machine up in power, we shall see that the window can be stretched further."

Vannis demonstrated with each machine, making the soccer ball slower and slower.

"Unfortunately," he said when they had finished with the fourth computer, "to interrupt the code, we need far greater speed of intercept. This machine will begin to show us what is needed." They had stopped at the forty-megabyte PC.

Again, Vannis did his magic at the keyboard. On the screen, a new figure had joined the game. Another player tried to intercept the ball. He was much too slow.

"I can bring him almost within reach of the ball," Vannis said, "but he can't get close enough to kick it, let alone deflect it. We need still more power."

Intrigued and secretly amazed by Vannis's prowess, Stolybin said, "What about the terminal? The defense computer should have enough power, surely."

"I hope so. However, the particular computer we're using is tasked with other things. We're only going to be able to use a free portion of its memory."

"Are you telling me that a computer that can launch a screen of intercontinental ballistic missiles can't handle this?"

"No, Comrade Colonel. That is not what I meant. I'm just explaining that it would depend on the amount of power available to us at any given time."

"You worry about making it work. I'll handle the power requirements."

"Very well." Vannis turned to the terminal and began to tap swiftly.

On the large screen, the familiar soccer scenario suddenly materialized in a manner that clearly demonstrated the vast reserves of power driving the program. Vannis slowed the action down, but now the intercepting player was moving at a speed that allowed him not only to reach the ball but to kick it out of the way. It missed the goal.

"Excellent!" Stolybin cried. "You've done it!"

Vannis shook his head. "This is only the beginning."

Stolybin stared at him. "You said you needed to intercept the ball. There is sufficient power. You've just proved it."

"No, Comrade. What I want to do is have the ball intercepted at such a speed that the original player will think no one else has kicked the ball." He hesitated. "I don't mean the figure in there knows what's going on—"

"I think I can understand that part, Ivan."

"Of course. Of course. What I need to do is make the intercept seem so fast to the player that's performed the original kick that it will be quite invisible. The ball will go into the net, but it will be a different one, though no change in its apparent trajectory will have occurred. For that, I will need enough power not only to make the intercept, but to do it during the flight time of the missile."

"You are quite certain you can do all this?"

"Positive."

"You'll have all the power you need," Stolybin vowed. "This is quite remarkable, Ivan. You're a genius. I've always known that."

Vannis permitted himself a hesitant smile. "The Comrade Colonel is kind."

"I'm not being kind. This is the truth. All right, Ivan. Keep at it. We may need your wizardry in a hurry."

The general was waiting when Stolybin returned to his office.

"Does he know what he's doing?" the general asked immediately. "He must. You're looking pleased with yourself."

"He can interrupt the missile command and substitute another. We can take over the missile in flight."

Stolybin described the method in as great a detail as he could.

"We can make it do whatever we want, within the flight time," he continued. "We can make it go off course, destroy itself, or"—he looked straight into the general's eyes—"hit a target of our choosing."

The general merely squinted at him through smoke.

"The kind of power needed," Stolybin went on, "would not make this method practicable as a defense measure."

"We don't need it for defensive purposes. We need just one missile to hit one target. Everything else will follow in its wake." The general nodded with satisfaction. "Good. Good. Another idea of yours that has worked. So your trip was worthwhile, after all." He showed no embarrassment. "Captain Vannis can have all the power he needs."

"I've already told him."

The general's eyes were like stone. "You have, have you?"

"I didn't think you would mind."

"I don't," the general said, and walked out.

That night in his apartment, with the great feline body of Tokareva straddling him and writhing away vigorously, he felt a great surge of power build within him. He rolled her onto the bed, reversing their position and thrusting himself deep into her.

She gave a sudden squeal both of surprise and pleasure and answered his pelvic movements with powerful ones of her own. They slammed and heaved at each other until they appeared in imminent danger of rolling off the bed and thudding to the floor. They probably would not have noticed if they had.

Tokareva gave prolonged keening wails that were punctuated only by her pauses for breath while Stolybin answered her with grunts and growls. They went on like this for some time, her magnificent legs now flailing, now locking him into place, until at last, great shudders took hold of their bodies. When it was all over, she lay back with a long sigh of contentment.

"Oh, Sergei," she eventually said in a hoarse whisper. "Something must have gone well for you. You were like a conqueror! Mmmm!" She rubbed a caressing hand along her inner thigh. "What could have happened today?"

Stolybin was staring at the darkened ceiling. Each time he made love to Tokareva, he felt he was paying the general back. He could not help it. He doubted whether he would ever forgive the general for touching her, for dumping him into that infernal waste for all those months. But today he felt he had subtly gained a few advantages over the general. Vannis's method of interception was going to work. The general had not thought of Vannis. The general would not have known how to utilize Vannis's talents. The general . . .

The general, the general. Screw the general.

The night is mine, Stolybin said to himself. And Tokareva is mine.

He turned to her to kiss a cheek made damp by their recent exertions. Her hand traveled slowly down his body, and stopped.

"What?" she said, voice thick with passion. "Already?"

"It's going to be a long night," he said, "unless you're feeling tired."

"Not me," she said, and proved it as only she could.

Kent, England. Midnight.

Sir James West was staring at his own darkened ceiling, unable to sleep. He had dozed fitfully, but deep slumber continued to evade him. It had been like this for several days.

No one, since the meeting on the bridge, had contacted him. No letters, notes, or mysterious phone calls had intruded upon his life. Yet his equilibrium was seriously disturbed. What were they playing at? It was as if no one had ever brought the raging nightmare of his guilt back to the surface from where it had retreated all those years ago.

There was a faint stirring next to him, then more pronounced movement.

"Still having trouble, dear?" came the sleepy voice of his wife. "You really should have a word with Colin Layton. He might be able to help."

Layton was their local GP, their doctor for several years.

"I don't need to trouble Colin. Go back to sleep," West told her gently. "I'm sorry I disturbed you."

"You didn't disturb me. I can catch up on my sleep easily. You know I've always been able to fall asleep at the drop of a hat. I'm worried about you. I might be able to help."

West shook his head in the gloom. "You've been a great help to me over the years, Madge, but this is beyond even your resourcefulness."

She raised herself from the bed to touch him gently. "Jimmy," she said, using the term of endearment from their youth, "I don't like it when you talk like that. It worries me so."

He patted her hand. "You go to sleep, my dear. I'll just go to my study for a while."

"Jimmy! You're not—"

"No, no, no. I'm not about to do anything silly. You go back to sleep. I'll be along soon."

West climbed out of bed, under the unseen, anxious gaze of his wife, and picked up his dressing gown from a bedside chair. Then he went quietly out of the room. She stared into the dark, but did not attempt to stop him.

In his study, West turned on a single wall light that gave subdued illumination to the room. Three of the walls were taken up by floor-to-ceiling bookshelves, some with locked compartments.

He went to his inlaid pedestal desk, opened a drawer, and took out a key from a small, lacquered box. He went to one of the bookcases and opened a compartment. There was a box in there, too, larger, with a combination lock. He took it back to his desk and opened it.

Resting on a lining of black velvet were two

gleaming pistols. One was his old service revolver, the other a Makarov PM automatic, a small Soviet army eight-shot handgun he had "acquired" while still in uniform. He inspected both weapons carefully, touching them almost with longing, an intense expression upon his face.

He replaced them slowly and shut the box. Unhurriedly, he put the box back in its compartment. He then returned the key to his desk, turned off the light, and went back to bed. A decision had been made.

He slept soundly.

Moscow. Christmas Eve.

People's Deputy Belov was trudging through the snow toward his apartment thinking there was not much to cheer about when a man, preoccupied and hurrying, collided with him.

Belov stumbled, but did not actually fall. The man grabbed him by an elbow to steady him before hurrying on after a mumbled apology. It was not until he had removed his coat in the apartment that he found the envelope in one of its pockets.

The note inside simply said there was a growing conspiracy to topple the government and that Belov should be careful. There were no details, and no suggestions of likely dates when this would supposedly happen.

"I want names," he muttered. "I need something more to show Gant."

As for his own safety, he did not spend time worrying about it. If they intended to kill him—whoever "they" were—they would do so at a time of their own choosing. His task was to preempt their plans for the country before they turned their lethal attention upon him.

"But I need more," he said. He could only wait for

his mysterious helpers to keep passing the information on to him.

He had no intention of trying to discover their identity. Apart from the possible added danger to himself, he would certainly be placing his informants in jeopardy and thus cause his supply to dry up. It was obvious from the quality of the information that his sources were people very deep within the party and/or the military hierarchy.

Belov looked about the dingy confines of his home. It was going to be a bleak winter.

In his office, Stolybin was looking at a map of the Mediterranean countries. The general was standing by, seemingly content to let Stolybin be in charge.

Stolybin traced a finger around a small island. "They can't use Malta as a base the way they did twenty-five years ago. Things have changed a lot since then."

"Sicily?"

Stolybin shook his head. "I wouldn't think so. Not Sardinia either. Too obvious for this test." Stolybin tapped a finger on another island that looked like a stubby raindrop about the size of Malta, over to the northwest. "That's my choice."

The general studied the island carefully, frowning a little.

"I agree," he said. "We should keep observation on the other places, but concentrate on this island. When they move, we'll know. I'll see to it."

During the Christmas holidays, the crews of Selby and Hohendorf drew duty while Bagni was able to spend three days with his parents in Fiesole near Florence. He told them virtually nothing about his new unit. Stockmann elected to remain on the base.

*   *   *

In the Mediterranean, a nuclear-powered submarine of the fast Alfa class with a submerged speed of forty-plus knots, began to do a quiet patrol beneath the waters around the island Stolybin had indicated.

In outer space, a satellite was moved from its original orbit to a geosynchronous one over a section of the western Mediterranean. This, too, would concentrate on the area around the same island.

The shift of orbit was not given much attention by the world's intelligence gatherers. All interest was focused on the Middle East as the world waited for another war it did not really want.

Which was precisely what Stolybin and the general had expected.

10

November One. 1600 hours, the first week in January.

Darkness had long descended upon the snow-covered base. The sky was clear, and though the land was cold, there was no wind. The sometimes fierce Moray storms of winter had so far spared the unit their worst attentions. There had been snowfalls and strong winds, but nothing that had prevented the November aircraft from operating normally. In fact, the area boasted a relatively mild climate, and those who were not familiar with it would hardly believe that a reasonably warm nine degrees Celsius had been recorded while supposedly warmer parts of southern England had shivered at freezing temperatures.

But this night, November One was itself registering a temperature of minus one Celsius. In Zero One squadron operations room Wing Commander Jason, in flying overalls, was addressing the crews who would be flying out on the detachment to the Mediterranean.

"I suppose," he was saying, "you're all quite relieved to be going to warmer climes. This, however, is not going to be a holiday. You have all proved to me during the past weeks that you have learned to operate the new missile with professional competence. It remains to be seen whether you will perform as well during the live firing exercises."

"And the missile, sir. Let's not forget *its* performance. I mean, we don't know how it will perform on a real shoot."

"Thank you, McCann," Jason said with heavy patience, "for the reminder. I think I can safely say I am aware of the untried nature of that particular weapon." His eyes were fixed upon McCann. "Anything else?"

"Uh . . . ah . . . no, sir."

"Must be a record of some kind."

Everyone glanced at McCann with knowing expressions of amusement. He wisely kept his mouth shut.

"I shall have the lead of the first pair," Jason continued, "in Eagle One, with Axel and Wolfie in Eagle Two on my wing. Mark, Elmer Lee and yourself will be in Eagle Three. You have the lead of the second pair. Nico and Hank Stockmann will be on your wing in Eagle Four. All right?"

"Yes, sir," the group said in unison.

"The second pair will take off one minute after the first," Jason went on. "There's no need for me to go over the flight plan. I trust you're all fully clued up on it."

Everyone nodded. Jason would not have expected otherwise. There was a rendezvous en route with a tanker, for refueling.

"Good," Jason said. "Don't miss that bloody tanker up there in the dark. If any of you goes into the drink or hits a mountain because of lack of fuel, I'll find you even if you're dead and sort you out. Got it?"

"Yes, sir," they chorused, hiding smiles.

He looked at them each in turn, nodding with satisfaction. "Our maintenance and support people, as you know, took off some hours ago. They should have things ready by the time we arrive. We've got a good man in command, so all ground support will be spot on."

"Who's in command, sir?" Only McCann would ask.

"Flight Lieutenant Pearce."

"Boy. I really needed that."

"Do you have a problem, Captain McCann?"

"Sir, no, sir."

Jason gave McCann the benefit of a long stare. "Right, gentlemen," he then said. "See you at our destination."

Jason went out, followed by David Milner, a squadron leader and weapons systems instructor, who was to be his backseater for the detachment.

"The guy's haunting me," McCann muttered to Selby as they filed out to head for the kitting room. "Why Pearce, for God's sake?"

"Perhaps you should stop having naughty dreams about his lady love."

"I'm not having any dreams about her," McCann retorted in a fierce whisper, "and definitely not 'naughty' ones, as you call it."

Selby grinned and wiped an imaginary dribble off McCann's lips. "Then why are you salivating?"

"That's not saliva. That's foaming rage because that gorilla's going to be in my space."

"You can always wish her fond farewells as we take off. I hear she's on duty in the tower tonight."

McCann paused, looking at Selby suspiciously. "I thought you didn't want me to think about her," he said as he moved on to catch up. "Besides, the Boss will hear."

"The lesser of two evils. If you say bye-byes to her, we may all get some peace for a while."

"Hey, you two," Stockmann said behind them.

"Stop bickering. Save it for the cold night upstairs." He grinned at them.

"Your problem, James Henry Stockmann the Third," McCann told him, "is that you're a marine. A passable aviator, as you guys like to call yourselves, but still a marine, and everyone knows a marine's got no soul."

Stockmann took no offense. "A hog am I, and proud of it. See you ladies upstairs. Come on, Nico, let's get our underwear on. It's mighty cold out there."

Karen Lomax watched as the barely distinguishable shapes, vividly marked by the twin tongues of blue-white flames of their afterburners, roared down the runway. Etched in pinpoints of light in the darkness it led, seemingly without end, into the inky gloom of the night.

The first pair lifted off, the four nozzles of their afterburners glowing furnaces that rose swiftly heavenward, navigation lights blinking like multicolored fireflies.

This time, she knew who the crews were, and as she waited out the minute pause between takeoffs she wondered whether McCann in Eagle Three would break communication procedures again. Since that last time, he had behaved himself. Clearly, she thought, the wing commander must have leaned on him.

Now the second pair were rolling. The burners came on with a quadruple explosion of sound, and four searing tongues lit the dark with their glare.

Her eyes followed them as she listened to their crews talking to the other controllers. The rules were being strictly obeyed.

She cut in when there was a pause. "Have a good flight, Eagle Three."

"Hey! What about Eagle Four?" came from Stockmann.

"You too, Eagle Four."

"That's more like it."

"Thank you, November." There was surprise in McCann's voice, which, for him, was somewhat subdued.

"You're welcome."

"See?" McCann said to Selby. "She must like me a little."

"I had an itch once. I grew quite fond of it when it wasn't there anymore. Come on, Elmer Lee. We've got a long flight in the dark, and a tanker to meet for some juice. Let's have our minds focused on the job in hand, shall we? Besides, I did try to help you. I took you to Morven's New Year's Eve party, and you practically ignored Zöe. Do you realize that most of the guys back at the unit would be pawing the ground with smoke coming out of their nostrils, if they ever caught sight of her? You don't know when you've got a good thing going."

"Sez you?" McCann remarked skeptically, knowing of Selby's fractured relationship with Kim Mannon. "I went to that party for the same reason as I went to Aberdeen with you the last time—to stop you from giving your kid sister a hard time over Axel Hohendorf."

"Don't bring Morven into this," Selby told him with a distinct lack of warmth.

For once, McCann did not reply with a smart retort, knowing when to leave well enough alone. He made a swift check of his systems, then glanced over his left shoulder as Selby reefed the Tornado around to head south, on the first leg of their journey. Far below in the darkness, clusters of light marked the villages, towns, and isolated dwellings of human habitation.

Selby well remembered the New Year's Eve party. It had been a lively affair, celebrated with the kind of verve Scotland was known for. Hohendorf had been there, too, naturally, and on the stroke of midnight, Morven had seized him, giving him the most sensual kiss Selby had ever witnessed. That his sister was doing the kissing made him uncomfortable.

Then Kim had grabbed hold of him. "If I didn't know you better," she'd said, "I'd be worried. Stop looking at them and concentrate on me." Then she had given him one of her own specials.

He repressed the thought as the memory of what had developed from their own kissing began to excite him. The cockpit of Eagle Three was no place for thoughts either of Kim Mannon, or of Morven and her relationship with Axel Hohendorf.

He settled onto the new course and put the accelerating aircraft into a gentle climb. He had canceled the burners, but the speed continued to build as the Tornado rose into thinner air. Transit level was to be 50,000 feet. With wings at midsweep, they would make good time, although they could go much faster than the seven-hundred-knot cruise Jason had set for the first leg. At full bore with wings swept, the ASV could complete the 1,600-mile journey in less than an hour. But that was a waste of fuel, which would also leave them trying to run the engines on air.

He glanced to his right. A little to the rear, he could see the winking nav lights of Eagle Four. Bagni was maintaining good separation and good formation.

He checked his displays, tapping through the menus. All systems were working smoothly. He knew McCann would be doing his own frequent checks, ensuring the continuing integrity of the backseat systems, ready to spot the slightest anomaly.

Through the wide-angle head-up display, Selby could see into the night. He had slaved the FLIR system—the forward-looking infrared—to it, and this enabled him to see clearly, as if he were looking at a black-and-white photograph of the world, slightly tinged with the palest, greenish amber. The FLIR virtually gave him a window in the dark, through which all was depicted clearly. The HUD symbols still glowed as normal, presenting him with relevant information for any given requirement. At the moment, the HUD was in navigation mode. Beyond it was the night, but it was night whose darkness was relative. Through the cockpit's bubble canopy, the stars shone brightly in a clear sky, bathing the two aircraft in a ghostly light that seemed both colorless and insubstantial. They seemed to float, motionless, waiting like hungry sharks ready to pounce upon an unsuspecting prey.

Within the snug fit of his lightweight, yet strong helmet, Selby could hear the aircraft's lullaby, the subdued sounds of its workings, as if it were itself alive, breathing softly at him.

"Gawd," McCann's voice said without warning, drawling in wonder. "You know, no matter how many times I do this, it always gets me when we come up at night. This is so darned beautiful."

For once, he was not playing a cassette. He would not have dared with Jason somewhere out there in the lead, even though the wing commander would not have heard. The music would have been on cockpit channel only, unless McCann inadvertently transmitted it, which was why he had erred on the side of caution.

Selby did not say anything, but he agreed with McCann. Night flying held no terrors for him, and he was able to appreciate the beauty of the winter's darkness. People did not realize, he thought, how much actual light there was in what seemed like impenetrable gloom on a clear night, even without a moon.

"Right," McCann was saying, "one-seven-one."

Selby banked the Tornado gently onto the new heading. In Eagle Four, Bagni would be doing the same as Stockmann gave him the change of direction.

The two aircraft settled into the new course, linked by an invisible umbilical cord to the lead pair, now twelve miles ahead.

"Yeah," McCann said after a while, again looking about him. "The night is beautiful."

"Elmer Lee."

"Yo."

"Do we have Karen Lomax to thank for this sudden explosion of poetic inspiration?"

"Who's Karen Lomax?" McCann asked shamelessly. "Next way point in thirty seconds. Right, right . . . one-zero-zero. Want to go auto?"

"I'll stay with it," Selby replied.

He had the option of relinquishing control of the aircraft to its onboard systems, allowing it to fly on whatever heading had been programmed. But he preferred a hands-on flight all the way to destination. The necessary concentration would keep both Kim Mannon and Morven out of his mind.

Cluttered thought processes had no place on the job in hand. McCann, he felt, should be as ruthless about his own preoccupation with Karen Lomax. Mistakes could be expensive, even fatal.

He decided to say nothing more about it to McCann. At least, not during the flight.

"AARA Hotel in nine minutes," McCann announced. "Tanker at seventy-four miles."

They had crossed France and were now over the

Mediterranean, in a gentle descent to 27,000 feet, to the waiting tanker orbiting in the air-to-air refueling area known as "Hotel." Though the entire flight could have been made with the fuel load they'd had on takeoff, Jason, never one to waste an opportunity, had decided to include a refueling exercise in the flight plan.

All four aircraft were being flown by crews who were highly experienced refuelers, but as Selby well knew, mistakes could still be made. He'd known a pilot with several hundred hours on the type of aircraft he'd been flying, who had inexplicably misjudged his approach and had turned both himself and the tanker into a fireball. That had been in daylight.

Selby looked out beyond his HUD at his infrared world and promised himself never to fall into the trap of a hasty approach.

In the backseat, McCann had the tanker on his displays. One showed a videographic image, with a constantly updating readout of speed, altitude, heading, and distance, plus estimated time of arrival at the refueling point, according to the given velocity of the Tornado. Selby eased the throttles back, aiming for an exact match of speed with the tanker aircraft, a converted Lockheed Tristar KC1, by the time they were close to the tanker's trailing fuel line. After that, it would be a matter of easing the speed up just enough to plug neatly into the shuttlecocklike drogue basket. The ASV's sleek nose helped to cut down the air turbulence that sometimes caused less streamlined aircraft to weave about, leading to pilot-induced oscillations.

"The Boss and Eagle Two are plugged in," McCann was saying, studying another display that showed a plan view of the tanker and its two "chicks." Though the fuel lines were not depicted, the positions of the smaller ASVs behind the large KC1 showed quite clearly. They were at their respective fueling stations.

"Tanker now at fifty miles . . . six minutes to Hotel. Tanker speed stabilized at four hundred knots. We'll have to wait."

They had reached 32,000 feet and Selby brought the throttles further back as the descent to 27,000 continued.

"We'll have their lights soon," McCann said. The night was as clear over the Mediterranean as it had been over the Moray Firth.

At 410 knots now, with just a thousand feet to go for refueling height, the Tornados of Selby and Bagni crept up upon the tanker and its companions, giving Jason and Hohendorf time to refuel. Soon they could see the Christmas-tree pattern of the navigation lights, now seemingly motionless in the night sky, the larger KC1 slightly above, with the smaller ASVs suckling at each unseen wing.

Before long, it was their turn as Eagle One and Two disengaged and peeled away. Through the FLIR head-up display, Selby could see part of the great body of the converted airliner as he carefully eased the Tornado forward, the crooked arm of the ASV's refueling probe now extending from its flush-fitting housing on the left-hand side of the nose, just beneath the windscreen. Two refueling warning lights were mounted, one above the other, within the far right-hand top corner of the cockpit instrument panel. The top light, with "RDY" marked upon it, had come on. The probe was ready to receive.

In the HUD, the Tristar seemed to be just part of an aircraft, the FLIR etching out upon the night only that section that came within the confines of the HUD. Beyond this, the remainder was a dark, looming shape.

Selby aimed the probe toward the drogue basket with its circle of orientation lights. He made contact smoothly and the fuel began to flow. Presently, the second light glowed "FULL."

Selby disengaged. The probe was retracted, and reducing speed slightly to clear the tanker, he banked steeply and climbed, knowing Bagni, too, had completed and was following.

"Stylish work," McCann said from the back as they regained transit height. "You've been practicing, my man."

Selby grinned in his mask, but said nothing. If everything went as smoothly, they'd be back at November One in no time. A few days of well-earned leave would enable him to patch things up with Kim.

The ancient Phoenician island that was to be their temporary base was somewhat smaller than Malta and was roughly eighty kilometers from the nearest North African coast. The missile trials, however, would be taking place well over a hundred miles from land, above the open sea.

An advance party had already been established several weeks previously, and up-to-date navigational aids and landing systems had been installed on the old wartime airfield. Though the runway itself had been improved, it had not been greatly lengthened. However, the ASV's extremely short landing and takeoff capabilities ensured that this would not be a problem. Pearce's engineering team, having long since landed, was waiting to receive the incoming Tornadoes.

Ahead of him, Selby could see the runway lights and the fast-moving navigational beacons of Eagle One and Two as they ran in for the break prior to landing. With Bagni on his wing, Selby followed. The runway lights appeared at his left wingtip as he banked hard halfway along, lowering the wheels as he brought the wings level. Bagni made his own break a moment later, slotting neatly behind.

While they were still at some altitude, Selby had thought they could easily have been coming in to land upon an aircraft carrier. The island, beyond the area of the HUD, was invisible on the dark blanket of the surrounding sea, only its sparse illuminations and the glowing path of the runway lights betraying its existence. At low altitude, however, the HUD showed some ferociously high ground.

With the head-up display now switched to landing mode, he watched the luminous yellow-green bars of the instrument landing system—the ILS—begin to move toward each other as he lined up his approach. The short bars—one horizontal, the other vertical— merged until they formed a perfect cross. A spot-on approach.

He carried out a smooth touchdown, nosewheel dropping with hardly a jolt, thrust reversers slowing the aircraft down. Soon they were at taxiing speed. There was plenty of runway left.

"Home for the next few weeks, Elmer Lee," he said.

McCann was looking about him unenthusiastically. "People actually *live* here?"

"If the briefing had it correctly, about nine thousand of them." The control tower was giving taxiing instructions. It was a female voice, a controller from November One, but not Karen Lomax. Selby acknowledged, then continued to McCann: "We're guests here, so remember not to upset the locals. Talk to Nico Bagni. As an Italian of Sicilian descent, he might know a little more about this place."

McCann held on to his disenchantment. "All this and goddamn Pearce. I'm such a lucky guy."

"You never know, Elmer Lee. You might actually get to enjoy it."

"You've got to be kidding."

Moscow. Thirty-six hours later.

The general stormed into Stolybin's office. In one hand he held out a sheet of paper toward Stolybin, smacking at it with the back of the other.

"This thing you've left on my desk," he began, "why did I not have it before? A detachment has arrived on the island, has fired the first missiles, and I've only just been told?"

Stolybin was calm. "I myself have only received the information within the last few minutes, Comrade General. I passed it on immediately."

The general was not mollified. So great was his outrage, he had actually forgotten his cigarette. This only served to make his temper worse.

"Are you saying," he said quietly, "that the satellite did not even pick up the deployment, and that until the submarine detected the destruction of a target drone, we had *no* idea that the unit had arrived?" The general's voice rose to a crescendo as he finished speaking.

Stolybin maintained his calm. "There was a temporary malfunction in the—"

"I don't want to hear about temporary malfunctions!" the general shouted. "There is no such thing as a temporary malfunction. Something works, or it does not. The satellite did not work, and we might well have remained totally ignorant of the timing of the deployment had I not had the foresight to post a submarine surveillance unit. We have lost thirty-six hours! This could mean the difference between success and failure!" Deprived of his customary cigarette, the general's ill-humor increased. Baleful eyes stared at Stolybin.

"How do we know the wretched satellite is going to perform the interception when we need it?"

Stolybin wisely did not mention the fact that the general's demand for speed had correspondingly increased the possibilities for failure. There was less time for double-checking. Stolybin liked to check everything over more than twice to avoid a screw-up, but the general's insistence had precluded this. Stolybin's instinct for survival told him that the general would not welcome criticism, and he wisely kept silent.

Instead of cringing under the general's attack, however, he took the bold course.

"It will work, Comrade General," he stated with a confidence he did not truly feel. "Your inclusion of the submarine was inspired thinking; careful, too. By giving us this backup, we lost only some hours."

"Only!" The general was not quite apoplectic, but he was rapidly approaching that state.

Stolybin went on smoothly: "They have completed the first of the firing trials, and our submarine was able to track one of the missiles to termination. We have the first timings, speed, and range. It makes depressing reading, on the one hand . . ."

"And on the other?"

"I'll come to that later, if the Comrade General will permit."

The general nodded reluctantly, eyes far from friendly.

"It's depressing reading," Stolybin continued, "because the missile performs even better than we had dared suspect, and worse, we have nothing in the pipeline to either match or exceed it. The fully operational version may well surpass it by a very wide margin. As you know, Comrade, we have discussed the theft of one, but discarded that route as impractical in the circumstances. Our best chance, therefore, is to discredit it and have the project canceled. This will give us time to work on our own missile, though with the way things are, this might never happen."

"This is not news to me," the general said. "That is why I initiated this operation in the first place."

Stolybin doubted this, but kept his opinion to himself and nodded.

"Precisely, Comrade General. Now for the more hopeful side. We have been able to analyze the missile's flight time." He picked up a sheet of paper and passed it to the general, who frowned at it.

"A bunch of figures," the general said, looking up from the paper. "It tells me nothing."

"To Captain Vannis it says plenty. He will compare each successive flight that we can monitor, either by submarine or satellite and, by comparing these, will be able to construct a program for the interception."

"Will he be in time?"

"He'll be in time."

"Your neck depends on it, Sergei."

Stolybin did not doubt that, but he had his own insurance policy. The general's use of his first name was not cause for imprudence.

"I'm well aware of that, Vasili." Despite the implicit threat, it was safe, however, to use first names.

"I know you think I'm pushing too hard," the general said, almost conversationally, "but time is not on our side. It is not on the nation's side. The Foreign Ministry is rudderless, and the Presidency . . ." He made a sound of disgust. "And as for the republics, if anything, matters have got worse. Soldiers from the different republics are shooting each other now. How can this happen? How can we *allow* it to happen? We are receiving food parcels like some third-world country. Our people are being humiliated. At the end of last month, I could not believe that our people were traveling to Poland, of all places, to buy food. *Poland!* I talked to an old veteran of the Patriotic War the other day. He told me taking food parcels makes him ashamed. This is a man who commanded a tank company, and is highly decorated."

The general's malignant eyes fastened upon Stolybin. "If there is not to be a civil war even bloodier than the Revolution, we must change things before it is too late. We must regain our status in the world. The international community must learn to respect us once more—or at least to fear us. And that, Sergei, is where the real power lies. It is time to stop the foreigners from dictating to us and involving themselves in our affairs. They're destabilizing us. I don't want their wretched hamburgers and their jeans. I don't want their stinking capitalism. I want the Soviet Union back as its old cohesive self. Freedom." He almost spat the word. "Freedom to do what? To call oneself a deputy and argue interminably about what to do? To kill each other in our streets? To starve? To beg from foreigners?" The general thumped Stolybin's desk with a clenched fist. *"No!"* he roared, eyes glaring. *"No, no, no!"* He punctuated each no with a thump.

Stolybin watched all this warily. It was the longest time he could ever remember having seen the general without a cigarette, and in a peculiar way, this made him seem all the more fearsome. Though he partly sympathized with the general's sentiments, he did not throw the blanket of blame upon foreigners. The Revolution had itself been betrayed by incompetence, self-servers, and narrow ideology. He did not think this was the sort of thing the general would want to hear. But then his mood had changed again suddenly.

"Sergei Grigorevich," the general went on with unnerving calm, "I am depending upon you, and I expect results. I want you to make quite sure your Captain Vannis does his job. I want that missile taken over and reprogrammed. I want no mistakes, and I want speed."

"It will all be done, Vasili Vasilievich."

The general stared at him. "The Motherland is relying on you."

That night, Stolybin made fierce love to Tokareva, feeling as if he were emptying his anger, frustration, and fear into her magnificent, feline body. She seemed to thrive on the diet, her own passion matching his vigor. Instead of burning each other out, they appeared to be increasingly revatilized.

Whatever the nature of the engine that drove their desire for each other, he was certain it was not love.

Two days later, Stolybin knocked on the door to the general's office.

"In!" the general ordered.

Stolybin smoothed down his uniform tunic and entered. The inevitable cigarette was in his superior's mouth, but there were no wreathes of smoke. Anyone entering the office for the first time would have been surprised by this, until his ears became attuned to the subdued whir of powerful extractor fans. The general, it seemed, did not like polluting his own space. Stolybin had grown used to the anomaly.

"Have you news for me?" the general asked immediately.

"Yes, Comrade General. Captain Vannis is now happy with his program. We are ready to conduct the first trial."

The general's heavy-featured face creased in a sudden smile. "Good. Good! The special unit has been standing by for some time. Are you both ready to move immediately?"

"Yes," Stolybin replied.

"Good," the general said once more. "I'll be coming with you, but not Tokareva, of course. Be ready to travel within the hour."

"Yes, Comrade General."

"All right. Go and prepare Vannis."

An aircraft of the PVO—the Air Defense Force—took them to an airfield two hundred miles east of Moscow, where they were shown to a small underground room. Here, Vannis would be expected to work his magic. A smaller duplicate of his working environment had been constructed, with two computers in place of the five in Moscow.

The room was strictly forbidden to all but those authorized by the general himself. The officer who had accompanied them but had not entered was an air-force colonel, who was not introduced.

Above their heads, two of the advanced Su-27 Flankers, sporting the foreplanes seen in Deputy Belov's clandestinely supplied photographs, roared unheard into the air. They lifted off with remarkable speed, pulling into a steep climb in a manner that spoke of enhanced agility rather than raw power.

Vannis had switched on the systems, and as they warmed up, the radar echoes of the two Flankers were depicted on one of the monitor screens. They were moving swiftly to their appointed stations. A third echo appeared. The remotely piloted target drone was airborne.

"If you will put on these headphones, Comrade General," Vannis said, using the highest rank out of respect and protocol, "you will hear the pilots. You too, Comrade Colonel. There's an extra set for you."

Stolybin and the general donned the headphones and waited.

On one of his screens, Vannis had a version of the soccer player he had previously shown Stolybin. The program had been inserted.

The three of them listened as the Flanker pilots maneuvered into an attacking position on the drone. Only one aircraft would fire. The other was there to record the shoot. Together with the film from the shooter aircraft, an overall analysis would be made. There would also be recordings of the radar traces, plus the computers' own recordings.

"They're getting ready," Vannis said. He paused, then went on, "He's achieved lock. Now he's firing."

As the missile left the Su-27, Vannis's fingers seemed to skim across the computer keyboards. One screen showed the player on the move; the other, a trace of the missile in flight.

Now the second player had appeared and had neatly intercepted the first. Then the second player was in full control of the ball and was taking it in another direction.

Stolybin found himself switching his attention back and forth between the two screens. The missile trace was still following its inexorable path toward the drone. If Vannis did not succeed soon, the missile would destroy the drone. If he failed with a missile that was much slower than the Western weapon, and possessed only a hastily constructed code, what chance would he have against the real thing?

But Stolybin felt a mounting excitement. A new set of goalposts had appeared, and the second player was running with the ball toward them. He glanced at the second screen. Was the missile trace beginning to veer?

At first, he refused to believe it, but the missile

was definitely veering off course. As he watched, the deviation became greater until it was actually traveling away from its intended target. On the screen with the soccer player, the ball had been shot through the second set of goalposts.

The missile kept going off course, until its fuel ran out.

The general removed his headphones slowly. Vannis and Stolybin were looking at him anxiously, awaiting his comments.

The general gave a thin smile. "Captain," he said to Vannis, "you have just become a major."

Two more firings that same day achieved similar success. The general returned to Moscow, looking very pleased. Stolybin and Vannis remained to carry out night firings. They would return the next day.

"It won't be as easy with the Western missile," Vannis said to Stolybin. "We'll be dealing with a difficult code, and have far less time to carry out the intercept and takeover. My little animated sequence with the soccer players is not necessary for the interception, of course, but I wanted the comrade general to see how it was being done."

"I'm sure he appreciated it," Stolybin said. "He'll appreciate it even more if you do gain control of the Western missile."

Vannis suppressed his euphoria. He knew he had just received a warning. Newly promoted majors were just as expendable as underpromoted captains.

Frankfurt, Germany. 1800 hours.

People's Deputy Belov looked out upon the lights of the city and felt a deep sense of foreboding. Days before, he had received the confirmation he had been expecting. This time, there had been no deliberate collision by a total stranger. He had found the envelope

with its single sheet of paper in his coat pocket. He had
no idea how or when it had been put there. On it was
the list of names he had brought out to the West; names
that spoke of treachery; names that included his own
fellow deputies, the military and KGB of many different ranks, and even some within the upper reaches of
the party. All, according to his anonymous informants,
were involved in a plot to overthrow the current government.

He didn't know what to believe. Was the information correct? What if it were all malicious lies to discredit the very people accused of plotting civil war?

If that were so, it would be the first time that his
informants had given him incorrect data. Belov had
then decided to trust the information. If true, not just
the Soviet Union, but the stability of the whole international community was in serious jeopardy. Given the
situation in the Middle East, this would make the situation in the republics even more volatile, with civil war
a virtual certainty. As for the Western nations, they
would not necessarily escape. A sudden influx of refugees from the East would pulverize their economies and
destabilize their societies.

Was that perhaps what the plotters hoped for, a
situation that would lead to a national mobilization
against a destabilized and weakened former enemy?
Wasn't the West already making deep arms cuts?

Belov found himself shivering. It was a waking
nightmare. If with Gant's help he blocked the plotters,
perhaps he could help protect the fledgling peace.

He stared out into the dark street below, scanning, out of habit, for a possible shadower. No passerby
looked like a likely candidate. Having been arrested
several times during the pre-*perestroika* days, he had
tried to become adept at spotting surveillance teams.

Belov had been taken to a house in a secluded lane

off the Siesmayerstrasse near the Grüneburgpark. His knowledge of Frankfurt was sketchy. He had no idea where he was, though he had been assured that the house was safe. There were armed men within the building, courtesy of Gant, who would himself arrive in the morning. They would then fly off to a destination unknown to Belov, with a small team of political and military advisers to discuss the situation, based upon the information he had so far supplied.

Belov glanced down at the street once more. He was not particularly worried about his own safety, but was eager for his meeting with Gant to take place. Like the previous time, no one had bothered to check up on him on his way out of Moscow. Perhaps his informants were also able to keep hostile elements off him long enough to facilitate his departures. He had no way of knowing.

He was glad he had no immediate relatives to worry about. Being single, he had no wife and children who could be used as pawns in games of emotional and political blackmail. His friends and various associates could take care of themselves.

"Better than I can of myself," he murmured ruefully. He had always felt that his election as deputy had resulted from sympathy for the number of times he had been flung in prison during the days of the underground movement.

It never occurred to him that he was genuinely respected by those who knew him well.

Belov scanned the well-lit street for a third time. No one to cause him worry. He could sleep well tonight. No one was on his tail, after all.

But he was wrong.

Whitehall, London. 1815 hours.

"Come in," the minister called in answer to a

knock. He had paused in the act of picking up his brief-case. He now took the case and stood waiting. "Ah, Charles," he said as Buntline entered. "Glad you could make it. Just wanted a quick update before I left. Any news?"

Buntline shook his head. "I'm afraid not, Minister. At least, nothing that gives us any clue as to what's going on. Stolybin's not been seen for some time, although I'm certain he's still in Moscow. He's not living at any of the apartments where we'd normally have expected a member of the privileged to be. That means wherever he's being housed was deliberately chosen to avoid scrutiny by interested parties."

"So we're no closer to discovering what he's currently working on."

Again, Buntline shook his head. "The one thing I am quite certain about is that whatever it may be, it's not going to bring us any joy."

"Do you still think the overthrow of their government is a part of it?"

"Given the situation there, that remains on my list of possibilities." Buntline briefly passed a thoughtful finger along his chin. "And as I do have some understanding of the way Comrade Stolybin works, I believe he'll be involved in something quite labyrinthine. It will be devious, and unexpected."

"Well," the minister said, "do keep an ear to the ground, Charles."

"Many ears are already there, Minister. Of course," Buntline continued in a contemplative voice, "we should not rule out sabotage."

The minister was skeptical. "Sabotage?"

"We're still in the dark, Minister, and therefore at a distinct disadvantage. We've got to consider everything. Even in the era of arms agreements, there are bound to be some Western assets his hard-line masters would like to nobble, from battlefield nuclear weapons to—"

"Surely not. In these times? And why? And please don't mention the Middle East. After all, they're backing us on this one."

"For the moment," Buntline said mordantly.

The minister surveyed him speculatively. "Is there ever a time when you're prepared to take things at face value?"

"Never," replied Buntline with the certainty of one who had played in too many dirty games and knew better.

"I see. So what are we left with?"

Buntline stuck his hands in his pockets and paced the minister's office for a few moments before perching on the edge of the large desk. He tended to do that on occasion, and the minister had long ago chosen not to mind.

"During the past few days," Buntline began, "we've picked up some brief bursts of transmission. However, there was no indication of their source. The satellite picked them up almost by accident. It was on a trawl, so to speak, and these transmissions were minnows caught up in the main bulk of the catch. We've been able to place all the others except those."

"Why should they have anything to do with Stolybin? They could be anything, even communication with one of their own satellites whose transmissions might have been degraded by the atmospheric conditions prevailing at the time."

Buntline stared at the minister, surprised at his understanding of the finer points of high-tech eavesdropping.

"I don't like anomalies," Buntline said. "Those transmissions may be nothing, but I'd like to *know* they're nothing."

The November One deployment island in the Med-iterranean. 0800, the next day.

"Do you feel any better about this place, Elmer Lee?"

It was Nico Bagni who had asked the question. He had taken a slightly morose McCann under his wing and had elected to show him around the island for the duration of the deployment, when time off from flying permitted. They were free for the day, but there was a night shoot scheduled later on for the crews of Selby and Hohendorf. They had therefore decided to use the morning for a brief look around.

Bagni had proved to be a mine of information, having been taken to the island during his childhood by his Sicilian relatives.

McCann stared at the tall volcanic mountain that Bagni had said was called Monte Grande.

"It's got some interesting features," he conceded. "Got to make sure we don't hit that thing at night," he added, pointing at the basalt tower. Their air charts had indicated its height as 836 meters, nearly 2,800 feet. "Hell, that piece of rock's higher than some of the stuff up in Scotland. Meaner, too." He had brought a camera with him and took a picture of it, using a zoom lens. "I wouldn't try some of your upside-down stuff with that mother."

Bagni gave a fleeting smile. "So you know about that."

"Yeah. Hank Stockmann told me about the little trick you and Axel Hohendorf pulled. Just don't let the Boss find out." McCann pointed briefly to some squat boxlike structures with shallow, domed roofs. "What did you say these are called?"

"*Dammuso,*" Bagni replied. "They were built in the fields by the ancient Arab farmers who came here hundreds of years ago. Many of the names of the villages have an Arabic origin. This is rich soil, you know. Very, very good for grapes. Do you like sweet wine? You must let me introduce you to some. Moscato is the best. My parents still have some shipped to them."

"You really do know this place."

"From childhood, of course. To a child, it was an adventure coming here. All these rocks and mountains and high cliffs, everything so close in this small place in the middle of the sea . . . it was for me a magic country." Bagni glanced at McCann. "You think perhaps this is a crazy thing for a man who flies a super-technology airplane to talk like this?"

McCann shook his head. "No, Nico. I don't think that at all. We all have our secret, magic countries. Thank you for showing me yours."

"So now you will not think this is just a piece of rock in the middle of an ocean."

McCann grinned. "No, Nico. I won't."

"Then let me show you more of my magic country."

Later, back at the deployment base, Selby accosted Bagni. "Thanks, Nico. Whatever you're doing, it's working. Elmer Lee's not thinking so much about his little problem."

Bagni was self-deprecating. "I was only showing him the things people miss when they come to a place like this."

"Whatever. You still have my thanks."

"This problem . . . is it serious?"

"A little affair of the heart." Selby did not give further explanation.

Bagni nodded sagely. "Ah. We all have those. I did not see my Bianca when I went to Fiesole at Christmas. She was in Tokyo, where she is having—how would you say?—a new distribution for her fashions. She does well. The name Bianca Mazzarini is now known from Milano to London and Paris and New York, and soon in Tokyo." He glanced over to his right, where the four, sleek ASVs of the detachment were neatly lined up. "She hates competing with those. She tries to understand, but it is not easy. She thinks we are more in love with our airplanes than with our women. When I ask her if she would stop her work, she finds *that* difficult to answer." He smiled ruefully. "She also loves her work . . . but I think there is a little truth in what she says about us."

Selby stared at the aircraft, which were being crawled over by the attentive ground crew, and said nothing. Kim, Morven, and now Bianca Mazzarini—all felt threatened. If there was an answer to this apparent conflict of interests, he did not have it.

"Are you looking forward to the shoot for tonight?" Bagni was saying.

Selby glanced at him with a slight shrug, then up at the cloudless sky. The January sun was warmer than expected, even for the southern Mediterranean.

"Should be interesting," he said.

* * *

In Frankfurt, People's Deputy Belov was relieved to see Gant.

After their greetings, Gant said, "We'll be taking off for Cannes this afternoon. Some people will be boarding the plane there. Then we'll do a night flight for our destination. We'll spend a few days going over everything we've got, at the end of which time, we should have all the hard evidence we need and a good case to give those guys on the Hill in Washington. Wake a few people up about their Peace Dividend."

Belov looked at the eagerness in Gant's face and wondered whether he had chosen the right channel for his protest about events in his homeland. But he had come this far. The halfway mark had long since been passed, and it was in his own interest to continue.

It was too late to think of turning back.

That afternoon, Frank Benno filed the flight plan for Gant's specialized 707. Another pilot was filing his own flight plan at the same time. They chatted amiably. Benno thought nothing of the man's slight accent. English, after all, was the international language of aviation, and a foreign accent in Europe was unlikely to cause interest among aircrew at an airport.

Benno did not see the man glance briefly at the 707's flight plan and note its destination.

Moscow; Stolybin's office. 1500 hours.

Stolybin looked at the message he'd just received and gave a feral stretch of the lips that would not seem like a smile to an onlooker, but that was what he meant it to be.

He stood up, walked around his desk and up to the general's door. He knocked.

"In!"

"This just came in," he said as he entered. He

went up to the general's desk and handed the message over. "They've taken off. Their current destination is Cannes."

The general read the short message, then looked up. "Are we ready?"

"We have had to bring things forward—"

"I don't want to hear excuses! Are we *ready?*"

"We are ready, Comrade General."

"Good."

Stolybin was not happy with the speed at which the general wanted the operation carried out. Rushed operations could lead to unforeseen mistakes.

But he did not say so. The general would not want to hear.

Gant's 707, with Frank Benno at the controls, banked steeply as it prepared to land at Cannes. The airfield did not normally accept aircraft as large as the Boeing, even though it had a recently lengthened runway. Jet users were usually restricted to small, twin-engine executive aircraft. Gant had, however, managed to obtain special clearance.

He, or someone working on his behalf, had persuaded the authorities that his 707, with its more powerful, thrust-reversing engines, had exceptional short-field performance.

Benno, with his vast experience of both fighters and the intelligence-gathering RC-135s, now watched as the southern coast of France wheeled beneath his wing. He was bringing the aircraft in almost like a fighter. Carrying much less weight than original design capability, it handled crisply, the extra power of the engines giving the impression it could actually fly like a fighter.

He leveled out, and there was the runway, bang on the nose. Gant had said a civilian flying training school was permanently based at the airfield. His own flight information had confirmed this. He kept a wary eye out for the small Robin DR-400 airplanes, but none was in sight. The collision avoidance radar on the 707's advanced flight deck instrument panel showed nothing to worry about.

Benno began bringing the nose up as his copilot eased back the four throttles, selecting the power setting he had requested.

The landing was carried out smoothly, thrust reversers coming on powerfully to stop the aircraft long before it ran out of runway.

"Hell," Benno said with a grin to the copilot. "I've taken big birds into tighter places than this."

The copilot, who did not have Benno's varied and sometimes clandestine experience, could only look at the unused remaining length of runway with relief.

He had thought it much too short and had fully expected to be plowing off the end.

"Hey," Benno said as they taxied to their specially allocated place on the airfield, "don't look so worried. We're down in one piece, and with plenty of runway to spare. Ol' Frankie always comes up with the goods."

"Nice landing, Frankie," came Gant's voice on their headphones.

"Wha'd I tell you?" Benno said to his copilot, trying hard not to sound smug, and not succeeding.

The hard-eyed man had been waiting all afternoon. He had piloted in a small prop-driven Cessna 172 that bore French registration. He also carried a pilot's license that was French. The license was not his, and he was not French. He had spent most of his waiting time working on his aircraft. To those who bothered to ask, he explained that he was sorting out an electrical problem.

The man watched with no more apparent interest than other people present as the big Boeing taxied to its parking place. This was, he noted, well away from other aircraft. When it had stopped and the engines shut down, two men got out and positioned themselves at the front and rear of the airplane. Obviously guards, the man judged. Their stance said it all.

Almost on the heels of the first two, another pair of men left the aircraft to walk to the airfield buildings. The hard-eyed man decided they were the pilots, though they wore ordinary suits instead of civilian uniforms.

From where he had parked his own aircraft, the man could clearly see into the administration offices. One of the people from the Boeing was busy filling out a form while a third man looked on. The hard-eyed man had not seen him until that very moment. The attitude of the newcomer was one of authority, though the pilots were not deferential. Clearly then, he was with the local aviation authorities. As if to confirm this, the official took the completed form and disappeared.

No one else left the Boeing.

The hard-eyed man continued to work on his Cessna.

Cannes airport. 1845 hours.

The man lay on his stomach, less than thirty meters from the Boeing. No one had seen him make his slow and quiet approach when darkness had fallen. As if wanting to maintain as low a profile as possible, the 707 was just a shadowy outline, which pleased the man immensely. He was close enough to hear the soft footsteps of the guard by the tail. Both guards were the same ones who had first come out of the aircraft, and the man felt their reflexes would have slowed down considerably. Boredom on duty had killed many a sentry.

The man continued to wait. The dark sweater and trousers he wore effectively blended with the night; and the soft, rubber-soled boots on his feet muted his footfalls while giving him excellent traction for a sudden sprint. He had an automatic with him, and though this had a silencer, he hoped he would not have to use it. Killing the guards was not something he intended to do.

He was not afraid of killing, far from it. But in this instance, it would be counterproductive. What had to be done must be done without detection. A killing would greatly displease those who had sent him on this mission.

Waiting caused him no problems. He was noted for his patience on such jobs. Once, he had been tasked to eliminate a very important man in a small country. His target had been guarded day and night. But he had waited for a whole week, burrowed in the vast grounds of his target's mansion. The killing had eventually been carried out, and instead of making good his escape, he had returned to his burrow for a further week while the entire country was scoured for the unknown assassin. By the time he was ready to leave, the government had fallen. This job was child's play by comparison. Among the weapons he now carried was a strange grenade launcher.

The hard-eyed man inched his way closer, then stopped. A light flared suddenly, starkly illuminating the features of one of the guards. The one by the tail lighted a cigarette, and its end glowed brightly as he drew strongly upon it. The flare of his lighter died.

"Jesus, Hagen," the other said in a harsh whisper. "How many times do I have to tell you not to smoke near the goddamn airplane?"

The guard called Hagen muttered something that was not particularly pleasant. He continued to smoke. Soon there was a low-voiced argument. The guards approached each other until they reached a wing. They stood beneath it and continued arguing.

Suddenly the man froze, flattening himself against the ground. A shaft of light had come from the Boeing as a door was opened and someone stood in the doorway.

"What the hell's going on out there?" the newcomer demanded.

"It's Hagen," the first voice said. "He's lit up."

"You and your smokes, Hagen," the one on the airplane said with some annoyance. "Someday a sniper will take a bead on your cigarette and blow your fucking head off."

Hagen was unrepentant. "Hasn't happened yet."

"It needs only one time, buddy. Now put that cigarette out or I'll have your ass."

"Yes, sir," Hagen said, though none too respectfully.

The light from the Boeing went out. The hardeyed man raised his head slowly to look. Hagen and his companion were dark shapes near the wing. They seemed to be arguing in whispers. It was the opportunity he wanted.

Spreading himself on the ground as if at a rifle range, he aimed the launcher at the tail of the 707 and fired. There was the barest sound, followed by a soft thump at the rear of the aircraft.

The whispered argument stopped suddenly.

"Did you hear something?" came Hagen's voice, edged with a sudden tension.

The man had reverted to lying still. He imagined the one called Hagen with gun drawn, peering about him.

"I heard nothing," came the other man's voice. "All that smoking has screwed up your senses."

"You leave my smoking out of this. I heard something, I tell you."

There was a long silence. Then: "Bullshit, Hagen. You're hearing things. Go back to the tail, and keep off the cigarettes."

Hagen moved off with angry steps.

The man continued to wait. It was another half hour before he decided to move, inching back slowly on his belly, then crawling, only rising to a crouch when he was a good distance from the aircraft. He made his way safely off the airfield. By the time he had gotten back to his small hotel on the Rue d'Antibes, he was dressed in a suit and looked as if he'd been out for a casual stroll.

What he had fired at the Boeing was a small cylinder five centimeters long and five centimeters in diameter. On making contact with the airframe, the cylinder's powerful magnets had attached to the metal. Out of its protruding end, a barometrically operated whip aerial no more than ten centimeters long would extend when the aircraft was airborne.

The object was not a bomb, but an extremely powerful transceiver.

Cannes airport. 1925 hours.

Three men were boarding the 707. They were followed by Hagen and the second guard. No one noticed the small cylinder attached to the tail.

The engines were started and the Boeing began to taxi toward the runway. Its engines roared as the throttles were pushed to takeoff thrust. The big airplane rushed down the lighted runway, a huge shadow that appeared to switch the airport lights on and off as it went. Then it was heaving itself into the air, taking less time, it seemed, than a smaller plane. Soon its navigation lights could no longer be seen.

Gant's 707 had headed south within the Marseilles flight information region, but along its western border with Barcelona FIR. The plan filed by Benno had indicated that on handover to Barcelona, the 707 would head southwest, ostensibly for Tangier, in Morocco. But that did not happen.

Instead of following his flight plan, Benno banked the aircraft left and descended, as he had been instructed by Gant. He would take the Boeing right down to five hundred feet, and his new heading would put him on a course that was southeast and over the open sea.

The copilot was staring at his altimeter as it wound rapidly downward, then compared it with the readout from one of the flight deck displays. The digits were madly counting down.

"You're taking this thing down to sea level at *night*?" he asked anxiously. He had to clear his throat to keep himself from squeaking.

"Not sea level. Five hundred feet."

"Five . . . five *hundred* feet!" His voice squeaked.

"Going below prying eyes. Five hundred feet is high."

"We might hit something!"

"Relax. I've taken Herk gunships down much lower at night, over jungle. Don't worry about it. We won't be staying down here long."

The gunships Benno had mentioned were two versions of the ubiquitous Lockheed C-130 Hercules. Designed as a four-engine turboprop transport, the C-130 had become one of the world's great aircraft. Benno had flown two of the gunship versions on special operations, the AC-130H and the AC-130A. The jungles he'd talked about were in Latin America. Had the copilot been aboard either of them, he would not have found five hundred feet over the Mediterranean so terrifying.

"How long have you been flying for Gant?" Benno now asked.

The copilot's eyes seemed to be staring far away. "Three . . . three months. Nothing like this, though. You know, campaign stuff with our regular first pilot."

Benno nodded. "I've done some of those."

"Why did you leave?"

"I didn't leave. I'm not permanent staff, if you see what I mean."

The copilot didn't see, but decided not to pursue it. It was the first time he'd raised the matter. Benno's private arrangements with Gant were none of his business. Even though Benno's style of flying scared him, he could not deny that the man in the left-hand seat was a pretty good pilot.

The copilot watched as the aircraft's heading changed once more.

"What about the flight plan we filed at Cannes?" he asked belatedly.

"Gant's got fixers to handle that. Don't worry about it. Come on, guy. When were you born? Yesterday?" Benno said. "Gant would not've had you on this baby tonight unless you'd been pretty well checked out. So why the worry?"

"Like I said . . . it's my first time. I'll be okay."

"Now you're talking."

The copilot was still feeling a bit queasy about the nighttime low flying, but he said nothing more about it.

Sensing the other's continuing unease, Benno said, "In case you're worried about our hitting anything, remember our little bag of tricks." He tapped at the collision avoidance display. "We've got a 360-degree coverage, and a thirty-mile range. Plenty of avoidance time."

The November detachment. 2030 hours.

Wing Commander Jason looked on as Hohendorf, Flacht, Selby, and McCann completed suiting up.

"Don't forget what I said at the briefing, gentlemen," he told them. "We're rather close to the shores of North Africa, and we all know what that means." He gave them a tight, vanishing smile that was more of a warning. "We wouldn't want to shoot down any strangers in the night, would we?"

"As if we would," McCann said. "Sir." He wanted to give his usual grin, but thought the better of it.

Jason's eyes fastened on him. "Just the drones, McCann. Just the drones. There's a good chap."

"Yes, sir."

Jason gave McCann the benefit of a neutral stare before saying, "Good luck, gentlemen. Let's maintain our performance so far. A lot of people would like to see us fail with this missile. Let's prove them wrong."

After Jason had gone, Selby turned to McCann. "One of these days, Elmer Lee."

"Hey. What'd I do?" McCann looked aggrieved.

"The Boss was making a serious point."

"Hell, I know that."

"You could have fooled me. Come on, let's put you in your cage."

As they walked out to their aircraft Hohendorf caught up with Selby.

"A nice clear night, for it," he began. "Our first 120-mile shot. Let's hope no one wanders into the area."

"You mean our chums south of here?"

"Yes. They like playing with the U.S. Navy."

"And get shot down for their pains."

"Exactly."

"I have a feeling the Boss wouldn't like it if we shot them down."

"And if they fire at us?"

Selby gave that some thought. "You've got the lead for tonight's mission, Axel," he then said. "I'll back any decision you take."

"Thanks, Mark," Hohendorf said, and walked on to his own aircraft.

As he began his preflight check of his ASV Selby remembered the thoroughness of the briefing. The two target drones would be flying at different altitudes, and the first Tornado to detect any of the two would launch a missile. Their own reaction times, as well as the performance of the missile, were equally on trial.

He had no worries about friendly aircraft blundering into the area designated for the shoot. The danger area would be on flight information notices, and flight plans for the period had also been checked. Nothing was going to be closer than two hundred miles, well out of range.

He completed his checks and climbed into the front cockpit. Already ensconced in the back pocket, McCann had warmed up his equipment and was going through yet another series of checks. No one was going to leave anything to chance.

"Are we in business?" Selby asked, after securing his mask.

"We're in," came McCann's voice on the 'phones. "Let's roll."

Selby started the engines and turned on the FLIR head-up display. The HUD painted its infrared picture upon the dark world outside the ASV. The time was 2050 hours.

* * *

In the 707's luxurious master study, Gant was saying to Belov, "We won't be going to Tangier, Alexei."

"No?" The people's deputy was mildly surprised.

"No. For some time, we've had the feeling you've been followed. Now don't look so alarmed. It's all right. We can handle it. We've planned for such a scenario. Back at Cannes, we filed a flight plan, openly, for Tangier. Except, of course, we're a long way from there right now."

"But won't that be noticed by the authorities?"

"Not if a 707 is on its way there."

"But you said . . ."

Gant smiled. "I said *a* 707. Not ours. A shadow aircraft is making our flight. Some, er, friends have taken on the special flight for me. When we went off the radar, they came on at the same time. To anyone who's interested, we're still on the way to Tangier."

"You have friends who can do this?"

"I told you we could handle it," Gant replied with some satisfaction. "We're heading for one of the Greek islands. The guys in the conference cabin are going over all the stuff you've given us, and when we get to our destination, we'll be meeting with one more person, then we'll be into some serious talking."

"My country is running out of time," Belov said, somewhat sadly. "I hope we can do something."

"We can," Gant assured him.

Gant did not say that the man waiting at their destination was another disaffected people's deputy. Gant liked to hedge his bets. For all he knew, Belov's sincerity and his apparent friendship could not be taken at face value.

The stakes he was playing for were too high, Gant had long decided. Two trumps were always better than one, especially if you didn't know whether the other guy could trump your first.

Very few people knew of the second deputy, whose information was even hotter than Belov's.

Washington, Gant thought. Here I come.

He smiled comfortingly at Belov.

In the special control center that had been constructed for him, newly promoted Major Ivan Vannis stared at one of his monitors. He was feeling very pleased with himself. Everything was working smoothly. The traces on the monitor had come via the air defense main computer, which had itself been fed the information by the already positioned satellite. The defense computer had then enhanced the traces.

"They were very clever," he now said to his companions, "but our little unit is telling us exactly which one is of interest. We can safely ignore the decoy."

The general and Stolybin were the only other people in the room.

"You are quite certain the correct aircraft was tagged?" the general asked Stolybin.

"Positive, Comrade General," Stolybin replied. He did not take offense.

"Good. Good. And you, Major, your work is that of genius."

Vannis almost puffed out his chest. "Thank you, Comrade General."

"Thank me when it is all over."

"Yes, Comrade General." Vannis knew it was much too soon to start feeling euphoric. A lot could still go wrong.

The general's wrath in such an eventuality did not bear thinking about.

They had not yet picked up the fighters, though the Alpha-class submarine, on station at temporary periscope depth, had acoustically recorded their take-off. It was obvious those particular aircraft had stealthy properties and would probably not even register before missile release betrayed the presence of the weapons.

This would give him less reaction time, but he was smart enough not to mention that little fact to the general. It would not have been appreciated.

His hope lay in the recognition code he had programmed into the small unit at the base of the 707's tail. Once he had burned through the missile's own code recognition program, all he would then have to do would be to get it to recognize the new code. It would then home inexorably on the Boeing. In theory. The speed of the missile and his being able to catch it at launch would determine how much time he actually had.

He hoped his anxieties were not evident to the hawklike scrutiny of his superior officers.

He kept his own eyes fixed upon the traces of the two 707s. The one going east was heading farther and farther away from the decoy aircraft, which was maintaining a much slower cruising speed, broadcasting its presence to all and sundry.

He concentrated on the eastbound Boeing.

You've got a surprise coming, he said to it in his mind.

Its altitude was given as 152 meters.

In the Boeing, the copilot found his attention constantly drawn to both the analog and digital altimeters. They both gave him the information he did not want: five hundred feet. For how long was Benno going to hold that altitude? This was not some gunship skimming the treetops of some hellish jungle in a dead-end part of the world. Besides, it wasn't exactly a smooth ride.

I'm five hundred feet above the sea at night, for

Chrissake, he worried. What am I *doing* here? This is an airliner, not a goddammed low-level bomber.

He glanced at Benno, whose hands in the subdued flight deck lighting appeared to be barely touching the controls.

Ex–military pilots never seemed to know when to quit thinking they were flying hot jets, the copilot mused anxiously. He had once flown with an ex–fighter pilot for a charter company. The pilot, ex–F-15, used to make approaches that looked fancy, but scared the shit out of the passengers. It wasn't long before he'd scared the hell out of the charter company, too. The last he'd heard, the pilot was flying jets for some third-world air force and getting all the scary flying he wanted.

That's not for me, the copilot thought, wondering about Benno.

He glanced once more at the left-hand seat. Benno was looking at him.

"Not much longer," Benno said.

The copilot did not feel convinced. He checked their heading as Benno made a slight alteration of course. North Africa seemed to be getting too close, this end of the Mediterranean.

"Do I get to know our destination?" he said, at last asking the question he had long wanted to. "It's not as if I'm going to get out and tell somebody."

Benno gave him a brief glance. "You worry a lot. You know that? What's bugging you? Do you think those bozos out there to our right might get it into their heads to send a bunch of fighters over? Hell, we're two hundred miles from the nearest coast."

"They're always messing with the navy—"

"And getting reamed for their pains."

"So who knows what they might do? What's two hundred miles to a jet fighter? Maybe fifteen, twenty minutes if they're just stooging around. A lot less if they're somewhere out there already."

"Relax, will you?" Benno said. "We're not on any-body's radar, and just to dump another worry you may have, we're not going far enough east to enter the Gaz."

The "Gaz" was Benno's word for the Gulf avoidance zone, an area that was being shunned by many civilian operators. The western boundary of the zone went south from Cyprus to Aden.

"We're going to Greece," Benno continued, after a quick scan of his instruments. "Well out of danger. Okay?"

"I guess."

"That's what I call a real positive answer," Benno said dryly.

"Well, Elmer Lee?" Selby began. "Anything for me?"

McCann gave one of his exaggerated sighs. "You pilots kill me. I'll let you know, Mr. Impatient. We'll get there before Eagle Two."

Eagle Two, Hohendorf's Tornado, had gone low, almost skimming the dark surface of the sea. It was something at which he excelled, and during his Marine-flieger days, when the Baltic was his stomping ground, it was something only the most hardened of backseat-ers could take with equanimity.

Selby knew this, and did not relish the thought that out there, low in the darkness, Hohendorf might find the first target before him. He also knew that McCann was well aware of the unspoken challenge. That had been the true meaning behind McCann's words. He looked out through the HUD upon his infra-red world and curbed his impatience.

In the back, McCann checked all his systems yet again. Everything was on-line, and nothing was on the radar, except Eagle Two ten miles away beyond their left wing.

"All riiiiight!" he said with sudden excitement.

"Don't keep it all to yourself," came from Selby. "What have you got?"

McCann had identified the trace that had suddenly appeared on one of the multifunction displays, which now showed an image of the first drone, complete with bearing, speed, and altitude.

"We're in business, ol' buddy," he now said to Selby. "We've got our drone. One thousand feet, six hundred knots . . . boy, they've given us a fast one here . . . bearing one-one-two. Range 160 miles. Hey, my box of tricks is working well tonight."

Selby banked hard right to come onto the drone's course. He felt very pleased with McCann. The backseat wizard had done it again. The range of 160 miles was virtually at the performance limits of the ASV's radar in track-while-scan mode, but McCann had managed to squeeze a little extra out of it to enable them to acquire the target before Hohendorf. Hohendorf's position down on the deck may have cut a few miles off the range of his own scanning radar. It could mean that Flacht, in the backseat, had not engaged look-up mode, or that they were simply not pointing in the right direction.

That state of affairs would not last for long. Eagle Two would soon acquire. Selby knew his slight advantage was being eroded by the second.

"Good job, Elmer Lee," he now said to McCann. "Let's not lose it."

"Leave it to ol' Elmer," McCann said with satisfaction. "That's one drone for the deep six."

"The deep six? What's this? Joined the navy, have we?"

"We're over the sea, aren't we? 'We're in the navy now. . . .' "

"Oh no, Elmer Lee," Selby pleaded. "No singing. Please. Just don't lose that drone."

"Who? Me?" McCann put an extra edge of injured pride into his voice. "I've got this baby solidly hooked."

12

Hohendorf, still at low level, said to Flacht, "How are we doing, Wolfie?"

Flacht, in the act of making a brief sweep of the radar in look-up mode, had caught the sudden change of course by Selby and McCann in Eagle Three; but he missed the drone.

"Eagle Three has just altered course," he said urgently. "They may have something. Let's follow. Go left, one-seven-five. Give them time to settle down, then we'll correct."

Hohendorf was already banking hard into the turn. "Shall I climb?"

"No. Stay down. We'll sneak in behind them, then run on ahead. Now go left, one-zero-zero. That puts them a little off our nose, but hold it there. Whatever they've seen, we'll get it soon. Let's have more speed."

Hohendorf pushed the throttles forward, but did not go into afterburners. No point in lighting up the night. Ten miles was no distance on such a clear night, and Eagle Three might be keeping a good lookout.

The Tornado leaped forward eagerly, gaining swiftly upon Eagle Three high above.

"We have the drone!" Flacht announced after a few moments. "Range 140 miles and closing."

"Scheiss!" Hohendorf said with feeling.

Flacht knew exactly what was going on in the other's mind. It was obvious Selby and McCann had made the first acquisition. But all was not lost.

"Go into 'burner,' he suggested to Hohendorf. "It doesn't matter if they see us now. Getting into missile range first is what matters."

He felt the barest of double thuds as Hohendorf complied without questioning his advice, and the ASV accelerated with renewed vigor. The drone's speed was just over six hundred knots, but as the Tornado's own speed began to build impressively it was as if they were reeling in the distant target.

Selby and McCann, he knew, would soon realize what was going on.

"Oh no, you don't," McCann said. "Gimme some speed, my man," he added to Selby. "Eagle Two have come around to our heading, almost, and have cranked up. They must have acquired."

"You don't have to tell me twice," Selby said, slamming the throttles forward.

Eagle Three hurled itself into the night. It was now a race to get into missile range.

"Have you found those fighters?" the general asked Vannis, a touch of impatience in his voice.

Vannis tried to reason without sounding insubordinate. "Not yet, Comrade General. It will be difficult. Our best chance is to wait for the missile launch. They won't have stealth capabilities"—*I hope*, he didn't add—"and the flare of their exhausts should also help us."

"Will that give you sufficient time for the interception?"

"Yes, Comrade General."

Vannis dared not voice his uncertainties and glanced at Stolybin for moral support.

Stolybin's eyes were cold.

And so, he thought philosophically, I am really on my own.

He had not expected otherwise, but had cherished the slight hope nonetheless, if only in recognition of what he had so far accomplished. As it now appeared, failure would bring swift retribution.

He was determined not to fail.

"In range!" McCann announced as 130 miles to target was passed. "We have lock-on. Patching it over to you."

One of the multifunction displays in the front cockpit now had a repeat of the tactical situation, and Selby switched the head-up display to air-to-air. The targeting box immediately appeared within the infrared window of the HUD.

"I'm slaving it to the helmet sight," he told McCann. As he did so the glowing green targeting box now also appeared upon the gloom of the night when he looked away from the HUD, with the indicator arrow showing him where to look when the box was out of vision.

"I think they've given us one of those agile drones," McCann said. "The guys controlling it will also try to jam the missile when the drone's systems pick it up."

"Then we'll just have to make sure they don't succeed."

On the sea below, a guided missile frigate from one of the NATO nations was responsible for the launch of the target drones. Aboard was a launch team from the November Project, with instructor pilots to fly the drones by remote control from a specially set up control center.

On the bridge of the frigate, the officer of the watch scanned the darkness with night-vision binoculars. No drone, or the attacking fighters, could be seen. The night seemed empty.

The officer of the watch continued his search of the night. There were also sailors on deck, with their own binoculars and wearing helmets with built-in radios, who would communicate with the bridge if they sighted anything airborne or seaborne.

The sailors saw nothing.

Selby had the drone firmly in the box. Though nothing could be seen within the pulsing rectangle, the lock-on cue told him that a launch now would score a hit. This effectively meant destruction of the target.

The missile was drooling, and the box solidified into a bright red etching upon the night. The single tone came on.

Selby pressed the release button on the Tornado's control stick.

"Missile launched!" he exclaimed.

The bright fire of the Skyray's motor pinned the ASV in a glare that made the launch aircraft appear to hang in midair, a predator of the night startled into sudden immobility. Then the glare rapidly faded as the missile streaked away.

"Jeez!" McCann said in awe. "Will you watch that thing go! Oh shit," he added.

"What? What's happened?"

"Eagle Two has launched at our bird. Goddammit."

Selby was unperturbed. "We were there first. They'll be eating scraps."

"Hey!" McCann sounded puzzled.

"What now, Elmer Lee?" Selby asked with a familiar, long-suffering tone of voice.

But McCann was staring in some confusion at the missile attack display. For the briefest of instants, the screen had blinked, and equally briefly, the targeting box had disappeared. He frowned at the screen, wondering what had happened. The symbology was back, but the blink should not have occurred. He always checked his equipment, and there had been nothing wrong with the systems at missile launch. He was absolutely sure of it. Further, he was certain the targeting box was now in the wrong place.

"That's one hell of an agile drone they've sent us," he remarked to Selby, "or they've launched the second one and the missile's switched to it. What a time for the thing to go wrong." He sounded disappointed. "Has your box moved?"

Selby had already checked his own MFD, the HUD, and the helmet sight. The boxes had moved. He didn't like it. Perhaps the second drone had been launched as McCann had said, or the original drone was supremely agile and its operators had taken evasive action, just in case, despite the fact that the drone's own sensors would not yet have picked up the Skyray. Even so . . .

"Check that Eagle Two is well out of the way," he said to McCann.

"I already have. They're safe."

"Let's be thankful for small mercies. So what have we got? A very agile drone? Or the second one?"

"Even if it is a second one, the missile should not have switched. Dammit. After all the work we've done. Everything checked out 100 percent so far."

"Just goes to show there's always something waiting 'round the corner to catch you out. Let's keep monitoring and recording. The Boss is going to love this."

"Tell me about it," McCann said gloomily.

He began to worry. What had happened? Had it been his fault? Had he perhaps pressed something inadvertently and redirected the missile?

He couldn't see how that could have happened. Wasn't he the wizard of the backseat? Everyone knew how meticulous he was with his systems.

But how to explain the strange behavior of the missile?

He made a decision. Only seconds had passed since launch, but the missile was accelerating to Mach 6 plus. McCann knew from the earlier trials that impact would occur less than 1.55 minutes from now.

"I don't feel right about this," he said to Selby. "We should abort. I know it should do that anyway if it's got the wrong target in its sights. But it hasn't, man."

Selby registered the serious edge to McCann's voice and decided it was right to play safe.

"All right, Elmer Lee. Do it." Hohendorf would get the score, after all. "I'll warn Eagle Two that we've got a rogue."

McCann uncaged the missile destruct button on his left-hand console and pressed.

Nothing happened. The missile was still locked on target.

"It's not responding!"

"What? Try again."

McCann pressed a second time, and continued pressing. The missile flew on inexorably.

"Jesus," he said softly.

* * *

The general was looking on, a satisfied expression upon his face.

When the first missile launch had come on the monitors, Vannis had attacked the keyboards of his computers with a blur of fingers. He had also turned on the graphic display of the soccer player, which, as on previous occasions, had been intercepted by a second, who now ran with the ball toward a second set of goal-posts.

Then the second missile had been launched.

Again, Vannis's fingers had done their magic, though a thin film of sweat had appeared on his drawn cheeks. The launching of the second missile had given him a sickly pallor. He had not expected *two* of them. Though he could have left the second weapon to its legitimate target, this would only have registered as a 50-percent failure for the missile. The West would have been reluctant to scrap it under such conditions. Both missiles failing would prove conclusive.

There was also the general.

Vannis heaved a loud sigh of relief as a third player appeared with a ball and was intercepted by a fourth. Now the two interlopers were running toward the second set of goalposts.

The general slapped his thigh and grinned hugely. "Good work, Major. Very good work! What will happen when they strike our target?"

"The computer will give us a flare to show its destruction." Vannis had to work hard to stop a tremor in his voice. The general frightened him even more with that grin.

He glanced furtively at Stolybin. There was no expression at all on the colonel's face.

Vannis suppressed a shiver as he watched the players run unerringly toward the goal. On another monitor, the missile traces stalked the unsuspecting Boeing.

"About time," the copilot said with relief as Benno began a gentle climb. "For a while there, I thought you wanted to turn us into a"—he paused, astonished—"ship. A ship! *A ship!* Dead ahead! Lights on the water! Pull up, for Christ's sake!"

Benno had seen the lights and was pulling firmly. The Boeing reared, nose high, striving for altitude. In the cabins, people tumbled off their seats. Drinks went flying, coffee spilled onto expensive upholstery. Anyone standing at the time fell heavily, to be pinned to the floor by the sudden force of gravity.

"What if . . . what if that's a missile boat out there from . . . from—" The copilot stopped, not daring to say what he was clearly thinking.

Benno said nothing. On the flight deck speakers, Gant's startled voice demanded to know what was going on. Benno ignored that, too.

The frigate's radar operators had picked up the low-flying trace and were a bit slow to react, perhaps because nothing was expected in the area. However, they still acted with reasonable speed. They warned the officer of the watch, who in turn alerted the captain.

On the deck, the lookouts could not believe their eyes as the huge aircraft suddenly filled their binoculars. Where had it come from? And why was it so low? Was it hostile? You never knew these days.

Although the ship was put on alert, no one was going to launch a missile. Everybody remembered the Airbus incident in the Gulf.

They ducked involuntarily as the aircraft swept over.

* * *

McCann was still trying to abort the missile—and failing. He had informed base by secure data link of the problem, and of his attempts to destroy the Skyray. But now a new radar echo had appeared, just within range of the ASV's track-while-scan mode. Its bearing corresponded with that of the target the missile had chosen.

"Hey, Mark," he began. "I've got a new echo here, bigger than the drone, and it's giving me a creepy feeling. Where in hell did that come from? Nothing like that is supposed to be in this area."

"What are you saying?" Selby asked tensely.

"I'm saying I've got an echo that shouldn't be there, man . . . and our missile's locked onto it. It's way bigger than the drone, but the missile seems to think it's the target."

Selby was shocked into silence.

"You're hearing me, man?" McCann was saying. "We've got some serious shit here. I don't know where that thing's come from, but it's no goddamn drone."

Selby's voice was calm when he spoke. "Let me try my destruct button again." He had tried his duplicate missile abort button, but that hadn't worked either. He was equally unsuccessful as he tried once more. "Both buttons together," he continued urgently. "Now!"

But as before, their combined efforts had no effect. The missile was a runaway.

McCann stared at the time-to-impact readout: 0.0.20.35, it said.

"Twenty-point-three-five seconds of missile flight time left," he announced, his voice full of horror. "We can't do anything to help whoever's out there." His eyes widened in shock as he looked at the attack display. Another track was speeding toward the same target. "What the hell?"

"We've got an abort?" Selby put in hopefully.

"No such luck. If this kit is working properly, I

think Eagle Two's missile is locked onto our target. I've also got identification. You won't believe this. It's a Boeing 707!"

"What? Are you sure?"

"What do you think, I'm making jokes here?"

Aboard the frigate, the deck crew stared in morbid fascination as twin streaks of light followed in the wake of the aircraft that had passed over the ship. Stoically, they waited for the inevitable.

Hohendorf's voice was studiously calm on the radio as he spoke to Selby and McCann. "We have a runaway, and it is locked on the same target. This is not good."

They could imagine both him and Flacht desperately trying to abort their own missile, though the controlled timbre of Hohendorf's voice did not betray this.

As the moments ticked away Hohendorf finally gave in to his sense of frustration and despair.

"Ah scheiss!" came clearly on their headphones.

On the Boeing, the copilot was watching the collision avoidance display. A great terror took hold of him when he saw the double trace gaining rapidly upon them.

"Look!" he shouted at Benno. "It was a missile boat! They've alerted the fighters! Oh my *God*. They think we're a bomber!"

Benno glanced at the display and instantly knew the traces for what they were. No fighters currently flying could move as swiftly. His air-force training took over and he instinctively began to take avoiding action, intending to go into a ninety-degree turn in an attempt to foil what he was certain were missiles.

Though the refurbished 707 was more powerful than its sister aircraft and handled more crisply, it was not a fighter. Benno's fighter-pilot reaction to the threat, heaving the 707 onto its left wingtip, was like trying to get a motorcycle-style response from a truck with a trailer in tow. Though if anyone from the outside had been able to see it, the Boeing's antics would have seemed spectacular, to missiles of the caliber of the Skyray, it might as well not have bothered.

It began its turn, but was painfully slow in doing so.

Benno, knowing all was lost, barely had time to say softly, "Sweet Jesus . . ."

The copilot opened his mouth to scream, a sudden, raging anger in his eyes as he looked at Benno.

The scream was stillborn as the 707 detonated in a vivid double explosion that flared like a sunburst in the night. A third explosion, as fuel tanks were consumed, scattered its remains over a vast area of sea. Blazing pieces, like so many Roman candles, appeared to flutter down in slow motion in the darkness, to extinguish themselves in the water.

Soon there was nothing left in the gloom of the Mediterranean night to show that an aircraft had died within it.

The sudden, red-gold blast of light had painted the frigate like a still life upon the black surface of the sea. As the Boeing expired in what seemed like a monstrous shower of shooting stars, the crew of the ship stood openmouthed.

Then the captain ordered a search for survivors.

In the two distant Tornadoes, the Selby and Hohendorf's crews saw the merging of the radar traces and the subsequent flaring on their display screens and felt a great horror descent upon them. They informed base of the outcome and headed back.

From the backseat of Eagle Three, McCann said bitterly, "Target down."

The general and Stolybin were slapping each other on the back and laughing. Vannis stared at his monitors, hardly daring to allow the enormity of what he had just done to sink in. He did not see Stolybin's eyes fasten upon him speculatively.

The general stopped congratulating Stolybin and turned to Vannis. "Major, you have just done the Motherland a great service. It will never be forgotten. From now on, your career is on the rise. You are a man of utmost value. I want you to shut everything down and wipe all your disks clean. This means both hard and floppy disks. Nothing must remain in memory. Do I make myself clear?"

"Yes, Comrade General." Vannis did not question the order.

"Good. Now I must talk with the colonel. You carry on here."

Vannis watched them go. Then he sat down slowly and touched the computer keyboards one by one. From here, he had killed an airliner over the Mediterranean and, in so doing, had secured a successful career for himself. The general had said so.

He wondered if he could trust the general.

"When all trace of what we've got in that room has been removed," the general was saying to Stolybin in his opulent office, "kill him."

Stolybin's eyes were fixed upon his superior. "Do you mean the major, Comrade General?"

"I was not aware my words were ambiguous."

"I want to be quite certain I've got the right person."

The general's feral eyes did not blink. "I do mean

Major Vannis. I also expect you to tidy up any loose ends. I'm certain you understand me."

Stolybin understood only too well. When studying the file of the general's earlier operation to stop development of the British missile in 1965, he had come across one of the general's "loose ends."

A fisherman from Malta had talked about seeing the destruction of the air-force plane. Sometime later, the fisherman had met with an accident at sea. A sudden wave, submarine-shaped, had silenced him for good.

This time, the loose ends were different. No one from outside the Union needed to be silenced. So far. Killing James West would be counterproductive, as the subsequent investigation into his death might well unearth information that could jeopardize the current operation. James West was best left to the merciless gnawings of conscience.

"I understand," he now said to the general.

Too bad about Vannis.

"First," the general was saying, "we must ensure that the foreign press knows about that downed airliner immediately. Our NATO friends might try to hush it up. We must help them to come clean." He gave one of his rare, but totally malevolent grins. "The story must not originate from the Motherland . . . obviously. America, I think. Mmm?"

"I'll see to it."

The general nodded with satisfaction. "I'm very pleased with you, Sergei. It was well worth getting you back into circulation. Things are beginning to move at last out there. The republics are being sorted out. Good news, eh?"

"Certainly looks like it."

"It's only the beginning," the general said ominously.

* * *

A grim-faced Jason was waiting on the flight line as the two aircraft taxied to their parking spaces, well away from the quiet civilian section of the airfield.

From their cockpits, the four airmen saw the lone figure, silhouetted by the detachment working lights as the Tornadoes were marshaled to a stop. By the stillness of his pose, they knew this was no welcoming reception. They shut down the aircraft systems, then climbed out slowly. The ground crew, who normally greeted their return with bantering, were uncharacteristically mute.

The funeral had already started. Quite probably, not only the 707 and all in it had died out there above the dark sea, but several careers, and even the November program itself.

Understanding full well the catastrophe that had been wrought, they walked silently toward the waiting form of their commander. They felt doubly distressed because they also knew what the demise of his idea for a fully integrated defense system for Europe would do to him. At their hands, his dream may well have died.

They stopped before him, helmets in their hands, and waited for condemnation, anger, and frustration to rain upon them. None of these was forthcoming.

He looked at each in turn, lights and shadows playing upon the face beneath his peaked cap, his probing eyes barely visible beneath its own mantle of darkness.

"Gentlemen," he said quietly. Yet the unhurried voice carried above the background noise of the aircraft maintenance crew.

He turned and began walking back to the refurbished World War II building that served both as detachment offices and home. They followed him silently.

The building was large enough to provide comfortable mess accommodations, with a separate area to house the operational section. He led them through corridors to the debriefing room, still in their full kit. People passing by stared sympathetically, but said nothing.

Jason did not speak until they were all in the briefing room and the doors shut. He removed his cap slowly, wiped his forehead with the back of his hand while still holding on to it, then placed it carefully upon a plexiglas-covered chart table.

"I don't know what happened out there," he began. "I do know the kind of crews you are, and I can see by your faces the kind of hell you're going through. There will be no recriminations from me. However, the shit is beginning to hit the fan. If we are to find out exactly how this appalling tragedy occurred, *everything,* no matter how apparently insignificant, must be set down in the reports I expect from each of you.

"Every monitoring and recording system on both aircraft will be checked, and their details analyzed. Everything we've recorded on the ground, and those of the frigate responsible for the launching of the drones, will be collated and studied minutely. All will be put together to give as comprehensive a picture of what really happened tonight as is humanly possible."

Jason paused, eyes not rejecting them as they had feared.

"They will be after our necks, gentlemen," he went on. "The Court of Inquiry will be our first hurdle. Depending upon its findings, screams for courts-martial may well be heard, then for dismissals from service, and eventually, the end of the November Project." Then a fire came into the eyes. "That, however, is not how I intend to finish. Our best defense is to believe in ourselves, to give every detail on the incident, to hold nothing back . . . to fight those who, for their own dubious reasons, would like to close us down. I will not give them the satisfaction and I shall use every wile at my command to ensure that they do not succeed. I happen to believe that what we're doing is the future of NATO-evolved defense.

"Now, gentlemen . . . some people will probably say I should ground you all after what has happened, until the results of the Court of Inquiry, or courts-martial, are known. I will not ground you, because I do not believe what has taken place is your fault. I may well be accused of blind faith. Perhaps so . . . but I would be a poor commander if I did not believe in the very personnel I have myself chosen. Again, this may lead to a further accusation that I cannot accept that I may have been wrong in my choices of people. I am prepared to meet that one head-on.

"Not unexpectedly, we shall be returning to November One tomorrow. This detachment has ceased forthwith. After you have unkitted, I expect you to compile your first reports of the incident. There will be others, but I want your impressions while it is still sharp in your minds. Very well, gentlemen. That is all."

He picked up his cap and let himself out of the briefing room.

Los Angeles, California. 2310 hours, Pacific Standard Time.

The night editor of a respected newspaper answered a telephone call that had been transferred to her.

"This had better be good," she said, irritated by the interruption.

"You judge," the unknown caller retorted. "Check a story that NATO fighters have just shot down a civilian 707 over the Mediterranean tonight."

"What? Who is this! How do you—"

"Check it, or miss a scoop." The line went dead.

The editor replaced the receiver with a slow, steady hand, then replayed the message on the machine that automatically recorded all calls. She listened to it three times before summoning a male colleague.

"Check this out, Larry," she said, then played the call for a fourth time.

He said nothing for a while.

"Well?" she asked.

"If we ignore it," he said at last, "and it's a true story, we've missed out on a major scoop. News will get around that we got it first and did nothing. People will think twice about giving us anything once that gets out. We'll look like dorks."

"Not so good."

"If this is some hoax and we do act on it . . ."

"Big egg-on-face time. We'll look like dorks."

"Yeah. I'd hate to be an editor."

"Larry, if some civilian jet has just been blown out of the sky by NATO fighters, I want in on it. I can't let this go."

"Just remember other young, ambitious editors have been burned on things like this. We won't mention names."

"I know, I know." The editor paused for thought, then scribbled swiftly on some notepaper. "How about this?"

The man called Larry leaned over to study what she had written.

" 'Did NATO fighters down an airliner over the Mediterranean Sea last night?' " he read aloud. " ' 'At eleven-ten P.M. the offices of this newspaper received a strange call.' " He stopped, then said to her with some approval, "Playing it both ways. You're not saying we

accept the story, only that we received it. So whichever
way it goes, we're smelling sweet."

"I wouldn't have put that last part quite like that,
Larry, but yes, it's the general picture. Do we run with
it?"

"I'd say yes. But you know where the buck stops."

"Thanks for reminding me."

She decided to print.

The man who had made the call had spoken without the slightest trace of a foreign accent.

Moscow. 1130 hours, the next day.

Stolybin sat at his desk pondering upon the fact
that by now the story would have been leaked to the
American newspaper. An unknown editor would be
wrestling with a decision to print. The time over there
was not yet one o'clock in the morning, but the decision
would have to be made soon.

He had not liked the idea of the early leak. His
preferred method would have been to let matters take
their course. Let the bodies be washed up on diverse
beaches and fishermen find bits of wreckage either
floating or tangled in their nets. *Then* would have been
the time to plant the story. It would have looked more
convincing, as if someone had done some investigating.
The current way, in his opinion, was too risky.

But the general wanted speed.

Stolybin thought of his insurance policy. Secreted
in the apartment of a foreigner, who was unaware he'd
been burgled, were tiny tapes he'd made of his dealings
with the general, his own reports of the details of the
operation, and actual conversations with the general
himself. The latest included the general's order con-
cerning Major Vannis.

Tokareva did not know of the hidden tapes. Stolybin would not have dreamed of taking her into his con-

fidence. In such matters, survival was all. What she didn't know about, they couldn't get out of her later.

If things did come apart, he was determined to ensure that the general would not be giving orders to someone else to terminate him like the unfortunate Major Vannis.

He intended to be no one's scapegoat.

13

By the time the detachment had returned to a som-
ber November One and the first court of inquiry con-
vened a day later, the news had spread internationally.
The headlines of the national tabloids were variations
on a theme.

NATO FIGHTERS BLAST CIVIL JET! they screamed.

The more serious papers were less shrill but not
less accusing. ACCIDENT? OR INCOMPETENCE? one inquired. Its defense correspondent went on to suggest
possible explanations, none of which bore much resemblance to what had actually occurred. The correspondent even wrongly identified the fighters as Tomcats,
which did not please the U.S. Navy.

No one mentioned the identity of the passengers
on the stricken jet. That bombshell had yet to be disclosed. The 707 was variously described as a 747, a
DC-10, an Airbus, and a Tristar. Only on the international scene was the correct description given, beginning with the Los Angeles newspaper that first broke
the story. But the correction would come soon enough,
and with it, the identities of the victims.

The Court of Inquiry, after due deliberation of the
known facts, did not blame the crew of the two fighters,

but it did not exonerate them either. More courts were promised.

Within four days, the identities of the victims were at last known, and Jason found himself facing a group of hostile people in a Whitehall chamber. His inquisitors were made up of members of Parliament, senior service chiefs, and the minister. There were other neutral-looking people who took no part in the proceedings, but who surveyed him with keen eyes. There was also a senior American air-force general.

Air Vice Marshal Thurson was present, sitting to one side, giving silent moral support. He had backed Jason's line from the beginning.

The only other person in the room whom Jason could conceivably consider less hostile was a face he recognized.

"Do you remember me, lad?" the broad tones of the MP queried.

"I do, Mr. Beresford," Jason replied. "You visited us when . . . er . . . when we lost Flying Officer Palmer."

"We do seem to meet under unfortunate circumstances."

"Yes, sir."

"And this one is particularly unfortunate. As we now know, a United States congressman *and* a Soviet people's deputy were on that plane your men shot down."

"With respect, Mr. Beresford—"

"I'm not finished, lad," Beresford, who prided himself on being a man of the people, cut in mildly. The words, however, had the force of a slap across the face.

Jason held on to his sense of outrage and shut his mouth. The countenances facing him seemed universally unforgiving.

"As I was saying," Beresford continued, "a congressman and a deputy were on that plane, on a mission of peace. Do you have any idea, Wing Commander, of the heat this is generating in both Moscow and Washington? They want your head, and those of your pilots, and I don't mind telling you there are many in this country who want your expensive little operation closed down. I shouldn't be at all surprised if the same is being said by our European partners." Beresford paused, waiting to hear what Jason would say.

They all waited.

Firmly controlling the anger he felt at the over-whelming self-interest he felt behind the masks of these apparent seekers after the truth, he coldly made up his mind to speak calmly.

"Several weeks before deploying the detachment," he began, "every precaution was taken to ensure our intended operating area would be free of other aircraft for at least two hundred miles—322 kilometers—well outside the range of any air-to-air missile anyone possesses."

"Excuse me, Wing Commander," another MP, not of Beresford's party, interrupted. "But can't a missile continue beyond even its extreme range?"

"Not unless it can refuel," Jason said, poker-faced.

"Hmm," the MP said, clearly not certain whether he had been put in his place.

Others looked at Jason suspiciously.

"If I may continue, gentlemen," he said politely. When the minister had nodded barely perceptibly, he went on: "The area was, in effect, made an exclusion zone. Any current airchart will show the designated danger area, with altitude limitations. In this particular case and in the interests of safety, the danger area was given an unlimited designation. This means from sea level upward, well beyond the service ceiling of any civilian aircraft.

"Even at the risk of letting potential enemies know something special was taking place—they read the same international charts, after all—special NOTAMS were issued—"

"NOTAMS?" another MP asked.

"Notices to airmen."

"Ah. I see. Please continue."

"The measure of our success in clearing the area," Jason said, "may be judged by the fact that with the single exception of the Boeing 707, no other aircraft strayed within the area. I have no idea whether you gentlemen can guess at the number of aircraft traversing the skies above the Mediterranean at any given moment, but I assure you that airspace is busy. Yet, not one of those aircraft entered the danger area."

"Are you saying, Wing Commander," a third member of Parliament intervened, "that the 707 breached airways rules?"

Jason looked at them all. "I was of the impression that this was already known. My own inquiries lead me to believe that Congressman Gant filed a flight plan that was deliberately misleading."

"Who told you?" the minister demanded.

The air vice marshal spoke. "I did, Minister. I made some inquiries which yielded information the Wing Commander requested."

"Are air vice marshals in the habit of running errands for wing commanders?"

Thurson was not intimidated. "When I see one of the best officers of the service being pilloried before all the facts are known, I consider it my duty as his superior officer to secure such information as is needed to get at the truth. Congressman Gant did file a bogus flight plan. A shadow aircraft flew the documented plan." Thurson glanced at the American general. "Per-

haps General Bowmaker can tell us who supplied that
second aircraft."

Before the air-force general could reply, the minister cut in smoothly. "We are not here to inquire into
the general's knowledge of flights by other, similar aircraft, even assuming he did have such information.
Please continue, Wing Commander."

"Congressman Gant's flight plan led the traffic
control authorities to believe he was heading southwest," Jason said in his deliberately calm voice, "while
he actually went east. I cannot believe his pilots did not
study the charts for the area, which leads me to con-
clude they deliberately ignored the warnings that were
clearly indicated in—"

"That's speculation, Commander," General Bowmaker put in. "We cannot confirm this."

"Granted, sir." Jason looked at the American officer's silver wings. "You're a pilot, sir. Would you ignore the warnings on a chart, unless you were ordered
to?"

Bowmaker gave the question some thought, rais-
ing a hand briefly to the minister, who was again about
to censure Jason.

"I do have some sympathy for your position, Commander," Bowmaker said. "In your place, I'd probably
be saying the same things. But what I would or would
not do is not at issue here. Don't misunderstand me. I'm
not on this inquiry to try and bury you, though to judge
by some of the remarks I've heard so far, I could almost
believe that is its aim."

Jason sensed a kindred spirit in Bowmaker. He
did not glance at the faces of the other members of the
group, but he could see on the periphery of his vision,
the stiffening of features. They did not like what the
American was saying.

"I'm here," Bowmaker was saying, "as an observer from the Alliance. I shall be reporting on the matter to my fellow colleagues on the NATO staff. Go on with your report."

But Jason was forestalled by another MP. "Even allowing for the fact that an aircraft did stray into your area, Wing Commander," came the supercilious voice, "what were your men thinking? I'm given to understand that they are highly trained, handpicked by you yourself. Surely, they are able to distinguish between an airliner and a target. Are we then to assume that your writ holds sway if a stray aircraft, for whatever reason, enters your restricted area, leaving you at liberty to shoot it down if you see fit? Do the men of your special unit consider themselves judge, jury, and executioners—"

The air vice marshal, who had been listening with increasing outrage as the MP warmed to his theme, leaped to his feet and turned a furious expression upon the minister.

"Minister, I strongly protest!" he exclaimed sharply. "The member of Parliament is using this tragic incident to score cheap, vested-interest points!"

The minister turned to the MP. "The Honorable Member for Strowley South should withdraw his uncalled-for remarks."

The MP took his time about it while everyone waited. Thurson remained standing, his eyes fiercely turned upon the member for Strowley South.

At last, the MP said, with as little grace as possible, "I withdraw my remarks."

The air vice marshal sat down slowly, still glaring at the MP.

The minister looked at Jason. "I add my apologies for those remarks, Wing Commander Jason." He nodded to Jason to continue.

"The chart warnings," Jason said, deliberately excluding the loudmouthed MP, "must have been deliberately ignored. I can see no other reason for such a blatant disregard of normal operating procedures. I believe the senior pilot was a former military man and, indeed, was still on the reserve list. I have every confidence in the abilities of my crews," he went on, this time speaking directly to the MP. "They are quite exceptional men. Their response to the crisis, which took them completely by surprise, was swift, professional, and in total accordance with emergency procedures. As a matter of fact, they began taking corrective action upon their own initiative, well before such procedures would have demanded it of them. Further, they informed base immediately they suspected anomalies."

"If not the aircrew, then the equipment?" The member for Strowley South was not going to give up easily.

"One of the backseaters—"

"Backseaters? What are they?"

Jason was patient. "The crew member in the backseat. The navigator, the weapons systems—"

"Thank you, Wing Commander. I think I've got the message." The other members of the committee allowed the MP his say, in accordance with the terms of the inquiry, but their expressions showed they did not necessarily like doing so. "One of your backseaters . . . what did he do?"

"The backseater in question," Jason continued, maintaining his patience, "reported a glitch in the—"

"A glitch?"

Jason could not restrain a sigh of exasperation. This drew a hard stare from the MP.

"A fault," Jason said.

"Why didn't you say that in the first place?"

Jason glanced at the air vice marshal pointedly, as if to show he was nearing the end of his tether.

Thurson fixed him with a stony look. Jason was expected to get on with it.

"I shall try to be more explicit in the future," Jason said neutrally. "The suspected fault in one of his systems was momentary, the barest blink on one of the displays."

"And what would cause such a . . . er . . . blink?"

"A number of things, including interference from an outside source."

The member for Strowley South pounced, as if scenting blood at last. "Interference? I thought your super airplanes were immune to such things. That's why vast sums of taxpayers' money were spent on them."

"They are hardened against—I'm sorry—immune. The system recovered in virtually the same instant—"

"Then why did it go wrong?"

"I am coming to that." Jason allowed some steel to come into his voice. The MP's eyes jumped in surprise. "This occurred *after* launch of the missile. Subsequent attempts to abort—destroy—both missiles by the launch aircraft failed, despite simultaneous operation of the destruct buttons by both members of each crew. Had the problem been with one missile, I would have assumed a fault on the aircraft, or the single missile. Two such failures lead me to other conclusions."

Beresford had been listening patiently to the exchanges. "It could also mean the design of the missile is at fault," he now suggested.

"With respect," Jason said to him, "I think not. We carried out tests with the same crews the next morning and deliberately aborted the missiles. All systems worked perfectly."

"Perhaps it's to do with your nighttime systems."

"Again, I have to disagree, sir. There is nothing wrong with the systems."

"Well, something went wrong, lad. An airliner was shot down by your missiles, and people are dead. We can't get away from that, can we?"

"No, sir," Jason agreed soberly. "But I think it was sabotage."

"Sabotage?" The MP for Strowley South was at it again. "Are you now telling us that your security is at fault? That anyone can gain access to your aircraft and equipment?"

"The security at November One is tight," Jason said coldly. "There are forms of sabotage that do not necessarily require on-site activity."

"Then how was this sabotage carried out?"

"I don't know, but I intend to find out." Jason paused, and looked at each member of the inquiry committee in turn. Watching him, the air vice marshal stiffened expectantly.

"I know," Jason began, "that some people in this room would like to see the November Project terminated. The reasons given would concern cost and the so-called Peace Dividend. There is nothing wrong in working for peace. Contrary to belief in some quarters, most people in uniform actually hate going to war . . . more so than some politicians.

"The object of the November Project is to create an evolved force that would have the clear political mandate for action in an emergency, with its command structure already in place. Such an arrangement would avoid the confusion we have seen in the Gulf. I firmly believe that an integrated force is the way forward. It will be cheaper for all the countries involved, and certainly more efficient. If one has to go to war at all, it is patently ludicrous to commit valuable lives to such an endeavor without ensuring the capability to wage it fast and furiously, and hopefully, within the shortest space of time.

"I do realize that national and political attitudes will make this difficult to achieve, but there really is no other choice. Killing the November program may satisfy current wishful thinking, but it won't change the requirement. You may want my head, gentlemen, and the heads of my aircrew. Very well, you may have them.

"But the next time you think of peace dividends and cutbacks, think long and hard of the Baltic, but especially ponder upon the fate of Kuwait. Being relatively unarmed did not help them. Better still, go there, and see the evidence for yourselves."

The minister was on his feet, shaking with barely suppressed anger. "How dare you! How *dare you* lecture us! We are not the ones whose actions are being questioned. *You are!*"

The air vice marshal was also on his feet. "Wing Commander Jason, wait in my office." It was an order.

"Sir," Jason said, and went out.

The minister rounded upon Thurson. "I was not finished with him! If this is a ploy to protect him, Air Vice Marshal—"

"No ploy, Minister."

"That man is insubordinate! He ought to be dismissed from the service."

"I believe he has just offered his resignation, Minister."

"What? He resigns when he's told to!"

"You may have to accept my resignation as well, Minister. I happen to agree with the Wing Commander. If you will excuse me, Minister. Gentlemen."

Thurson let himself out while the committee stared at each other.

"Are we going to allow this?" the MP for Strowley

South demanded. "Are we letting the military dictate to us now?"

The American general stood up. "Please excuse me for a moment, gentlemen." He went out after Thurson and caught up with him in the corridor. "Air Vice Marshal."

Thurson stopped and turned round.

"Your boy's got guts," Bowmaker said. "He shook those sanctimonious bastards in there. Like you, I think he's right."

"About the November Project? Or the sabotage?"

"Both."

"I see."

"I'll make my report to the NATO chiefs and get them to keep their respective governments off your backs while you check out the sabotage theory."

"Thank you."

"I'm a pilot," Bowmaker said, "as your wing commander observed. People always blame the pilot when something goes wrong and they don't know why. I hate that. I hope, for your sakes, it is sabotage. Now I'd better get back in there and see if a little foreign influence can smooth ruffled feathers."

Thurson held out his hand. "Thank you, General."

"You can buy me a scotch someday."

"You're on."

They shook hands.

Jason was waiting in the air vice marshal's functional-looking office, in another Whitehall building. He was standing, looking out of a window that appeared to be streaming tears. London was having one of its wetter days of the winter.

He turned as Thurson entered, bringing himself to attention.

"At ease, Christopher," the air vice marshal said. "Take a seat. Had some tea yet?"

"Mrs. Davidson's organizing it, sir." Jason sat down.

Mrs. Davidson was Thurson's civilian secretary, a friendly and efficient woman in her forties. She came in with the tea, gave the wing commander a mug, then a sympathetic glance as she left.

The air vice marshal remained standing. "Well," he began. "You certainly do like living dangerously."

"I'm sorry, sir. I allowed my feelings about politicians to get the better of me. But I felt they were ignoring the real issues behind the November program."

"That's as may be, but you're an officer of Her Majesty's Royal Air Force, whatever the status of the November program. In a democracy, the military are subject to the politicians, whatever our misgivings about their competence. I would not like to live under a military dictatorship. Would you?"

Jason looked startled. "Of course not, sir."

"Glad to hear it. Even the most incompetent politician is preferable to a dictator. Besides, military men make terrible politicians, as any brief perusal of a world atlas will prove. Now tell me about this sabotage idea of yours."

"As you know, sir," Jason commenced, "we carried out exhaustive live tests with the missile since the incident. We removed the warheads, replacing them with a small charge that was just sufficient to enable us to blow them up during the abort sequence. Although we were worried about the number we had to use, we wanted documented proof that would satisfy even the most skeptical. We fired those weapons under all possible conditions, given the time we had. They performed flawlessly, even when fired under extreme G-loadings."

"You do realize those very skeptics will quite

likely point out that you cannot recreate the exact conditions under which the fatal incident occurred."

Jason nodded. "Yes, sir. I do. However, my prime purpose was to demonstrate the total reliability of the systems, as well as the competence of my crews. I believe the only way those missiles could have gone rogue on us was by some kind of outside interference. Our aircraft systems are hardened against jamming. This means the missiles were got at during flight."

Thurson stared at his subordinate. "Do you realize what you're saying? The Skyray B is phenomenally rapid. An intercept from launch to impact must be nigh on impossible, and that's without having to get at its code."

"Someone's managed it. That's my absolute gut feeling, sir."

Thurson drank some of his tea thoughtfully. "Your doubting inquisitors might again consider that an attempt to shield your aircrew. I managed to stall their bringing the personal lives of those involved into the equation—at least, I got the minister to sit on it—but the Investigation Branch have dug deeply and discovered the, er . . . somewhat confused emotional undercurrents—just a minute, Christopher. There's no need to leap protectively to their defense. Hear me out. I am on your side.

"Hohendorf and his wife are estranged, and to complicate matters even further, he appears to be having an affair with Selby's sister. Selby is not pleased by this, whatever his outward demeanor, and is himself involved with the daughter of a rather well-known tycoon, who just happens to share the same club as the minister. Then there's McCann." Thurson paused again, this time as if to say a silent prayer. "It occurs to me that the only one with a normal life among them is Flacht. Although I suppose if he's so locked in with their method of flying, there must be something slightly peculiar about him, too."

"If you were to assess each of them professionally, sir, how would you rate them?" Jason said quietly.

"That's a silly question, Wing Commander. You know what I think of their capabilities. I'm playing devil's advocate. I'm trying to say what I know will be said, unless you come up with the right answers. I have to tell you there is not much time. The wolves are baying for blood."

In the minister's office, Buntline was looking out on the wet traffic packed nose to tail when the minister entered.

"Thank you for waiting, Charles," he said, a preoccupied look on his face. "Not surprised you couldn't stay in there any more."

Buntline had been one of the silent observers in the inquiry room.

"I'd had enough, Minister," he said. "I also think the wing commander may have had a point."

"Insufferable man!" the minister said, taking his seat at his desk. "When I was a young man, wing commanders knew their place."

Buntline let the remark go.

The minister continued. "You don't really believe his wild story, surely? It's an excuse."

"I don't think so, Minister. A man who has put so much of himself into something he passionately believes in would not be prepared to throw it all away without good reason. While he was being questioned I watched him carefully. I did not see a man intent on dodging his responsibility. He was genuinely shocked by the incident. This was a man so confident in the capabilities of his entire organization that something like that seemed unthinkable. I've been doing some of my own digging into the affair. I believe there is more than enough to raise my own suspicions about what happened."

"It is the nature of your job to be suspicious."

"Precisely. Which is why I decided to look beyond the obvious. The whole story about Gant and Belov set my antennae twitching, especially the parts we've managed to keep out of the papers. For example, the Los Angeles paper which got the first call about the incident."

"What about it?"

"The newspaper got an anonymous call late in the evening, conveniently in time to allow the night editor to catch the first issue of the next day. The caller's voice was perfectly American."

"Why shouldn't it be?"

Buntline restrained a sigh. Did the minister expect someone operating in the United States to have a thick foreign accent?

"It occurs to me," Buntline went on, ignoring what he considered a question not meriting a reply, "that with all eyes on the Middle East, Stolybin, or those controlling him, would consider this the ideal opportunity to launch a covert operation."

"How can you be certain?"

"As certain as I am about the fact that the person who rang the Los Angeles newspaper did so with *prior knowledge* about the downing of the 707. I've checked. Only a very few in the intelligence community over there had the slightest idea *at the time*. They descended upon the hapless night editor like a ton of bricks to find out where she'd got the story."

The minister was reluctantly coming around to the conclusion that Buntline was on the right track. "So where does that leave us?"

"For a start, I think we may have found out what

Comrade Stolybin has been up to, perhaps only a small part of it."

"But if the wing commander is correct, it would mean the missiles were intercepted during flight. Which is probably what he was hinting at, I suppose."

"I have a feeling he could well be right."

"But is that possible?"

Buntline shrugged. "Anything is possible these days. If a satellite can photograph the sandwich that someone's eating, or in some cases, an ant, why not intercept a missile?" Buntline paused suddenly. "Satellite," he murmured softly. "Bursts of code among the general traffic. A satellite that was moved . . . no one took much notice." He stopped paused once more. "But how . . ."

It was almost as if the minister had gone away. Buntline put his hands in his pockets and began to pace while the minister stared uncomprehendingly at him. He paused again, in midstride.

"Excuse me, Minister," he said abruptly. "Something I must check."

He hurried out before the minister could say anything.

Sevenoaks, Kent. 1630 hours.

Sir James West had spent most of the day privately dwelling upon twenty-five years of guilt. He had slept even worse than previously, after the news of the Boeing 707 had been made public. All the old horrors of his past had returned with a vengeance, in a reply of what had gone before. It was 1965 again, twice over.

When those people had blackmailed him into visiting the special unit in Scotland, he had waited with trepidation for them to betray him. And when that had not happened, he had suffered even more from the uncertainty. But now the waiting was over. He knew what he had to do. He could no longer protect his wife, or his son, by his silence.

The rain that had been falling steadily upon London for most of the past few days had given this part of Kent a miss for the day; but angry clouds scudded overhead, hustled along by a strong wind. An hour before, West had entered his study, his decision made. But so far, he had spent the time thinking about his past life, and of the things he had done.

He now opened the drawer of his desk at which he had been sitting and took out the same key from the small lacquered box as he had done previously. He then went to the compartment in the bookcase that housed the gun box. He took the box back to his desk and opened it, staring at the pistols on their gleaming black velvet. He took out the Makarov PM, turning it this way and that, studying it, as if seeing it for the very first time.

He laid the pistol on the desk, pushing it to one side, then shut the box and put it on the floor next to the desk. He took a pad of letterheaded paper from another drawer and picked up a pen from the desk to carefully lay it on the paper. He stared at his handiwork.

He would write a letter each to his wife and son, telling them the whole story. A third letter would be written to the minister who had arranged the visit to the November base. After that, the Makarov would give him merciful release. There would be no more blackmail.

He never got the chance.

The years of guilt and its accompanying stress finally took their toll in a sudden spasm of savage pain that seemed to engulf his entire body, devouring him. His mouth was wrenched open, but only a strange and terrible rasp came out of it. His hands clawed ineffectually as he tried to stop the pain, but his battle was already lost.

He fell to the floor still gasping, body constricted, then suddenly the struggles ceased. His body began to relax into the unnatural stillness of death. It was 1645 hours.

The Makarov, unneeded, lay gleaming upon the desk, untouched.

It would be many hours before Lady West, accustomed to her husband's long periods in his study, would look in on him. The first person she would contact would be Colin Layton, the family doctor.

Whitehall, London. 2100 hours.

Buntline had spent the time since leaving the minister probing into old files. As a thorough intelligence man, he hated to overlook anything that might give the slightest clue to the solution of a particular problem. Those who did not understand his methods tended to think he wasted valuable time on the tiniest of aspects of any given matter requiring his attention. Conversely, he firmly believed that tiny fragments, which by themselves seemed unimportant, were part of a greater picture that was clear for all to see, if only they'd take the time to look.

It was this belief that drove him to take the wing commander seriously. Buntline had little time for what he considered to be prima donna airmen. But a job was a job, and it should be done properly. His antipathy for fliers did not blind him to the true focus of his task: the neutralization of whatever operation Stolybin and his masters were running.

The files had taken him to a missile incident in 1965, which he studied with avid interest. The name James West rang several bells in his mind. He accepted that he could be wrong, but he did not believe in coincidences. He checked out every file, every computer record that related to James West. By midnight, he decided a visit to Sevenoaks was required, if only to dispel a growing suspicion. He had to be certain. Accusing James West wrongly would bring the wrath of both the minister and sundry heavyweights down upon him. His visit, therefore, would have to be circumspect. He would be able to judge by the replies he received whether his suspicions were well founded.

He decided to go first thing in the morning.

14

November One. 1100 hours (the next day).

Wing Commander Jason did not like the conclusion he had come to. It seemed crazy. Yet no matter how he looked at it, he saw the same thing.

He got up from his desk and went to a window. The gales that had lashed this part of Scotland since the detachment's return from the Mediterranean had subsided, but the snowfall had been heavy. Though all runways were fully operational, plenty of snow lay on the ground beyond the taxiways, roads, and flight lines. The Grampian landscape was itself clothed in a thick mantle of white.

A sudden roar signified the takeoff run of a pair of Tornadoes. Neither was manned by the crews of Selby or Hohendorf.

Jason went back to his desk and reluctantly picked up the phone. He selected the scrambler to enable him to speak without fear of eavesdroppers. He punched in a number. It was a direct line to the air vice marshal.

"Thurson," came the brisk voice.

"Chris Jason, sir . . ." Jason briefly hesitated, then continued. "Sir James West—"

"Good Lord. How did you know?"

Jason moved the phone slightly away, staring at it in mild confusion. What was the AVM on about?

"Know what, sir?"

"That's he's dead."

Jason froze.

"Christopher! Are you there?"

"Er . . . yes. Yes, sir."

"How did you know Sir James West was dead?"

"I didn't, sir."

"What? But you just—"

"If you'll pardon the interruption, sir, that was not why I called. I'm a bit shocked, actually. Rather unexpected . . . then again, perhaps not, if my suspicions are correct."

It was Thurson's turn to pause; then his voice was very quiet when he said, "What the devil are you trying to tell me?"

"I don't know how to put this, sir. If I'm wrong—"

"Perhaps you should let me be the judge of that." There was another pause as Thurson's voice faded, clearly speaking to someone else. "Christopher, something's come up. I'll call you back." Thurson's voice had taken on a sudden urgency.

Jason replaced the receiver, convinced the interruption had to do with Sir James West.

"We did it ourselves," he said to the phone.

Thurson was back within half an hour, his voice very strained as he spoke.

"A can of worms has opened up down here," he said. "I'm coming up to you. I shall have . . . company."

"Yes, sir."

There was not a choice.

*   *   *

Two and a half hours later, the HS 125 CC executive aircraft landed at November One. Jason met the air vice marshal, who was accompanied by a civilian he vaguely recognized.

"Wing Commander Jason, Mr. Charles Buntline." Thurson's tones were crisp and almost abrupt as he made the introductions. "For the purposes of this visit, you'll assume Mr. Buntline carries the rank of Air Commodore." He did not look as if he enjoyed having to say it.

That made Buntline ostensibly two ranks higher than Jason, who glanced at his superior questioningly. But Thurson gave him no comfort.

He took Buntline's outstretched hand. "Mr. Buntline."

"Wing Commander."

They did not speak again until they were in Jason's office.

"Jacko Inglis has been informed of our visit," Thurson began, "but there's no need for him to attend."

Inglis, the group captain with overall command of the base, was clearly not going to be privy to whatever Buntline had in mind.

"Air Vice Marshal Thurson tells me you have apparently come to the same conclusions as I have," Buntline said.

"That depends upon what you mean, sir," Jason said.

"I mean Sir James West," Buntline told him coldly.

"Bringing him up here was not my idea," Jason said, with equal chill. "I responded to orders from my superiors."

"I do know the background, Wing Commander. I would not have come up to see you. You might well have been coming to see me . . . under escort."

Jason's eyes narrowed, then he glanced at Thurson, who was studiously looking elsewhere.

"Sir James, as you now know," Buntline went on emotionlessly, "is dead. Massive heart attack in his study. I am about to give you information which I would not normally pass on to you." He paused, eyes fixed upon Jason's. "However, there is a way to neutralize the situation. But first, tell me what led you to suspect Sir James West."

Jason again glanced at Thurson, somewhat awkwardly. Thurson's gaze still held no message.

"I'm not sure I'd make it a solid accusation."

"There's no need to be circumspect, Wing Commander. There is nothing you can say about James West that will surprise me now." Buntline spoke with some irony.

"When I returned from London, I did some research into the files we hold about the genesis of Skyray, to clear up something that had been nagging at me since the incident," Jason said. "I tied the events of 1965 with his visit here, and with the way he wanted to know how the missile was directed to target. We did not give him the code, of course, but he was shown how a hypothetical code would function. Even that was clearly sufficient for someone to write a fast breaker program that could then hunt out the code itself and impersonate, or usurp, it. Mr. Eldridge, who is our programmer, suggests this to be the only way it could have been done. Whatever was done had to operate at incredible speed. The risks of failure were very high."

"Clearly a risk they intended to take," Buntline said grimly.

"The missile is coded differently now, with a tertiary sentry added. If Sir James were to carry out the same mission, the code breakers would be occupied by this sentry system while the missile continued on its way uninterrupted."

"One is tempted to ask why such a system was not inserted in the first place."

"With respect, Mr. Buntline," Jason said evenly, "no one can guarantee the total security of any system. Until a breach has occurred, you cannot know what form it will take. You can plan for the expected and sometimes the unexpected, but there is no such thing as infallibility. If we began to think that and took 100 percent security for granted, we would be guilty of the worst kind of negligence. My crews acted commendably and swiftly. They had no idea of what they were facing, yet they took correct action. Had the abort systems not been ignored by the missiles, both weapons would have exploded long before reaching the airliner."

There was a brief silence in the room. This was suddenly disturbed by the roar of two ASVs sweeping past prior to breaking for entry into the landing circuit. Buntline could not control an involuntary start.

Jason had the grace to hide the smile he felt coming.

Buntline glared at him, suspecting his thoughts.

"James West was not found for some time," Buntline said. "It was his habit to spend several hours in his study, and his wife thought nothing of it when he was not seen for most of the day. She discovered him only when she went to call him for dinner, and immediately called their doctor.

"Like you, I decided to act upon a hunch. However, I do have other . . . er, indications which led me to take an interest in his activities. Last night, I decided to pay him a morning visit. I was thus the first 'official' person, so to speak, to know of his death. Lady West was quite startled to see me, and before long, she had told me of a visit he had received from a couple pretending to be army friends of his son. Nonsense, of course. They were KGB. Their visit ties in neatly with all that has occurred since."

Buntline paused, then went on. "I'm not going to give you details of James West's treachery over the years. That is not within your province. However, I believe this operation was conducted with some haste. Why, I have no idea, but it has given us a window within which to take some corrective action. We're going to mount a little operation of our own, and your two crews—those involved in the incident—will be required for escort duty."

Jason frowned at Buntline. "Escort duty? Am I allowed to ask whom, or what, will they be escorting?"

Buntline was almost cheerful. "Certainly. You may, and I'll be happy to answer."

Jason was not so sure he wanted to hear the reply.

"They'll be escorting a Boeing 707," Buntline said, "in the same area where Congressman Gant's was shot down. Gant and Belov will be continuing their secret journey."

Jason stared at him before turning to the air vice marshal. "I thought Gant and Belov were dead, sir. We're supposed to have shot them down."

"They are dead," Buntline said calmly.

Jason did not look at him, but kept his eyes upon the air vice marshal.

"Mr. Buntline has all the information," Thurson said.

Reluctantly, Jason again turned to the civilian.

Buntline's tiny smile showed triumph. "They are dead," he repeated, "but we're about to resurrect them."

Jason waited.

"Word will get around," Buntline went on, "so that the right people will hear that Gant and Belov

were in fact not on the aircraft at all. That doubles—
out-of-work actors—had taken their places, and in fact,
the real trip is soon to be undertaken. The one that
caused the incident was a dry run. That will be the
story."

"In the press?"

"Of course not in the press, Wing Commander."
Buntline managed to sound both exasperated and irritated. "You leave the disinformation to me. Your part
is to supply the crews, and to present yourself aboard
the 707."

Jason ignored service protocol. *"What?"*

Buntline did not seem to mind. "To make this
work properly," he said with infuriating calm, "we
need extra bait. In addition to Gant and Belov—de-
ceased—we felt it would add to the attraction if it were
whispered in the right earholes that the architect of the
November Project would also be on that flight, in an
advisory capacity." Buntline now allowed his lips to
stretch in an identifiable smile, but his eyes carried the
chill of a frozen wasteland.

Jason's own eyes remained locked upon Buntline's. "Sir," he began to the air vice marshal, "did you
agree to this?" He was asking Thurson to confirm a
betrayal.

"Mr. Buntline has the minister's approval," Thurson replied stiffly.

"Am I being set up for sacrifice to save other
necks?" Jason asked tightly, striving hard to keep his
anger in check. "Or is this another way to kill the
program?"

Buntline cut in before the air vice marshal could
speak. "I'd advise caution with your words, Wing Commander. I know you seem to enjoy a certain . . . autonomy . . . out of all proportion to your rank—"

"I offered my resignation."

"Which has not been accepted . . ."

"So you'll kill me instead."

Buntline's eyes were suddenly dangerous. "Are you afraid, Wing Commander?"

"Of course I'm afraid. Everyone's afraid of dying. The trick is to—"

"Then the confidence you expressed in your crews appears to have been misplaced."

"I have every confidence in my men."

"I'm very glad to hear it. I'd hate to think I'd be entrusting my life to incompetents."

"Your life?"

Buntline's eyes widened in feigned innocence. "But of course, Wing Commander. I'm going to be aboard that aircraft with you. I never ask anyone to do something I would not be prepared to do myself. Thought I'd mentioned that."

He looked like someone who felt he had won the argument.

Moscow, 1830 hours.

Major Vannis climbed out of the official car that had brought him close to his home. The small apartment had been found for him, courtesy of Stolybin, at the start of the operation.

He felt satisfied with his lot. The comrade colonel found good apartments, gave him a staff car, and had gotten him advanced to major after years in the promotion wilderness. True, it was the general's hand on the actual recommendation, but that would not have happened if the colonel had not first selected him for the mission he has so successfully completed.

Vannis began to walk home. It was only a short distance, and he liked the exercise after a day in the confines of his new office. The room where he had carried out his electronic magic had been thoroughly cleared, and his new job collating computer-extracted intelligence from international communications was not as exciting, but the colonel had promised more excitement from time to time. The way things were shaping up, he was certain there would be other occasions.

With life looking quite promising, Vannis walked briskly but carefully, half listening to the receding sounds of the staff car as it accelerated away. His cautious steps were due to the hard-packed snow, and every so often, his boots crunched on small patches of ice.

He was negotiating a larger patch when a man came running up from behind. Vannis did not hear the dark approaching shape until it was almost upon him. He whirled, losing his balance. He skidded and staggered onto the icy road, trying to regain stability. But his frantic movements only made matters worse. He began to fall.

From around a corner, a car suddenly slid into view, engine roaring, its back end swinging from side to side as its driver tried to counter the motion. Like an unstoppable juggernaut, it hurtled toward the tumbling Vannis, broadside on.

The driver made no move to evade.

The sliding mass hit the helpless Vannis with full force, crushing his body sickeningly as it went. The last coherent thought in his mind before he went under the heavy vehicle was that he'd been hit by his own staff car.

He did not die immediately as the sounds of the racing engine died away, but expired slowly on the cold ground.

The man who had run at him had disappeared in the winter night. It was as if Vannis had never been.

* * *

Whitehall, London. 1030, the next morning.

Buntline entered the minister's office unsummoned.

"All in place?" the minister inquired as Buntline appeared.

"We've been working all night to see how much could be done in the time available," Buntline said. "I'm confident we'll have things well organized. The trick is to have the mission running before—if that's liable to happen—the bodies of the real Gant and Belov was up somewhere and are identified. Of course, there may well be nothing left of them. If the records are correct, very little was found of that Canberra crew in 1965."

"And Stolybin?"

Buntline smirked with grim satisfaction. "If Comrade Sergei is involved, as my gut reaction tells me, he'll be up to his neck in it when he or his masters believe they failed. I wouldn't give much for his chances. They'll have to do something to try and recover the situation. They can't use the missile trick again because they'll assume we'll have taken some kind of corrective action, or withdrawn it from service.

"Gant apparently had some important information—hard facts—about, for example, the shifting of top-class military equipment further east to keep them out of the arms-cuts discussions, and a more sinister program to destabilize the Soviet Union itself. Unfortunately, documentary proof went down with the aircraft. We're going to try and convince Stolybin that proof still exists. So while the news media's making a big production about the downing of the 707, our people will manufacture a story line that will be fed down the intelligence grapevine."

"But will they take the bait?"

"If we make it look as if they got at the information all by themselves."

"And the November people? Were they in agreement?"

Buntline's grin was full of malicious pleasure. "I bounced the wing commander into coming aboard our decoy. We'll certainly have our escort. Those men of his will do anything to protect him. If they're as good as he keeps maintaining, he'll have nothing to worry about."

"We do have evidence of their prowess."

"All the better, Minister," Buntline remarked smoothly.

"You're virtually taking the man hostage. I intensely dislike his insufferable insubordination, but even so . . ."

"Name of the game, Minister. We need to neutralize this threat."

The minister stared hard at Buntline. "Sometimes, Charles, you can be a cold fish."

Buntline was unperturbed. "Someone has to be. We've got our 707," he went on before the minister could comment, "the RC-135 version, courtesy of some help from General Bowmaker. Seems he's taken a liking to Wing Commander Jason."

"What would you expect?" the minister said testily. "The man's an American. They like people who go against the established order. They think it shows guts. Still drunk on 1776, I shouldn't wonder."

Buntline chose to ignore the minister's petty prejudices. There were Americans he knew in his line of business, any one of whom he'd swap for ten of the minister.

"I do hope this works, Charles," the minister was saying. "If it comes apart, I'll have to take some steps to limit the damage."

Buntline understood the code. The minister would

distance himself from the proceedings and claim ignorance. Heads of state did that all the time, after all. It should be routine for a minister. In the Baltics, it was a rogue army commander working on his own initiative. If things went wrong, the minister would quite probably say it was an unauthorized operation and drag the November unit into the mess for good measure. Two birds with one stone.

"I feel confident about this," Buntline said. "They thought with all attention on the Middle East, they could mount such an operation unobtrusively, among other adventures like the ones they've pulled in the Baltic. In the case of the 707 incident, they moved hastily. That may well prove to be their undoing."

"As long as it isn't ours."

Buntline said nothing.

Two days later, Stolybin sat in his office studying transcripts of clandestine activities from different parts of the globe—satellite eavesdropping, telephone intercepts, computer hackings, rifle microphones, laser transmissions, and all other versions of secretive listening at the disposal of his team.

He was bothered by something. If true, it could put him in serious jeopardy.

Out of all the pile of information, something small, like a deadly virus, was beginning to surface. What focused his attention were no less than three mentions of Gary and Little Bear. Code names, certainly. Places? People? Or neither?

But that was not all. Gary and Little Bear, according to the transcripts, were traveling.

Stolybin frowned. It couldn't be that easy. Gary was in Indiana, where Gant had come from; and Little Bear, in that context, could only be Belov. Belov had been a smallish man. It had to be Belov. The code name was the sort of thing the Americans would go for.

But how could they be "traveling"? They were dead, blown to smithereens by NATO missiles.

He decided not to say anything to the general. Not yet.

But he was going to keep an eye on developments. If the transcripts had gotten it right, he was going to need his insurance policy. It would also mean Ivan Vannis had been killed for nothing.

If something had indeed gone so seriously wrong, it was because the operation had been carried out far too quickly for his own liking. But the general had wanted speed. Even so, the general would be most unforgiving of failure.

Stolybin looked into the immediate future and felt distinct unease.

By the end of the day, he could no longer ignore the implications. More up-to-date transcripts confirmed the worst. He decided to see the general. Putting the inevitable off for much longer would work against his own interests.

He knocked on the general's door, carrying the relevant information and his interpretation of it on a single sheet of paper.

"In!"

Stolybin entered, trying hard not to feel as if he had just put his head between the jaws of a very hungry predator. He went up to the general's desk and placed the paper down upon it with outward calm.

The general squinted up at him through a rising veil of smoke, ignoring the paper for the time being. The eyes that peered through the pungent cloud seemed indeed like a predator's.

Instead of reading the paper Stolybin had

brought, the general picked up one of his own and looked down at it.

"You are going to tell me," he began, not looking up, "that we hit the wrong target. That Gant and Belov are not dead and that we blew up two out-of-work actors instead." The eyes now fastened upon Stolybin. "How am I doing?"

Taken by complete surprise, Stolybin nevertheless stood his ground. His own eyes did not waver.

"You are correct, Comrade General."

"Thank you, Comrade Stolybin," the general said with heavy irony. "It makes me feel secure to know you consider my information correct. *For how long were you going to keep this from me?*" he yelled suddenly, pounding at his desk with such fury, his fist seemed to bounce off it.

The cigarette flew out of the general's mouth and landed on the polished toe of Stolybin's left boot. He picked it up and carefully placed it in the general's ashtray.

The general glared at it, then at Stolybin. "Put it out. Do you think I'm going to smoke a cigarette that's been on your boot?"

Stolybin did as he was told.

"Well?" the general went on. "What have you to say in explanation for this mess? I warned you I would not take failure lightly."

Stolybin stood rigidly, though not quite at attention. "I wanted to make certain the information on the transcripts was correct. I was not aware the Comrade General was using other sources."

The general made no apologies. "I can use whatever source I want. The fact that both yours and mine have obtained the same information means there must be some credibility in it. They made a song and dance about the destruction of the aircraft, hoping we would accept the deaths of Gant and the traitor Belov as fact, leaving those two free to embarrass us at a staged international press conference. No doubt they would choose a time guaranteed to create maximum effect, perhaps while we're engaged in restoring order in the republics."

He slammed at his sheet of paper with an open palm. "According to this, they'll be taking the same route as that other plane that you so confidently destroyed."

The biting edge to the general's words forewarned Stolybin of the way things would be going. Had success been achieved, the general would have claimed it. Shooting down the wrong aircraft was, of course, Stolybin's mistake.

Stolybin chose to remain prudent and did not tell the general that if he'd been given sufficient time to mount the operation, he would most probably have discovered the impostors.

"Why should they take the same route?" the general was demanding. "Why go into an area where one airplane has already been shot down?"

"They will have looked upon it as a tragic accident," Stolybin suggested. "Why should they think otherwise? And further, even if they suspect we had a hand in it, which I doubt, they'll assume we would never expect them to use the same route. Hiding in plain sight. It's a trick I've used myself to good effect. Many of my people have. No one ever looks for you in the obvious place, precisely because it *is* obvious."

"Yes, yes. All very intellectual, but it does not get me those two. I want them. *I want them!* Whatever they're planning has to be stopped. I want their flight closely monitored, and I want them shot down. This time there will be no mistake. At least," the general finished grudgingly, "it appears the missile has been taken out of service. Your efforts were not a total failure."

Stolybin wisely kept his mouth firmly shut.

"I'm activating a special detachment," the general went on. "Six of our new aircraft will be making a courtesy visit to a friendly North African country, clandestinely. There will be no national markings. It will be an independent deployment." His lifeless eyes stared at Stolybin. "That means highly secret. Do you have a dissenting point of view?"

Stolybin well knew the general's "special detachment" had been on standby for some time, but he felt it was the wrong solution. He didn't tell that to the general.

"No, Comrade," he replied instead.

The general nodded, not really expecting a different answer. "The Sukhois will be used, the new Su-27TP that you saw at that base. They're not yet on the service inventory and their deployment will serve as a test of their range capabilities. Their job will be to shoot down the real target. The fancy electronic games that your Latvian enjoyed playing are no match for dependable firepower from an unbeatable Soviet aircraft, as you will see."

The general paused to give Stolybin a sideways look. "Your eyes are jumping about, Colonel. If you're worried that the West may note the detachment's movements, I'd think they would be more preoccupied with their little problem in the Middle East." His own eyes danced with a lively malice. "Very fortunate for us, that mess out there. I want you to keep a twenty-four-hour listening surveillance on everything to do with Gant and Belov, right up to the moment of their arrival in the air above the Mediterranean. I shall arrange a warm welcome for them."

Scarcely believing the general was mad enough to

carry out this plan, Stolybin tried to be conversational. "Who will be the pilots?"

"Politically sound ones who do not accept our retreat from Central Europe." The general almost snapped as he spoke. The withdrawal of Soviet forces from the western borders with NATO was something that ate at him. "Like me, they hope we'll soon remedy that situation."

As the general talked Stolybin became more certain he would need the tapes hidden in the foreigner's apartment. The general wanted to risk no less than six of the operational prototypes in the drive to eliminate his quarry.

As if knowing part of what was going on in Stolybin's mind, the general said, "Some of the information we passed to Belov was genuine. We had to risk it, or his story would not have hooked a political opportunist like Gant. And as for Belov, we cannot risk having him spill his guts to the world. *We'll* spill his guts for him."

Stolybin was not sure whether it was meant to be a macabre joke. But the general was not smiling.

"The Su-27TP has an even longer range than the standard version. There'll be a stop at Odessa to fill the tanks. The remaining two thousand kilometers from there to our hosts can easily be done without further refueling. Armament will be carried in the support aircraft, which will be on site a day before we arrive. The engineers will then arm the aircraft on landing. We'll tell our hosts we're carrying out tests. We have done that in the past. Another tragic accident will occur, and people will merely say how dangerous that part of the Mediterranean has become. Given the current situation, it won't be difficult to make that acceptable."

"Why six aircraft, Comrade General?"

The general stared at Stolybin for a long time before replying. A fresh cigarette was in his mouth. "I like to be certain of my results," he eventually replied. "Had you done your work, the entire operation would have been successful, and just like twenty-five years ago, no one would have been the wiser. People would have blamed the Western military, and we would have prevented a dangerous man from having the chance of becoming the president of the United States one day. As for the traitor Belov, he has a strong following and could have caused us serious problems in the future. And finally, the new Western missile itself. As far as I can tell from what we now know, that is the only thing you have succeeded in stopping. I had great expectations of you, Colonel. I am beginning to think I may have made a mistake." The general's eyes seemed to film over, as if to hide the real thoughts going through his mind. "I would like to be proved wrong . . . for your sake."

Seething with resentment because of the way the general was taking the credit for what had gone well while blaming him for what had not, Stolybin forced himself to remain silent. It was what he had expected. It was why he had taken the precaution of taping their meetings from the very beginning.

"I have full confidence in my pilots," the general went on, rubbing it in. "As I've just told you, they are politically sound. For example, they feel we are on the wrong side in the Middle East. Given the slightest chance, they would happily offer their services and aircraft to fly against the Western fighters over there. Well? What do you think?" The question was shot without warning, as if to test Stolybin's own political soundness.

"Why not? It would be interesting," Stolybin said calmly.

15

Late January had brought a thaw to the Grampian landscape, with only the mountain peaks retaining their white caps of snow. A period of rain, sometimes heavy, had replaced the snowfalls, leaving barely a breeze in their wake. Even the temperatures were unseasonably high, and almost springlike.

At November One, it was two A.M. on a particularly wet night and high tails of spray rose behind two Tornado F-3S's as they roared down the main runway to lift themselves into the streaming darkness, the white-hot plumes of their afterburners baking the air behind them. November One, in accordance with the principles that governed its existence, was always at work.

Away to the south-east, in Edinburgh, Mark Selby awoke suddenly, screaming. Kim Mannon, next to him in bed, was startled out of sleep and frantically groped for the switch of her bedside lamp. She turned it on and reached for him anxiously.

He was sitting bolt upright, face held tightly in his hands. His fingertips and his thumbs dug into his skin, as if he were trying to blot out a terrible vision.

"Oh God, oh God, oh God," he whispered repeatedly.

She put her arms about him, holding him as she would a frightened child. His body did not respond, but she refused to let go. Despite the thin film of sweat that covered his upper body, he was strangely cold to the touch. Outside, the rain pounded at the windows.

After half an hour, he began to relax and she tightened her embrace as she felt the easing of the tension within him.

He brought his hands down to his sides. "Oh God," he said again. He had been silent for some time, and the words came out in a long groan. "I thought I'd left that well behind. Sorry, I woke you."

"Oh Mark. Do you think I mind?" She kept hugging him. "I'm worried about you. Was it your friend again?"

He nodded. "But worse."

Before he had been selected for November One, he had been flying the IDS version of the Tornado, the low-level attack variant. A close friend's aircraft had taken his slot because of a fault in his own, and had crashed during the training mission. The friend had not ejected and had burned to death. Selby had nightmares for long months, seeing the burning face in his dreams, looking accusingly at him. After he'd met Kim Mannon, the nightmares had stopped. Now they were back with a vengeance, except that this time, new faces had entered the flames. They were faces without features, faces from a burning 707.

He had not told her about what had occurred that terrible night over the Mediterranean, but he felt she already knew.

"I know something's very wrong, Mark," she now said, "and I know it can't be just the old crash you told me about. I'm not going to ask you to tell me. I just want you to know that whatever it is, I'm on your side."

He looked at her. "But if you don't know—"

She placed a gentle finger upon his lips. "Shhh." She moved the finger to kiss him. "And I don't want to. Whatever it is, I am always going to be here."

"And Reggie?"

"Reggie, as Elmer Lee would say, can take a hike."

He continued to look at her intensely. Like anyone who had either read a newspaper, listened to the radio, or even briefly watched television, she had to know of the fate of the Boeing. While most people had no idea about what had really happened, her instincts would have locked onto his private torments.

"You know, don't you?" he asked to her softly.

The dark eyes gave nothing away. "What you think I know does not matter. What matters is that I love you." She caressed his cheek with a warm hand. "Just remember that." She gently but firmly pushed at his chest to make him lie down once more, sliding against him beneath the covers and placing one of her legs across his bare lower body. She snuggled close. "Try to get some sleep now."

But the heat of her upper thigh had aroused him, so he pulled her on top of him and they made a very slow and gentle love.

After that, sleep came easily to him.

In Aberdeen, Hohendorf was also awake. He listened to the rain as he lay, eyes wide open, in the glimmer of the bedroom. Breathing softly in the crook of his left arm was Morven, the curves of her warm body fitting neatly into his.

In the morning, he would be returning to November One. From there that evening, in the company of

Selby and McCann's Tornado he'd be taking off for the Mediterranean, with Flacht in the backseat. Ever since the Boss had told them they had been selected for special escort duty, he had felt a small knot of tension in his stomach. It didn't help that the Boss was himself going to be on the aircraft to be escorted. Whatever trouble was expected, he knew they had to protect that plane at all costs.

He turned his head slowly so as not to wake Morven. In the twilight created by the street lamps through the partially drawn curtains, he could see her face quite clearly. Only her head was visible from beneath the quilt. In sleep, her face he thought, had the repose of a child who felt safe. Part of her mass of dark hair had fallen across an exposed cheek, while the rest was spread across her unused pillow.

He wondered if he'd see her again. Anything could be waiting above the Mediterranean, but whatever it was, it would not be allowed to take this away from him. Like the mystery Boeing 707, there was always the unforeseeable. But even so . . .

Would she miss him?

He banished the thought from his mind. Thinking like that was asking for trouble, blunting instincts and clouding the brain. In the air, such a state of affairs could kill you. He had known at least two people who had gone out that way. Though in his thoughts always, Morven was firmly put on hold whenever he flew.

He resisted the temptation to stroke her face, fearing that, too, might wake her. He wanted this moment to observe her in the half-light, to imprint the picture upon his memory.

The destruction of the 707 had caused him some anxiety, but he had not allowed it to affect his own capabilities. He had assessed the tragedy, carefully going over all the actions he had taken. The 707 had strayed into a well-notified danger area. Then the Skyray had inexplicably gone rogue at the worst possible time and had failed to respond even to the emergency commands. There was nothing that he could have humanly done to save the aircraft. It did not make him feel any better, no matter how many times he analyzed it; but allowing this to affect his performance in the air was unthinkable.

Morven made a tiny sound and he looked down at her. Her sleep was undisturbed.

A fond look came into his eyes. Who would have thought that after his disastrous marriage to Anne-Marie, he could have found someone who was so completely what he wanted, and needed?

"You have no idea how much I love you," he said, so softly the words barely came out.

"But I do know," she said.

He was startled to see her eyes come open.

In married quarters at November One, Wolfgang Flacht slept soundly. The accidental shooting of the 707 had disturbed him, but like Hohendorf, he had looked at the incident as objectively as he could and had forced himself to overcome the potentially destructive sense of culpability that had threatened all four members of the crews of the two ASVs.

Before going to bed that night, he had spent a little longer with the children at bedtime and read them an extra story.

His wife, Ilse, had noted the change but had stilled the fears she felt.

While he slept peacefully it was she who lay awake.

Elmer Lee McCann's dreams were full of erotic fantasies of Karen Lomax. On his return from the deployment, she had sought him out in the mess to say how sorry she was. What had gladdened his heart was her belief that he had not made a mistake.

For all that, she was still solidly engaged to the formidable Pearce. But it didn't matter. His dreams were his own.

In the current one, Karen Lomax's lithe body brought a smile to his sleeping face. He tightly hugged the pillow that in his superheated dream was Karen Lomax, clad only in the blue of her RAF sweater.

November One, 1630 hours.

Tenente Colonello Mario de Vinci was a small, neat man with quick dark eyes and a finely groomed head of black hair. He was one of the two deputy commanders who assumed command during any time that Jason was absent from the base. His colleague was the Marineflieger Fregattenkapitän Dieter Helm.

Da Vinci was taking the mission briefing.

"Gentlemen," he concluded to the four men before him, his English strongly laced with Milanese undertones, "you have already received all the flight information necessary for this mission. There is not much more that I can say to you, except that if trouble comes and the Boss's plane is shot down, he will come back to haunt you." He paused, giving them a grim smile. "You'll also have to answer to me, and to Dieter Helm."

Helm, tall and angular with wavy blond hair, was standing to one side of the podium in the small room being used for the briefing. He gave the merest trace of a smile.

"Call sign for the mission," da Vinci added, "is Nighthawk. Selby and McCann have the lead in Nighthawk One. Hohendorf and Flacht will be Nighthawk Two." He picked up his cap from the lectern and stepped down from the podium. He went up to each man to shake hands. "Good luck. I expect to count you all back in."

Helm had also come up to shake hands. "That also goes for me."

The two men went out, da Vinci with quick, brisk steps, putting his cap on as he left.

"I wish somebody had told us what to expect," McCann said as they walked to their aircraft in the hardened shelter.

"They would have," Selby told him, "if they had any idea."

McCann paused by the entry ladder. "What if the missiles go ape again? Hell, I don't want to be responsible for sending the Boss down in a ball of flame."

"We've got our fail-safe button, so if it does go rogue on us for a second time, we've got the autonomous destruct code."

Trials with the missile, using a totally separate set of commands to destroy it, had worked perfectly and was now standard fit on all November aircraft. Even if for some reason the missile was successfully jammed while in flight, the independent destruct system would work unhindered. Skyray had performed as expected, even in an intense electronic countermeasures environment.

McCann began to climb the ladder as Selby began his check of the Tornado ASV.

"Dreamed about Karen Lomax last night," he said.

Selby did not pause in his preflight inspection. "I wouldn't say that too loudly." He glanced to his left, where one of the ground crew was standing. "News might get back to our rugby star. Then where would you be?"

"Up shit's creek?" McCann suggested.

"As long as you know."

Satisfied with his inspection, Selby climbed into the front cockpit.

In another HAS, Hohendorf and Flacht were fully strapped in and ready to go.

"Did you think about the Boeing last night?" Flacht asked as they finished their pretaxi checks.

"A little. No worries."

"I slept like a baby, so Ilse told me. She didn't do so well, though. She stayed awake most of the night."

"Why?" Their conversation was punctuated by call-outs of various systems checks which they confirmed to each other. "She's a pilot's wife. She knows the risks."

"That doesn't worry her. I think she's a little worried about this mission."

"But she doesn't know what it is, any more than she knows what our normal missions are."

"That's what I mean. She's never worried like this before. What do you think is waiting for us out there?"

Hohendorf paused before replying. "We must expect anything, Wolfie. We're fully armed. We'll just have to see what turns up."

"Nighthawk Two," came on their headphones. "Ready to roll."

"Nighthawk Two ready," confirmed Hohendorf, and eased the throttles forward.

The Tornado ASV nosed its way out of the hardened aircraft shelter. Hohendorf briefly dabbed at the toe brakes to test them. The aircraft dipped its nose momentarily as the powerful brakes took hold and were released. The ASV continued on its way, nosewheel turning onto the yellow guide strip that would lead it to the taxi track.

Up ahead, the winking nav lights of Nighthawk One led the way.

Moscow, 2000 hours.

Stolybin sat in his office, studying the day's harvest of information. The six Su-27TPs had made their flight without incident, and to judge by the clandestinely gathered communications traffic, the occasion had gone unremarked.

Hardly surprising, he thought. With everybody's attention divided between events in the Baltic republics and the Middle East, six Su-27s in transit could easily be overlooked. Satellites, like all machines and their makers, were fallible. They didn't always see everything.

"And we are not immune," he murmured to himself.

There had been no sightings of the second 707, although traffic intercepts still confirmed it would be on its way. Perhaps the general had the right idea, after all, he thought sourly. Blow the thing out of the sky with a couple of well-directed missiles from the Su's, and the world might well chalk it up to yet another terrorist outrage. Which, all things considered, it was.

But Stolybin still had his nagging doubts. Terrorist outrage or not, two similar incidents in the area, even allowing for its volatility, was pushing luck too far. His innate caution made him feel uneasy. The general may have carried out a highly successful operation in 1965, but this was the nineties. Today's adversaries were a lot less gullible, and technological advances had transformed the potential battleground.

Stolybin was decidedly unhappy. If something went wrong, he knew the general would dump it all on him. He had no intention of ending up like Vannis.

The general had looked in just once during the day and had left his office early, saying he had things to attend to.

For some reason, that also caused Stolybin some anxiety.

After a rendezvous with a waiting Victor K2 tanker to take on fuel, the two ASVs went on to land on the deployment island in the Mediterranean. The flight had been without incident, and no clandestine eyes either at sea, or in space, noted their arrival. The general's satellite had been switched to watching the gameplay in the Middle East, while the Alpha-class submarine, though still meant to be on station, was preoccupied with playing hide-and-seek with a U.S. Navy Los Angeles–class hunter-killer sub that had come on the scene, apparently from nowhere.

The Soviet boat, with its submerged speed of more than forty knots that allowed it to outrun most torpedoes in a straight sprint, and with its anechoic coating, which lessened its chances of detection, was faster than the American vessel; but the LA-class boat carried extremely sensitive sensors, specially dedicated to hunting the Alpha prey.

Beneath the waters of the Mediterranean, the game went on.

On the island the next day, the two ASVs and their crews spent the hours waiting. They were primed and ready to go. The aircraft, their air-superiority gray paintwork static while at rest, gleamed dully beneath their open-rigged temporary shelters. Reclining in plain deckchairs next to the silent predators, fully kitted out but with their helmets placed upon their laps, the crews waited tensely.

Throughout the day, food and drink was brought

to them. They left the chairs only long enough to obey calls of nature, while about them, the ground crew lolled, talking quietly among themselves. Beyond the shelters, another group was playing soccer, and beyond the area itself, the island went about its business. It was a clear, warm day.

The waiting went on until a bloodred sun, heralding the coming of night, hovered above the horizon. There was, however, plenty of light still left in the sky.

"This is like those old war movies," McCann said. "Here we are sitting in these things all day, waiting for something to happen." He tapped at his helmet. "The kit's sort of different . . . but if those guys back then felt anything like I do . . ." He paused, to lean forward and peer beneath the Tornado at the second aircraft, next to which Hohendorf and Flacht were sitting. Hohendorf was reclining as if he hadn't a care in the world, eyes closed. "Yo, Wolfie," McCann called to Flacht. "How's it going?"

Flacht turned a calm face toward him. "It goes well." He patted his flight gear. "A pity I could not have taken this off. Maybe I could have got a tan today, eh?"

Whatever McCann had been about to say in reply was suddenly interrupted. Just beyond the shelter, an airman wearing helmeted headphones had been slowly pacing. When he stopped, body stiffening as he listened, everyone paused to stare at him expectantly.

Abruptly, he whirled to face the aircraft, eyes on the waiting fliers. *"Launch Nighthawks!"*

The studied tranquillity of the day erupted in a burst of activity. The ground crew hastened to their appointed tasks while the aircrew hurried up the ladders and dropped into the cockpits. The Tornadoes had already been preflighted, and all systems checked. Engines were started and the aircraft were rolling; even as the canopies were closing, the backseaters were switching their avionic equipment from standby to active.

Within a very short space of time, it seemed, the ASVs were hurtling down the runway, afterburners blazing, to launch themselves into the glowing sky. Wheels swiftly tucked in, they climbed steeply, standing on their tails as they went for the upper reaches of the heavens.

McCann glanced behind him, past the tail, as they rocketed upward. The fast-receding island seemed to burn in the golden rays of the dying sun, a molten bauble in the darkening sea.

"God," he murmured softly in wonder. "I love these takeoffs."

At 60,000 feet they leveled out and, with wings fully swept, set off at high speed for the RC-135, to mount the preplanned combat escort. Very conscious of the fact that their commanding officer was aboard the aircraft, they were ready to counter anything that might jeopardize its safety.

Over to their left the sun, still just above the horizon, bathed the sky in a great fan of orange gold that gradually faded into grayness and then into a faint darkness the further east it went. There were no clouds.

In that part of the sky, the tiny shape of Nighthawk Two was barely distinguishable as it held station in wide combat station.

"Wonder what the Boss expects to happen," McCann said. He studied his displays. "Sky's clean. So far. Perhaps this will turn out to be a—hold it. I've got something!" He waited for the system to identify the trace positively. Soon the image of the RC-135 came up on another display. "Yep. It's the Boss. Bearing zero-four-eight. Speed 380 knots . . . they're cruising . . .

altitude 20,000 feet. Everything seems okay. Range,
154 miles."

"Just keep a sharp lookout," Selby told him. Already, a precombat tenseness had descended upon
them. "We don't want surprises. Give Nighthawk Two
a datalink alert."

"No need. They've just confirmed. We may have
excited a few radars in North Africa when we took off."

"As long as they just stay excited. We're not anywhere near them."

McCann had switched off the search radar, but
the system was not idle. It continuously updated the
position of the RC-135, based upon the heading, speed,
and altitude data it had received. Every now and then
it flashed concentric rings upon the display, with little
boxes dotted about, showing probable positions. All
McCann had to do was briefly give the other aircraft
the most fleeting of sweeps and one of the boxes would
flash, showing its actual position. The new data thus
obtained would be processed, and the procedure would
continue until the next sweep. The ASV's own radar
exposure was thus kept to the absolute minimum, not
enough to allow a positive fix by a potential adversary.

But they did not have that problem to deal with
for the time being, as they were well out of the radar
range of possible hostile fighters.

"He's still alone," McCann was saying of the RC-
135. "They've just acknowledged our presence on the
link. So what do we do now?"

"We wait," Selby said.

"Walk in the park, huh?"

"Let's hope."

Half an hour later, when their patrol circuit was pointing them eastward, the walk in the park came to an
end.

"Oh shit. We've got some bad company," McCann said suddenly in a tight voice. Two new boxes, flashing red, had appeared on the scanning display. He pressed a button on another display, and immediately the computers put an image onscreen. Identification, printed in red, began to appear and flashed at him. "Oh boy," he said. "This is not the company I like."

"Do you think you could let me in on the secret?" Selby asked sharply.

"Flankers."

"What? Are you out of your mind? What would Flankers be doing out here? They don't sell these things to—"

"Whether they do or not, they're here, buddy. My kit says we've got Su-27 Flankers . . . and get this: *variants unknown.* Insufficient data! It's trying to give me an image of what it thinks it's seen."

"Variant unknown," Selby repeated, astonished. "What is all this?"

"I haven't got the answer. Oh boy."

"What? *What?* Come on, Elmer Lee."

"The kit's got an image here that *is* a Flanker, but sort of different. It's got foreplanes. Man, that's mega-agility. Those are very, very new babies. The latest of the late models. If they want a tangle, you're going to have to make like a magician. Bearing's one-seven-nine, speed six hundred knots, altitude 40,000 feet."

"I'm arming Skyray, just in case." Even as he spoke Selby was rapidly assessing the tactical situation. Where had they come from, and more importantly, what did they want? "Let's see what you've got, and let Nighthawk Two and the Boss know."

"Done." McCann put a duplicate of the display on one of Selby's MFDs. Swift datalink messages went out to the other aircraft.

Selby quickly studied his MFD. The Flankers

were still 140 miles away, but that range would give them visuals in less than twelve minutes, if the Flankers continued on course. The time would shrink even further if the ASVs turned to face them.

"I'm quite sure those Flankers would not be sold to any of the North African countries," Selby said. "Nothing this new, that's not even in official service—as far as we know, which isn't saying much . . . so we're still left with two questions. What do they want? And who are they?"

"Beats me," McCann said. "The RC-135 has already picked them up, and Nighthawk Two confirms. Hey!" McCann stared at the display. The two Su-27s had sharply altered course. Their new heading sent a sudden chill through him.

In the front cockpit, Selby waited patiently for McCann to explain his exclamation.

McCann, wanting to be certain of what he thought was happening, punched a button on the tactical display. Immediately a line extended from the Flankers' new course, stretching itself across the display. He then tapped another button. This time, a second line extended from the RC-135. Both lines met and intercepted each other.

"Go, go, *go!*" McCann shouted in his mask. "They're after the Boss! I'm informing Nighthawk Two and warning Jackdaw." Jackdaw was the RC-135's call sign.

Selby did not waste precious time questioning McCann's evaluation. If McCann said that was the tactical situation, then it was so.

He slammed the throttles into combat burner. The Tornado F-3S streaked forward, curving to intercept the Flankers. All the combat and tactical data were now on his screens. The head-up display glowed with the missile attack symbology showing "Sky B" at bottom left, denoting selection of a Skyray B for the first shot. Helmet visor was down, and the sight activated. He was ready.

"Nighthawk Two is taking up position," McCann said. "It's a two-on-two. They haven't seen us yet. They must think Jackdaw's all alone. Are they in for a surprise. Question: do we shoot before they do? I mean, they're probably only going to do a visual check."

"Do you want to take a chance with the Boss's life?"

"Hell, no. But—"

"He must have been expecting this. He must have known. I'm not going to take any chances. We engage."

"You've got the lead. You're the boss."

"Yes. Tell Nighthawk Two to watch the situation, but be ready to engage. If those Flankers launch from close range, then Jackdaw's had it. There won't be time for us to save them, and an aircraft that size isn't going to outmaneuver an air-to-air missile from one of those things."

"They've got chaff and flares aboard. They might escape the first shots."

"I'm not taking the chance," Selby said firmly. "But I'm willing to let them know we're around. Give the Flankers a burst of the radar."

McCann gave the Su-27s a prolonged sweep, long enough for the distant aircraft to know they'd been scanned, before switching down. The warning receivers on the Flankers should have gone crazy, but they would not have time to know where the potential threat was coming from. They were also still beyond the range of their own radars. The ASVs might as well have been invisible as far as the Flankers' radars were concerned, until the range closed.

The Flankers could well be following standard Eastern Bloc procedures and be operating under ground-controlled intercepts; which was probably how they had picked up the RC-135. It was well known that many of the states that purchased Soviet aircraft tended to follow these procedures. But Selby very much doubted that the aircraft out there, homing in on Jackdaw, were client-state purchases.

"Look at them go!" McCann said urgently.

The radar traces of the Flankers had suddenly diverged in frantic haste, clearly trying to find the source of the radar that had scanned them. Then abruptly, they returned to their original course.

"Shit!" McCann said. "They're not letting go! They're really after Jackdaw!"

"No doubt about their intentions now," Selby said grimly.

No fighter pilot in his right mind would have ignored a radar warning, unless he was already tasked to do so in order to concentrate on a specific target. Selby mulled over various scenarios as the Tornado charged into the attack.

The Su-27s' odd behavior could either mean that they had not expected opposition and, having been caught out, were determined to press on, or that they had a backup lurking around somewhere.

"Watch out for a backup pair hiding out there," he warned McCann. Su-27s, with their big Lyulka engines, were no easy meat.

"Don't worry. I'm on it. So far, we're all alone. Nighthawk Two's selected their target. We're on the other one. All yours."

The RC-135 was heaving around in a steep turn. Jason, strapped by a full harness to a seat that faced forward on the right side of the rear fuselage, studied the slightly paled complexion of the man sitting opposite in a rearward facing seat. Similarly secured, Buntline looked as if he would gladly be elsewhere.

"It would seem," Buntline began as calmly as he could, "that you may have been right, after all, Wing Commander."

Each wore headsets and could hear communication between the crew of the RC-135. Nothing could be heard from the escorting Tornadoes.

"As you mentioned before, Mr. Buntline, you yourself suspected other hands being involved."

Buntline nodded, looking sick as the big aircraft reversed its turn. "Does he have to maneuver so violently?"

"He's got to try and degrade the missile solution of those Flankers out there, while the ASVs maneuver into optimum attack positions."

The RC-135 went into another steep turn.

Buntline swallowed. "Why . . . why can't we hear the Tornadoes?"

"Secure data link. There will be no voice communication. No point giving anyone any ideas about what we're up to."

"Well, I hope your men are as good as you maintain." Buntline looked anxious.

"You've already had evidence of their capabilities, Mr. Buntline."

"Yes, but I wasn't dependent upon them for my continuing survival."

Jason fought back the smile he felt coming.

At one hundred miles out from his target, Selby saw the box in the sky, telling him where the Flanker McCann had selected was positioned. The box began to pulse, and the Skyray B began its deathknell sounds. There was still plenty of light to the day, despite the fact that the darkness to the east was encroaching upon the fiery spread of the sunset. The targeting box had framed the brightest part of the sky, it seemed. The box was continually on the move, following the targeted Flanker with deadly accuracy.

The box glowed brightly upon the golden fire of the sky. The Skyray began to slaver. Selby launched his first shot.

The missile left the Tornado with an explosive hiss, surging away with phenomenal velocity.

"Gawd," McCann said. "I'd hate to be on the receiving end of that. That sucker out there won't know anything about it until it's too late."

The traces on the displays seemed to bear him out. The Su-27s made no move to evade. On the tactical screen, he watched in awe as the missile streaked toward its target, the computer-generated trail somehow seeming demonic as it lengthened across the display. Then suddenly the trace made a frantic darting leap, to no avail. A bright flaring on the screen told the story.

"One down," McCann said gleefully. "And the other! Nighthawk Two's just got theirs. Splash two Flankers."

Selby was scanning the sky about him, refusing to give in to euphoria. "Just watch out for their friends, Elmer Lee. If they want Jackdaw so badly, they're not going to let him escape out of here, if they can help it."

"I'm watching."

On the RC-135, a loud cheer came on the headphones as the crew recorded the destruction of the Su-27s.

"It seems as if you're going to live a little longer, Mr. Buntline," Jason said with a straight face.

"Can we get out of here before they have more ideas like that? I think we've made our point. We now know it was sabotage."

"It might not be as easy to make good our escape."

"What?" Buntline's eyes opened wide with un-
veiled horror. "There's plenty of friendly airspace we
can reach—"

"Unfortunately, our maneuvers would have prevented us from covering sufficient distance, and besides, if they've got more fighters out there, they won't
necessarily have to invade friendly airspace. All
they've got to do is launch a missile. It will do all the
invading. Missiles don't respect invisible boundaries."
Jason studied Buntline interestedly. "This is the aspect
of air fighting most people never experience, and never
will."

"I prefer to do my fighting on the ground. My
work sometimes puts me in . . . er . . . difficult situations.
But this waiting . . ."

"Each to his own," Jason said. "I won't deny I'd
rather be in one of the fighters than in here, where I
can't actively control what occurs or, at least, respond
to it."

"Exactly how I feel."

"I still prefer to be up in the air."

Buntline was looking at Jason with some respect.
"I don't think I'll ever underestimate what you fliers do
from now on."

"When you're feeling safe again, you will."

"Looks like you were right, ol' buddy," McCann said
sharply, staring at the tactical display. "We've got two
more Flankers heading for Jackdaw. I've transferred to
you, and Nighthawk Two—aaah! Dammit, Mark!
There you go again!" His voice faded abruptly.

Selby had hauled the Tornado into a tight turn,
racing to counter the new pair of Su-27s that had appeared on the scene. McCann strained against the sudden onset of high G as the ASV hurtled on an
interception course.

"Oh hell," he went on as he regained his voice. "We've got real trouble here. I've got *two* more in the game."

"You're joking," Selby said.

"Nope. Wish I were. These guys are throwing assets at Jackdaw. What in hell's going on? Why do they want him down so badly?"

"Your guess is as good as mine, Elmer Lee. All I know is that we've got to stop them or we're dead as well."

"The first two are 110 miles from Jackdaw, and 100 from us. The second pair are close to the island, but they're on their way. Nighthawk Two is in a good intercept position for them."

"Looks like a division of labor for us. Tell Axel and Wolfie they've got the pair coming up past the island. We're going after the leaders."

16

The RC-135 was heading north at 25,000 feet doing six hundred miles an hour, nearly its maximum speed. The Flanker chasing it was doing 1,700 mph. It was no contest.

Buntline, face pale, looked at Jason. "I didn't expect four more."

The wing commander seemed unperturbed. "As you've heard, the ASVs are countering."

"It's two versus four. No matter how good they are, one missile at us will be enough. One of your crew is trying to head off the one that's chasing us while the second Flanker has broken off to attack *him*. Doesn't that mean he'll have to concentrate on his own defense?"

Jason shook his head. "The primary target will be the Flanker that's after us. The ASV can cope with multiple targets. As for the second pair of Flankers—in reality the third they've launched against us—the other ASV is engaging. That will neutralize any attack from those two."

"I wish I had your confidence. I'm not belittling your men's capabilities, but four versus two is still two-to-one odds. We can't outrun our hunter, least of all his missile."

"You can rely on my aircrew."

Buntline glanced anxiously out of the small port-hole window, as if expecting to see the nose of an Su-27 pointing at him.

"We gotta hurry, man," McCann was saying. "That guy's going to get into missile range of Jackdaw pretty soon." He watched as the second Flanker began to work its way around on the display. "And his buddy's trying to come around on our tail. The second guy's still way behind—130 miles—well out of his missile range, but let's not let him get too close."

Selby was concentrating on the Su-27 that was chasing Jackdaw with such single-mindedness, it did not even take avoiding action.

"Like me," he muttered to himself.

"You say something?"

"No, Elmer Lee. Just keep our tail covered. Ah! I've got the box. Skyray armed."

That part of the sky above the canopy was almost evenly demarcated. To their right and east, the gray had deepened, while over to their left and west, it still carried its golden fire. The targeting box had fixed itself squarely upon the divided sections and had begun to pulse almost immediately.

Selby glanced to his right and left. The sky was clear of other aircraft. Beyond each shoulder, the swept wings of the ASV gave it the semblance of a giant moth. In the cloudless air it appeared to be hanging, unmoving, despite its 1,900-mile-an-hour rush.

Soon, "In Range" was showing on the head-up display. The box blinked faster, then solidified into a baleful red. The Skyray gave its gleeful tone. Selby squeezed the missile release.

"Let's hope we don't total the Boss instead," McCann said. "That Flanker seems awfully close."

"Thanks for the act of faith," Selby remarked dryly. The Flanker was, in fact, still a good eighty miles from its intended target, though to the Skyray that was no distance. The Flanker would have wanted to get as close as possible to its target, to make quite sure perhaps with a two-, or even a three-missile shot. "The Boss will be okay."

"Well, you've just ruined that guy's day." McCann had been monitoring the Skyray's progress on the TAC display. "He's taking avoiding action. Screwed his shot up, too. No release at this time." There was a pause, then he went on excitedly. "Oh yeah! No missile release . . . ever. There he goes in a lovely flare. Three down, and three to go. Now we're cooking."

Selby brought the throttles back with relief. Jackdaw was safe. The extra-long reach of the ASV had seen to that. Skyray was a long-distance killer. No doubt about that.

As the Tornado began to decelerate he said to McCann, "I hope you're keeping an eye on his friend. He's going to want blood for this."

"I'm watching."

Bip bip bip . . .

Selby abruptly rolled the ASV onto its back and pulled on the stick, reversing his direction suddenly. The bipping died.

"I thought you were keeping a good lookout," he said in a voice that was edged with sarcasm as the aircraft plunged seaward from 40,000 feet.

McCann was unperturbed. "He's being hopeful. He's well out of missile range and is just trying to spook us."

And bloody succeeding, Selby thought grimly.

"It's quite possible," he said, "he's carrying a tool kit that does have the range."

"Nope. He'd have shot one off by now. Uh! Hell. You're at it again. I really hate it when he does that. I really do."

Selby had pulled hard out of the dive, rolled ninety degrees while pointing skyward, and pulled on the stick once more. The Tornado darted in the new direction at six hundred knots and at 30,000 feet.

"All right, Elmer Lee. Where is he?"

"Bearing two-one-five, at 35,000. Range sixty miles."

"*What?* He must be nearly in range. Why hasn't he fired? I don't believe all the crap about their not having decent weaponry. That's one certain way of getting roasted."

"He's seen what we've done and knows he can't take us at our kind of long range. I reckon he's going to come close in, if he can. He wants to mix it, because he feels he's got the better agility."

"He's in for a shock."

"I'd still prefer it if we zapped him at extreme range," McCann said. "I'm sort of partial to the soft bit in this backseat . . . me."

"He's awake now. He knows we're out here. He's not going to make it easy. Range?"

"Fifty miles, and closing. Every time we maneuver for a shot, he wriggles out of the way. Thirty-five miles."

The two aircraft continued their distant ballet of death, using great areas of sky as they feinted for advantage while keeping out of missile-launch envelope. They were like two knife fighters linked by an invisible cord about each wrist, ducking and weaving, but unable to make the one strike that would spell the destruction of one of them.

Their arena, the divided sky, slowly changed color as the sun continued its way down. It seemed as if years had passed since the very first pair of Flankers had been shot down. In reality, the time was measured in fleeting minutes.

"He's still coming in," McCann announced, watching the trace on the display. "Thirty miles. Well within range of our Kraits."

Selby's head was constantly on the move, searching the air about him for the first signs of a darting shape against the gold and dark of the sky.

"We're well within his range, too. He's good, Elmer Lee. We're going to have our work cut out."

They were at 15,000 feet and climbing steeply on afterburners. Selby glanced at the fuel readout. Okay for juice, for the time being. They had been carrying underwing tanks at the beginning of the escort patrol, using the fuel therein. These had been jettisoned at the onset of combat, to both lighten the aircraft and to increase agility. There was still plenty of internal fuel left, provided they didn't take too long to sort out the wily Flanker. Turning and burning was a fuel-hungry business.

One moment your tanks were telling you they could take you anywhere, the next your engines were trying to run on air. Bad news for you, good for your opponent. A kill for him. All he'd have to do was stand off and, if he felt charitable that day, wouldn't waste a missile on you. Instead, he'd wait while you ejected if you wanted to live, and your precious multimillion-pound aircraft would obey the laws of gravity to head terminally downward.

If he felt charitable.

Selby didn't think the man who fought so implacably was feeling charitable. Three colleagues down did not a samaritan make.

"Hey, man," McCann said. "Are we going to send this guy to the happy hunting grounds or what? He's after our ass. Twenty miles."

Selby replied with a grunt as he hauled the Tornado into a tight eight-G turn. "If you'd like . . . to . . . swop . . . grunt . . . seats, you're sodding . . . well . . . welcome. What the . . . hell . . . do you . . . ah . . . think I'm—"

Beep beep beep beep!

"Oooh *shiiit! He's launched!*" McCann yelled in his mask.

"Decoy! Decoy!"

McCann swiftly hit the decoy button and a small canisterlike shape was jettisoned from the whirling ASV. The decoy began sending out signals to make the incoming missile think it was the intended target.

Selby racked the Tornado into another tight turn, leveled the wings, and hauled upward, putting distance between them and the decoy.

A sudden flaring told them the ruse had worked. The decoy had died for them.

"This guy means business, man!" McCann was saying. "He's not playing." He was now looking out of the cockpit, constantly scanning about him, hunting out the swift-moving speck that could grow in an instant into a shape of menace. He gave his displays the briefest of glances to check the Flanker's range. "Fifteen miles. Well within visual, but where the hell is—got him!"

Something had streaked across the of a violent, red-gold sunset. McCann turned his head, following the shape.

"Okay, Mark. I've got the joker and he's your meat. He's running in for our six." McCann had twisted in his seat as far as the inertia system of his harness would allow, to check the vulnerable region behind the tail. He turned around again just as Selby rolled the

ASV onto its back and hauled on the stick in a split S, reversing direction.

The Tornado was now turned toward the Su-27 in a head-to-head. Selby armed a Krait, and immediately the box framed the incoming shape. The Krait began to howl.

But the Flanker was not having any, refusing to risk a head shot in case it missed. It broke hard, reversed the turn, and shot past upside down, crossing above the ASV from right to left. Its shadow fleetingly touched the gray Tornado.

"Sweet mother," McCann murmured softly as his eyes followed its progress. "That is some ship."

"That sort of admiration can get you killed," Selby said. "Admire it all you want, *after* we've shot it down. Meanwhile, keep those eyes of yours working and use that tricky paintwork."

"Already done," McCann said, "and the eyes are wide open."

The Flanker pilot, a lieutenant colonel with plenty of combat experience gained from seconded service with various client states, was baffled. He blinked several times as he extended the distance between himself and his adversary, prior to returning to the fray.

It had seemed, for a brief moment, that the other aircraft had actually disappeared.

Not possible, he thought. This close, it was registering on his radar warning receiver. It must have been the strange lighting conditions. He'd have to watch that. What you couldn't see could kill you. He had no intention of allowing that to happen.

McCann was again watching the tail.

"Here he comes," he warned. "Dammit! He's launched! Go, go, *go!*"

Beep beep beep . . .

"Decoy, Elmer Lee!"

The missile was infrared homing this time, heading for the heat of the ASV's engine nozzles.

McCann released an IR decoy, which burned immediately with an intense fire. Selby rolled upside down again and pulled hard on the stick, keeping the engines out of afterburner and allowing gravity to give him speed. He reversed the turn, but kept plunging down toward the relatively cool sea, letting the decoy superheat the air in his place.

The ASV hurtled past 15,000 feet. Time to start pulling out soon, or the water was going to be as hard as a brick wall.

"Decoy gone, missile gone," McCann announced, and felt a huge relief as the Tornado's nose began to rise. "He's too eager, Mark. That's his weak spot."

"We need something in our favor," Selby remarked grimly. "He's already had two launches."

"Yeah, but more importantly, two misses."

Selby pulled the ASV out of the dive, then unloaded the wings by pushing the stick slightly forward. This had the effect of making the entire aircraft momentarily weightless. At that very instant, he slammed the throttles into combat burner. Developing maximum thrust, the engines had virtually no load to push, with the result that the ASV rocketed upward, accelerating, it seemed, like a ballistic missile in level flight.

"The homesick angel," McCann said crowed. "Now that I like!"

"You're a speed freak. Now where's that Flanker?"

"Don't worry. I've got him. I've got him. He's at 20,000, wondering what to do next. He can't be feeling good about those two misses. Bearing three-three-five, range twenty miles. And here he comes again. Listen, Mark . . . we've got to get a lock on this guy. One Krait is all it'll take. He can't dodge our babies."

"First catch your rabbit. The helmet sight's pointing, but he keeps slipping out of the envelope. Those foreplanes are giving him some tight turns."

Selby grunted against another punishing weight as nine Gs came up on the HUD symbology as he racked the Tornado into a turn to confront the Flanker.

"I want that bastard," he said tightly. He could feel his body oozing sweat in response to the tenseness of the fight and the crushing forces of gravity. It was as if a giant hand were trying to squeeze all moisture out of him.

The Flanker pilot couldn't believe both his missiles had missed. Whoever was in that other plane knew his stuff. It was never in steady flight for more than a moment, and even though he'd had brief locks on it, the missiles had never achieved a solid lock-on. On top of that, it definitely seemed to change color from time to time. It had to be the sunset.

He decided to try another line of attack. Subterfuge was called for. Subterfuge, followed by the attack from an unexpected quarter.

"There he goes!" McCann said, neck craning to watch as the Su-27 shot past above them upside down for the second time. "I think he's going to pull something sneaky. He's gone past our tail and is rolling upright. Now he's climbing. Hell . . . he's slowing down! Now he's rolled 180 . . . shit, he's going for a tail slide. What the hell?"

"I know what he's up to," Selby said. "Two can play. I think we've got him, Elmer Lee."

"Oh yeah? You think he knows that?"

"Trust me."

"Oh boy."

As soon as McCann had warned him about the Flanker's moves Selby had brought the throttles back and extended the airbrakes. As the aircraft slowed, the wings began to spread. He pulled into a climb. There was plenty of energy left, though the deceleration was quite rapid. He rolled through 180 degrees so that in relation to the Flanker, both aircraft faced their undersides to each other in the climb. The Tornado was slowing down faster, falling behind.

"What are you doing?" McCann asked in a voice that sounded extremely nervous and high.

"Trust me," Selby repeated.

"You mean I've got a choice here?"

"Not unless you'd like a swim."

"That's what I figured."

The Tornado had begun to hang in the air, still upright. Soon, its nose would fall forward to plunge it into a dive, to gain the momentum through the air so that its wings could work again and turn it once more into a flying machine. But to begin with, it would have to slide, tail-first.

Selby was not worried about the effects of reverse airflow on the engines. He had tried this maneuver several times before, without the slightest degradation in performance.

"I don't know what you two guys are doing," McCann said, "but this is no airshow. Nobody's down there to cheer. Just the cold sea."

Selby did not reply. He armed the Krait. The box on the helmet sight began hunting. No warning was being given to the other aircraft. The targeting arrow had appeared and was pointing in the direction of the as yet unseen Flanker.

McCann forced himself to remain quiet. Once or

twice he caught himself holding his breath. The cockpit had an unreal sense of quietness about it. The world seemed to have paused.

Then suddenly the nose was dropping, and there, still above them, was the Flanker, its nose still pointing heavenward. Then it, too, was dropping, but too late.

Selby got a nice tone as the targeting box stopped pulsing and glowed a solid red. He pressed the release button, and the Krait seemed to shoot off eagerly even as the ASV's nose fell into a steep dive. Selby shoved the throttles forward. The engines responded immediately. A brilliant flash lit the sky above and behind, and the shock wave buffeted the Tornado as it hurtled downward.

Selby brought the nose up and circled the combat area. Pieces of the Flanker, flaming and tumbling like monstrous burning leaves, fell toward the dark sea far below. No parachute was visible.

They watched silently, until all the pieces were gone.

"He never had a chance to get out," McCann remarked soberly.

"Doesn't look like it. Any more of his friends around?"

McCann studied his displays. "Seems there's just one left. Nighthawk Two's onto him. Must be a hell of a fight going on. They're over by the island. Must be dark down there now. Jackdaw's circling. Maybe they're going to land on the island when Axel and Wolfie have finished off the last guy. Know something?"

"Why don't you tell me?"

"You're a hell of a pilot. You know that?"

"Bet you say that to all the boys." Selby was pleased.

* * *

Aboard the RC-135, Jason and Buntline had received the report on the combat.

"It would appear, Wing Commander," Buntline said, "that your faith in your men has been amply vindicated. No use my pretending that this will not help your program."

"As I said at the investigation, the time will come when the necessity of the program will become apparent even to those most against it. The air combat that has just taken place underlines the situation in the Middle East, which has already proved we need the November type of system for Europe. We can no longer dance to our own tunes as and when it pleases us. That way lies confusion, and danger."

"Easier said than done. The politicians need to be convinced."

"I don't have to do any convincing. Reality will do it for me. The only danger is the length of time that may take, and what damage circumstances may first do."

"You sound very sure of yourself, Wing Commander."

"That's where you're wrong, Mr. Buntline. I am not sure whether even what has happened today will be enough to keep the wolves at bay."

The burning rim of the sun had disappeared beneath the horizon, but its afterglow continued to light the upper reaches of sky. Down near the sea, where Nighthawk Two prowled, a dimness that was not quite the dark of night had settled.

"Is he still following, Wolfie?" Hohendorf asked.

"We're towing him nicely. He's at five thousand feet, range forty miles."

"I want him closer, and lower."

"He can't run for home, because he knows we'll

intercept. He has to fight his way out. He must be very lonely out there." Flacht read a message that had come via the data link. "Nighthawk One says they'll wait upstairs as watchdog, unless we need help."

"Tell them thanks, but no. No help needed. They can wait for us up there."

"All right. I'll let them know."

They had taken out the last remaining Flanker's partner at long range, but like the one that had fought Selby and McCann, this Su-27 also wanted the close-in arena.

He must be another veteran, Hohendorf decided. Already, they had been feinting around each other, with neither gaining any advantage. That was when Hohendorf had decided to change the game. He was now heading back to the island, luring his adversary behind him. He had turned on the FLIR head-up display, and through its infrared window he could see the island's greenish-amber shape.

Suddenly he pulled on the stick. The ASV leaped skyward. Instantly, the Flanker began running in for a quick shot.

"He's on his way," Flacht said, calmly.

"Let him come in."

The ASV, wings fully swept, hurled itself up toward the light, a fleeting arrowed shape. The forward-looking infrared system was in auto mode. It was light-sensitive, and as the aircraft climbed into the paler regions of the sky it gradually reduced its effect until the ambient lighting was sufficient to make the standard, daylight head-up display usable.

This left Hohendorf free to concentrate on the fight at any level, without having to worry about visibility. As far as he was aware, the known variants of the Su-27 did not as yet have an FLIR capability, which meant the Flanker pilot was already at a disadvantage in a close-in fight, given the current lighting conditions. But ther was still the Flanker's infrared search-and-track scanner, which had a 120-degree scan envelope. The IRST was also slaved to the pilot's own helmet sight.

Even so, Hohendorf was not unduly worried. He had his plan, and he was putting it into operation.

"Are you using our paint, Wolfie?"

"Yes. I've programmed it. He's going to have problems visually acquiring us in this light."

Beep beep beep bmmmmmmmmmm . . .

Hohendorf instantly broke out of the climb and headed downward.

"An eager launch, Wolfie," he said, grunting hard as the G-suit squeezed at him under the pressure of the high-G turn he was making. He reversed direction as Flacht released decoys. "He's not . . . waiting for the right . . . moment. An anxious man. Good."

Bmmmmmmmmmmmmmmm . . .

"His missile's still with us," Flacht said, voice still remarkably calm, all things considered. "Are you going to do something about it? Don't dance with this thing too long." Flacht was now studying his TAC display. "It's getting close."

Hohendorf twisted and turned across the sky, heading ever downward and closer to the island. A sudden brightness told them the missile had consumed itself on a flare.

"A miss," Hohendorf said, as if marking off a score. "He won't like that. Into the dark we go."

The HUD slowly metamorphosed into its FLIR mode, its ghostly window peering into the ever-deepening gloom. To Flacht in the backseat, it was like diving into the underworld.

Hohendorf glanced at the threat-warning display

with its concentric ranging circles. The Flanker was still there, following.

"Well, Wolfie?"

"He's coming down. What are you planning?"

"I'm taking him down to the mountain."

"The old volcano?"

"The edge of it. It's a dead volcano. There's no ash. Our engines will be okay."

The volcanic mountain at nearly 2,800 feet the highest on the island, was the one Bagni had pointed out to McCann on the first deployment. To the west of it was a deep, crescent-shaped valley, and to its south was another, similarly shaped, but longer and narrower. This was to be the battleground.

"You're not going to do your mountain-climbing trick, are you, Axel? Not in the dark," Flacht asked, with a trace of anxiety.

"Don't worry, Wolfie."

Flacht gave a sigh of resignation. "He is going to do it."

"Where is our friend?"

"Coming down like a bird of prey." Flacht twisted briefly in his seat to look back, beyond the tail. High above, where there was still light, something glinted fleetingly. A cockpit canopy.

"Good, good," Hohendorf said as they plunged ever deeper into the darkness.

They were over the island now, and Hohendorf took the ASV into the southern valley, standing the aircraft on a wingtip as it curved along the crescent. The valley was itself seven kilometers long from end to end. No distance at all.

Hohendorf brought back the throttles. Airspeed was reduced, but the Tornado was still hurtling toward the end of the valley, which narrowed to an apex that was a six-hundred-foot cliff.

"Looks as if you've succeeded," Flacht said. "He's come down into the valley." He sounded puzzled. "Why would he do that? He's reducing his options. He can't feel confident down here."

Beep beep beep beep bmmmmmmmmmm!

"There's your answer, Wolfie," Hohendorf said tightly, and hauled the ASV steeply up the dark face of the cliff, made an eerie green by the FLIR window.

Flacht released several flares to divert the incoming missile as the Tornado went perpendicularly up past the cliff face. There was a violent explosion as the missile impacted upon the cliff, and what sounded like a shower of hailstones peppered the aircraft, but it did not falter.

Hohendorf rolled the ASV ad pulled it back down, heading toward the mountain.

"Close, eh, Wolfie?" he said. "Here comes our mountain."

The Flanker pilot could barely see the fleeting shape ahead of him. His heart was still in his mouth from having only just managed to pull clear of the cliff where his missile had hit. Now he doggedly followed his quarry, knowing that if he broke the engagement, he was as good as dead. The other pilot would simply give chase and shoot him down with one of the long-range missiles that had so easily taken out his colleagues, well before he'd have a chance to reach safety. He had no choice but to continue the battle.

His infrared sight was helping in the poor light conditions, but the view through his HUD was unaided. As a result, he flew gingerly past the high ground.

Hohendorf went closer to the mountain slope, rolled the aircraft onto its back, and climbed. Outcrops of rock shot invisibly past the canopy. Flacht was silent.

Hohendorf smiled. Wolfie was probably shutting his eyes.

The Flanker pilot saw, but refused to accept the evidence of his own eyes. The glowing exhausts in front of him had definitely performed a 180-degree roll. But why? Incredibly, the vague shape seemed to be climbing. . . .

The pilot gave an involuntary yell as the dark mass of the mountain appeared to be suddenly upon him. His terrified shout was accompanied by an instinctive jerk of the stick, and the agile Sukhoi kicked its nose upward and bolted for the safety of the upper air.

Hohendorf saw the trace on the threat display hurtle past.

"I've got him, Wolfie! He's made the mistake."

Hohendorf rolled the ASV in the climb. A little backward pressure on the stick, and immediately the targeting box framed a patch of now dark sky. The box pulsed, then solidified. The selected Krait had achieved lock-on and was giving its chilling howl. The Flanker had obviously realized too late that it had been suckered, for the targeting box had begun to dart about, unerringly following its desperate, evasive movements.

Hohendorf fired.

The missile left the rail, climbing vertically toward the weaving target. Within the briefest of moments, the sudden bright flaring marked the end of the last Flanker. Hohendorf rolled the ASV away to avoid the fiery wreckage that plummeted downward. He didn't think the pilot could have gotten out in time.

"All right, Wolfie," he said. "You can open your eyes now. Tell Nighthawk One we're joining up."

There was no reply from the backseat.

"Come on, Wolfie. Are you going to sulk all the

way back to base? What's a little upside-down mountain climbing between friends?"

No reply.

"Wolfie? Wolfie! Come on, Oberleutnant. Enough
is enough."

"It hurts," came weakly from the back, at long
last.

Hohendorf felt a sudden spasm of fear. Wolfie was
hurt. But how? Abruptly, the victory over the Flanker
tasted bitter.

"Wolfie, what happened?" Hohendorf asked urgently. "Can you tell me?" Dear God. Had he killed his
backseater? Wolfie musn't die.

There was no further sound from the back.

Hohendorf went to voice communication. "Nighthawk One from Two. We've taken hits. Returning to
base. Warn Jackdaw. Cover us. Nighthawk." He went
back to cockpit frequency. "Wolfie?"

"We copy," came McCann's shocked voice. "We're
coming in. You guys okay?"

"Wolfie's not so good."

"Oh hell. Hang in there. Be with you soon. We'll
warn base."

There was still an ominous silence from the backseat. Hohendorf felt a heavy weight descend upon him,
and while this did not affect his flying, it took away all
the elation he had felt on destroying the last Flanker.

What was he going to tell Ilse? Had Wolfie been
hit because they had gone too close to the ground? Had
he . . .

He checked himself. You had to employ every ruse
in air combat. It was no use pretending otherwise. Air
fighting was a dangerous game, but he didn't feel any
better about Wolfie, who might well be dead in the
backseat.

He flew on into the night, back to the airfield on the northern end of the island.

The RC-135 was also heading for the island. It was originally due to return to its base on another shore of the Mediterranean, but Jason had insisted that he should be dropped off at the airfield. One of his men was hurt, perhaps dead. He had to be there.

Looking at Jason's anxious face, Buntline said, "Those men are rather like sons to you."

"I wouldn't put it quite like that."

"No need to be embarrassed, Wing Commander. You have every right to be proud of them."

"It's the price they have to pay, that's the hardest to live with. Although we all know the risks, it doesn't make it any easier. Wolfie Flacht has a wife and young children. I hope to God she's not a widow tonight."

Hohendorf landed as gently as he could. Throughout the remainder of the flight, there had been no communication from the backseat, despite repeated calls from him.

As he taxied the aircraft toward the flight line, he had the uncomfortable impression that the ASV was now a hearse, taking Flacht on his last journey. One of the ground crew marshaled him to a stop, and as soon as he had switched off the engines and the systems he snapped the release of his harness and began climbing out of his cockpit, to go over to the backseat.

Another member of the ground crew had put a ladder against the aircraft, and a member of the waiting medical team was scrambling up. Another ladder was put in place.

"If you'll get down please, sir," the medic said quietly, "it will be easier for us. We can help him now."

Hohendorf stared into the rear cockpit. Flacht's

body seemed lifeless, his helmeted head with its visor down lolling to one side. It was impossible to tell how he was without a look at his features.

"Please, sir," the medical man repeated urgently. "The longer you wait, the longer it's going to take us to get him out."

"Yes. Yes."

Hohendorf hurried down the ladder to stand a little distance away, watching with a deep anxiety as people swarmed over the aircraft to remove the inert body in the backseat.

His eyes strayed over the airframe. There were several jagged holes in it, but nothing very big. Shattered pieces of cliff face from the missile explosion? Or shrapnel from its warhead?

They were bringing Flacht down. Something dark was dripping from the flying gear. There seemed to be a lot of it. There was, he thought, an unnatural looseness about the body. He hurried to the ambulance.

Again, he was stopped. "We must get him to the hospital detachment as quickly as possible, sir."

"He's my backseater! How can you stop me—"

The medic was kind. "I know how you feel, sir."

"How can you? You don't know!"

"Take it from me, sir. I do understand, but if we're to save his life . . ."

Hohendorf felt a powerful relief. "You mean he is *alive?*"

"Yes, sir, but barely. The longer we stay here arguing . . ."

Hohendorf stepped back. "Of course. Of course."

The medic parted with kind words. "Hitch a ride, sir. Come down to the sick bay." He climbed into the back of the ambulance, which was already moving, and shut the doors.

It roared swiftly away, just as Nighthawk Two landed.

Hohendorf, Selby, and McCann were all standing in the narrow corridor, still in most of their flight gear, waiting. None of them spoke. Every time a member of the medical staff walked past, their bodies stiffened expectantly. Eventually, a woman officer they recognized as the detachment's senior medical officer came up to them. She carried the rank of a squadron leader in the RAF.

She had a small medical tray in one hand, which she held toward them. The other hand picked up a thin sliver of metal, scarcely more than two inches long. She held it up.

"That, gentlemen, is the cause of all our problems."

"That?" McCann said. "It's no bigger than a paper clip."

"How is he, doctor?" Hohendorf asked quietly.

"He lost a lot of blood. He could have died, but he's a fit young man. He'll be all right. We're putting him on a casevac flight back to November One tomorrow."

The detachment had an executive twin jet that had been converted for casualty evacuation.

The doctor handed them the tray. "I expect he'll want to see this. But don't keep my tray." She dropped the sliver of metal back into it.

McCann poked at the splinter with a forefinger. "Where was it, Doc?"

"A few millimeters from his heart." She looked at Hohendorf. "He was very lucky. The shock put him out, but if he'd been conscious, he would have been screaming with the pain and might have tried to pull this out. He might have touched the heart and killed himself." She shook her head in wonder. "One in a million. He'll probably live forever now. Now, if you'll excuse me, I must see to my patient."

"Can we see him?"

"I'm afraid not. Strict doctor's orders. You'll be able to see him back at November."

As she left they turned to see two men in flying overalls approaching. One of them was Jason.

"How is he?" he asked.

"He's okay," McCann answered, then held up the sliver. "The docs took that out of him, a whisker from the heart. Missile splinter."

Jason looked at Hohendorf. "Close."

"Yes, sir."

"But not close enough. That's what matters in the end. Can he be visited?"

"The doctor's forbidden it." Hohendorf gave a tight smile. "But we're not wing commanders."

"Hmm." Jason turned to his companion. "Gentlemen, Mr. Charles Buntline. He insisted on meeting you."

Buntline held out his hand to each. "That was excellent work today. I am very sorry about your colleague. What you've done has implications far beyond what happened up there. It won't be forgotten. This has to be brief. I have a plane to catch. Thank you, gentlemen."

Buntline left, accompanied by Jason, who soon returned to join them. A heavy aircraft could be heard taking off.

"Get some decent rest tonight," he told them. "We'll be going home tomorrow." He turned to Hohendorf. "Your aircraft will be ready by morning. Do you mind having me in the backseat?"

"No, sir."

"Good. See you in the morning."

* * *

Whitehall, London. 0900 hours, two days later.

"So Charles," the minister began as Buntline entered the large office. "None the worse for wear I see, after your little adventure."

"Alive and kicking, Minister. Those pilots of Jason's are quite exceptional people."

"Et tu, Brute? What's this? Become a fervent supporter of the turbulent wing commander, have we?"

"Perspectives tend to change when your life's on the line. The only reason I am in your office today is because of those crews. It's my opinion that Wing Commander Jason's onto something with his November program."

The minister digested what Buntline had said. "Well," he eventually began, rubbing a forefinger against his right ear, "I can see he has made a convert of you."

"Let's look at it another way, Minister. There are, as we know, rather a lot of opposition to the idea, for all sorts of reasons. If, as seems quite likely, the November Project is the way for the future, anyone who was seen to be in the vanguard—so to speak—could gain some very strong, valuable points. Farsightedness against political myopia. Such a thing would do wonders for a career and, of course, would make Air Vice Marshal Thurson more amenable when . . . er . . . surgical jobs arose for the November units to undertake."

Buntline paused, allowing his seductive words to work their magic. The minister was ambitious. It did not mean his backbone would become any stiffer when things got tricky, but that was the way of the world.

The minister had stopped rubbing his ear. "I'll think about it," he said.

Buntline did not smirk. The minister had taken the bait.

"And now, Charles," the minister went on, "when you came in, you looked like a cat that's been at buckets of cream. You still look it."

Buntline nodded. "I've had an interesting two days. My American contacts were able to gain access to Gant's secret papers. Seems he had taken no chances and had made copies of everything. Whatever was lost when his aircraft went down will not leave much of a gap in what we've found out. I've made a full report, but the short version is that Gant possessed solid facts about hard-liner plans for a reversal of their current fortunes in the Soviet Union. The assassination of both Gant and Belov was part of it. Stolybin was up to his neck in that section of their program. I'd hate to be in his shoes right now." Buntline spoke with a malicious glee. "As for the Peace Dividend, that's beginning to look somewhat tattered.

"However," he went on, "Stolybin is small fry. There's a KGB general who's his boss. That same gentleman was here in 1965 with the rank of major, masquerading as a cultural attaché. It seems as if he wanted to emulate his earlier success. He would have, had Wing Commander Jason not been so stubborn."

"All right, Charles," the minister said. "You've made your point. Let me have the report soonest. I'll see it receives the proper attention."

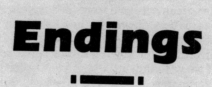

Endings

November One, base hospital. 1000 hours.

Hohendorf, Selby, and McCann were making their way out of Flacht's ward. At the door, Hohendorf paused to look back. Flacht was sleeping peacefully. At the bedside, Ilse sat close by, holding on to one of his hands.

Hohendorf went back to her. "Ilse, I . . ."

She turned to look at him, eyes moist. "You must not blame yourself, Axel. It could easily have been you. Who would have brought the plane back? Perhaps I would have lost my Wolfie then." She returned her attention to her sleeping husband. "As it is, I still have him. He'll be well again soon."

"If . . . if you would like him to stop flying, I'll understand. The wing commander has also said—"

"No!" she interrupted in a fierce whisper. "How can you say that? I will never tell Wolfie to stop. Don't you understand? He will not be my Wolfie if I take him away from his flying." The moist eyes showed a powerful determination. "There will be no pressure from me."

Hohendorf leaned forward to kiss her on the cheek. "Wolfie is a very lucky man." He touched her shoulder briefly, then went out to rejoin Selby and McCann, shutting the door quietly behind him.

He caught up with them in the highly polished corridor. As he reached them someone came around a corner, causing McCann to halt in his tracks.

Karen Lomax. She was carrying what looked like a box of sweets.

"I think we should carry on, Axel," Selby said.

"I think you may be right."

McCann stayed where he was as they walked away. She came up to him and stopped, a shy smile on her lips.

"Hello."

McCann swallowed. "Er . . . hi. Going to see Wolfie?"

Tiny spots of color stained her cheeks. "Well, actually, I've come to see Geordie Pearce."

"Oh." Faintly. "Er, and what's he done?"

"Broke his leg in a rugby tackle."

McCann wanted to laugh, but thought the better of it. "I'm real sorry to hear that," he lied, and compounded it by adding, "Hope he gets better soon."

"Thank you. And I hope your Wolfie is up and flying before long."

"He will be. Look," McCann went on, emboldened by the temporaily immobilized Pearce, "why don't we have a coffee later?"

Her eyes speculated briefly. "Why not? I'm having lunch in the mess today. We can share a table if you'd like."

"I would."

"That's fine, then. See you later."

"Yeah. Later."

McCann watched her walk away, loving every movement. "Dangerous McCann," he remarked softly. "That's me."

He hurried on to catch up with Selby and Hohendorf.

They were walking slowly away from the hospital.

"We work so well in the air," Hohendorf said, "we really ought to make things easier between us on a personal level."

"Part of me agrees with you," Selby told him.

"And the other? The part that concerns Morven?"

Selby gave a deep sigh. "Look. I—"

McCann came running up. "Hey guys, I've just got me a date."

Selby and Hohendorf looked at each other.

"Have you checked your insurance policy lately?" Selby asked McCann.

Hohendorf looked on, amused.

"C'mon, guys. Give me a break."

"Oh, you'll certainly get that when Geordie Pearce finds out you're playing around with his woman," Selby said. "A broken neck."

McCann grinned. "Well, he'll have to catch me first. Right now he can't run too good. He's back there in the hospital." The grin widened. "Broken leg."

Moscow, 1300 hours. The same day.

Stolybin had studied all the reports. When the first had come in days before, about the Alpha-class submarine being chased off station by an American hunter killer that would not give up, he had sensed a rising disquiet. Now the destruction of the six high-value operational test aircraft, together with the loss of six equally highly valued pilots, showed the extent of the clever trap that had been sprung upon the general.

But Stolybin knew the general would not see it like that. He would conveniently forget the warnings about being too hasty. He would look for a scapegoat to save his own neck.

"Me," Stolybin muttered.

He had cleared his desk of what little he thought would be necessary. Always aware of the precariousness of his position with the general, he had traveled light. When the recriminations began, his tapes would give the real picture. The general was not going to get away with taking him down.

He put some papers into his narrow, brown briefcase and picked up his cap from the desk, where he had placed it since his arrival early in the morning. He put the cap on and began moving toward the door. The general had not been seen for two days.

The connecting door slammed open. Stolybin retained sufficient control of himself and was not startled. He turned around slowly. Even before he looked, he'd smelled the general's eternal cigarette.

"And where do you think you're going?" the general barked. His eyes seemed to burn with a hellish fire, as if they wanted to fry Stolybin on the spot.

"I have just cleared my desk, Comrade General," Stolybin said calmly. "I was about to hand in my keys, then tender my resignation to you. I'd have come to you first, but you were not here."

"Couldn't you wait?"

"Comrade General, I'm a realist. I know I'm to be the casualty in this. I'm merely saving you the trouble."

"Since when have you learned to read my mind? Who said I was about to fire you?"

Stolybin was genuinely surprised.

The general came further into the room. "There. You see? You don't know everything. So we've lost this one. These things happen."

Stolybin refused to believe his ears. What was

hidden behind those words? How could the general write off such an expensive operation so easily?

"I haven't been here," the general was saying, "because I've been having some high-level discussions with those who want our Motherland back. Come. You've proved your soundness to us. They would like to meet you. You'll be back in time to enjoy Tokareva tonight. I have a car waiting. I'll meet you outside."

The general returned to his office, leaving Stolybin to stare at the closing door.

Stolybin went cautiously out to the large courtyard. Tokareva was there, with his own staff car.

He went up to her. "I won't be needing the car till later. I'm going to see some people with the general."

Her eyes narrowed slightly. "Shall I follow?"

"No. It should be all right. Wait here for me."

"Are you sure, Sergei? Do you trust him?"

"These days, who knows who can be trusted?"

The eyes widened. "Does that include me?"

"No, Tokareva. For me, you're special."

She smiled. "Keep remembering that." Her voice dropped. "He's here."

Stolybin turned. The general was waiting.

The car was on a snowbound road out of Moscow. There were just three people in it: the general, Stolybin, and the driver.

Stolybin looked out at the wintery landscape. It was covered with a white blanket of snow, and there was nothing to see except sparse collections of flecked trees.

"We must meet away from prying eyes," the general explained. "The place we're going to is owned by a comrade general in the army. It is well secluded."

The road became a wide bend that went through rows of tall trees. The road behind went out of view.

"Not too long now," the general said. "We won't see it until we're practically there."

Stolybin glanced out of the rear window.

"Expecting someone?"

Stolybin settled back in his seat. "Habit. I always like to check."

The general gave a fleeting twitch that could have been a smile. "Spoken like a true surveillance man."

Since entering the car, the general hadn't smoked.

Some distance behind, Tokareva drove at an easy speed, keeping out of sight of the car up ahead. She wondered whether Stolybin realized the danger he was in. Maintaining separation between the vehicles, she followed.

"Very soon now," the general said.

Stolybin looked out of his window, but could see no buildings. A wide expanse of snow, with a forested area in the distance, greeted his eyes. The other side of the car showed a variation on the same landscape theme.

"It's up ahead," the general said. "Around this bend. There's a track to some trees. The house is behind the trees."

The general shifted position. Stolybin took no notice. Was he being taken to a secret court-martial? Or did the general have one of his special prisons behind those trees?

The pain, when it came, was such a surprise, that Stolybin had opened his mouth to scream before he realized he'd been shot. As the pain filled his entire being and the sounds refused to come out of his mouth, he distantly heard the general speaking.

"All right. That's far enough. Stop here."

Stolybin was vaguely aware above the waves of pain that the car was stopping and pulling off the road. There seemed to be an unnatural warmth that was sticky pouring into his clothes, soaking through his uniform and greatcoat. His cap had fallen to the floor of the car when the force of the bullet had thrown him against the door.

The general climbed out as the car stopped, pulling his own greatcoat about him. He walked around, opened the other door, and pulled Stolybin unceremoniously out. He dragged him a little way from the car, ignoring Stolybin's faint cries of pain.

"All right," he said to the driver. "You can go."

The driver did not argue. He turned the car around and drove back the way they had come.

The general waited until the car was some distance away before turning back to the dying Stolybin. He hunched down on his heels and turned Stolybin roughly onto his back. Stolybin began to shiver in the snow. Flecks of white spotted his hair and face.

"Well, Sergei," the general began conversationally, "you were right. There have to be casualties for failure. I did warn you." He reached into a greatcoat pocket and pulled out a microtape. He held the tiny cassette above Stolybin's clouding eyes. "What were these for? Insurance? We've got them all. It was clever of you to pick that foreign journalist's apartment instead of yours, but not clever enough. We were close to you all the time. Very close."

The general smiled. "I don't suppose you can talk," he went on in the same conversational tone. "Never mind. I'll talk for both of us. You see, I did sleep with Tokareva. Ah, I can see by your eyes that you find that hurtful. Too bad. I slept with her several times. She's really my operative and kept a close eye on you for me." The general actually laughed. "We both know how close. It was she who followed you to the journalist's apartment. All we had to do after that was search it for your little hiding place. The apartment was bugged by us anyway, but you already knew that. Which was why you thought a normal operative on surveillance duties would not make much of a KGB colonel on my staff paying it a visit.

"I have to say you were not seen. Except, of course, by Tokareva. Don't take it so hard, Sergei. She wants to survive. You'll get a chance to see her for the last time. She's picking me up. Ah. Here she comes."

Very faintly, Stolybin thought he could hear the sound of an approaching car. All feeling seemed to have left his body. His eyes could not move, and the day was getting darker. Then she was looking down at him, no expression on her face at all.

To Stolybin, it was the ultimate betrayal. The world went dark.

Tokareva stared down at the body.

"Have you destroyed the tapes?" the general asked her.

She did not look around. "Yes, Comrade General."

"This is the last one." He dropped it to the ground and raised a booted foot to stamp upon it.

Tokareva turned. The single shot echoed in the cold stillness.

The general's eyes widened in horror. His boot never landed on the tape. He staggered back, hands clutching at his stomach. His staring eyes were fixed upon her.

"You . . . you!" he gasped hoarsely. "Who . . . who are you? Wh-why?"

She did not answer, but kept looking at him until he fell heavily into the snow, dying as he hit. She put the pistol away.

She stooped to pick up the tape, carefully brushing the moisture off it. She then put it in a pocket. She had not destroyed any of the tapes.

She next went over to Stolybin's body, bent down on one knee to brush the snow off the still-warm face. She kissed the lips that were turning blue.

"Sorry," she said. She looked back at the general. "Target down."

She stood up, got into the car, and drove back along the snowbound road.

Behind her, the two bodies lay in chill companionship.

Off Malta. Some days later.

The fisherman looked at the strange thing that came up with the fish in his net as he hauled it in. Frowning, he pulled at the net until the baffling object slid aboard, partially hidden by the thumping fish as they struggled ineffectually to get free. Half the net was still in the water.

He parted a section of the net carefully and cleared the fish off the object. It was a white helmet, with a small red star on each side.

The fisherman turned the helmet over and felt his stomach heave. There was a head in it, and the fish had been feeding. He threw the helmet away from him with a horrified cry. It arced far away from the boat, tumbling as it went. Pieces fell from within it. It splashed into the water, rolling over once before sinking.

The fisherman released the net and gave the fish back to the sea.

Born in Dominica, Julian Jay Savarin was educated in Britain and took a degree in history before serving in the Royal Air Force. Mr. Savarin lives in England and is the author of LYNX, HAMMERHEAD, WARHAWK, *and* TROPHY.

⚓ HarperPaperbacks *By Mail*

NIGHT STALKERS *by Duncan Long.* TF160, an elite helicopter corps, is sent into the Caribbean to settle a sizzling private war.

NIGHT STALKERS— SHINING PATH *by Duncan Long.* The Night Stalkers help the struggling Peruvian government protect itself from terrorist attacks until America's Vice President is captured by the guerillas and all diplomatic tables are turned.

NIGHT STALKERS— GRIM REAPER *by Duncan Long.* This time TF160 must search the dead-cold Antarctic for a renegade nuclear submarine.

NIGHT STALKERS— DESERT WIND *by Duncan Long.* The hot sands of the Sahara blow red with centuries of blood. Night Stalkers are assigned to transport a prince safely across the terrorist-teeming hell.

TROPHY *by Julian Jay Savarin.* Hand-picked pilots. A futuristic fighter plane. A searing thriller about the ultimate airborne confrontation.

STRIKE FIGHTERS— SUDDEN FURY *by Tom Willard* The Strike Fighters fly on the cutting edge of a desperate global mission—a searing military race to stop a fireball of terror.

STRIKE FIGHTERS—BOLD FORAGER *by Tom Willard.* Sacrette and his Strike Fighters battle for freedom in this heart-pounding, modern-day adventure.

STRIKE FIGHTERS: WAR CHARIOT *by Tom Willard.* Commander Sacrette finds himself deep in a bottomless pit of international death and destruction. Players in the worldwide game of terrorism emerge, using fear, shock and sex as weapons.

MORE ACTION AND ADVENTURE
8 ACTION-PACKED MILITARY ADVENTURES

These novels are sure to keep you on the edge of your seat. You won't be able to put them down. **Buy 4 or More and Save.** When you buy 4 or more books, the postage and handling is *FREE*. You'll get these novels delivered right to door with absolutely no charge for postage, shipping and handling.

Visa and MasterCard holders—call

1-800 331-3761

for fastest service!

MAIL TO: Harper Collins Publishers
P. O. Box 588, Dunmore, PA 18512-0588
Telephone: (800) 331-3761

Yes, please send me the action books I have checked:
☐ Night Stalkers (0-06-100061-2) $3.95
☐ Night Stalkers—Shining Path
    (0-06-100183-X) $3.95
☐ Night Stalkers—Grim Reaper
    (0-06-100078-2) $3.95
☐ Night Stalkers—Desert Wind
    (0-06-100139-2) $3.95
☐ Trophy (0-06-100104-X) $4.95
☐ Strike Fighters—Sudden Fury (0-06-100145-7) .. $3.95
☐ Strike Fighters—Bold Forager
    (0-06-100090-6) $3.95
☐ Strike Fighters: War Chariot (0-06-100107-4) $3.95

SUBTOTAL. . . . .$_____

POSTAGE AND HANDLING*. . . . .$_____

SALES TAX (NJ, NY, PA residents) . . . .$_____

            TOTAL: $_____
             (Remit in US funds, do not send cash.)

Name_____

Address_____

City_____

State_____Zip_____ Allow up to 6 weeks delivery. Prices subject to change.

*Add $1 postage/handling for up to 3 books...
FREE postage/handling if you buy 4 or more.   H0071